"Drop 'em," he instructed.

"If you say so."

She let the devices fall to the dusty cement floor. F'lun targeted them with the twice-stolen disruptor. A crimson beam disintegrated the transponders. He smirked at Spock as the glow of the atomized capsules faded away.

"So much for that. Bet you thought you could outsmart us."

"It seemed worth the effort," Spock replied.

"So now what?" Chapel asked, rolling down her sleeve. A bouncer reclaimed the medkit, laser scalpel and all.

"Now we talk, but not here," F'lun said. "You have questions, we have questions, so you're coming with us."

His gaze darted to a trapdoor at the rear of the room. Evidence of a lower level, Spock speculated, or an underground escape route leading to another location? He considered whether to resist or not. With his Vulcan strength and Starfleet combat training, he might be able to subdue their foes, despite their greater numbers, but there was no guarantee that neither he nor Chapel would be harmed in the melee, and even if they should make their escape unscathed, it would not bring them any closer to the answers they sought.

"Will we find Doctor McCoy where we are going?" he asked.

"You're asking the wrong person." F'lun adjusted the disruptor, switching it to the lowest setting.

"Seriously?" Chapel said. "Again?"

STAR TREK™

THE ORIGINAL SERIES

A CONTEST OF PRINCIPLES

Greg Cox

Based on *Star Trek*
created by Gene Roddenberry

GALLERY BOOKS

New York   London   Toronto   Sydney   New Delhi

Gallery Books
An Imprint of Simon & Schuster, Inc.
1230 Avenue of the Americas
New York, NY 10020

First Gallery Books trade paperback edition November 2020

GALLERY BOOKS and colophon are registered trademarks of Simon & Schuster, Inc.

For information about special discounts for bulk purchases, please contact Simon & Schuster Special Sales at 1-866-506-1949 or business@simonandschuster.com.

The Simon & Schuster Speakers Bureau can bring authors to your live event. For more information or to book an event, contact the Simon & Schuster Speakers Bureau at 1-866-248-3049 or visit our website at www.simonspeakers.com.

Manufactured in the United States of America

10 9 8 7 6 5 4 3 2 1

Library of Congress Cataloging-in-Publication Data

Names: Cox, Greg, 1959– author.
Title: A contest of principles / Greg Cox ; based on Star Trek created by
   Gene Roddenberry.
Other titles: At head of title: Star trek the original series
Description: First Gallery Books trade paperback edition. | New York :
   Gallery Books, 2020. | Series: Star trek: the original series
Identifiers: LCCN 2020028888 (print) | LCCN 2020028889 (ebook) | ISBN
   9781982134709 (trade paperback) | ISBN 9781982134716 (ebook)
Subjects: LCSH: Star trek (Television program)—Fiction. | GSAFD: Science
   fiction.
Classification: LCC PS3603.O9 C66 2020 (print) | LCC PS3603.O9 (ebook) |
   DDC 813/.6—dc23
LC record available at https://lccn.loc.gov/2020028888
LC ebook record available at https://lccn.loc.gov/2020028889

ISBN 978-1-9821-3470-9
ISBN 978-1-9821-3471-6 (ebook)

Historian's Note

The events in this story take place in the final year of the *U.S.S. Enterprise*'s five-year mission.

PROLOGUE

Planet Vok
Sector 8491

"VOTE!" scrolled the window.

Bloj stepped back to admire the effect. The new smart-glass window at the front of his downtown art gallery worked just as advertised. The blunt imperative scrolled continuously from the top of the window and back again, spelled out in bold phosphorescent purple letters that appeared almost three-dimensional when viewed from any angle. It was a clear spring morning, awash in sunlight, but the glowing message still popped. There was no way any passing driver or pedestrian could miss it, which was precisely the idea.

"What do you think?" he asked Lesh, who was standing beside him on the sidewalk outside the gallery. Vintage carnival posters, both classical and abstract, could be viewed through the transparent portions of the window, beyond the scrolling "VOTE!" A handheld remote allowed Bloj to tinker with the color, luminosity, and scroll rate of the message, as well as edit the text if necessary. "Pretty dramatic, isn't it?"

"It's eye-catching, all right," his nephew said, his worried tone and expression betraying a certain lack of enthusiasm. Lesh glanced nervously up and down the sparsely populated sidewalk; it was early enough that the street wasn't bustling yet, although the neighborhood was already beginning to stir. The younger man, whom Bloj had hired as a favor to his sister, eyed the window with visible discomfort. "Maybe too much so. Are you sure you want to be so . . . provocative?"

"Times are changing," Bloj said. "We don't have to watch what we say like we did under the old regime."

"So they say," Lesh said skeptically. "But it's not as though that regime is ancient history. You certain you aren't jumping the gun here? Maybe we ought to wait until *after* the election before getting too political?"

"After the election could be too late. We need to make our voices heard now, at long last." Bloj contemplated his modest gallery, which had been shut down more than once over the years. "I've spent too much of my life having to appease government censors and propaganda officers. Now that we can finally speak our minds, I intend to take full advantage of our new freedoms, no matter—"

A hover truck pulled up to the curb, hissing loudly to a stop as it settled to the pavement. The men turned toward the vehicle, which was emblazoned with the emblem of a local EPS repair service. A weathered steel door slid open, disgorging the driver, who strode toward them, displeasure written over her all-too-familiar face.

"Oh, flux," Lesh moaned.

Bloj's own spirits sank, despite his convictions, but he stood his ground as the hefty technician approached, her tool belt jangling from her waist. He braced himself for an ugly confrontation; he and Prav had clashed before over artwork she deemed insufficiently "patriotic." He suspected that she had also reported him to the authorities in days gone by.

"What's this?" she demanded, scowling at the window.

Bloj refused to be intimidated, even though Prav was a head taller than him and younger and in better shape as well. Platinum-blond dreadlocks framed her bellicose features. Silver epaulets on her shoulders betrayed her loyalty to the old regime.

"I would think the message is self-explanatory."

His answer did not satisfy her. "Who are you voting for?" she asked. "As if I can't guess."

"Doctor Ceff, of course. Not that it's any of your business."

"Figures." Prav snorted in disgust. "Should've known you'd support that spineless professor. It's as though you and your sort can't wait to tear down everything that has kept us strong and secure for generations. Bet you want to appease those barbaric scum on Ozalor, too. Let them steal Braco from us without so much as a fight."

"Ceff represents a more enlightened, more peaceful future for all of us," Bloj said. "I'm sorry you can't see that."

Prav came closer, invading Bloj's personal space. She loomed over the elderly gallery owner. "Oh, I see you just fine. I see that traitors like you are in for a big surprise when the General takes power."

"*If* your General wins the election," Bloj corrected her before resolving to get back to work. He knew better than to get sucked into a pointless debate when there was obviously no common ground to be found. "You vote your way and I'll vote my way, and we'll see who ends up surprised."

"We shouldn't even be voting in the first place," Prav snarled. "Everything was fine before subversives like you divided us."

"Speak for yourself, please. That's not how I remember it."

Bloj began to turn away from Prav, but she surprised him by snatching the remote from his hand and hurling it at the window with all her strength. The device shattered the smart glass. Jagged shards rained down onto the sidewalk.

"Oops," Prav said with a smirk.

Fury consumed Bloj. "You ignorant bully! You had no right!"

"What are you going to do about it, old man?" Prav raised her fists, spoiling for a fight. "Show me what you've got, art collector."

Bloj had never been a brawler, not even in his youth, but he was sorely tempted to oblige her. He trembled with rage, his fists clenched at his sides. He had put up with the likes of Prav for too long. That she thought she could still get away with such tactics infuriated him.

Just when I thought things were getting better!

"Leave it, Uncle!" Lesh grabbed his arm to restrain him. "Don't let her bait you. She's just looking for an excuse to flatten you!"

"Listen to the boy." Prav snickered as she headed back to her vehicle. "And you might want to think twice before trying to stir up any more trouble. Don't think we're going to forget whose side you chose once this idiotic election is over."

"You can't stop the future," Bloj said, his voice thick with emotion. "The military isn't in charge anymore!"

"Right," she scoffed. "Keep telling yourself that."

She got into her hover truck and cruised away, leaving the vandalized window behind, its shattered message littering the pavement.

"You see, this is just what I was worried about." Lesh released Bloj's arm once Prav was well away. He shook his head at the wreckage. "This election has everyone worked up. You need to be more circumspect."

"But I wasn't even promoting any one candidate over another," Bloj protested, still shaken by the encounter. His heart drummed even as his blood boiled at the injustice. "I was just urging people to vote, that's all."

"These days, that's enough to set some folks off," Lesh said. Broken glass crunched beneath his boots as he inspected the damage. "I told you before, you're staking too much on this election. Chances are, the whole thing is rigged anyway, so why risk antagonizing people over it?"

Bloj was dismayed by his nephew's cynicism. "That's not true. Good people have fought long and hard to make this election happen. Why, the Federation is sending its own experts to observe the election to guarantee that it's conducted fairly. The eyes of the entire quadrant are upon us. There's no way anyone can steal this election!"

"That," Lesh said dubiously, "remains to be seen."

One

Captain's Log, Stardate 6784.1: *As the* Enterprise *nears the end of its five-year mission, we are en route to Vok, an independent world in a sector bordering the outer reaches of the Federation. The planet is about to hold its first free election after being ruled by a military dictatorship for more than a generation. Because tensions are running high, the Federation has been invited to oversee the election as a neutral observer, which may prove challenging given that the results of the election could affect the future of not just Vok but two other neighboring planets.*

"With apologies to Charles Dickens, this is essentially a tale of three worlds," Commissioner Imogen Dare informed various senior officers of the *U.S.S. Enterprise* in the ship's main briefing room. A distinguished Federation diplomat, she was a human in her late fifties, with silver hair and shrewd brown eyes. Her civilian attire was well tailored and professional. "Vok, Ozalor, and Braco."

Captain James T. Kirk listened attentively. He was already familiar with the gist of the mission, but he let Dare take the lead on this briefing. Although he had never met her before she came aboard at Starbase R-3, she'd made a good first impression in that she didn't strike him as being as overbearing or self-important as some other high-ranking dignitaries he could name. He hoped that boded well for their joint assignment.

"More than two thousand years ago, an apocalyptic interstellar war pretty much wiped out civilization on all three worlds, each of which occupies its own solar system within a common sector," Dare continued. "After centuries of struggle, their respective peoples have only now climbed back up from post-atomic dark ages to modernity, although much of their early history remains in dispute, surviving only as conflicting legends and scraps of unreliable data. At this point, they are only just warp capable again; in Earth terms, they're somewhere between Zefram Cochrane and Jonathan Archer, which means they've made contact with the Federation, but are probably still generations away from joining us."

Graphics on a viewscreen accompanied her briefing. At present, a star chart demonstrated the three planets' relative proximity to one another. Kirk noted that each world was only a solar system away from the others, making them only a few days' travel from one another at warp speed. Just as significantly, their sector bordered various outlying Federation colonies and outposts, giving the United Federation of Planets a vested interest in preserving peace in the region lest any conflicts spill over into Federation territory.

"Vok is our destination," Dare said, "but their relations with their neighbors are key to understanding the politics involved, as well as all that is at stake."

The image on the screen zeroed in on one particular Class-M planet.

"Ozalor is Vok's ancient adversary and rival. As noted before, much of the sector's history was lost to time and the war, including the particulars of who exactly initiated the conflict, but the enmity between Vok and Ozalor has endured in the collective memories and myths of both peoples long after the cataclysm sent them back to the dark ages. These festered and grew during the millennia or so that they had no contact with each other, prior to rediscovering warp travel in the last century or so. We're talking thousands of years of bad blood, congealed into the bedrock of both resurgent civilizations."

"There's a grisly image," Doctor Leonard McCoy said. He was seated at the conference table along with Spock. Yeoman Zahra was also on hand to take notes on the meeting. McCoy shook his head. "Too bad there's no such thing as a cultural anticoagulant when it comes to clotted feuds and prejudices."

"If only," Dare said. "These days Ozalor is a modern, reasonably high-tech monarchy, with whom, unfortunately, the Federation does not have formal diplomatic relations, due to a tragic misunderstanding a few decades ago."

"The *Pericles* affair," Spock stated. "A most regrettable occurrence."

Kirk recalled the incident. A routine first contact had taken a bad turn, leading to a Starfleet landing party being taken hostage. An ensuing rescue attempt had also gone amiss, resulting in fatalities on both sides. Relations between the Federation and Ozalor had been frosty ever since, despite sporadic attempts on the UFP's part to mend fences. Ozalor preferred to keep the Federation at arm's length and so Starfleet had given the system a wide berth.

"Very much so, Mister Spock," Dare agreed. "And, for better or for worse, the fact that Vok is on friendlier terms with the Federation doesn't help matters as far as the Ozalorians are concerned."

"I can see that," Kirk said. "Hard to win their trust when we're already forging ties with their ancient enemy. That's a tricky nut to crack, diplomatically."

"And beyond the purview of this mission," Dare said. "But rest assured that we can't talk about the presidential election on Vok without understanding its rivalry with Ozalor, particularly where Braco is concerned."

The focus of the viewscreen shifted to the third planet under discussion.

"Braco is a major bone of contention. Both Vok and Ozalor lay claim to the planet, which is believed to be the ancestral home of both peoples, while the planet's own population is divided in their loyalties, with some claiming allegiance to Vok and others to Ozalor. After years of strife and civil war, a tentative cease-fire is in effect, with the planet being jointly administered by a provisional government representing both factions, but the planet's long-term status and loyalties remain precariously unresolved. The possibility of a proxy war, with Vok and Ozalor supporting opposing forces, or, worse yet, a hot war between Vok and Ozalor, remains a very real possibility . . . and a major issue in the presidential election on Vok."

"How so?" McCoy asked.

"On one side you have the hardliners, headed by a General Gogg, who is affiliated with the old military regime. He and his fellow hawks feel strongly that Braco belongs to Vok and resist any sort of compromise on the issue. On the other side, you have Doctor Ceff, an intellectual and reformer who is committed to working out a peaceful solution to the Braco issue." Dare paused to take a sip of water before proceeding. "Frankly, the Federation would prefer that Ceff win the election, but we need to fall over backward to avoid any hint of favoritism. We can't take sides if we're to fulfill our role as impartial observers."

"Understood," Kirk said. "What challenges do you anticipate us encountering once we reach Vok?"

"Difficult to say, Captain. An executive committee is temporarily in charge of the planet's government, but tensions are running high in anticipation of the election, with threats and accusations flying back and forth between the rival camps and unrest simmering amongst the populace. Among other tasks, securing a fair election may entail preventing voter intimidation, not to mention protecting the safety of the candidates and their supporters."

Kirk nodded. He wanted to believe that elections and bloodshed were incompatible, but galactic history suggested that democracies sometimes experienced violent birth pangs—and didn't always survive. The descent of the First Sybellan Republic into anarchy came immediately to mind, as did the bloody Ballot Wars of Tammuz VI and too many other cautionary examples. Nobody wanted to see Vok turn into another failed state or dictatorship.

"You can count on the *Enterprise* and its crew, Commissioner, to provide whatever assistance you require."

"Thank you, Captain Kirk." She swept her steely gaze over her audience. "Let me stress the importance of ensuring a peaceful transition of power on Vok. Beyond the humanitarian aspects of our mission, the last thing anyone wants is war and chaos spreading into neighboring sectors. Fair elections on Vok won't resolve all the tensions in the region overnight, but, fortune willing, they'll bring greater stability to the sector . . . and that's in everyone's best interests."

McCoy sighed. "I'll stick to medicine if you don't mind. Politics brings out the cynic in me."

"You're not alone there," Dare conceded. "Ambrose Bierce once defined politics as 'a strife of interests masquerading as a contest of principles.'"

"Let's hope for more of the latter," Kirk said, "and less of the former."

"I wouldn't count on it," McCoy said.

"So I understand you've been to Vok before?" Kirk asked Dare as the landing party prepared to beam down to Yant, the planet's capital city, to meet with the presidential candidates. He was decked out in his dress uniform for the occasion.

"That's right," she replied. "Years ago, as a junior member of the diplomatic corps, I helped establish formal relations with Vok. One of my first big assignments, actually, so I have a personal attachment to the planet and its inhabitants. It's a terrific world, full of natural beauty, a rich culture, and warm, welcoming people, even if, politically, they've gone through some difficult times over the last few decades. The military staged a coup twenty-seven years ago, during a severe economic downturn, but the people are ready to try democracy again."

"I look forward to getting to know them," Kirk said.

The *Enterprise* had made good time getting to Vok. The election was still more than a week away, giving them time to get settled in to observe the proceedings. For this initial meeting, Kirk had kept the landing party to a minimum in order to seem less like an occupying force. Only he, Dare, and Yeoman Zahra occupied the transporter platform. Spock had the bridge, while McCoy had seemed happy to stay put in sickbay for "medical reasons."

"I'm allergic to politics," he'd insisted.

Bones never did like dressing up for formal occasions, Kirk recalled.

"Any word from the planet, Mister Scott?" he asked the engineer, who was at the transporter controls.

"Aye, sir. We're receiving the exact coordinates now. Just needed a moment to provide the proper passwords to get past a few extra layers of encryption." Scott frowned at the inconvenience. "A bit of a bother, if you ask me."

"Better safe than sorry, Mister Scott. We're meeting with the future leaders of the planet at a crucial juncture in their history." Kirk shrugged. "Can't blame the Vokites for wanting to take all prudent safety precautions."

"I suppose not, sir," Scott conceded. "Regardless, we're ready when you are, Captain."

"Very good, Mister Scott." Kirk glanced to confirm that Dare and Zahra were in position. "Energize."

As ever, the transport was near instantaneous. Kirk and his party suddenly found themselves in a large, well-lit parlor boasting the garishly colored walls and furnishings favored on Vok. Only a handful of individuals were present, all humanoid in appearance; like many alien species, Vokites were more or less indistinguishable from humans at first glance. Kirk recognized the rival candidates. Opaque windows provided privacy from prying eyes.

A young man in a conservative Federation business suit stepped forward to greet them. A slight accent indicated Neptunian roots. Kirk recognized him as Steve Tanaka, Dare's advance man, who had come ahead to lay the groundwork for the mission.

Fashionable sideburns framed his youthful countenance; a pencil mustache provided a rakish flair—or possibly just represented an attempt to look more mature. Dare had spoken highly of Tanaka on the voyage here.

"Commissioner, Captain Kirk, Yeoman, welcome to Vok."

"Good to see you again, Steve." Dare glanced around. "I take it everything is in order?"

"You bet," he said. "Per your instructions, I've arranged a larger, more public reception later this afternoon, complete with vid opportunities and press coverage, but this gathering is just for the principals, to give everyone a chance to meet outside of the public eye."

Kirk saw the wisdom in that. Less chance of political posturing if nothing else. He also observed that there didn't seem to be a lot of mingling going on; both camps were keeping to themselves, eyeing each other warily from opposite sides of the room. He didn't need a psycho-tricorder to pick up on the tension between them. It was just as well that phasers or any other kind of sidearm had been banned from the occasion.

He was pondering how best to break the ice when the reform candidate, Doctor Ceff, took the initiative. Loose, neon-bright fabrics swirled about her short, roundish form as she crossed the room. A warm smile, rosy cheeks, and laugh lines added character to her features. A pile of fuzzy auburn hair contributed several centimeters to her height. She came forward, accompanied by an older man, who bore a distinct familial resemblance to Ceff, and a younger woman, who struck Kirk as roughly the same age as Chekov back on the *Enterprise*.

"Allow me to introduce my right and left hands," Ceff said after a few pleasantries. "This is my brother, Div, who also happens to be my campaign manager."

"Pleased to meet you," the man said. His auburn hair and rosy complexion matched his sister's, while his smile was perhaps a tad *too* broad. He shook Kirk's hand vigorously. A sweaty palm left

Kirk wishing for a discreet way to wipe his own hand off afterward. "The way I see it, my job is simply to make sure the voters get to know and appreciate my sister as much as I do. Beyond that, she sells herself."

Ceff chuckled indulgently. "Did I mention that Div used to work in marketing before joining my campaign?" She turned toward the younger woman. "And this is Prup, my number-one policy advisor. Don't be fooled by her tender years; she's one of the best students I ever taught back in my academic days and she has a prodigious grasp of the issues and how they affect the average citizen. I like to think she keeps me honest . . . and in touch with the younger generation."

"The professor is too kind," Prup said. Her straight blond hair was parted down the middle. A pale blue dress, suitable to the occasion, flattered her slender figure. A data slate was tucked under her arm. "She taught me everything I know."

"I certainly hope not," Ceff replied, chuckling again. "I'm counting on you to keep me informed of what I don't know, even when I don't want to hear it."

"My attitude as well," Kirk agreed. "I depend on my crew to provide me with information as well as their expertise and judgment. And I like to think that they're comfortable expressing their opinions, sometimes quite forcefully."

"Oh, I can attest to that," Dare said lightly, "particularly where your chief medical officer is concerned."

"I'll have to take your word for that," Ceff said. "Barring any unexpected medical emergencies."

"Knock on wood," Kirk said, taking a liking to Ceff so far. He reminded himself, however, that he needed to be evenhanded when dealing with the candidates vying for the leadership of the planet. He turned toward the opposition, who were standing a few meters away. Unlike Ceff and her people, who'd wasted no time approaching them, General Gogg and his supporters made the new arrivals come to them.

"General." Dare crossed the room to address him, followed by Kirk and the rest of the Federation party. "A pleasure to meet you at last."

"Commissioner, Captain."

Gogg was a tall, imposing presence, whose rigid bearing betrayed his military background even though he had traded in his uniform for a crisply pressed dark suit, with only a single medal testifying to his service. Cropped black hair had gone gray at the temples. Sharp, severe features matched his saturnine expression. A deep voice rumbled from his chest. His hands remained clasped behind his back.

"Thank you for making the time to meet with us today," Dare said.

"I could hardly surrender the field to the enemy," Gogg declared.

"The opposition, you mean," Kirk said. " 'Enemy' seems a bit strong for a peaceful election."

"I am not one to mince words," Gogg said. "This is a battle I intend to win . . . for our world's sake."

Kirk chose not to press the point. "Fair enough. We're just here to make sure everyone plays by the rules."

One of Gogg's aides snorted in derision. "Sure you are."

"I assure you," Dare said, "we take our role as impartial observers very seriously."

"I don't know," the aide said. "You lot looked pretty cozy with Ceff and her fellow subversives just now. Everyone knows whose side the Federation is on."

"That's enough, Sozz," the General said curtly. "Captain Kirk is a soldier with an honorable record. He and his associates must be accorded respect."

"Thank you, General," Kirk responded. "I can only reiterate what Commissioner Dare just stated. We're not here to interfere in your election."

Gogg looked squarely at Kirk, more or less ignoring Dare. If the diplomat was offended by this, she did a good job of hiding it. Kirk could only assume that she judged this a battle not worth fighting at the moment.

"I will take you at your word, Captain," Gogg said. "I have reviewed your career and find it most commendable. As a fellow military man, I am reassured that you are a soldier, not a politician."

"I appreciate the vote of confidence," Kirk said. "But, if you'll forgive me, aren't you a politician these days?"

"Don't remind me," Gogg said, sighing heavily, "but it's a sacrifice I'm prepared to make to protect our society from those who would weaken us. I am confident that, in the end, Vok will choose a strong leader to maintain order and hold on tightly to what belongs to us."

"Such as Braco?" Ceff asked, joining the conversation. "Surely, that is negotiable. Why not strive for a long-term solution that respects the claims of all?"

Gogg bristled. "The sacred birthplace of our species means so little to you? You would barter away our heritage, embolden our foes?"

"Ozalor doesn't have to be our foe," Ceff argued.

"Not our foe?" Gogg said. "Have you forgotten the billions they slew in The Leveling, the cities they laid waste to, the hundreds of centuries of hardship our people have endured because of Ozalor's perfidy? You dishonor our martyred ancestors with every word out of your seditious lips."

"That war was millennia ago, and Ozalor suffered as much as Vok," Ceff stated. "We need to look to the future, not the past."

The General huffed indignantly. "Maybe you can blithely dismiss our history, but I for one will never relinquish our proud heritage . . . or our rightful claim to the planet that spawned us."

"But that's never been proven," Prup chimed in. Ceff's young protégée looked up from her slate to add her own two cents. "And even if Braco *is* where our species evolved before colonizing Vok

and Ozalor, doesn't that mean Ozalor also has a legitimate interest in Braco?"

"You dare place the enemy's 'interests' on the level of your own
people?" spat the General's outspoken aide-de-camp. His face
flushed angrily. "That's nothing short of treason!"

"I'm sure that's not what my young associate meant." Div attempted to spin Prup's words. "Nobody has greater respect for
Vok's proud heritage than my sister and—"

Prup did not allow Div to speak for her. "Are you questioning
my patriotism?" she shot back.

"I'm calling you a traitor," Sozz said. "You and the rest of—"

"Everyone cool their engines." Kirk stepped between the two
factions in hopes of de-escalating the increasingly heated confrontation. He briefly wondered if he should have included a
couple of security officers in the landing party, while taking some
comfort in the knowledge that Zahra was trained in self-defense
and could handle herself in a tight spot if necessary. "Let's keep
things cordial."

"An excellent suggestion, Captain Kirk," Dare said. "These are
important issues and there will be plenty of opportunities to debate them, but perhaps now is not the time or the place? This is a
social occasion."

Kirk recalled Khan Noonien Singh's observation, a few years
ago, that social occasions were often just war concealed. Did General Gogg feel the same way? Did Ceff and her people?

"Very well," Gogg said. "There is little point in wasting breath
on those who cannot hear. Better to make my case to the people."

"On that we can agree," Ceff said. "This election is about convincing the voters, not each other."

Steve Tanaka spoke up. "Speaking of whom, perhaps now is a
good time to introduce you to the state-of-the-art computer that
will be tabulating the vote."

"By all means," Dare said, no doubt grateful for the change of
subject. "That's your field of expertise after all." Her voice con-

veyed total confidence in her aide. "I confess that Steve is much better versed in the technical aspects of modern suffrage than I am."

"Thanks." He crossed the room to address a vibrantly yellow steel wall. "Tanaka to VP-One. Requesting terminal access."

An amber-colored sensor beam, issuing from the ceiling, illuminated him for a moment.

"Biometric scan confirmed," a bodiless voice replied. *"Allowing access."*

The wall retracted into the floor, exposing a sophisticated computer terminal. Banks of processors, bedecked with blinking lights, flanked a central control pedestal facing a large circular screen that currently provided a view of a spherical satellite orbiting the planet. It was difficult to judge the size of the satellite against the vacuum of space, but it conveyed the impression of heft. Kirk understood that the satellite had been designed and built on Vok, albeit with technical assistance from the Federation.

"Meet Vok Populi," Tanaka said, grinning at the pun, "or, more simply, VP-One. The actual computer is in orbit above our heads, waiting to receive and tally the votes of every eligible adult on the planet come Election Day, which will last for one entire planetary rotation in order for VP-One to receive ballots transmitted directly from voting stations all over the globe, without any need for intermediary relays. Our goal? A completely automated system, eliminating any possibility of humanoid error or tampering. VP-One is autonomous and incorruptible, at least as far as possible."

Kirk frowned. Memories of Landru and M-5 and other rogue computers compelled him to play devil's advocate. "Are we sure that's wise, placing that much power in the hands of a machine?"

"I understand your concerns, Captain," Tanaka said, seemingly unfazed by Kirk's query. "I studied under poor Doctor Daystrom back in my undergrad days, so I understand where you're coming from. Let me assure you that, bottom line, VP-One is just a glorified calculating machine, not a genuine artificial intelligence with any possibility of developing its own agenda, nor is it tied into the planet's defense grid or anything like that. Heck, it's actually programmed to self-destruct if it's ever irretrievably compromised, not that such a breach is remotely possible. Advanced duotronic firewalls and algorithms allow VP-One to detect and avert any attempts at fraud or hijacking." He beamed at his pride and joy. "Trust me, we've taken every precaution."

"Glad to hear it."

Kirk had no desire to undermine anyone's confidence in the election results; that would be contrary to his mission. He figured, however, that it was better to address such issues head-on rather than let them go unspoken. In the long run, answering any worrisome questions in advance could only increase the odds of a fair and uncontested election.

"Nevertheless," he said, "might I suggest that some of my people conduct a review of the system, strictly in the interest of added redundancy. In particular, I'm thinking that I'd like my science officer, my chief engineer, and my communications specialist to look over the specs, if only to provide fresh eyes."

"I'm not sure that's necessary, Captain," Tanaka said. "Between me and my Vokite collaborators, we've already gone to extraordinary lengths to perfect VP-One and our voting centers."

"No doubt," Kirk said, not wanting to question the other man's efforts. "But given the importance of the election, why not err toward overkill when it comes to reviewing the systems in place?"

The captain knew he would feel more comfortable having the hardware, software, and transmission networks checked out by Scotty, Spock, and Uhura, respectively.

"Why not, indeed?" Dare said. "The *Enterprise* is at our disposal, so it would be foolish not to take full advantage of its gifted crew."

"Well, when you put it that way," Tanaka conceded. He nodded at Kirk. "Please let your officers know, Captain, that I will be happy to provide them with whatever technical specs they require."

"Thanks," Kirk said. "I appreciate your cooperation."

Tanaka shrugged. "That's what I'm here for. Now then, does anybody else have any questions?"

Prup raised her hand, as though still in a classroom. "I'm already fairly familiar with the basics of the systems, but I wouldn't mind a chance to go over some specifics with you in detail . . . although perhaps not at this particular moment."

"Naturally," Tanaka agreed. "Talk to me later about scheduling an appointment."

Gogg stepped forward. "I would prefer one of my own lieutenants attend any such conference."

"That can be arranged," Tanaka said amiably. "If that's acceptable to both parties."

"No problem here," Prup said. "We're all about transparency."

"Within reasonable limits, naturally," Div added. "Wouldn't want to give away our entire playbook before Election Day."

An electronic chime caught Tanaka's attention. He consulted his personal communicator.

"Ah, it's time for that public reception. We don't want to keep the press and various other dignitaries waiting. If you'll excuse me for a moment." He turned back toward the viewscreen. "Tanaka to VP-One. Secure terminal."

"Acknowledged. Securing."

The concealing wall slid back into place. Tanaka guided Kirk and the others toward a bank of waiting lifts.

"If you'll follow me, the media—and a full buffet—await."

"What about security?" Sozz asked warily. "How do we know this reception will not expose the General to unnecessary risk?"

"All the customary measures are in place," Tanaka said. "The guest list has been vetted and revetted by all concerned. There's no cause to worry."

"Easy for you to say," Sozz said. "We cannot take any chances with the General's safety, not with so many radicals and subversives about." He squinted suspiciously at Ceff and her entourage. "There are those who would stop at nothing to seize control of the state."

"Is that directed at us?" Prup objected. "Please! If anything, it's your diehard supporters who are more likely to resort to force to get their way, just like the old military regime did."

"Lies and propaganda," Sozz said. "It's well known your side tolerates no opposition to your so-called reforms."

Prup produced her data slate. "Would you care to back that up with facts? Perhaps consult the actual numbers regarding death threats against Doctor Ceff and assaults on nonviolent advocates for change?"

"Manufactured numbers," Sozz said. "The truth cannot be found in whatever spurious 'facts' you have on your device."

"Actually," Div said, "we're quite conscientious when it comes to our data collection and projections."

Sozz laughed harshly. "I wouldn't trust your data if you swore to it on the lives of your misbegotten forebears."

"Hey," Div objected, "there's no call for that kind of personal insult."

"I quite agree." Ceff confronted Gogg directly. "You mind calling off your attack dog, General Gogg?"

"He is merely speaking his mind," Gogg stated. "I cannot fault him for the passion of his views. Perhaps you should concentrate on reining in your own subordinates instead."

Kirk was about to intervene again when Dare beat him to the punch.

"Candidates, please!" she said. "We're about to go before the public. Is this really the picture you want to present to Vok?"

"Why not?" Sozz stated. "Why sugarcoat the truth about the combat we're engaged in?"

"Well, there's the truth and there's the *truth*," Div said. "Presentation matters."

Spoken like a salesman, Kirk thought, but he knew what Div meant. "*Electoral* combat, you mean. As I understand it, the message we want to convey today is that this contest will be fairly fought, with both sides in agreement regarding the rules of engagement, so maybe you shouldn't look as though you're ready to come to blows? This is supposed to be a *peaceful* election, correct?"

"Quite right, Captain," Dare said. "Let's put our best faces forward, so that whoever wins the election will do so without dispute."

She strode over to the lifts, which opened to receive them. Kirk found himself grateful that they wouldn't all have to squeeze into the same lift. That could make for an extremely uncomfortable ride, in more ways than one.

"Time to shake hands before the world," Dare said. "Smiles, everyone."

Easier said than done, Kirk thought.

TWO

"We're approaching the planet, Doctor."

Lieutenant Peter Levine was at the helm of the *Galileo* as the shuttlecraft sped through space toward Braco in response to an urgent medical emergency. McCoy shared the passenger area with Nurse Christine Chapel as the Class-M planet came into view through the forward portholes. Drifting clouds obscured unfamiliar continents.

"About time," McCoy muttered. "No offense, Levine. I know you're flying this shuttle as fast as you can. I'm just anxious to get there before it's too late."

The distress signal had reached the *Enterprise* several hours ago, alerting them to a serious outbreak of Rigelian fever in a remote mountain village on the planet. As the potentially fatal disease was not native to Braco, the local doctors apparently lacked the experience and resources to cope with the outbreak; in particular, they were desperately in need of ryetalyn, a rare mineral needed to cure the disease. Fortunately, McCoy had taken pains to keep an adequate supply of ryetalyn aboard the *Enterprise* ever since the fever had spread like wildfire through the ship two years ago. That supply was now on *Galileo*, waiting to be administered to suffering patients on Braco.

"No offense taken," Levine said. He was a trim, dark-haired security officer whose muscular build bespoke many rigorous workouts in the ship's gymnasium. He was also the captain of the gamma shift bowling team. "I understand that every second counts."

Kirk had been tied up in meetings on Vok when the alert

reached the *Enterprise,* so Spock had authorized the relief mission in the captain's absence. McCoy and Chapel had wasted no time getting underway. *Galileo* had made good time, but McCoy hated the idea of being too late to save even a single life.

One of the unfortunate side effects of space travel and exploration was bacteria and viruses spreading from planet to planet and sector to sector, despite the most stringent of precautions. McCoy hoped that it wasn't a Federation citizen who had brought the fever to Braco, but he fully intended to stop the spread of the disease. They could trace the source of the fever later, once the initial outbreak was under control. Maybe after the *Enterprise* completed its mission on Vok.

"Entering the atmosphere," Levine said. "There may be some turbulence. Buckle up."

He wasn't joking. Thunder and lightning shook the shuttle, making for a bumpy descent. McCoy glanced over his shoulder to make sure the ryetalyn was stored securely at the rear of the spacecraft.

"It'll be fine, Doctor," Chapel assured him. "No need to worry."

"Who said I was worried?" he groused. "And how the devil are you keeping so calm on this roller coaster? Did you help yourself to a tranquilizer when I wasn't looking?"

"No," she quipped back, "but I'd be happy to administer one to you if you'd like."

"That won't be necessary." He settled back into his seat to ride out the storm. "Just feels like my innards are about to slingshot through time."

"Won't be much longer," Levine promised. "I'm dropping below the cloud cover to get away from the turbulence."

True to his word, he piloted them out of the storm. The roiling clouds gave way to clearer skies as *Galileo* descended, then leveled out at a lower altitude. The surface of the planet came into view. McCoy's eyes widened at the sight of a vast glittering expanse that appeared to stretch on for hundreds of kilometers. Empty plains, seemingly devoid of life, reflected the fading sunlight as though carpeted by Spican flame gems in a wide variety of hues.

"Well, that's something," he said. "What are we looking at?"

"The Sea of Glass," Chapel replied. "A souvenir of an atomic attack on the planet millennia ago. Legend has it that it was once as smooth and glossy as a mirror, but time and the elements long since shattered it into a sea of tiny glass particles, most no larger than a grain of sand." She gazed out at the sparkling vista. "Hard to believe that something so tragic could create such beauty."

McCoy looked over at her. "How do you know all this? Have you been here before?"

"No," she said. "But it was a long flight, so I had plenty of time to do some reading on the way here."

He noticed the data slate resting in her lap. He guessed that she had been reading up on Braco while he'd been reviewing the latest medical literature on Rigelian fever.

"A very efficient use of your time," he commented. "Spock would approve."

Almost instantly, he regretted the remark. As far as he knew, Chapel had gotten over her hopeless crush on Spock, but she was no Vulcan; her feelings could be hurt.

She took the compliment in stride, however, looking not at all bothered. "Thank you, Doctor. I figured it couldn't hurt to learn the lay of the land."

Guess she's moved on after all, he thought. *Good for her.*

The shuttlecraft cruised over the glass sea until a range of rugged gray mountains appeared on the horizon. Sparse vegetation dotted the slopes as the lifeless glass gradually surrendered to a slightly more habitable landscape. Desert scrub marked the outskirts of the scintillating wasteland. Twilight approached as the planet's sun sank toward the mountains.

"The signal is coming from just up ahead," Levine reported. "Heading in for a landing."

Galileo slowed its approach. As they drew closer to their des-

tination, weathered steel buildings could be seen nestled in the
jagged foothills at the base of the mountains. Squinting, McCoy
glimpsed what looked like a mining camp all right, complete with
towering ore breakers, refineries, and dormitories, all built into
the stark, granite slopes and gorges. Solar panels and communications dishes cluttered the rooftops, but McCoy was disturbed
to spy little or no signs of life or activity. The sun was already
beginning to set in the east, but no lights were coming on in the
doorways or windows.

"Looks pretty quiet," McCoy said. "They know we're coming?"

"I've tried hailing them," Levine said, "but no response. All I'm
getting is the same distress signal on a continuous loop."

Chapel and McCoy shared a concerned look. "You think we're
too late, Doctor?" she asked.

McCoy didn't want to think so. He could be as pessimistic as
the next physician, and maybe more so than most, but he wasn't
about to pronounce the patient dead before doing everything he
could.

"Let's not assume the worst. Maybe everyone is too caught up
with the crisis to notice our approach." He eyed the disturbingly
desolate mining camp. "In any event, we'll find out soon enough."

Galileo touched down on a paved landing pad at the foot of
the hills, below the town. The landing party gathered up their
gear and supplies and exited the shuttlecraft. A brisk wind chilled
McCoy's bones, making him wonder if he should have put on a
jacket over his uniform. All three humans had been inoculated
against Rigelian fever before leaving the *Enterprise,* so there was
no chance of them contracting the disease or spreading it when
they departed, provided they maintained proper sterilization
protocols. They glanced around the landing pad, which appeared
empty except for a few rusty vehicles that looked as though they
had been sitting there since Pike captained the *Enterprise*. Weeds
sprouted through cracks in the pavement. Only rustling brush
greeted them.

"No reception committee?" Levine asked.

"Apparently not," Chapel said.

"This is damn strange," McCoy said. "It's not as though I was expecting a red carpet, but where is everybody?"

The lonely stillness puzzled him. If the outbreak was as bad as advertised, the place should be swarming with emergency medical personnel. Even if the local doctors and nurses were ill equipped to combat the fever, you'd think they'd be on hand to treat the victims' symptoms and try to ease their distress.

"That's what I was wondering," Chapel said. "Perhaps the whole area has been placed under quarantine?"

"Maybe," McCoy said, "but there still ought to be doctors caring for the patients inside the restricted zone, unless somebody decided to callously write off the entire town in order to contain the infection."

Sadly, such heartless measures were not unknown. Plague-ridden communities had sometimes been walled off by panicked authorities, both in Earth's past and on other worlds. It was hard to imagine that such atrocities could occur in a warp-capable civilization, but McCoy had seen too much to think that technological progress always went hand in hand with ethical advances. Just look at the Klingons and the Romulans, for example.

"I don't know," Levine said. "In that case, wouldn't there be barricades and guards to keep people from entering or leaving the quarantined area? Nobody ordered us away."

"Good point," McCoy said. "Are we sure we have the right co-ordinates?"

"Absolutely." Levine activated his tricorder. "I'm picking up some life signs up ahead, although it's hard to get a clear reading from this distance."

That's encouraging, McCoy thought. "Guess we need to get closer, then."

A steep pathway, cutting between two tall ridges, led up to the town. Moving walkways had once assisted visitors, but, like the derelict vehicles on the landing pad, the people conveyors had obviously been out of commission for some time. The long-term neglect could not be attributed to the recent outbreak; McCoy could only assume that the mining outpost had fallen on hard times long before the fever struck. He shook his head at the forlorn conditions; he'd seen failed colonies in border systems that were less run-down. How many people still lived here, and how many of them were left?

The path was poorly maintained, and the fading sunlight didn't make it any easier to navigate. McCoy stumbled over a bulge where a thick root had warped the paving. Chapel grabbed his arm to keep him from falling.

"Watch your step, Doctor."

"I'll do that." McCoy regained his footing. "Thanks for the assist."

"Anytime." She let go of his arm. "Last thing we need is another patient on our hands."

Assuming there are still fever victims left to treat, McCoy thought. He was starting to have his doubts about that. This place felt like a morgue, not a community teeming with sick people. Was it possible even the doctors had succumbed to the fever already?

To McCoy's slight amazement, they made it to the top of the path without breaking their necks. An empty square provided no ready answers. Silent buildings surrounded them. No faces appeared in the darkened windows. Weeds clotted the gravelly floor of the square. A collapsed roof rendered a nearby storage shed unusable. Dislodged solar panels littered the ground. A derelict zee-gee forklift had toppled over onto its side. Vines had grown up around the wreck. Stagnant puddles filled depressions. A small lizard-like creature, no more than eight centimeters long, slithered away from the newcomers' approach, vanishing into a murky sewer grating. Nothing else seemed to notice their arrival. Nothing else seemed to be there to notice.

"It's like a ghost town," Levine said.

"Not *like* a ghost town." McCoy looked around, his eyes adjusting to the dimming light. "No fever could do this in only a matter of days. Something's not right here."

"Hello?" Chapel called out, raising her voice. "Is anyone here?"

Her voice echoed off the silent walls encircling them. McCoy grew increasingly uneasy. "You might as well save your breath, Nurse. I'm getting a bad feeling about this house call."

Levine looked apprehensive as well. He glanced back the way they'd come. "Maybe we should turn around and—"

A bright yellow disruptor burst came from one of the darkened windows, striking Levine before he even knew what hit him. He collapsed onto the weeds and gravel.

It's an ambush! McCoy realized. *They lured us here like lambs to the slaughter!*

"Run!" he shouted to Chapel, drawing his type-1 phaser to cover her. He glanced over at Levine's fallen form. Shallow breathing indicated that the security officer had only been stunned, not killed, thank goodness, but McCoy was torn between helping Chapel escape and attempting to take Levine with them. Crouching down, he fired his phaser at random windows, but wasn't entirely sure where the disruptor burst had come from or even how many ambushers they were dealing with. What was the point of this attack and who was behind it? Why go to so much trouble just to ambush a Starfleet medical team?

Are they after the ryetalyn? he wondered. *That might fetch a pretty penny on the black market.*

"Hurry, Doctor. We need to get out of here."

Christine rushed to Levine's side instead of fleeing as instructed. She aimed her own phaser at the looming buildings, but she had no better idea where to fire than McCoy did. Their attackers could fire from cover, while the landing party was out in the open. Whoever had staged this ambush had planned it well.

"Blast it, Christine, I told you to run!"

"Not without you and Levine." She tugged at his unconscious form. "You think we can manage to get him to—"

A second disruptor burst, striking with pinpoint precision, took Chapel out. She dropped limply beside Levine, leaving McCoy the last man crouching, as it were. He was a sitting duck and he knew it.

"Show yourself, you bushwhackers!" he shouted at his faceless opponents. "This is no way to treat a doctor!"

A brilliant saffron blast cut off his complaints.

Three

Vok

"Excuse me, Mister Spock," Yeoman Mears said. "Would you care for a cup of tea?"

Seated in the captain's chair on the bridge, Spock looked up from the data slate he had been reviewing, paused to assess his current need for liquid refreshment, and calmly replied in the negative.

"No, thank you, Yeoman. That will not be necessary at this time."

"Aye, sir." She turned to exit the command circle. "Sorry to interrupt you."

"No need to apologize," Spock said. "I am not so easily distracted."

Indeed, he was more than capable of multitasking, as demonstrated by the fact that he was presently commanding the *Enterprise* in the captain's absence, while also conducting an in-depth analysis of the computer software operating the VP-One satellite meant to tabulate the results of the upcoming election on Vok. His gaze returned to the slate, where lines of code scrolled down the display screen for many thousands of virtual pages. The slate was slaved to the nearby science station, allowing him remote access to the myriad databanks he was accustomed to having at his fingertips. It would have been more convenient, of course, to simply work at his usual post, but he grasped the psychological and symbolic importance of not leaving the captain's chair unoccupied, even if such concerns were not entirely logical. He resisted the temptation to cast a glance at the science station; such an action would come dangerously close to sentiment or wishful thinking, neither of which was worthy of his Vulcan heritage.

He scanned the computer code at a rate that allowed for both speed and thorough comprehension. Much remained to be reviewed, but so far he was impressed by the quality of the coding. Although it lacked the sophistication of Vulcan programming, it was a robust, solid piece of software that appeared more than sufficient to the crucial task it was designed for, while being prudently secure from outside interference or sabotage. As he studied the various routines and subroutines and sub-subroutines, Spock employed a stylus to annotate the program, suggesting a number of subtle changes to improve the efficiency and security of the system, which he intended to pass on to Steve Tanaka for implementation. That Commissioner Dare's protégé had made significant contributions to the program could be seen in the code itself; Tanaka's signature was woven through the system in the form of certain protocols characteristic of modern Federation duotronics. Indeed, Spock could discern the legacy of Doctor Richard Daystrom in VP-One's software, not unlike the way an ancestor's genes could be found entwined in the DNA of a living being. It occurred to Spock that, in a way, VP-One was a hybrid like himself, given that it was born of both Vokite and Federation technology.

One hoped it felt less conflicted.

"Mister Spock," Lieutenant Uhura said, "I'm receiving an emergency transmission from Nurse Chapel."

Chapel?

Spock was immediately concerned and intrigued. He consulted the chronometer installed between the helm and navigation consoles. By his calculations, Chapel, Doctor McCoy, and Mister Levine would have reached Braco approximately three hours and thirty-four minutes ago; although it was somewhat unusual that they had not yet reported back to the *Enterprise*, he would expect them to be entangled with the medical crisis. What emergency had they encountered on Braco and why was Nurse Chapel hailing them, not Doctor McCoy? Had something happened to the doctor?

"Do we have visual?" Spock asked.

"Yes, Mister Spock," Uhura said. "The signal comes via sub-space relay."

"On-screen, please, Lieutenant."

"Aye, sir."

Christine Chapel appeared on the main viewer, looking some-what the worse for wear. Her blond hair was mussed, while her blue nurse's uniform appeared uncharacteristically soiled and rumpled. Lieutenant Peter Levine could be seen behind her, peer-ing over her shoulder. He also appeared to be in less than pristine condition, while his grim expression complemented her worried one, both of which foretold bad news in store. Spock noted that they appeared to be transmitting from an office of some sort, pre-sumably on Braco.

"Mister Spock," Chapel said. *"Is Captain Kirk available?"*

"The captain is on Vok, dealing with political matters," Spock said. "Is Doctor McCoy with you?"

"I'm afraid not." Her tone indicated a significant degree of emotional strain. *"We believe he's been kidnapped!"*

Despite his Vulcan nature, Spock had served among humans and other highly emotional beings long enough to register that a heightened state of tension now existed on the bridge. In truth, he was troubled by the news as well, although he would not allow that reaction to affect his judgment or behavior. What was re-quired now was information, not emotive displays.

"Please elaborate, Nurse."

"Yes, Mister Spock, I'll do my best."

With admirable concision, given her obvious distress, she recounted how the landing party had arrived at the alleged site of the fever outbreak only to discover an apparently abandoned ghost town, where unknown assailants had targeted the party with disruptors.

"Levine and I were both stunned by the sniper . . . or snipers. When we regained consciousness a few hours later, we were still where we fell, but there was no trace of Doctor McCoy."

"Which implies that he was the true target all along," Spock deduced. "Hence the fabricated medical crisis to bring him to the site of the ambush."

"He is still alive, isn't he, Mister Spock?" she asked hopefully. *"If they had wanted to kill him, they would have left his body behind, so they must have taken him."*

"Your logic is sound," he reassured her after his fashion. "Although we cannot rule out more dire scenarios, it is far more likely that McCoy was removed from the site alive."

"Thank heavens for that," she said. *"I couldn't bear it if I thought we'd lost him."*

"What about you and Lieutenant Levine?" Spock asked. "Are you well?"

"A bit shaken up, and bruised in places from collapsing onto gravel," Chapel said, *"but nothing serious."*

Spock accepted her expert assessment. "Have you contacted the local authorities on Braco?"

"Yes, Mister Spock. I'm broadcasting to you from the planetary police headquarters in the capital city of O'Kdro. We would have contacted you earlier, but the Galileo's *communications systems lacked the range to reach the* Enterprise, *and there seemed no point in searching a ghost town, so we flew to the city and got in touch with the authorities . . . all of which took longer than it should have."*

"Do not blame yourself, Nurse. Your circumstances were less than ideal," he said. "Your decision to immediately seek out the local authorities was a logical one. Do they have any information or insights regarding Doctor McCoy's apparent abduction?"

"They say they're looking into it," she said, frustration evident in her tone, *"but if they've learned anything, they haven't told us about it."*

Spock recalled that, due to Braco's disputed status, the Federation had no formal embassy or presence there. As he understood it, both Vok and Ozalor claimed the planet as the birthplace of their race, with rival factions on Braco claiming allegiance to one neighboring planet or the other. The abduction of a Starfleet medical officer, on a mission of mercy no less, could certainly be seen as a politically delicate matter by the planetary authorities; Spock would not be surprised if local officials wanted to carefully manage the situation or perhaps even cover it up, which suggested that the *Enterprise* could not necessarily count on the full cooperation of the Bracon authorities.

"*To be honest, Mister Spock, I'm at my wit's end,*" Chapel said. "*Even if we wanted to search for Doctor McCoy on our own, we have no idea where or how to begin. Or should we return to the* Enterprise?"

Spock considered the options, weighing the safety of Chapel and Levine against the need to locate McCoy. Logic dictated that if the anonymous snipers had wished to harm or kidnap the rest of the landing party, they would have already done so, which implied that Chapel and Levine were in no immediate danger on Braco. Then again, the unknown nature of the attackers and their motives precluded any definitive assessments of the threat. Leaving Chapel and Levine where they were was an acceptable risk.

"I must confer with the captain, but for the present remain on Braco to monitor the situation. I take it no one has claimed responsibility for the abduction or made any demands for McCoy's safe return?"

"*Not that I know of, Mister Spock,*" she said. "*I almost wish somebody would, just so we would know what has become of him. Not knowing anything is torture.*"

"Insufficient data is often worrisome," he sympathized. "Inform us immediately of any new developments. I expect a swift response from Captain Kirk. No doubt assistance will be dispatched to Braco shortly."

"*Thank you, Mister Spock,*" she said. "*I shudder to think what the doctor could be going through right now.*"

"I share your concern," Spock said. "In the meantime, I urge you and Lieutenant Levine to take every reasonable precaution with regard to your own safety. Without more information, we have no way of knowing how close by his abductors may be to you . . . or whether they will strike again."

"*Don't think I haven't thought of that,*" Chapel said, "*but if there's anything we can do to get Doctor McCoy back, then we're not going anywhere.*"

"*That goes double for me,*" Levine chimed in.

Spock admired their dedication to duty and concern for the doctor's welfare. He took comfort in knowing that Levine was on hand to provide security. He had been caught unawares before, but the young officer was surely on high alert now.

"Stand by for further instructions," he said. "*Enterprise* out."

"*Who is behind this, Spock?*" Kirk asked. "*And why McCoy?*"

At Spock's request, Lieutenant Uhura had relayed the transmission to the desk viewer in his quarters, where he had retired to converse in private with Kirk. The captain was presently on Vok with Commissioner Dare, conducting an inspection tour of various major metropolitan voting centers, while also advising on global voter education campaigns, taking part in the negotiations over the terms of the forthcoming presidential debates, and other activities pertinent to the task of observing the election.

"The identity of the ambushers is unknown," Spock replied. "As to why they chose to abduct Doctor McCoy, one can only assume that the kidnappers were in need of a physician of his caliber. It is perhaps significant that Federation medicine is generally more advanced than is typical for this sector."

"*But why not just ask for McCoy's help?*" Kirk wondered aloud. "*He didn't think twice about rushing off to Braco in response to a medical emergency, which they obviously counted on, so they could hardly expect him to refuse any legitimate request for medical assistance.*"

"I concur," Spock said, "which suggests that the kidnappers have a strong motive for not going through conventional channels, perhaps because they need McCoy for some unlawful or highly confidential purpose." He pondered that possibility before moving onto another. "Or it could simply be that McCoy was seen as a high-value hostage."

"Then why have there been no demands? No ransom requests?"

"An intriguing question," Spock said, "whose answer is most likely to be found on Braco."

"My thoughts exactly," Kirk said. *"My first instinct is to return to the ship and immediately set course for Braco at maximum warp, and yet . . ."*

Kirk hesitated, as though reluctant to follow the thought to its inevitable conclusion.

"You have a larger mission," Spock finished for him, "which you are not at liberty to abandon simply because of one missing crew member."

"But this is Bones we're talking about, Spock! I know I can't postpone an election just to go searching the sector for one man, but it's hard to put politics above the safety of one of my best friends. One of our best friends."

Spock could not dispute that designation. Despite their significant differences in temperament, and frequent verbal sparring, Spock valued Leonard McCoy as a personal friend as well as a man of great character. It was for that reason that Spock had chosen both Kirk *and* McCoy to stand beside him at *Koon-ut-kal-if-fee.* McCoy had saved Spock's life on more than one occasion, so he too felt an urgent need to rescue McCoy from whatever peril the doctor now faced, and with as much alacrity as possible.

"Nevertheless, as the commissioner would surely remind us, this is not just any election. It is a turning point in the history of this planet and possibly this entire sector as well. Its outcome will have consequences extending beyond Vok and its home system, perhaps even so far as to impact the interests of the Federation. Far more than ordinary 'politics' is at stake."

"I know, I know," Kirk said, visibly wrestling with the dilemma. *"But maybe Dare and Tanaka can see to matters on Vok while we hunt for McCoy. They're the diplomats after all."*

"The commissioner is counting on the full resources of this ship and its crew. Starfleet did not dispatch the *Enterprise* to Vok simply to ferry Dare here and move on. Observing the election is our mission as much as theirs." A new thought occurred to Spock. "Indeed, it is not impossible that McCoy was abducted for the express purpose of luring the *Enterprise* away from Vok and our mission."

"But by whom?" Kirk asked again. *"The Klingons? The Romulans? The Orions?"*

"Unlikely," Spock stated. "This region of space is well beyond their respective spheres of influence. It is only the Federation that has colonies and outposts just a few systems away. Although we cannot rule out the possibility that rival powers have long-term designs on this sector, it strikes me as more probable that Braco's own fraught political status is relevant here."

He saw no need to remind Kirk of the planet's history, given their recent briefings on the subject and the fact that Braco was a major issue in the Vokite presidential campaign. No doubt the captain had already heard more than enough on the topic—from both sides.

"What do you suggest, Spock?"

"You and the *Enterprise* are needed here. Let me take a shuttlecraft to Braco to investigate Doctor McCoy's disappearance. Mister Scott can assume command while you are occupied on the planet, while my skills are perhaps better suited to searching for clues." He allowed himself a wry smile. "My father is the diplomat, not I."

"Don't sell yourself short," Kirk said, *"but I take your point . . . even if I don't want to."* A scowl betrayed his frustration. *"I won't*

lie. *I hate the idea of delegating this assignment to anyone else, but if I trust anyone to find Bones and bring him home safe, it's you.*"

"I will endeavor to justify your confidence in me."

Kirk nodded, his decision made.

"*Very well, Mister Spock. The mission is yours. Assemble whatever team you require. I assume you intend to leave for Braco with all deliberate speed?*"

"That is my intention. The *Copernicus* is already being prepped for departure."

Spock regretted taking another of the *Enterprise*'s shuttlecrafts to Braco when the *Galileo* was already there, but time was of the essence. The kidnappers were already several hours ahead of any investigation; McCoy could be anywhere on the planet—or in the sector—by now.

"*Be careful, Spock. I don't want to lose you too.*"

"That would be most regrettable," Spock agreed.

Four

Vok

Acrobats tumbled across the stage of a capacious outdoor amphitheater built into an immense crater left behind by The Leveling centuries ago. Throngs of men, women, and children packed tiered benches carved into the southern half of the crater, facing the huge arched proscenium before them. Jugglers and clowns performed to the lively beat of local musicians, who occupied bleachers at the back of the stage. Contortionists literally twisted themselves into living hoops and ladders and tightropes, turning their bodies into platforms upon which their fellow entertainers executed graceful feats of gymnastic dexterity. Sparkling capes and tights, liberally bedecked with sequins and costume jewelry, delighted the eye. A tumbler took a swig from a gleaming metal flask, then exhaled a burst of phosphorescent green plasma into the air above his head, drawing gasps and cheers from the audience, who were here for a political rally in support of Doctor Ceff's campaign. Kirk was impressed by the turnout, as well as by the energetic performers warming up the crowd prior to the speeches.

"See what I meant about Vok having a rich and vibrant culture," Imogen Dare said to Kirk as they watched from the wings. The high acoustic shell above the stage provided shade from the bright afternoon sunshine. "Years of political strife have not squashed their zest for life and self-expression. The carnival arts are a vital aspect of their culture, occupying a role comparable to, say, subsonic throat-singing among the Slemomites or cloud-diving to the Jiploo." A nostalgic smile lifted her lips. "I got pretty good at juggling during my first stint here years ago."

"I can imagine," Kirk said. His archery had improved during his cultural survey of the planet Neural back in the day. "When on Vok . . ."

"Precisely."

Thoughts of Neural reminded Kirk of the dangers he and McCoy had faced together the last time they visited that primitive world. That Bones was missing troubled Kirk, making it hard to truly enjoy the Vokite entertainers' artistry and showmanship. Nevertheless, he had thought it best to attend the rally after being invited to do so by the campaign. Beyond simple courtesy, he saw it as an opportunity to get a real feel for the mood on the ground, as opposed to merely gazing down on Vok from the bridge of the *Enterprise*. He was here to observe the election after all.

The campaign had lucked out as far as the weather was concerned. A clear blue sky and abundant sunlight had encouraged attendance; Kirk estimated that at least a thousand people had turned out for the event. He assumed most of the audience supported Doctor Ceff, but he had to imagine that there were some dissenters present as well. Scanning the folks crowding the seats, he spied a few surly faces whose unhappy expressions were unrelieved even by the pre-rally entertainment. Silver epaulets, which he had come to understand symbolized loyalty to the old military regime, were boldly displayed by a few clumps of spectators, drawing dirty looks from their neighbors. Ceff was clearly in for some heckling.

Fine, Kirk thought. *Just as long as heckling is all they have in mind.*

He mentally reviewed the security procedures in place. Automated sensors scanned the entrances and seating areas for weapons. Local and Starfleet security personnel were stationed throughout the amphitheater; the latter were discreetly armed with inconspicuous type-1 phasers set on stun. An invisible force field shielded the stage.

"Ceff should be coming out anytime now," Dare observed. "In theory."

Kirk knew the candidate was prepping backstage while conferring with various consultants, staff members, and well-wishers. By his calculations, the event was already running a bit behind schedule.

"I wonder if any political rally has ever started on time," he said.

"Not in my experience," Dare said. "Although I wouldn't be surprised if the General's events are run with military precision."

Kirk reminded himself to attend one of Gogg's rallies as well, simply in the interests of parity. "Unless the realities of civilian politics prove less amenable to that sort of discipline."

"Quite possible," Dare said. "I remember one time on Benecia—"

Div emerged from backstage, interrupting Dare's anecdote. The campaign manager appeared somewhat harried, but still greeted them heartily.

"Commissioner, Captain! Glad you could make it! Hope you're enjoying the entertainment!"

"Very much so," Kirk said. "I'm impressed by their energy and talent."

"Thanks!" Div took a moment to wipe his brow. A headset kept his hands free. "They came highly recommended."

Onstage, the plasma-breather was displaying another trick in his repertoire. A compact rod expanded into a lethal-looking spear with a sharp point at each end; tilting his head back, he eased the length of the spear down his throat in the manner of a traditional circus sword-swallower, all while hanging upside down from an antigrav trampoline upon which two other performers were juggling flaming torches. Kirk repressed a wince even as he admired the man's daring. Juggling struck the captain as a less risky hobby.

"Ouch," Dare said.

"My thoughts exactly," Kirk said.

"I'm sure he's done it a hundred times before," Div said before being distracted by a voice over his headset. "What's that?

She's ready to go on? Fantastic. Cue the entertainment to wrap it up."

Concealed lights, visible only to those onstage, signaled the performers, who took their final bows before scurrying off the stage, some of them brushing past Kirk and Dare on their way backstage. The musicians filed out of the bleachers as well, to be replaced by rows of local dignitaries and lower-ballot candidates. Scattered cheers and applause rewarded the departing acts, even as the audience sat up straighter in anticipation of the main event. Kirk noticed that many of the performers lingered in the wings to see and hear Ceff. An amplified voice rang out from the loudspeakers, assisted by the innate acoustics of the amphitheater.

"Brothers and sisters, fellow citizens, people of Vok, thank you for your patience. Now let's welcome the person you've all been waiting for, the future president of our planet . . . Doctor Ceff!"

Ceff strode onto the stage, waving and beaming at the crowd. Cheers drowned out any boos or hisses. Basking in the warm reception, Ceff let the din die down before speaking. Standing at center stage, without any podium, she addressed the audience.

"Good afternoon, everyone! I'm enormously grateful to you all for joining us. Regardless of whether you're for us or against us or undecided, the very fact that you've taken the time to come out today proves that you care deeply about the future of our world, as well as our relations with our interplanetary neighbors—"

"Traitor! Appeaser!"

A man sporting silver tassels on his shoulders hurled a translucent globe at Ceff, only to have it splatter against the force field guarding the front of the stage. Azure energy briefly crackled and flared as a viscous blue ooze slid harmlessly down the invisible screen between the stage and the audience. Not being a native, Kirk wasn't sure exactly what had been thrown at Ceff, but he was relieved; the field had proved a wise precaution. He watched with approval as a security team from the *Enterprise* moved quickly to remove the offender, in part for his own protection. Kirk briefly feared that a larger donnybrook might erupt in the stands, but, aside from some shouting and fist-shaking, his people managed to swiftly contain the situation. Kirk made a mental note to commend the team later, even as anonymous campaign workers scrambled to clean up the mess at the base of the stage and Ceff did her own part to calm the crowd.

"It's fine," she assured her listeners. "I'm fine. Everything is under control, thanks to the terrific work of people responsible for making this a safe environment to discuss the serious issues affecting us all. Let's not allow one intemperate protest to divert us from what brought us together today." She paused to let the crowd settle back into their seats. "Obviously, this election is provoking heated feelings and, honestly, that's to be expected. This is new ground for all of us, so there's bound to be some growing pains, but the whole point of the election is to give us a means to settle our differences peacefully and in an orderly fashion. It's about communicating our views, without rancor or violence, and letting the people choose for themselves."

Kirk listened to the speech while keeping his eye on the audience. He didn't want any more unexpected disturbances.

"We mustn't fear or oppose disagreement," Ceff continued. "That would make us no better than the old regime, who offered security at the expense of our liberty. Some say that this election is a dangerous mistake, that we can't be trusted to choose our own leaders, that peace means weakness or surrender, but I believe that we as a people are stronger than that, that we're more than capable of making our own decisions and charting our own course to a better future, on our own and as part of a larger galactic community."

Mixed cheers and jeers greeted her pronouncement. Kirk remained on guard.

"At this point, I'd like to take a moment to thank our friends from the United Federation of Planets for lending us a helping hand on our bold new voyage into democracy."

Ceff gestured for Kirk and Dare to join her on the stage, but Kirk hesitated, uncertain whether this could be seen as endorsement on the Federation's part. He looked to Dare to see what she thought.

"It's okay," she said. "I've got this."

Straightening her suit, she started toward Ceff while waving at the audience, some of whom probably wondered who exactly she was. Kirk trusted her to expertly finesse the situation in a properly diplomatic fashion. He was happy to cede the spotlight while he kept watch over the crowd. He had no idea if anyone in the audience was hostile to the Federation, but, after the incident a few minutes ago, he was still worried about a fight breaking out in the seating area.

"Look out!" Div pointed frantically at the rear of the stage. "He's got a spear!"

His cry electrified Kirk, who swung his gaze away from the audience to see the spear-swallower from earlier charging out from behind the bleachers at the back of the stage where the various dignitaries were seated, and where he must have been lurking all this time. He hurled his javelin at Ceff, who was several meters away. It flew toward its target.

"For the General!" he shouted.

No! Kirk thought. He realized too late that he'd been looking for danger from the wrong direction. The would-be assassin had flaunted his weapon onstage in front of all of them.

Kirk was too far away to stop the spear in time, but Dare was already halfway toward Ceff. Reacting quickly, she dove to shield Ceff from the attack. She knocked Ceff to the ground, then cried out in pain as the spear struck her in the back. She collapsed onto Ceff, still shielding the candidate with her body.

"Commissioner!" Kirk said.

Pandemonium erupted on the stage and throughout the amphitheater. Kirk sprang into action, intent on subduing the attacker, only to find himself blocked and buffeted by panicked bystanders scrambling for safety. Invited guests pushed and shoved their way off the bleachers, dashing for the exits. Scared people tried throwing themselves off the stage into the audience, only to bounce off the force-field curtain trapping them in with the assailant. A few braver souls, including Div and Prup, rushed toward Ceff and Dare, seeking to render assistance.

Unfortunately, the assassin was still intent on his target as well.

Instead of fleeing, the caped performer produced another expandable javelin from a pouch on his belt. Kirk drew his phaser, but he couldn't get a clean shot through the commotion. He was unwilling to stun fleeing civilians in the middle of a dangerous situation, especially when the full extent of the threat remained unclear. Kirk glanced about anxiously, wary of other hostiles. Was the assassin acting alone or as part of a larger, coordinated attack?

"Out of my way!" The man swung his javelin before him like a scythe, struggling to clear a path through the uproar to Ceff, who was still at the front of the stage. He was clearly not satisfied with just spearing Dare. "Let me at that traitor!"

Kirk glimpsed Prup and others trying to hustle Ceff to safety, despite her reluctance to abandon Dare. He was briefly torn between tackling the assassin and tending to the wounded diplomat.

"Say your prayers, subversive!"

The attacker closed in on Ceff, who wasn't getting away fast enough. Putting away his phaser for the moment, Kirk moved to intercept the assassin, shoving his way through the frantic mob with both hands, even if it meant tossing people out of his way without apology. He pushed forward in time to see the erstwhile plasma-breather take a swig from his flask. To his alarm, Kirk saw that the man was less than a few meters away from Ceff and those trying to remove her from the stage. Kirk pushed through the mob to reach him first. He shouted to get the assassin's attention, hoping to distract him long enough for Ceff to escape.

"That's far enough, mister! Drop that spear!"

The man turned to glare at Kirk. The crowd thinned between

them, so Kirk surged forward, drawing his phaser, but a gout of searing green plasma erupted from the man's mouth to scorch Kirk's outstretched arm. The blazing heat engulfed Kirk's hand. He screamed in agony and dropped the phaser, which was suddenly too hot to hold on to. He smelled his sleeve burning.

"Stay out of this, Starfleet!" the man snarled, exhausting his plasma breath. "This is none of your business!"

Kirk begged to differ. Despite the searing pain emanating from his burned hand, he charged at the assassin, who was still armed with a double-pointed javelin. Kirk wasn't going to let him get another shot at Ceff.

Not on my watch, he thought.

The man held on to the spear instead of throwing it, perhaps because he still wanted to use it on Ceff. He lunged at Kirk, holding the spear in front of him like a lance, but Kirk ducked and rolled beneath it, barreling into the man's legs like a bowling ball. The impact knocked the assassin off his feet, causing him to tumble face forward onto the stage. Kirk sprang to his own feet behind the other man, who started to lift himself off the floor, only to find himself on the receiving end of a flying kick to the skull that spared Kirk's injured fist from any further abuse. The assassin went limp, lying flat across his spear.

Should have stuck to carnival tricks, Kirk thought.

The captain stood over the downed assassin. Grimacing, he clutched his agonized hand to his chest and prodded the man with his foot to make sure his opponent was truly unconscious. Starfleet and Vokite security forces belatedly flooded the stage, securing the scene. From the looks of it, there were no other would-be assassins to be dealt with, thank goodness.

"Are you all right, Captain?" Lieutenant Yaeger asked.

Kirk glanced at his hand. It was red and blistered and hurt like the devil, but it looked like nothing sickbay couldn't handle . . . eventually. He had more urgent matters to attend to first.

"I'll manage, Lieutenant."

He lurched across the stage toward Dare. Steve Tanaka was already at her side, looking understandably distressed. Someone—Tanaka?—had extracted the spear from Dare's back, but there was a worrisome amount of blood in evidence. Dare groaned upon the floor of the stage, proof at least that she was still alive. Tanaka was trying desperately to stanch the blood while shouting over the tumult.

"Help, please! We need help here!"

Kirk joined him beside her. "How bad is it?"

"I don't know!" Tanaka said. "I'm not a doctor!"

Dare stirred. "Ceff?" she managed. "Is she—?"

"Safe," Kirk assured her. "Just hang on now. We've got you."

"Where's that medkit?" Tanaka shouted to anyone within earshot. "We need a medkit, pronto!"

"We can do better than that."

Kirk flipped open his communicator, fumbling awkwardly with his left hand. "Kirk to *Enterprise*. Three to beam up. Alert sickbay we have incoming."

"Understood, Captain," Lieutenant Uhura responded. "I'm monitoring alarming news broadcasts from the planet."

Kirk wasn't surprised she was on top of things. He appreciated that she didn't press him for more details. There would be time enough to brief the rest of the crew later.

A moan drew his attention to Dare's attacker, who was being taken into custody by Lieutenant Yaeger. Kirk's pained expression darkened.

"On second thought, make that *four* to beam up . . . and have security on hand to receive a prisoner."

He wanted to interrogate the attempted assassin himself.

Five

Ozalor

The hiss of a hypospray roused McCoy.

He awoke with a headache, a bad taste in his mouth, and a tingling sensation on his upper left arm that indicated that he had just been dosed with something. Groggy and disoriented, he blinked and looked around. As his head and vision cleared, he found himself lying on a couch in a sumptuously appointed chamber ornate enough to make an Elasian royal jealous. Wood-paneled walls were trimmed with polished blown-glass moldings and wainscoting. Elaborately woven carpets, sparkling with iridescent fibers, protected gorgeous parquet floors. Sunlight filtered through silken curtains. A desk viewer and air filtration indicated that the old-school luxury boasted modern conveniences as well.

"What the—?"

Last he remembered, he was pinned down by unseen snipers in a ghost town on Braco. Then a disruptor burst had knocked him out and . . .

He sat up straight, which made his head spin.

"Where in blue blazes am I?"

"Welcome to Ozalor, Doctor. The Summer Palace in Borostosio, to be precise."

The speaker was an older man, possibly in his sixties, standing a few paces away. He was tall and lean and formal in bearing. A neatly trimmed gray beard adorned his gaunt, angular features. He wore a crisp tan uniform distinguished by a reflective silver sash across his chest. He placed a hypospray down on a lacquered wooden coffee table and offered McCoy a crystal goblet. "Have some water. You must be thirsty."

McCoy had more urgent concerns. Ignoring the proffered drink, he checked instinctively for his phaser and communicator, only to discover them conspicuously (if predictably) missing. Scanning the room, he spotted another individual: a trim young woman standing between him and the nearest visible exit. Clad in a utilitarian olive-green jumpsuit, she leaned casually against the door while whittling on a colored piece of quartz with a glowing knife. The white-hot blade vaporized slices of quartz, leaving no shavings behind as the woman worked on her miniature carving. Bobbed black hair and bangs framed her face, which was crossed diagonally by an old scar slashing between her eyes from the left side of her brow to her right cheek. She smirked at McCoy as though daring him to make a break for it.

Not until I have a better idea exactly what kind of mess I'm in, he thought, *and what's happened to Chapel and Levine.*

"My nurse?" he asked. "And the officer who was accompanying us?"

"Left behind on Braco," the man assured McCoy. "Unharmed aside from being stunned by our weapons, from which they have surely recovered by now. We had no intention of injuring or abducting them. It was only your company we sought."

McCoy was relieved to hear it, even as the full implications of what he'd been told sank in.

"Hang on. This is Ozalor?" That was a full system away from Braco. "How long was I out?"

The man shrugged. "As long as necessary."

The headache, the fogginess, the metallic taste in his mouth; McCoy figured it out. "You drugged me."

"For the duration of the trip," the man admitted. "It was the most convenient way to convey you to Ozalor without any fuss. My apologies for the extreme measures we took to secure your presence, but the times called for them." He gestured at their opulent surroundings. "Please consider yourself our guest."

McCoy snorted. "Where I come from, guests aren't invited via weapons fire. Let me guess, there was no outbreak of Rigelian fever on Braco."

"Merely a ruse to lure you to a suitable spot for extraction. Again, my apologies. We would not have gone to such lengths were we not in urgent need of your services as a physician."

McCoy was skeptical. "You look pretty hale to me."

"It is not I who requires your care." The man held out the goblet again. "Please, you should drink something."

McCoy was tempted. To be honest, his mouth felt as dry as Vulcan's Forge and tasted like an industrial refuse heap. He eyed the goblet suspiciously, then decided that his captors wouldn't have roused him just to drug him again. If they'd wanted to poison him, they could have done so anytime between here and Braco.

"If you insist."

He accepted the glass and took a tentative sip. The water was cool and refreshing, with no worrisome aftertastes, so he gulped it down. He had to admit that it made him feel a bit more like himself again. His headache began to fade. Curiosity infiltrated his overall indignation at being shanghaied across the sector.

"I don't believe I caught your name, sir."

"I am Count Rayob, majordomo to our exalted sovereign, Salokonos, *Yovode* of Ozalor." He gestured at his associate, the woman with the knife. "And this is Jemo. She will look after you during your stay here."

She dipped her head in acknowledgment. "At your service."

"My jailer, in other words," McCoy translated.

"More like your bodyguard," Rayob said, "if you must know."

"Bodyguard?" McCoy didn't buy it. A captive being assigned a bodyguard struck him as a damned peculiar notion.

"Bodyguard, babysitter," Jemo said. "Take your pick."

She put a few finishing touches to her carving, then blew on it to cool it down. She lobbed it at McCoy, who caught it instinctively. Glancing down, he found himself holding a miniature quartz caricature of his own face, complete with an exaggeratedly cranky expression. Or maybe not so exaggerated, to be honest. He couldn't help admiring the craftsmanship, but he was not about to be distracted or provoked by the gift. He still had plenty of questions he needed answered.

"Why would I need a bodyguard?"

Rayob sighed. "That requires some explanation, if I may."

"Not like I'm going anywhere." McCoy glanced at Jemo. "Am I?"

She shook her head.

"In that case," McCoy said, "I'm all ears."

"Very good." Rayob settled into a carved wooden chair across from McCoy, on the other side of the coffee table, where the empty goblet now rested. "But before we get down to matters of state, would you care for another drink? Perhaps something stronger this time?"

"Why not?" McCoy figured he was due a drink.

Rayob looked at his accomplice. "Jemo, if you don't mind."

"On it." She switched off her blade, which cooled to a silvery sheen before she slid it into a sheath at her hip. Crossing the room, she approached a framed silver mirror and addressed it. "Guest Suite Guya, refreshments."

The mirror retracted to reveal a built-in food slot, along with a manual control panel. Jemo deftly keyed in a command and a bottle and two glasses appeared in the slot. She retrieved the items and walked them over to the table, where she uncapped the bottle, then took a deep swig straight from it.

"For your peace of mind," she informed McCoy a gulp later. "You're welcome."

"How reassuring," he said dryly.

"Anytime."

She wiped her lips with the back of her hand, then poured two drinks for the men. The unnamed spirits were a deep caramel color. Rayob raised his glass in a toast.

"To your health, Doctor, and the health of the royal family."

Now we're getting to it, McCoy suspected. He had an inkling where this was going. He clinked his glass against Rayob's before sampling the vintage. It was a bit sweeter than a good bourbon, but prisoners couldn't be choosers. "I'm guessing that toast is not just a formality, and perhaps has something to do with why you brought me here?"

Against my will, he added silently.

Rayob nodded. "How much do you know of our world, Doctor?"

"Just the basics." McCoy thought back to Dare's briefing aboard the *Enterprise* not too long ago. "A hereditary monarchy, albeit a warp-capable one. You once fought a devastating interstellar war with your neighbor Vok, and you have a rather fraught history with the Federation, due to an unfortunate incident some years back. And apparently you're not above kidnapping Starfleet medical officers on occasion."

"Only with cause," Rayob insisted. "Suite, show us the *Yiyova*."

A voice-activated viewscreen manifested above the table. A holographic portrait depicted an attractive young woman with curly brown hair and thick, bushy eyebrows, who appeared to be in her teens by the standards of most humanoid species. She was elegantly posed in an embroidered gown, a warm smile on her face. Her right hand was placed over her heart, the better to show off a bracelet of polished agate; its prominence in the portrait suggested that the ornament held some symbolic significance. Sparkling hazel eyes conveyed a lively intelligence.

"Behold Avomora, beloved daughter of our sovereign, destined Heir to the Pellucid Throne of Ozalor," Rayob said. "The *Yiyova* by title."

McCoy assumed there was some nuance to the term that resisted universal translation. The holo had the look of an official portrait. "She's lovely."

"That is the least of her many fine qualities," Rayob said. "Despite her tender years, she is a lady of fine character and learning."

"Glad to hear it," McCoy said, with just a trace of impatience. "But what does that have to do with me?"

Rayob took a sip from his drink before answering. He examined McCoy thoughtfully. "May I count on your discretion, Doctor? As a physician, do you honor the seal of confidentiality where your patients are concerned?"

"That's between me and my patients, not me and my kidnappers," McCoy felt obliged to point out before attempting to allay the majordomo's concerns in order to keep him talking. "But, for what it's worth, I'm not one to gossip about medical matters."

Rayob appeared reassured. "That is as I anticipated. Your sterling reputation precedes you, Doctor."

"Lucky me. Now what's this all about?"

"This palace holds a secret, Doctor. Although the knowledge has been carefully kept from the people, the *Yiyova* is not well. She suffers from a debilitating illness that frequently leaves her incapacitated, while inflicting great distress and suffering on her royal person. Our own medical science has failed to relieve her of this ailment, which may ultimately threaten her ability to assume the throne when the time comes."

"I'm very sorry to hear that," McCoy said sincerely. His own predicament did not preclude his sympathy for any patient, even as he saw himself being reluctantly drafted into service. "Is there nothing your own doctors can do for her?"

"Our doctors? No," Rayob said. "Only Vumri."

He spat out the word (name?) with obvious disgust. He took another gulp of his drink as though to wash the taste of it from his mouth. Jemo's expression curdled as well.

"Who or what is a Vumri?" McCoy asked.

"A healer," Rayob said. "*Lossu* Vumri, to grant her the title due her, is one gifted with unique abilities beyond those of ordinary mortals. She alone has been able to relieve the *Yiyova*'s symptoms and ease her suffering."

A mystical healer with special powers? It sounded like superstitious hogwash to McCoy, but he was hesitant to jump to conclusions before he learned more. In a galaxy inhabited by telepaths and shape-changers and other unusually talented life-forms, not to mention all manner of exotic folk medicines, he'd learned not to be too presumptuous when it came to dismissing local legends and lore. Hell, he'd personally been on the receiving end of a Vulcan mind-meld more times than he cared to think about. Perhaps this Vumri's abilities were the real deal? Stranger things were possible on an alien world largely unknown to the Federation.

"I see," McCoy said. "So if your healer is helping her, where's the problem?"

"Vumri is hardly 'our' healer. She serves only herself," Rayob said. "Nor is she content merely to heal the sick. She takes advantage of her unequaled ability to treat Avomora to gain undue influence over our sovereign, at the expense of our world."

"Or maybe just at your expense?" McCoy challenged Rayob. "How do I know that the real problem isn't simply that this Vumri character is a threat to your own position at the court?"

Rayob stiffened, taking offense at the suggestion.

"I have devoted my life to the well-being of Ozalor and its rulers. This is not about my ambition. It is about what is best for my world, this sector, and perhaps even your own Federation."

His indignation struck McCoy as genuine. "How so?"

"Vumri does not seek peace between Ozalor and our neighbors. She clings to the ancient hatreds that once brought devastation to this entire sector. She zealously asserts our claims on Braco, urging more support to those who would bring the Birth World under our rule, even to the extent of fomenting civil war on that troubled planet, or, worse yet, actual conflict with Vok and its allies, including the Federation." Although softly spoken, his somber words relayed the gravity of his fears. "And as long as she alone can help his daughter, Vumri has our sovereign's ear."

McCoy nodded. What Rayob was saying matched up with

what Dare had explained during her briefing. Seemed as though hardliners on both Vok and Ozalor were unwilling to let go of the sector's tragic past.

"So what do you want from me?"

"To render Vumri superfluous," Rayob said. "If you, with your advanced Federation medicine, can find a better way to treat Avomora, or perhaps even cure her entirely, then Vumri ceases to be essential, weakening her hold on the royal family."

"Got it," McCoy said. "You want me to fix the princess so you can send this overly ambitious faith healer packing." He frowned, not entirely sure what he thought about that. Sticking himself in the middle of another planet's tangled court intrigues struck him as a risky proposition, in more ways than one. "I got to admit, I'm uneasy about poaching another doctor's patients."

"Vumri is no healer at heart," Jemo said with feeling. "She doesn't care about Avomora. She's just using the *Yiyova*'s affliction to gain power over the throne and further her own ends."

"Can't say I care for that idea either," McCoy admitted. If Vumri was indeed exploiting her position as a healer for political advantage, then McCoy already disliked her on principle. The fact that her hawkish politics were apparently counter to the best interests of the sector just made the scenario all the more disturbing. "If what you're saying is so."

"We speak only the truth," Rayob said, "but I cannot lie to you. You must be aware that these are perilous times. We are playing a dangerous game for the highest of stakes, and Vumri is a hazardous person to cross. Even with Jemo guarding you, I cannot fully guarantee your safety."

"Good thing you asked me first," McCoy drawled.

"Given the relations between the Federation and our world, along with the crucial need to keep the *Yiyova*'s condition a secret, that was never an option, Doctor."

"Easy for you to say," McCoy grumbled.

He finished off his goblet as he diagnosed his situation. Rising from the couch, McCoy stretched his legs by walking across the chamber to the nearest window and drawing back the curtain. That Jemo made no move to halt him suggested that the window was not a viable escape route even before he discovered the suite was several stories above the grounds outside. He gazed out over sunlit gardens, manicured lawns, sparkling pools and fountains, and, beyond the outer walls of the estate, rolling hills and verdant countryside. The so-called Summer Palace certainly lived up to its name; the contrast with that desolate ghost town on Braco was enough to give McCoy whiplash.

Pretty enough as cages go, he thought, *but still a cage.*

He wondered again about Chapel and Levine. In theory, they would have alerted the *Enterprise* to his abduction by now. McCoy liked to think that Kirk and the others were worried sick about him.

Well, except maybe Spock.

Jim won't give up on me, McCoy knew. The captain and the rest of the crew were surely trying to find out what had happened to him and were possibly already on their way to rescue him. Granted, the last time Starfleet tried to extract hostages from Ozalor it hadn't ended well, but McCoy had faith in Kirk and the others. He just hoped too many people, on both sides, wouldn't get hurt before the crisis was resolved. *This could get ugly.*

"Well, Doctor?" Rayob rose from his chair. "Will you lend us your expertise?"

McCoy turned away from the window. "You have some nerve," he said, his temper flaring. "You trick me, stun me, drug me, drag me halfway across the sector, then expect me to straighten out your palace rivalries?"

"You are a doctor, are you not?" Rayob gestured at the 3-D portrait of the Heir to the throne. "Forget politics and affairs of state. A young woman is ill and in need of care. Can you truly turn your back on her distress, without even seeing if you can help her?"

He's got me there, McCoy thought, scowling. *He would have to play that card. Blasted Hippocratic Oath!*

"Fine. I'll examine the patient, maybe even give you a second opinion, but don't think for one minute that I've forgotten how you got me here."

Rayob smiled in vindication, as though he knew all along what McCoy's answer would be, but he had the good manners not to rub it in.

"Of course not, Doctor. I can't imagine that you would."

Six

Braco

"Greetings, Commander Spock. We've been expecting you."

Spock beamed into the headquarters of the Bracon Tranquility Bureau, his shuttlecraft having touched down at the municipal spaceport outside the capital city of O'Kdro precisely twenty-seven minutes earlier. *Copernicus* had made it from Vok to Braco with commendable speed; nevertheless, the trip had cost the search party more than forty-nine hours that they could ill afford to spare. He appreciated the Bracon police force using their transporter to beam him directly from the spaceport to their downtown headquarters, sparing him an additional journey, given that transporter technology advanced enough to safely transport living beings, as opposed to inorganic cargo, was relatively scarce on Braco, being primarily reserved for major government agencies.

"We came as promptly as possible," Spock replied to the Bracon police officer greeting them in the transporter room. A tingling sensation, akin to static electricity, lingered from the crude Bracon transit beam. "Under the circumstances."

"Yes, a most unfortunate affair," the officer said. "Allow me to introduce myself. I am Chief Inspector Wibb. I have been placed in charge of this case and will serve as your official liaison during your stay on Braco."

Short in stature, Wibb wore plain clothes as befitting his rank. A three-piece slate-colored suit conveyed an impression of sober authority. Fulsome gray muttonchops framed his ruddy features, compensating perhaps for his receding hairline. Pince-nez glasses perched on his prominent nose, while the stem of a hard rubber pipe poked ominously from his vest pocket. A trio of olive-uniformed troopers flanked the inspector. Spock recalled that on Braco the police and the military were largely the same, or at best, separate divisions of the same overall agency.

"On behalf of the *Enterprise,* Starfleet, and the United Federation of Planets, we thank you for your cooperation," Spock said. "Recovering Doctor McCoy as expeditiously as possible is a matter of top priority."

"Of course," Wibb said. "Least we can do."

Spock stepped down from the transporter platform, accompanied by Lieutenant Jennifer Godwin. Recently transferred over from the *Yorktown,* the security officer had an impeccable record that had recommended her for this mission. White hair and a pair of rudimentary stubs protruding from her brow indicated a trace of Andorian ancestry, as did a perceptibly blue tint to her dark complexion. Three additional security officers remained upon *Copernicus,* to be called upon as needed. Taking stock of his surroundings, Spock observed that the transporter room roughly resembled those aboard the *Enterprise,* aside from the fact that the primary control console was larger and more cumbersome, requiring at least two operators, not unlike earlier generations of Starfleet transporters. He also noted that Nurse Chapel and Lieutenant Levine were not present.

"I do not detect my colleagues from the *Enterprise.*"

"They are waiting in a briefing room nearby," Wibb said, "but first, may I ask you to surrender your weapons?"

Both Spock and Godwin were armed, Spock with a type-1 phaser, the security officer with type-2.

"Is that necessary?" Spock asked.

"Standard procedure," Wibb replied. "No unauthorized ordnance is allowed within Bureau headquarters. That applies to *all* visitors."

"A reasonable precaution." Spock would have preferred to retain his phaser, considering the attack on the previous landing party. Then again, if he and Godwin were not secure in the heart of the regional police headquarters, their situation was more dire than anticipated. He handed his phaser to Wibb, then nodded at Godwin, who was waiting on his command. "Please turn over your weapon as well, Lieutenant."

"Aye, sir," she said, complying.

Wibb confiscated the sidearms and handed them off to a subordinate. "Your tricorder also, Commander Spock."

The Vulcan raised an eyebrow. "For what reason, may I ask?"

"Procedure. No unauthorized recordings on the premises."

"Would it not be sufficient to simply request that we refrain from doing so without permission?"

"I don't make the rules, Commander," Wibb stated. "I just enforce them." He held out his hand. "The tricorder, please."

If he were fully human, Spock might have been annoyed by the lack of trust implied by the request. As it was, he calculated that this was not a battle worth fighting when there were more important issues to be dealt with. He saw little point in antagonizing the local authorities at this juncture.

"I have much vital data stored on this device, regarding any number of ongoing tasks," he said. "I trust it will be returned upon my departure?"

"You will naturally be provided with a receipt for all personal effects."

That was not precisely what Spock had asked, but again he judged that there was nothing to be gained by prolonging this debate. Meeting up with Chapel and Levine, and progressing with the search for McCoy, was a more urgent objective.

"Very well." He took a moment to lock the contents of the tricorder against inspection, then provided the device to Wibb. "Shall we proceed to the briefing?"

"Certainly, Commander," the inspector said.

" 'Mister Spock' will suffice," he said.

"All right, then, *Mister* Spock," Wibb said. "Follow me."

Exiting the transporter room, the inspector led them through a maze of bland, utilitarian corridors to a numbered chamber, where Spock was relieved to find Chapel and Levine, the former seated at a rectangular conference table, the latter pacing restlessly. He observed that both of them had taken advantage of the last several hours to freshen up and change into fresh uniforms, presumably packed aboard *Galileo* in anticipation of their sojourn on Braco. They appeared to be in serviceable condition, physically. He hoped they had managed to attain sufficient rest and nutrition, despite any anxiety over McCoy's disappearance.

I may need them at their best, he thought.

The briefing room was stark and intimidating enough that Spock surmised that it served as an interrogation chamber as well. A viewscreen occupied the farthest wall; Spock suspected that whatever transpired in the room was monitored and recorded. Based on what he'd encountered so far, it seemed the planet's Tranquility Bureau ran a very tight ship.

"Mister Spock!" Chapel rose from her seat, her face lighting up. "Thank goodness you're here."

"Nurse, Lieutenant," he addressed the pair. "I am pleased to find you as well as can be expected, considering your ordeal."

"I certainly don't feel well, Mister Spock," Chapel said. "And I'm not sure I will be until I know Doctor McCoy is safe . . . and back in sickbay where he belongs."

"That is very much my goal," Spock said, "nor do I intend to return to the *Enterprise* without him." He crossed the room to join his fellow crew. "The captain sends his apologies for not seeing to this crisis personally. Alas, his mission on Vok demands his presence there."

"We understand, Mister Spock," Chapel said. "We all know Captain Kirk would be here if he could."

"Speaking of apologies," Levine said, "I'm sorry I dropped the ball so badly. I was supposed to provide security to the medical team, but those snipers caught me with my pants down."

Familiar as he was with the human idiom, Spock did not take the young officer's description literally.

"Personal recriminations will not help us recover Doctor McCoy," he replied, less interested in assigning blame than in achieving McCoy's safe return. "Your energies are better devoted to the task before us: determining who ambushed you, where the doctor is being held, and how he can be rescued."

"Yes, sir," Levine said, "but I still feel like I let Doctor McCoy down."

"Nonsense," Chapel said firmly. "I keep telling you, it's not your fault. We thought we were responding to a medical emergency. You had no reason to expect that we would come under fire." Her face flushed with anger. "It just makes me so furious, though. What kind of people attack a doctor on a mission of mercy?"

"That is foremost among the questions we need to answer." Spock turned toward Wibb. "Has your investigation yielded any pertinent results so far?"

The inspector indicated the seats around the table. "Please make yourselves comfortable while I apprise you of the current status of the case."

Spock and the others did as directed. "You have our full attention, Chief Inspector."

"Our investigation is ongoing," Wibb stated, remaining on his feet, "but as of yet we do not have a clear idea of what has become of your doctor."

Spock was disappointed but unsurprised by the inspector's statement, since he imagined Chapel and Levine would have been informed of any major breakthroughs had they occurred. "May I ask what you have learned?"

"Our forensic teams have thoroughly scoured the abandoned mining camp where the reported ambush occurred, finding no sign of Doctor McCoy's body nor any pieces of same, nor any trace of human blood, all of which we take as very encouraging indicators that your physician is still alive. We are also now quite confident that the kidnappers and their captive are not hiding in any of the deserted structures or tunnels at the site. Indeed, we found evidence that a small aircraft was recently hidden in the surrounding hills, from which we surmise that the attackers absconded with Doctor McCoy while his companions were still unconscious."

This struck Spock as a reasonable supposition. He remained troubled by how much time had passed since the abduction. McCoy could well have been shifted from any number of crafts and hiding places by now. It was even possible that he was no longer on Braco.

"What of the identity of the ambushers?" he asked.

"The snipers left little evidence behind," Wibb said, "but it's fairly easy to guess who is behind this heinous crime."

"And that would be?" Spock pressed.

Wibb's lip curled in disdain. "They call themselves the United Bracon Front, but they're nothing more than a terrorist organization waging a guerrilla war against the Provisional Government with no concern for public safety or tranquility. Their methods are despicable: rioting, bombing, sabotage, and, yes, even kidnappings. They may have covered their tracks at the old mining camp, but the UBF's grubby fingerprints are all over that cowardly sneak attack."

A handheld remote rested on the conference table. Wibb used it to activate the viewscreen. A montage of vivid images, both moving and static, paraded across the screen: smoking ruins, debris, violent street demonstrations, bank robberies, hooded hostages being roughly tossed into the back of unmarked vehicles, and other disturbing snapshots of crime and civic turmoil. A bold green banner, emblazoned with the Bracon symbol for the number one, was brandished by many of the demonstrators. Spock assumed the grisly montage had been compiled for the landing party's benefit.

"This group would indeed appear to be a logical suspect, well worth considering," he said. "Yet am I correct in understanding that there is no actual evidence pointing toward their involvement?"

"Not yet, but there will be." Wibb looked at Chapel. "You asked what kind of people would perpetrate such an appalling act, Nurse Chapel. Well, look no further."

A click of the remote brought up a candid photo that appeared to have been taken by a security camera. The slightly blurry image depicted an orange-skinned woman in her midtwenties, clutching a disruptor rifle in both hands. A vest, tunic, trousers, and boots seemed both practical and well worn. A tightly bound green bandanna effectively concealed and controlled her hair.

"Meet Hynn V'sta. The ringleader of the terrorists . . . and our number-one suspect."

Spock remained unconvinced, as well as increasingly concerned that Wibb had already made up his mind regarding the terrorists' culpability in this affair, to the exclusion of other possibilities. It would be regrettable if alternative lines of inquiry were being overlooked because Wibb was overly focused on one specific theory.

"On the other hand," Spock pointed out, "I gather that this particular dissident group has yet to claim responsibility for the abduction, or issue any demands for McCoy's return? They have asked for no ransoms, no political prisoners to be released? They have issued no manifestos?"

"No, nothing of that nature," Wibb admitted. "Frankly, I'm not sure what they're waiting for."

"Then what do you presume to be their motive?" Spock asked.

"Who knows?" Wibb shrugged dismissively. "To foment disorder, or perhaps create an interstellar incident that would embarrass the current government, making it look weak and ineffectual. They could even be trying to spark division among the ruling coalition. You never know with these fanatics. Bottom line: they just want to stir up trouble, pit Bracon against Bracon, Vokites against Ozalorians, just like in the bad old days."

Spock had thoroughly familiarized himself with the political situation on Braco. After centuries of civil war and unrest, with some factions urging closer ties to Vok and others to Ozalor, the planet was presently administered by a provisional government supposedly representing both sides in equal numbers. The highest executive level, in particular, consisted of a ruling council comprised of two Bracons, from opposite factions, as well as one "advisor" each from Vok and Ozalor. In theory, this provisional government was meant to be a temporary compromise, holding power only until Braco's final status was determined; in practice, this uneasy coalition had been the status quo for several decades now.

"Or maybe those filthy criminals just need a doctor to treat some loathsome disease they've contracted in whatever fetid lair they're holed up in," Wibb continued. "Or, worse yet, perhaps they need your medical officer's expertise to devise some hideous new bioweapon."

Chapel reacted in disbelief. "Doctor McCoy would never be party to such an atrocity!"

"Forgive me, Nurse Chapel," Wibb replied, "but the UBF might not give him a choice. You have to understand these are ruthless individuals with no respect for civilized codes of conduct."

"I must concur with Nurse Chapel," Spock said. "Doctor McCoy has faced mortal threats before, and endured torture as well." Spock vividly recalled the agonies McCoy had been subjected to on Minara II only two solar years ago. "I can also attest to the fact that he can be exceedingly stubborn when he wants to be."

"If you say so, Mister Spock, but this is my world," Wibb said. "You don't know these bastards the way I do. You don't know what they're capable of."

"Perhaps," Spock conceded, "but you have never met Leonard McCoy."

"True enough," Wibb said. "I hope you're right about him. In any event, the UBF surely had some malicious reason for setting that trap for McCoy."

Spock considered the trap itself. "What of the supposed 'emergency signal' that lured our medical team to your world in the first place?"

He had already ascertained, after consulting with Lieutenant Uhura back on the *Enterprise*, that the alert had registered as authentic enough, transmitted directly to the ship on an appropriate frequency, complete with the proper verification codes from the Bracon emergency services agencies. There had been no reason to suspect that the original signal was anything but genuine.

"A total fabrication," Wibb reported, "albeit cleverly disguised as an official distress call, narrowcast to the *Enterprise* specifically. We never even picked up on it until Miss Chapel and her guard alerted us to the ambush at the mining camp."

Spock nodded. "Who would possess the capability to commit such a hoax?"

"Sadly, all too many people," Wibb said. "Emergency distress codes and frequencies are not exactly closely guarded secrets, since that would somewhat defeat their purpose. It would be easy enough for a UBF infiltrator or collaborator to obtain the necessary parameters . . . and fake them as needed."

Spock resolved to institute a new verification procedure for all future distress signals to the *Enterprise* once this immediate crisis was resolved. At present, however, he had a more urgent item on his agenda.

"With your permission, I would like to inspect the ambush site myself, as soon as possible, as that would be the most logical place to begin our search for Doctor McCoy."

Wibb frowned. "I'm sorry, Mister Spock, but only authorized personnel are allowed access to the crime scene, which will remain sealed off as long as this case is active. I can assure you that the site has been meticulously searched. If there were any further clues to be detected, we would have found them." He shrugged.

"Granted, it doesn't help that a thunderstorm or three has swept over the camp since the incident, complicating matters."

"With all due respect to your own forensic investigators," Spock said diplomatically, "surely there can be no harm in allowing us to conduct our own survey of the site? I am under orders from my captain to make every effort to recover our lost crew member, even if they may strike you as redundant."

"I sympathize with your position, Mister Spock, but may I remind you that your captain has no authority here." His posture stiffened. "To avoid any further confusion, let me make things perfectly clear. This is *our* world and *our* investigation. You are being kept informed as a courtesy to the Federation, but *we* will be handling this case, not you. In fact, I urge you strongly not to interfere."

"We aim not to interfere," Spock stated, "but to work with you to achieve our mutual goal: Doctor McCoy's deliverance."

"I don't doubt your good intentions," Wibb said, "but as outworlders, you cannot grasp the harsh realities of modern Braco. Frankly speaking, the last thing we need are well-meaning visitors mucking things up and getting into trouble. And I certainly don't have the personnel to guarantee your safety if you go poking around those crumbling old mines."

"I thought you said your people had already confirmed that nobody was still lurking in that ghost town," Chapel said, quite incisively. "So why would we be in danger there?"

"Those old ruins and tunnels are hazardous in themselves," Wibb said.

"We are prepared to take that risk," Spock said.

"You may be, but I am not," Wibb declared. "You lot are my responsibility and I'm not about to let anything happen to you under my watch. One missing Starfleet officer is enough." He crossed his arms atop his chest. "The crime scene is off-limits, period."

"I see." Spock was rapidly coming to the conclusion that the inspector's definition of cooperation left something to be desired.

Although disappointed at being denied the opportunity to inspect the site himself, Spock took solace in the recognition that enough time had passed since the abduction that any surviving evidence might well have been washed away by the elements by now. It was even possible that the site had already been swept clean by the Bracon authorities in order to conceal some conspiracy or scandal they wished to keep under wraps. At this early stage of his own investigation, Spock could not afford to rule out any possibility, including a government cover-up.

"So what can we do?" Levine protested. "You can't expect us to just sit by passively while one of our own is missing!"

"That is just what I expect, Mister Levine," Wibb said. "Rest assured that the Bureau is on the case and will exert every effort to rescue your Doctor McCoy. Our agents are pressuring their usual informants as we speak. Mark my words, somebody out there knows where McCoy is, which means we will too . . . eventually."

"And if the doctor's captors are not the terrorists you suspect?" Spock asked. "What then?"

"We are pursuing other leads as well," Wibb said, "but the UBF is behind this, Mister Spock. I'd bet my salary on it."

"Vulcans do not engage in games of chance," Spock replied, "nor do we reach conclusions before fully examining the facts."

Annoyance showed on the inspector's less-than-stoic features.

"This is not Vulcan, Mister Spock. You would do well to remember that." He clicked off the video display. "I believe that concludes this briefing. As Nurse Chapel and Mister Levine can attest, accommodations for you and your entire party have been booked at one of our finest downtown hotels, only a few blocks from here. Allow me to personally escort you to your lodgings."

It was a statement, not a request.

"Thank you, Chief Inspector." Spock judged there was nothing further to be gained from the interview, given Wibb's generally unhelpful attitude. "I suspect I shall have more questions for you as your investigation progresses."

"As I hope to have happier news to convey in the near future." Wibb gestured toward the door. "Shall we?"

He led them out of the briefing room into the busy halls beyond. An old-fashioned elevator carried them down to the ground floor, where Wibb waved them past several layers of security, which, Spock observed, included checkpoints, force fields, and full-body scans. A response to the ongoing spate of terrorist attacks?

"Excuse me, Chief Inspector," Spock said. "Now that we are departing your headquarters, may I request the return of our equipment?"

Wibb sighed. "I suppose there's no harm in returning your tricorder to you, but the Capital Hotel has a strict no-weapons policy, the times being what they are. Only sanctioned security personnel are permitted arms. No exceptions."

"Even when one Starfleet officer has already been forcibly abducted, not very far from here?" Spock argued. "I am quite certain I speak for my colleagues when I state that we would prefer to be able to defend ourselves if necessary."

"What he said," Levine added. "I feel naked without my sidearm."

"The hotel is perfectly safe," Wibb said. "We are not talking about a desolate ghost town in the middle of nowhere. The Capital boasts first-class security, which is exactly why we are lodging you there . . . at the taxpayers' expense, I might add."

"And what if we should venture outside the hotel?" Spock asked.

"I would not advise that."

A very human sense of irritation tested Spock's equanimity. Wibb's seeming determination to keep the Starfleet contingent contained and out of the way posed an obvious obstacle to their mission. They could hardly expect to track down McCoy and his captors while confined to a hotel and obstructed at every turn.

Wibb snapped his fingers, then beckoned to a junior officer, who, somewhat grudgingly, returned Spock's tricorder to him. Spock recalled a human saying about being grateful for small favors; as a point of fact, however, he was feeling little in the way of gratitude at the moment.

"I'm a busy man," Wibb said. "Let us get on our way. The sooner you are securely ensconced in your suites, the sooner I can get back to finding your missing doctor."

They departed the building via a back entrance, perhaps to avoid attracting excess attention, and Spock received his first street-level view of the city proper. Downtown O'Kdro did not appear particularly inviting. Austere gray buildings of steel and concrete lacked aesthetic appeal, an impression not helped by the overcast skies and drizzle. As a child of Vulcan, a world of intense light and heat, Spock found the damp, clammy atmosphere distasteful, although he easily repressed that reaction. Steel barricades cordoned off the alley behind the Bureau headquarters, where an armored groundcar waited at the curb. A uniformed trooper was posted beside the car. She slid open the car's side door to reveal the passenger seats within.

"Kindly enter the vehicle," Wibb instructed. "Our destination is only a short drive—"

"Inspector Wibb!" an insistent voice called out from one end of the alley, less than nine meters away. "A few questions, please!"

The request came from an apparent civilian on the other side of the barricade, who was holding up a recording device of some kind. Blond hair and stubble contrasted with his orange skin. A rumpled overcoat and a knitted beret provided partial protection from the light rain dribbling down from above. His accent clearly pegged him as a Bracon.

"D'Ran Colc, Bracon Free Press!" he identified himself. "Is it true that a Starfleet medical officer was kidnapped here on Braco? Is that why you're hosting visitors from Starfleet?"

Wibb's ruddy countenance darkened. "No comment," he muttered, while briskly pointing out the reporter to the nearby trooper. She nodded and started toward Colc, who kept hollering his questions.

"Do you have reason to suspect the UBF? Does this have anything to do with the upcoming presidential election on Vok?"

Wibb turned his back on the reporter, ignoring the queries. "Into the car," he ordered Spock and the others. "Promptly."

"Commander Spock!" Colc shouted, trying another tack. "That is you, isn't it? What is the first officer of the *U.S.S. Enterprise* doing on Braco, and at police headquarters no less? Are you looking for a lost crew member?"

Spock arched his eyebrow. "He appears unexpectedly well informed."

"The car . . . now," Wibb snarled.

More troopers converged on Colc, clearly intent on getting him out of the way. Spock reluctantly slid into the vehicle along with his companions while Wibb claimed the passenger seat next to the driver. Spock silently committed the reporter's name and affiliation to memory, even as Colc loudly argued with the troopers.

"Hey, keep your hands off my newscorder! The public has a right to know what's going—"

The car door slid shut, sealing Spock off from the clamor. He watched through the vehicle's windshield as the troopers forcibly cleared Colc away from the barricade, which lifted to allow the car egress from the alley. Peering out through a one-way window, Spock saw Colc vigorously contesting his ejection as the car accelerated past him. A trooper seized the reporter's newscorder and hurled it to the ground. A heavy boot stamped down on the device before the car sped away from the scene, leaving the confrontation behind.

"Who was that individual?" Spock asked.

"Nothing but an irresponsible muckraker and all-around pain," Wibb said, scowling from the front seat. "He delights in airing dirty laundry without any care for its effect on public morale." The inspector turned his face forward. "My apologies for the unpleasantness."

"But how did he know about Doctor McCoy?" Chapel asked.

"I have no idea," Wibb said, "but I fully intend to find out. This matter is far too delicate to have wild reports made public before we are ready to make an official statement."

Spock was less concerned with public relations than with what else this Colc might know. "Is it possible he has access to information that could prove useful in locating Doctor McCoy?"

"You give him too much credit," Wibb scoffed. "He's a squalid purveyor of gossip and speculation dressed up as journalism. Don't waste another moment taking him seriously."

The inspector's low opinion of the reporter appeared unshakable, so Spock kept his own counsel for the time being. He observed the city from inside the car as it negotiated the congested downtown traffic. The view did nothing to alleviate his dismal first impression, although he now noted that the city streets and sidewalks appeared only marginally less locked down than the police headquarters. Armed troopers were a visible presence, posted at intersections and patrolling the neighborhood. Security checkpoints and barricades slowed both vehicles and pedestrians. Looking closer, Spock saw that O'Kdro was still scarred by the violent conflicts of the past and present. Scorch marks defaced walls and buildings. Craters, patched with varying degrees of success, pocked the pavement. A now-vacant lot was strewn with rubble. A gutted cathedral awaited restoration. The lingering residue of the civil war, he wondered, or the results of more recent terrorist bombings?

He felt the absence of his phaser rather more keenly.

Along with *Copernicus*, *Galileo* was also parked at the main spaceport on the outskirts of the city. Both shuttlecrafts were a potential source of fresh armaments, Spock reminded himself, should the need arise.

"Ah, here we are."

The groundcar pulled up in front of the Capital Hotel, whose ornate facade conveyed an impression of faded elegance, under-cut by the bars over the windows and the armed sentries posted at the entrance. Wibb peered at the sidewalk.

"No more annoying tattlers," he muttered. "Praise the Prime."

The door opened automatically for the passengers, who dis-embarked from the vehicle. A fringed awning shielded them from the rain, which was growing heavier, as Wibb hurried them past the guards into the lobby, which also held on tenuously to its prewar grandeur. Another elevator brought them to a brace of interconnected suites on the hotel's top floor. The luxurious accommodations certainly appeared to be more comfortable than the shuttlecrafts; Spock made a mental note to rotate shifts between the hotel and the spaceport, so that the same crew members were not left guarding *Galileo* and *Copernicus* indefinitely. A few scattered items, such as Starfleet-issue microtapes and a medkit, confirmed that Chapel and Levine had occupied the suite in the days prior to the rescue team's arrival. Spock's gaze fell on a desk viewer in a work alcove.

Convenient, he thought.

Wibb saw them installed in the suites before briskly mak-ing his farewell. "Please avail yourselves of the hotel's amenities, including the food service, saunas, entertainment library, and gymnasium. I particularly recommend the nutfruit stew, which is a delicacy not to be missed." He made his way toward the door to the hall. "In addition to the Capital's top-flight private security, I am also posting additional guards in the hall and lobby, simply as an added precaution."

"That may not be necessary." Spock indicated Levine and God-win. "We do have our own security team after all."

"Minus their weapons," Wibb said, indulging himself with a smirk. "Allow us an excess of caution with regard to your safety."

Spock could already see the onerous presence of the Bureau troopers as a possible impediment to his plans, since he had no intention of remaining sequestered in the hotel. He judged it impolitic to mention those plans.

"If you insist," he said mildly.

"I do," Wibb said. "I very much do."

Spock suspected that the troopers were meant to keep an eye on the Starfleet personnel in more ways than one. No doubt they would be reporting back to Wibb on the landing party's movements.

"And with that I take my leave, for now."

Wibb gave them a polite bow before departing, leaving Spock and Godwin alone with Chapel and Levine for the first time since *Copernicus*'s arrival on the planet. Spock glanced around the suite.

"May we speak freely?" he inquired.

"Aye, sir," Levine reported. "I swept the premises for monitoring devices first thing. Found a few concealed bugs, but they've been disabled." He chuckled quietly. "The Bracons haven't said anything about it. Guess it would be awkward to admit that they tried to spy on us in the first place."

"Well done, Mister Levine," Spock said.

"I almost wish that Chief Inspector Wibb would object, so I could give him a piece of my mind." Emotion colored Chapel's voice now that she felt free to voice her true feelings. "You see what we've been dealing with, Mister Spock? Trying to find out what Wibb and his people are doing is like pulling teeth the old-fashioned way. Sometimes it feels like Wibb is just humoring us."

"He does appear to be less than amenable to involving us in the investigation," Spock agreed, "although it is unclear whether he is actively attempting to obstruct us or if he is simply being excessively territorial."

"Either way, he's not going to make our job any easier," Godwin said.

"Indeed," Spock said, "which behooves us to find alternative sources of information."

He crossed the suite to the work nook and activated the desk viewer. "Computer," he addressed it.

"Welcome to Guest Services," a robotic male voice replied. *"How may I assist you?"*

"Can you access public databases and news sources?"

"Affirmative."

"Request contact information for the following individual: D'Ran Colc, Bracon Free Press."

If the police could not assist them, perhaps the press could.

Seven

Vok

"I demand political asylum!"

"You've got some nerve," Kirk shot back at the would-be assassin, who was now in custody aboard the *Enterprise*. He faced the man across the table in a briefing room near the brig. "You attacked a Starfleet officer, you critically injured a Federation diplomat, and you expect asylum aboard my ship? Think again."

The spear thrower had been identified as a native-born Vokite named Lom. A pair of stone-faced security guards were on hand to maintain order during the interrogation, while the ship's computer recorded the proceedings. Steve Tanaka was also present, filling in for Dare. The injured commissioner, currently recovering in sickbay after being operated on by Doctor M'Benga, was watching remotely from her sickbed. Kirk's hand, now bandaged after being treated with an anesthetic balm that also promoted healing, still smarted enough to gnaw at his temper.

"But I wasn't after you or that Federation woman," Lom insisted. Dark hair and eyes contributed to his matinee-idol looks. He was still clad in his theatrical outfit, although his cape and belt had been confiscated along with the rest of his personal effects. A bruised jaw served as a souvenir of the flying kick that had taken him out of commission down on the planet. "You just got in my way. I was after Ceff . . . as a political act."

"Sorry," Kirk said. "An assassination attempt is not going to earn you any kind of special status or protection, not on my ship."

They were lucky that Lom had failed to murder Doctor Ceff. Kirk could only imagine the strife that might have erupted on Vok had the candidate actually been assassinated. As it was, the incident was bound to exacerbate the volatile emotions surrounding the election. Kirk had briefly been in touch with both campaigns in the aftermath of the incident, but he suspected that more consultations would be needed. According to Uhura, the *Enterprise* was being besieged by hails demanding details and updates regarding Lom. Not that Kirk could really blame the interested parties on the planet; he had plenty of questions himself.

"Did anyone put you up to this? Were you working alone or with others?"

Lom smirked at him. "Wouldn't you like to know?"

"Answer my question, mister! You're not going anywhere until I get some answers."

The man's expression darkened. He clearly didn't like being bossed around.

"You have no authority over me, Starfleet! I report to the General!"

Kirk stiffened. "What do you mean by that?"

"I did nothing wrong!" Lom said defiantly. "I was merely following orders . . . from the General himself!"

The General?

Kirk was staggered by the implications of what he had just heard. He traded worried looks with Tanaka. He had to be careful here; too much was at stake to risk any sort of misunderstanding.

"Let me get this straight. You're saying that General Gogg personally ordered you to attack Doctor Ceff?"

"That's right." Lom leaned back in his seat, his arms crossed atop his chest, as though daring Kirk to call him a liar. A cocky grin lifted his lips. "And I can prove it."

Kirk frowned. "How?"

"Get me my gear and I'll show you," Lom said.

Kirk nodded at a security officer, who fetched the items in question. He watched alertly, along with the guards, as Lom removed a data disk from a compartment on his belt. The man handed the disk over to Kirk, who accepted it warily.

"No tricks?" Kirk asked.

"No tricks," Lom said. "I want to see your face when you watch this."

The disk was Vokite in origin, raising compatibility issues with the *Enterprise*'s systems.

"Allow me, Captain," Tanaka volunteered. It took a few minutes, which Kirk sweated out impatiently, but the young man managed to transfer the disk's contents to the ship's computer. An additional layer of encryption protected the file, but Lom gave up the password without hesitation. Tanaka looked at Kirk. "Ready when you are, sir."

Kirk braced himself for the worst. "Computer, display data provided by the prisoner identified as Lom."

"Displaying."

An image appeared on the room's main viewscreen. Kirk saw Gogg grimly facing forward in what seemed to be a transmission from an unspecified location. His stentorian tones issued from the screen:

"You understand what is expected of you? It has been arranged that your troupe will perform at one of the enemy's public spectacles. You will then have a tremendous opportunity before you to strike a decisive blow at a mortal threat to our great world. You must not let it pass by."

"And in exchange?" Lom's voice asked from offscreen.

"Fear not," Gogg said. *"Your family will be rewarded under the new regime, no matter what becomes of you. You have my word on it."*

The recording ended abruptly, the screen going blank.

"Is that it?" Kirk asked.

"Recording complete," the computer replied.

"You see," Lom gloated. "I'm not a criminal, I'm a patriot."

"One does not necessarily exclude the other," Tanaka said. "Sad to say."

Kirk had to agree with him, but he remained puzzled by what

they had just witnessed. "I don't understand," he said to Lom. "Even if General Gogg was behind it all, why would he allow you to record this . . . and why would you share it with us?"

"It was a show of good faith," Lom said. "I believe in the General and his promises, but he wanted to go on record for the sake of my family, so there could be no question of the rewards due them once he took power." He sneered at Kirk. "Just you wait. After the election, I'll probably get a medal along with a pardon. I'll be honored for my valiant effort on behalf of the cause . . . even if that subversive witch survived because of you and your Federation commissioner."

Kirk remembered Dare crying out in pain as the javelin struck her in the back. A medal was the last thing Lom deserved. Kirk shook his head, still trying to make sense of Lom's confession. Was he so convinced of Gogg's victory that he didn't realize what a blow this revelation could be to the General's campaign? Or was Lom simply determined to justify his actions by proving that he was acting under orders from Gogg?

"I wouldn't count on him getting elected," Kirk said, "not if what you say is true."

"Tell me about it," Tanaka said. "This is a bombshell that could blow up Gogg's chances of winning the presidency."

Lom didn't look too concerned. "You outworlders underestimate the General's support among the actual population, as opposed to the radicals and revolutionaries. When the time comes, the true voice of Vok will be heard."

"If you're so confident of victory," Kirk asked, "why bother assassinating Doctor Ceff?"

Lom shrugged. "Better safe than sorry. And who am I to question the General's orders?"

Scowling, Kirk issued an order of his own.

"Take him back to the brig."

Eight

Ozalor

"The coast is clear," Jemo said. "Let's go."

McCoy's new hosts hustled him down a back corridor toward the afflicted Heir to the throne. They were, by their own admission, in no hurry to advertise McCoy's presence in the palace, let alone on the planet, given Ozalor's lack of formal relations with the Federation, not to mention the little matter of a Starfleet officer having been forcibly abducted from Braco. To avoid attracting undue attention, McCoy had been made to change into local attire. A short-sleeved brown tunic, along with white slacks and sandals, were apparently everyday summer garb. His makeover also included a fake beard, since apparently Ozalorian men did not go clean-shaven in adulthood. The disguise itched like the devil. He fought the urge to scratch at it, while hoping that he would not be sticking around long enough to grow the real thing.

I have no intention of going native if I can help it, he thought. *Or even if I can't.*

At least his medkit and medical tricorder had been returned to him, albeit concealed within an inconspicuous briefcase. McCoy toted the case as they made their way through a series of service hallways, which they largely had to themselves, aside from an occasional member of the palace staff passing them on errands of their own. Rayob's authority granted tacit permission for McCoy to traverse the palace in his company; the disguised doctor drew a few curious glances from stray passersby but nothing resembling suspicion. Nevertheless, Jemo scouted ahead while Rayob and McCoy followed closely after her, with Rayob walking directly behind McCoy while quietly urging him on. His phaser, confiscated by his captors, was tucked beneath the majordomo's belt to ensure McCoy's compliance. Rayob had displayed the weapon to McCoy prior to their leaving the guest suite.

"Hasten, Doctor," he said in a low voice. "I would prefer not to tread these halls any longer than necessary. Vumri has eyes and ears everywhere."

"She's that popular?" McCoy asked.

"Hardly," Rayob answered. "Vumri has no friends, only pawns and opportunists, who either fear her rising power or hope to benefit from it." Contempt colored his voice. "Alas, there will always be those who chart their course by the prevailing winds alone, with no heed to conscience nor duty."

"Got it," McCoy said. "Folks are already planning to ride her coattails."

"Precisely," the majordomo said. "Unless you can change the way the wind is blowing."

No pressure there, McCoy thought. "About that, even if I can help your sick princess, how long exactly do you intend to keep me around as your 'guest'?"

"Let's not get ahead of ourselves, Doctor." His expression defined inscrutable. "You have yet to even examine your patient."

McCoy scowled. He wasn't looking to become the new royal physician indefinitely; he already had a steady job on the *Enterprise*, which he fully intended to get back to at the first opportunity.

"You'll forgive me if I find that answer evasive," he said.

"Consider yourself forgiven," Rayob said wryly. "In any event, here we are."

They caught up with Jemo in front of a large ornate archway that was filled by a tall silver mirror that reflected the corridor behind them. Jemo stepped forward and rapped gently on the mirror, producing a bell-like chime. Moments later, the silvered glass shimmered and the image of a woman replaced the visitors' reflections. A portrait of elegant middle age, she had dark hair done up in a bun and was dressed rather too expensively to be a minor servant, at least on the basis of McCoy's limited exposure to the palace's residents. She scrutinized them with a haughty expression. Her tone reflected annoyance.

"Yes?"

Rayob came forward, leaving Jemo to watch over McCoy.

"Good afternoon, Madame Bilis. We wish to call upon the *Yiyova* if she will have us."

The woman in the mirror peered at McCoy. "And who is the stranger?"

"An honored guest, whom I hope to present to Avomora."

Bilis, whom McCoy gathered to be a governess or chaperone of some sort, balked at the suggestion. "Now is not really a good time."

"Is she unwell?" Rayob asked.

"Not so much," Bilis hedged. "That is, I mean—"

"Why don't we leave the matter to Her Highness to decide?" He spoke more sternly, as though to remind her that being major-domo carried some weight. "If you will kindly convey our request to your mistress."

Bilis caved. "Of course, sir."

She vanished from the mirror.

"Who was that stuffy grande dame?" McCoy asked.

"Bilis, one of the Heir's attendants." Rayob sighed wearily. "She can be overzealous when it comes to protecting Avomora's privacy."

Jemo was blunter. "She's a stuck-up harpy who thinks she casts a bigger shadow than she does."

The mirror shimmered and Bilis reappeared. "The *Yiyova* will see you after all," she announced with a distinct lack of enthusiasm.

"Splendid," Rayob said. "We appreciate your cordial assistance."

Jemo snickered, eliciting a dirty look from Bilis, who nevertheless reached outside the border of the mirror to operate some unseen mechanism. McCoy expected the mirror to retract, but instead it sublimed into a silvery mist through which Rayob passed effortlessly. He beckoned for McCoy and Jemo to follow him.

Instead of dissipating, the mist remained within the confines of the archway. McCoy instinctively held his breath as he passed through it; he felt nothing but a staticky sensation as he stepped from the hallway to the antechamber beyond, where he found Bilis waiting in the flesh. She gestured toward one of three branching hallways. "If you'll follow me."

"No need." Jemo brushed past her. "We know the way."

The right-hand corridor led to a smaller archway. They entered a cozy study lined with shelves holding a generous assortment of knickknacks, microtapes, and bound albums, atlases, and encyclopedias. A miniature brass orrery, charting the orbits of Braco and its sister planets and moons, shared space with the fossilized tooth of some prehistoric predator. A plush wingback chair faced an open balcony looking out over the pastoral countryside beyond. The chair spun around at their approach. Its occupant's face lit up in delight.

"Jemo!" blurted Avomora, *Yiyova* of Ozalor.

McCoy recognized the crown princess from her official portrait, curly brown hair and all, although the real thing was rather more animated. She rose, perhaps a touch unsteadily, from her mobile chair to embrace Jemo, who gingerly hugged her back. Avomora winced anyway, although she tried not to show it. Jemo saw through her efforts.

"Bad day?" the bodyguard asked.

"Worse than some, better than others." Avomora shrugged, clearly putting up a brave front. "But let's not discuss that tiresome subject again." Her gaze lit on McCoy. "Who is this intriguingly new face?"

Rayob led McCoy toward the Heir. "Your Highness, allow me to introduce Doctor Leonard McCoy."

A flicker of dissatisfaction passed over the young royal's face at the word "doctor." McCoy couldn't much blame her. He imagined she'd seen more than her fair share of physicians and specialists.

"An honor to meet you, Your Highness." McCoy treated her to his warmest bedside manner, figuratively speaking. He hesitated, unsure of the proper etiquette. Was he supposed to bow or curtsy or what? He compromised by dipping his head momentarily.

Avomora did not appear inclined to stand on ceremony. "You're from the Federation!" she said with excitement. "Earth, if I'm not mistaken."

"Guilty as charged," he said. "Is it that obvious?"

"Your accent is quite distinctive, even through the automatic translator," she explained, "while, upon reflection, your name also has the ring of Earth." A sweep of her arm encompassed the numerous tapes and tomes filling the study's shelves. "I've made quite a study of the galaxy beyond our sector. An engrossing diversion for those times when I'm . . . ill-disposed."

McCoy noted that her chair contained a built-in tape reader and screen, not unlike those on the captain's chair back on the *Enterprise* or the biobeds in sickbay. Looking closer at the young woman herself, he saw that she appeared rather more pallid than in her official portrait. She was trembling, too, even though the room's temperature felt quite comfortable to McCoy. He got the impression that she was under more of a strain than she wanted to let on.

"Perhaps you should sit down, Your Highness," Bilis suggested. She hovered in the doorway, watching over the scene. "You mustn't tire yourself."

Avomora rolled her eyes, but grudgingly accepted the advice. She retreated back into her chair, drawing a quilted blanket over her lap and lower limbs as though chilled. The diagnostician in McCoy filed that observation away even as he made small talk to put his prospective patient at ease.

"You are clearly a scholar and a gentlewoman, Your Highness."

"And, I flatter myself, a fine judge of character despite my relative youth and inexperience." She graced him with a winning smile. "Please call me Avo. All my friends do, at least outside formal occasions."

McCoy appreciated the familiarity. "As long as I won't be sent to the dungeons for breaching protocol."

"The dungeons were turned into wine cellars and a fully equipped gymnasium a century ago," she informed him. "We may not be as technologically advanced as Earth or Andor, but we're hardly medieval."

"I never meant to imply otherwise," McCoy said. "And my friends call me Bones." He shrugged. "Some of them at least."

"What a curious nickname," she said. "From whatever is it derived?"

"That's too grisly a story for so lovely a day. Perhaps we should save that for a more appropriate occasion, preferably midnight during a thunderstorm."

"I look forward to it," she said, "although this is hardly storm season." She marveled at McCoy. "A doctor from Earth, no less." She looked at Rayob. "Does my father know of this?"

"I have not had occasion to mention it to him yet," Rayob confessed. "He is a busy man after all."

"Oh, very busy," Avo agreed, although her tone indicated that she knew full well that there was far more to the majordomo's omission than simply her father's demanding schedule. She returned to her attention to McCoy.

"Will you be with us long, Doctor Bones?"

McCoy glanced at Rayob, whose poker face would do Jim Kirk proud. "That remains to be seen . . . and perhaps we should just stick with 'Doctor' for now."

It occurred to McCoy that he might be able to convince the crown princess to allow him to return to the *Enterprise*, but he was uncertain if now was a good time to play that card. There was still a lot he didn't know about the treacherous political currents here in the palace. Openly accusing Rayob—and Jemo—of kid-napping a Starfleet officer, and to a member of the royal family no less, could have potentially explosive consequences, so he chose to play it by ear for the time being.

"Very well, Doctor, and I certainly hope you won't be depart-ing too soon. I've never met an Earthman before and fortune only knows when I'll have the opportunity again." Her pale cheeks flushed with enthusiasm. "You must tell me all about everything. Have you visited many worlds?"

She leaned forward in her chair, perhaps too abruptly. She gri-maced in pain and a shudder ran through her body. She sagged back into the chair.

"Your Highness!" Bilis shoved her way past McCoy and the other guests to reach Avomora. "You must not overexcite your-self. Shall I summon *Lossu* Vumri?"

"No!" Avo said forcefully, although the effort clearly cost her. She gripped the chair's armrests with white knuckles. "Not yet."

"But why torture yourself by waiting?" Bilis pressed. "You know what the *Lossu* said. You should call for her as soon as you feel one of your spells coming on—"

"That will be enough, Bilis," Avo managed. Her generous eyebrows slanted ominously, signaling her displeasure. "When I require Vumri's services, you will be the first to know." She ap-peared both embarrassed and annoyed to have her condition ad-dressed so blatantly in front of company. "For now, you will leave me with my visitors."

Bilis wrung her hands. "But *Yiyova* . . ."

"That will be all, Bilis."

"As you wish, Your Highness."

Bilis unhappily retreated from the study. Avo watched her go.

"That's better," the princess murmured. She took a few deep breaths to recover from the exertion. Her grip on the armrests loosened as though the spell was ebbing to some degree. "I swear, if she weren't my second cousin, thrice removed . . ."

Jemo regarded Avo with concern. "Never mind that self-important hanger-on. How *are* you doing?"

"Been better," the princess admitted. She looked ruefully at McCoy. "My apologies, Doctor, I regret you had to witness that. I resent being treated as an invalid, even if it's occasionally an apt description."

"Think nothing of it," he assured her. "Occupational hazard."

"I just wish I was in better shape to receive you." She glanced at Rayob. "I'm guessing that our faithful majordomo has apprised you of my . . . affliction."

McCoy recalled that the princess's illness was not public knowledge.

"That is so," Rayob said. "Doctor McCoy is a physician of some renown. I took the liberty of consulting him in hopes that he can provide his professional opinion on that matter."

"I suspected as much," Avo said, groaning, "and here I was hoping this was purely a social call. Nothing personal, Doctor, but I am weary of medical tests and examinations. Given a choice, I would gladly never discuss my condition again."

"Trust me, I get awful sick of sickness too," McCoy said, sympathizing. "Is that why you resisted calling for your healer?"

"That's *one* reason," she said pointedly. "I dislike being dependent on anyone, let alone the likes of Vumri." She seemed to share her visitors' distaste for the vaunted healer, whom McCoy had yet to encounter. "Please tell me you're not here to subject me to another diagnostic inquisition."

"No promises," McCoy said. "But how about we just chat a bit first?" He pulled over a much less impressive chair. "If you don't mind . . ."

"Please, make yourself comfortable, all of you," she said. "I was so excited by your company that I neglected my manners." She let her visitors find seats as she awaited McCoy's questions. "But hasn't Rayob already informed you of the particulars of my ailment?"

"To some extent," McCoy said, "but I'd like to hear it in your own words."

"Very well." Avo resigned herself to the inevitable. "It comes in waves, some more severe than others. Early on, there are simply chills, fatigue, lack of appetite, and an increased sensitivity to light, sound, smell, and touch. Sometimes that's as bad as it gets: unpleasant but hardly incapacitating . . . if I'm lucky."

McCoy gathered her symptoms were worse at present. "And when you're not so lucky?"

"The sensitivity increases, becoming more uncomfortably acute, so that dealing with the world becomes ever more excruciating, and I am forced to retreat to my chair. My body temperature swings back and forth erratically, so that I go from freezing to feeling overheated and back again, sometimes in a matter of minutes. And my nerves begin to hurt, beginning at the top of my spine, then radiating out to my extremities. Just a dull ache at first, but growing sharper as the wave crests. My body starts to twitch and I can lose control of my fingers, so that I become clumsy and have difficulty holding on to things. Sometimes my vision even blurs . . ." She cringed, recalling past ordeals. "It's horrible."

McCoy mentally catalogued her symptoms. Any number of possible diagnoses occurred to him, but he knew better than to jump to conclusions in the absence of any actual tests or scans. As he understood it, Ozalorians, along with Vokites and Bracons, were largely indistinguishable from humans, but that "largely" could make a world of difference where medical issues were concerned. Nebular influenza, for example, presented as a sudden fever for Izarians but could cause shortness of breath for Bolians. Similarly, different species of humanoids could react very differently to certain drugs and therapies. You wouldn't want to prescribe melenex to a Catullan unless you wanted to sterilize them for life, so McCoy was reluctant to make any snap judgments about Avo's ailment without further research.

"I'd like to help you, if I can." He cracked open the briefcase and took out his medical tricorder. "Would you allow me to conduct a few noninvasive scans? Strictly routine, I promise."

Avo eyed the device. "If you must, but I expect a sizable infusion of small talk in return."

"It's a deal."

He activated the tricorder and began a thorough scan of the patient, starting with her basic physiognomy and making his way through her nervous system, circulatory system, endocrine system, and other functions. A deployable hand scanner allowed him to target specific regions with greater focus than a standard tricorder would have permitted. He perused the readings as they streamed across the tricorder's display panel, while recording them for future study. Adjustable knobs allowed him to fine-tune the scans along a range of parameters as he pursued various hunches with no immediate success. An electronic warble accompanied the scans.

"Well, Doctor?" Rayob looked on intently. "Have you found anything?"

"No immediate red flags or irregularities," McCoy reported, finishing up, "but I never expected it to be easy. Anything obvious would have been picked up by your own doctors well before now. Plus, what I don't know about the finer points of Ozalorian medicine would fill databanks. It's going to take some time and effort to get to the bottom of this."

If we can, he added silently, not wanting to crush Avo's hopes before he even raised them. As it happened, he *had* reviewed Vokite physiology on the way to Vok, which might come in handy given that Vokites and Ozalorians supposedly shared a common ancestry, but he still needed to compare Avo's readings against those of other Ozalorians if he wanted to identify any telltale deviations from the norm. *Wonder if Jemo would consent to a full scan to help me establish a baseline for their species?*

"I understand, Doctor," Rayob said, unable to entirely conceal his disappointment. "I confess I had hoped for a more immediate end to the *Yiyova*'s maladies."

And a quicker departure for your rival, Vumri, McCoy thought. "I never promised you a magic bullet. I only agreed to examine the patient."

He wrapped up his initial scans, intent on analyzing them more thoroughly later . . . assuming the *Enterprise* hadn't come to reclaim him by then. To his annoyance, he found himself oddly conflicted when it came to the prospect of being rescued before he'd had a chance to help or cure Avomora. Now that he'd actually met the young royal, he hated leaving her in the lurch.

Seems like a nice kid, he thought.

"All done." He switched off the tricorder and lowered the hand scanner. "See, that didn't hurt a bit."

"I suppose not," she said, but a strained whimper escaped her. She clenched her jaw, clearly trying to bite back another groan. She squirmed uncomfortably in her chair and, trembling visibly, pulled her blanket up to her shoulders. The movements seemed to pain her, contorting her features, which grew steadily more ashen, as well as slightly green around the gills. Blinking, she turned her face away from the light pouring in from the balcony. An involuntary gasp escaped her lips. Tears leaked from her eyes.

"Avo!" Jemo was alarmed by the younger woman's turn for the worse. She wheeled about to confront McCoy. "What's wrong? What did you do to her?"

McCoy was suddenly all too aware of the ionic knife sheathed at the bodyguard's hip. "Whoa there! Let's not do anything hasty!"

"It's nothing he did," Avo said through her torment. "It's my gods-splintered spells, that's all." She raised a shaky hand to shield her eyes from the sunlight, which wasn't really all that glaring. "Somebody draw the drapes, please!"

"Right away, kiddo!" Jemo rushed to the balcony, forgetting all about McCoy for the moment, and yanked the drapes shut, casting the study into gloom. "There you go!"

Instead of experiencing relief, however, Avo clamped her hands over her ears. "Not so loud, I'm begging you."

"Sorry," Jemo whispered in chagrin. She made her way back toward the others, moving as silently as a shadow. "Didn't think."

McCoy found the bodyguard's practiced stealth rather disturbing. He could only imagine how good she was at sneaking up on people.

Something to remember.

Avo kicked off the blanket, sweating as though in a steam bath. Palsied fingers fumbled with a control panel on her armrest, trying to adjust what looked like temperature controls. "Shards!" she cursed in frustration, unable to get a grip on the knobs. She squeezed her eyes shut, trying to block out the world.

Rayob turned to McCoy in dismay, clearly anguished by the sight of Avo's suffering. Any doubts McCoy had regarding the majordomo's genuine concern for his princess evaporated. This wasn't just about politics and power struggles to him; he obviously cared about Avomora's well-being.

"Can you do nothing for her?" he asked softly.

"I don't know," McCoy said. "I've barely begun to study her condition. I don't want to make things worse."

Avo writhed in her chair. Her right eye blinked spasmodically.

Despite his reservations, McCoy found it hard to stand by while Avo suffered right before his eyes. Perhaps he could risk a mild sedative or analgesic? He extracted a hypospray from his concealed medkit and set it to a cautious dosage.

Maybe eight cc's of sonambutril . . . ?

Before he could administer the drug, however, a strange woman barged into the study as though she owned the place.

"Stand aside!" she ordered. "Let me to my charge!"

McCoy could guess who this was. *The notorious* Lossu *Vumri, I presume.*

The controversial healer was a tall, bald woman clad in a plain, dark-green robe and sandals. Esoteric symbols were tattooed onto her shaved pate, making her stand out from every other Ozalorian woman McCoy had encountered so far. Eerie white eyes also caught his attention, their faint gray irises so thin as to be almost invisible compared to her large black pupils. A simple rope belt held a few small pouches and purses, while her only jewelry was a clear glass pendant dangling on a chain about her neck.

Sure looks the part of a mystic, McCoy thought, *for what that's worth.*

He found himself briefly targeted by those unearthly eyes as Vumri gave him an icy look before rushing to Avo's side. Her husky voice held a peculiar vibrato.

"My poor child! I sensed your tribulations across the palace."

Bilis entered behind Vumri, a trifle sheepishly. "Forgive me, Your Highness, but the *Lossu* would not be denied."

McCoy could already see how Vumri could steamroll over the attendant. Heck, he was half-relieved by the healer's arrival as well. Avo was in a bad way; if Vumri could actually help her, he wasn't about to stand in her way.

"Child, why did you not summon me at once?" Vumri shook her head sadly before turning to dismiss McCoy and the others. "Leave us."

"No," Avo said weakly. "Don't send them away."

Vumri frowned. "But, child, you require care, not company. You are in no state to entertain guests."

"I don't care." Avo's face and voice were taut with pain, but she held her ground. "Let them stay."

"Very well, child." Vumri peered back over her shoulder at her unwelcome audience. She regarded them coldly. "Keep back and do not interfere."

Wouldn't dream of it, McCoy thought. He made a deliberate effort to keep what he'd already heard about Vumri from coloring his own first impressions of her. She wasn't exactly rolling out the welcome wagon, but then again, she had a suffering patient to tend to, so she could be forgiven for prioritizing Avo's care over any social niceties. Lord knew he could also be brusque and impatient when it came to anything getting between him and a patient in need. He stepped back to give her more room to work.

"Watch this," Rayob whispered to him. "You may find it of interest."

Vumri ignored them as though they weren't there, focusing on Avo instead. "Give me your hands, child."

Avo was in no position to reject the healer's ministrations. Complying, she held her trembling hands out before her; along with her general tremors, her fingers jerked and twitched randomly. Vumri grasped Avo's hands with her own. She tilted her head back and commenced a low humming that seemed to emanate from deep within her. The hum gradually rose in pitch and volume, becoming more of a trill. The atonal chant set McCoy's teeth on edge, yet seemed to genuinely soothe Avo. Her face and form relaxed visibly; her breathing grew deeper and more regular. Her eye stopped blinking.

Well, I'll be, McCoy thought.

He put away his hypospray for the time being, watching in fascination as the healer worked her magic on the apparently responsive patient. McCoy was not a big believer in faith healers in general, but he couldn't deny the evidence of his own eyes. He wondered what the science was behind Vumri's gift. He was tempted to try to scan her with his tricorder as well. As a doctor, he was always intrigued by the medical practices of unknown races and cultures. He was not so closed-minded as to think that the Federation knew everything there was to know about healing.

The trilling trailed off and fell silent. Vumri took a deep breath, as though she had just exerted herself, and spoke gently to Avo.

"There now, child. Better now?"

"Yes, *Lossu*," Avo conceded. "Thank you."

"You know I am ever at your service. Perhaps next time you will not hesitate so long before calling for me." She released Avo's hands, which no longer appeared to be twitching. "Sleep now. Regain your strength."

"Maybe just for a moment . . ."

Drained by her experience, Avo drifted off. McCoy had to admit that she looked much more comfortable than before. He was grateful on Avo's behalf. It was hard to begrudge Vumri her intrusion if it meant that the princess got some much-needed relief.

Vumri turned away from the dozing royal. "She will rest now . . . and feel much restored when she wakes."

"For a time, that is," Rayob said.

"True, but when the *Yiyova* needs me again, I shall be there for her." She faced her rival confidently. "You may rely on that, majordomo."

The enmity between them was palpable. McCoy tried to lighten the atmosphere.

"That was quite impressive," he said sincerely. "Tell me, how did you acquire your talent for healing?"

"It is a gift," she replied, "granted but to a few."

That meshed with what Rayob had told him prior to leaving the suite, that Ozalor had a long tradition of mystic healers said to be born with exceptional abilities, identified by such signs as Vumri's unusual eyes. They were exceedingly rare, but well documented in the planet's history and folklore, with the former perhaps hopelessly entangled with the latter. A recurrent genetic mutation, McCoy speculated, or a recessive trait that manifested only infrequently? Beings with special abilities beyond those of other members of their species were not without precedent in the universe. Even on Earth, some humans had significantly higher esper ratings than average.

Vumri had questions of her own.

"Who are you," she demanded of McCoy, "and what are you doing here?"

Again, McCoy was hesitant to spill all the beans before he fully grasped the possible repercussions. "Doctor Leonard McCoy." Phony whiskers or not, he figured there was little chance of pretending to be a local. "As you can probably tell, I'm not from these parts."

"A foreign doctor . . . in the *Yiyova*'s chambers no less." Her gaze drifted to the briefcase containing his medical gear, having no doubt taken note of his hypospray earlier. "I suspected as much."

"The good doctor is here at my request," Rayob stated.

"On whose authority?" she challenged him.

"My own, naturally."

Vumri was unimpressed.

"We shall see what our sovereign says about that!"

Nine

Braco

Scintillating blue steam rose from vents in the sauna floor as Spock took advantage of the hotel's amenities for reasons of his own. The chemically generated mist contained a mild astringent that had a bracing effect upon his bare skin. Although Vulcans had evolved in a much drier environment, he found the saturated warmth not unpleasant, reminiscent of the more popular tropic biomes on Illami IV. As it was extremely late into the night, the sauna was occupied only by Spock and a solitary Tellarite merchant snoring on the opposite side of the circular chamber, his porcine form largely obscured by the swirling vapors. Spock sat patiently on a concrete bench, his back against the wall, his modesty and dignity protected by a towel.

He hoped this excursion would not be in vain.

Footsteps slapped against the damp tile floor. A figure in a hooded bathrobe slipped into the sauna. Steam veiled their identity, but the timing was encouraging. The newcomer sat down beside Spock and spoke in a low voice that was nonetheless perfectly audible to the Vulcan's keen hearing.

"Waiting long?"

"No more than seven minutes, sixteen seconds," Spock replied.

"That long, eh?" D'Ran Colc chuckled as he shed his robe. "Sorry for the delay, but I couldn't exactly stroll right through the lobby to get here. A contact on the housekeeping staff snuck me into the building, then slipped me a guest pass to the sauna. The whole rigmarole took a little longer than anticipated, but I didn't want to take any chances."

"Understood," Spock said. "I appreciate the need to be circumspect."

He had reached out to the reporter via a confidential tip line on the Bracon news network Colc worked for, employing his Starfleet communicator rather than the hotel computer terminal in order to avoid alerting the Tranquility Bureau to his efforts. Subsequent communications with Colc, arranging this clandestine meeting, had been done via an encrypted frequency. The hotel sauna had been selected as a suitable meeting spot since it provided a reasonable expectation of privacy while not requiring Spock to exit the hotel or for Colc to brave the troopers guarding the penthouse suites. Not even Wibb's security detail had felt obliged to join Spock in the sauna.

"And I appreciate you contacting me in the first place," Colc said, arranging his towel.

"With all due respect to Chief Inspector Wibb," Spock said, "I am in need of alternative sources of information about the affairs of your world. You appear to be well informed on such matters."

Colc nodded. "Not to brag, but I have my sources, in both high and low places."

"And are they reliable?" Spock asked.

"More so than the 'official story' sometimes. You just have to remember, everyone has their own agenda."

"And what is your agenda, Mister Colc?"

"Me? I just like to find out for myself what's going on, then get the real story out." He shrugged. "Just naturally nosy, I guess."

"Chief Inspector Wibb is not an admirer of your particular brand of journalism," Spock observed.

"You don't say," Colc said sarcastically. Rather than being offended, he seemed distinctly pleased by Spock's remark. "The way I see it, a reporter who doesn't irk the Powers That Be isn't doing their job right. Folks like Wibb always want to control the narrative being fed to the public, so pests like me are bound to rub them the wrong way. We're the tribbles to their Klingons."

"An inventive analogy," Spock said. Certainly, Colc's unspecified sources had been reliable enough to alert the reporter to

McCoy's abduction despite the Bureau's best efforts to contain the story. "Are you willing to share the identity of your sources with me?"

"Not on the first date," Colc quipped. "But you offered to exchange information with me, so let's hear what you've got."

Spock nodded. "What do you already know about my colleague's abduction?"

"Ah, so there was a kidnapping!" Colc said, his eyes lighting up. "Tell me more."

"And what data do you have to offer in exchange?" Spock asked.

"Uh-uh," Colc said. "You go first."

"Very well."

Spock saw little point in haggling since he had no actual secrets to conceal. "I cannot help but note, however, that you appear to have no recording device on your person."

"Just this one here." Colc tapped his temple. "Obviously."

Spock allowed that the reporter was the best judge of his own memory. He glanced cautiously at the Tellarite, confirming that the fellow was still snoring obliviously, before briefing Colc on the particulars of the case.

"Approximately four days ago, by your time, the *Enterprise* received a report of a medical emergency on your planet . . ." He related what he knew of the ambush in the mining camp and McCoy's apparent abduction. "In response, Captain Kirk dispatched me to Braco to find and recover Doctor McCoy."

"Leonard McCoy, you say." Colc listened intently. "What can you tell me about him?"

"His professional career and accomplishments are a matter of record," Spock stated. "You should have no difficulty researching his background."

"Count on it," Colc said, "but what can you tell me about him as a person, his personality, his likes and dislikes? Does he have a girlfriend? A boyfriend? Pets?"

Spock frowned. "I fail to see how that is relevant to his disappearance."

"My readers aren't Vulcans. They're going to want a humanoid interest angle as well."

"I am not comfortable discussing the doctor's personal life and predilections," Spock said. "If you must paint a portrait of him, let me merely state that McCoy is a man of great integrity and feeling, a dedicated healer, and an undeniable asset to Starfleet."

"Friend of yours?" Colc pressed.

"I consider him such," Spock said, faintly embarrassed by the admission, "but I would prefer to discuss his possible whereabouts."

"All right," Colc said with a sigh. "Guess you can only squeeze so much warm and fuzzy stuff out of a Vulcan. Maybe I can get more personal info on McCoy later, perhaps from one of your colleagues."

"Possibly," Spock said. "We shall see."

"Let's table that for now, then," Colc said. "So where does the official investigation stand? Hard to get any info out of the Bureau when they won't even admit that an incident occurred."

Spock sympathized with the reporter's difficulty. "Chief Inspector Wibb can be less than forthcoming, but at present his investigation seems focused on one specific radical organization, the United Bracon Front."

"Figures." Colc appeared unsurprised. "Chances are, the Bureau would want to blame the UBF even if they weren't responsible, just to give them an excuse to crack down even harder on anyone remotely associated with the group. In fact, I'll lay odds that's the tack they'll take once the news finally goes public."

"What is your opinion?" Spock asked. "Could there be any validity to Wibb's suspicions?"

"It's not impossible," Colc said. "The UBF has never targeted neutral parties before, but they have been known to kidnap establishment politicians and bigwigs to secure the release of political prisoners, funds for their operations, and other concessions. Officially, the Bureau has a strict policy of not negotiating with terrorists, but private firms and wealthy clans have quietly paid out, or pulled strings, to get their people back." Colc adopted a more sympathetic tone. "If it's any consolation, the hostages are generally returned unharmed."

The "generally" in that statement concerned Spock. "And have any such hostages been killed?"

"Not that I know of, but I suppose it could have been hushed up. I don't pretend to know everything."

Ironically, Colc's admission of fallibility engendered more confidence than Wibb's unshakable certainty. The reporter struck Spock as a valuable guide to the finer points of Bracon society and politics.

"What precisely is the agenda of the United Bracon Front?"

"Well, if you ask them, they're all for an independent Braco, divorced from our ancient ties to Vok and Ozalor. They want our feuding interstellar siblings to mind their own businesses and keep their hands off Braco, so we can sort out our differences on our own." He snorted quietly, as though skeptical of the notion. "They also consider the so-called 'Provisional' Government a joke that has gone on way too long. They want a permanent Bracon government, minus outside interference, as opposed to a compromise coalition that has worn out its welcome."

"And what are your views on the subject?" Spock asked.

"I'm a reporter," Colc said. "I'm all about facts, not issues."

"But are you not concerned about the effects your stories may have on current events?" Spock said. "Science tells us that observing a phenomenon often affects the same. You must be aware that you may sometimes make news by reporting news, therefore becoming part of the story."

This dilemma was not academic for Spock. Although rescuing McCoy was his foremost objective, he was acutely aware that his mission could have political ramifications throughout the sector, perhaps even affecting the crucial election on Vok. For that reason, he intended to tread carefully. It worried him that Colc might be more cavalier in his approach.

"You're a scientist, Mister Spock, right?"

"That is correct," Spock said.

"So you get where I'm coming from," Colc said. "Scientists and reporters, we're a lot alike. We follow the facts wherever they lead, even if that's not always pretty. We'd rather discover the truth than settle for a comforting illusion."

Spock pondered the comparison. "Some would argue that scientists should give great thought to the consequences of their discoveries and bear the responsibility thereof. Look at Landru, Oppenheimer, or Subimore." He assumed Colc was knowledgeable enough of galactic history to grasp the references. "Perhaps the same might apply to journalists?"

"That's big-picture stuff." Colc flicked some sweat from his brow. "I'll leave that to the historians, philosophers, and academics to debate. Me, I'm just a workaday newshound, bouncing from story to story while trying to get my facts straight as best I can."

"I'm afraid I do not have the luxury of dismissing the big picture," Spock said. "My duty to Starfleet precludes that."

He wondered if trading information with Colc was indeed a prudent move. Could he trust this journalist to report what they uncovered in a responsible manner?

"Look at it this way, Mister Spock," the man said. "One way or another, this story is going to break. Wouldn't you prefer that I got it right?"

"You make a valid point," Spock said. "Inaccurate data too often leads to erroneous conclusions, resulting in negative consequences."

"See!" Colc said, grinning. "I knew we'd end up on the same page. So what else do you need to know from me?"

Spock chose to proceed with their arrangement for the duration.

"What do your sources tell you about whether the United Bracon Front is responsible for McCoy's abduction?"

"To be honest, I'm having trouble getting a straight answer," Colc said. "I'm not going to lie. I've got some contacts with ties to the UBF, but I can't get anyone to confirm that they're holding a Starfleet officer prisoner. Some deny it vehemently, others act like they have no idea what I'm talking about, while others just clam up if I start pushing too hard. Hard to say who is on the level."

"What of the group's leader, one Hynn V'sta?" Spock asked. "Do your contacts include her?"

"I wish!" Colc said. "I'd sell an organ to get a face-to-face interview with her, but she's deep underground these days, now that she's Public Enemy Number One as far as the Bureau is concerned." He chuckled. "V'sta's not going to show her face to anyone outside her inner circle, let alone yours truly. I'd have an easier time getting a private audience with the *Yovode* of Ozalor."

Across the chamber, the Tellarite stirred, belched, then ambled out of the sauna on his bare hooves, leaving his towel behind. Spock was grateful for the concealing steam as he waited for the Tellarite to fully exit their presence.

"I need to speak directly to someone affiliated with the radicals," Spock said. "Can you arrange a meeting with one of your more reliable contacts?"

"Not so sure about that," Colc said, making a face. "You probably ought to leave that kind of sleuthing to me."

"I disagree." Spock was growing weary of being asked to take a back seat in the search for McCoy. Whether the United Bracon Front was involved in McCoy's kidnapping was a question that required a conclusive answer, one way or another, and Spock was not inclined to delegate that vital task to a relative stranger. "As a reporter, you must surely appreciate the value of a primary source over secondhand accounts. I need to make my own inquiries, in person."

Colc scrutinized Spock through the steam. Perspiration rendered his features as slick as a Ba'ul emerging from its pool.

"In other words, you're not one hundred percent sure you can trust me."

"I lack sufficient data to adequately judge your credibility," Spock admitted. "No offense."

"Smart man," Colc said, shrugging. "Here on Braco, everyone has an ulterior motive. You don't want to take anything—or anyone—for granted."

"I will keep that in mind," Spock said. "Can you broker a meeting?"

Colc ran a hand through his damp yellow hair, which was now plastered to his scalp. "Even if I could set something up, how do you expect to slip past Wibb's troopers? 'Cause I'm pretty sure nobody connected to UBF is going to be willing to walk into the belly of the beast here, no matter how toasty this sauna is."

"Leave that to me," Spock said. "Can you arrange it?"

"Maybe," Colc said, "but it's going to take a whole lot of persuasion on my part, and I'm expecting the full scoop afterward. Anything you learn, you share with me, deal?"

"Naturally," Spock said. "As you said, I would not want you to get your facts wrong."

Worry showed on Colc's sweaty face.

"You realize I can't guarantee your safety," he said. "If V'sta and her crew did grab your friend, they might be inclined to snatch you too . . . especially if you walk right into their clutches."

Spock acknowledged the risk. He calculated, however, that his odds of rescuing McCoy were significantly higher by embarking on a deliberate course of action than they would be if he merely waited for Chief Inspector Wibb to complete his investigation. Risk, as Captain Kirk had once sagely observed, came with their mission.

"Your warning is duly noted," he told Colc. "Rest assured that I intend to take all reasonable precautions."

"I just hope that's enough," the reporter said. "For your sake."

Ten

"Well, this complicates matters," Dare said.

Kirk had been relieved to find her sitting up in a biobed in sickbay, looking better than you might expect for someone who had taken a spear to the back. A diagnostic monitor above the bed charted her vital signs, which appeared to be on the upswing. She was still notably paler than usual and winced when she moved too much or too quickly, but Kirk understood that she was lucky to be alive. According to M'Benga, if the javelin had lodged a few centimeters deeper or in the wrong direction, they would be holding a funeral service, not a bedside briefing.

"That's putting it mildly," Kirk agreed.

He and Tanaka had gathered around Dare's bed to confer with her in the wake of Lom's startling revelation. A nurse hovered nearby, going about her business. Sickbay felt strangely abandoned with neither McCoy nor Chapel present, but Kirk couldn't think about that now. The aftermath of the near assassination demanded his attention.

"I've been in touch with my contacts planetside," Tanaka said. "Even without any actual evidence yet, plenty of people are already accusing Gogg or his associates of being behind the attempt on Doctor Ceff's life, although he's emphatically denying it. Meanwhile, others are saying the incident is a false-flag operation, cooked up by Ceff to discredit General Gogg, and that's just one of myriad conspiracy theories." Tanaka sighed. "On the bright side, Commissioner, you're being acclaimed as a hero . . . at least by most people."

"Glad to hear it," Dare said wryly, "although taking a spear was not exactly part of my job description."

"Accept the praise," Kirk said. "You deserve it."

"If you say so." She leaned back against her pillow. "In any event, thanks again for the emergency beam-up. Not that I don't trust the doctors and nurses down on Vok, but there's nothing like Federation medicine when your life depends on it."

"Happy to oblige," Kirk said. He wished McCoy were on hand to add his own two cents.

"So what are we going to do about that recording Lom turned over?" Tanaka asked, getting back to the business at hand. "Any chance we can keep it—and him—under wraps until after the election?"

Dare shook her head, then grimaced as though the movement pained her.

"Withhold incriminating evidence about a major candidate? Not a good idea. We'd be compromising our neutrality in a big way, and possibly calling the result of the election into question if and when the truth got out."

Kirk agreed. "We can't appear to be part of a cover-up, not where an attempted assassination is concerned."

"I suppose," Tanaka said, "although accusing the General is going to be seen by some as the Federation interfering on Ceff's behalf." He lowered his voice so as not to be overheard. "Granted, her winning the election wouldn't be such a bad thing in the long run."

"There's no way around it," Dare said. "We have crucial evidence and need to turn it over to the civilian authorities on Vok, although we should give both campaigns a heads-up before the recording is made public, just so neither faction feels blindsided." She looked at Kirk. "How many people know about the recording so far?"

Kirk had anticipated her query. "I'm keeping the information on a need-to-know basis for now, and you can count on my crew to be discreet when it comes to any confidential details of our investigation, but we can't keep Lom locked up on the *Enterprise* indefinitely or compel him to keep his mouth shut. The authorities are already demanding that he be extradited back to the surface. I'm pushing things holding him in our brig as is."

Starfleet had no jurisdiction here. Even though both he and Dare had been injured, Lom was a citizen of Vok and the attack had taken place on his planet. This was a matter of Vokite justice.

"Lom's testimony is damning enough," Dare observed, "but that recording speaks for itself."

"Does it?" Kirk asked. "I'm not entirely ready to take it at face value just yet. I want my people to subject that recording to a full forensic analysis, just to make certain that it hasn't been faked or doctored somehow."

"You think that's possible?" Dare asked.

Kirk recalled nearly being court-martialed over a faked video replay in the *Enterprise*'s memory banks. "Anything is possible. We can't afford to jump to conclusions with a planet's future in the balance."

"I can assist your people in examining the footage," Tanaka said.

Kirk appreciated the offer. With Spock away, he could use all the extra brain power he could get. "Thank you, Mister Tanaka."

"In the meantime, however," Dare said, "we can't count on that recording being invalidated. We need to get ahead of this if it's not already too late. Can Lieutenant Uhura patch me into Vok's communications network? I need to set up meetings with both Gogg and Ceff."

She sat up and reached for the bedside computer terminal, only to suddenly grow faint. Her eyelids drooped and her head rolled unsteadily atop her neck as she sagged back against her pillow. The diagnostic monitor charted a precipitous drop in her pulse and blood pressure, signaling Nurse Alongi to scurry over to check on her patient. Kirk looked on anxiously, but he was re-assured to see that the nurse didn't appear too alarmed. Dare just needed a moment or two to regain her strength.

"Whoa," she said weakly, the blood beginning to return to her face. "If you don't mind, Captain, could you kindly ask your helmsman to stop spinning the ship around?"

"Only if you don't insist on pushing yourself too hard too fast," Kirk said. "You nearly died. You're allowed time to recuperate."

"But the election," she protested. "I need to speak with both sides, preferably in person."

"Belay that," Kirk said. "You need to rest. Leave the candidates to me."

Eleven

Ozalor

"You did what?" the sovereign demanded. "Do my ears deceive me?"

His Excellency, Salokonos, *Yovode* of Ozalor, was holding audience in his private chambers, his throne room having been deemed too public a venue for so delicate a matter. Nevertheless, he presided over the scene from a most impressive silk-lined chair that rested upon a raised platform overlooking the inner sanctum. His was the only chair in the room, so that the others were required to stand in his presence. At that moment, those in attendance consisted of Vumri, Rayob, Jemo, and McCoy, the last of whom scratched irritably at the fake beard glued to his face. Palace guards were posted along the perimeter of the chamber to discourage any bad behavior. A routine weapons scan had already turned up Rayob's concealed phaser, which he'd surrendered without protest. Sound-absorbing baffles on the walls and ceiling protected the privacy of whatever discussions transpired within the chamber.

"I'm afraid not, sire," Rayob replied. "I take full responsibility."

The truth had finally come to light. Unwilling to flat-out lie to his ruler, Rayob had confessed to spiriting McCoy away from Braco in hopes of curing the Heir to the throne. *Lossu* Vumri, who had instigated this audience, looked on smugly, not even bothering to conceal her satisfaction at seeing her rival in hot water. For himself, McCoy was relieved that, if nothing else, he no longer needed to worry about who knew what or to debate whom to tell about his abduction. Perhaps now something could be done about his involuntary stay on the planet. On Ozalor, he gathered, the *Yovode* was the final court of appeal.

And right now Salokonos wasn't happy.

"What were you thinking, Rayob? Kidnapping a Starfleet officer, and without even asking my permission?"

Salokonos was a stocky, barrel-chested monarch with a dense brown beard that would make a Klingon envious. Bushy eyebrows resembled those of his daughter, who was presently recuperating back in her chambers, presumably under the watchful eye of the ever-attentive Bilis. Like her, he wore a gleaming quartz wristband, but in his case, there were several rings stacked one atop another, of chalcedony, jasper, carnelian, agate, and onyx, so that practically his entire forearm was girded by the bands, which McCoy surmised to have some ceremonial significance. Beyond that, the *Yovode*'s attire was surprisingly plain and practical, albeit of evident quality and condition. An off-white linen tunic and trousers, along with a sturdy pair of boots, covered his regal corpus. Apparently, he preferred comfort to finery outside the public eye. Considerably darker was his expression, which could best be described as glowering. He scowled at the errant majordomo, who, to his credit, did not wilt before his sovereign's displeasure.

"Forgive me, Your Excellency, but I sought to protect you from any possible culpability in this matter. Plausible deniability."

Salokonos was not appeased.

"That's all very well and good, but I still have a kidnapped Federation citizen on my hands, and a Starfleet medical officer, no less. Now, what am I to do with him?"

McCoy raised his hand. "If I may, Your Excellency, I'm not inclined to press charges or create an interstellar incident here. Just let me contact my ship, maybe give me a lift back to Braco, and I'm willing to let the whole kidnapping thing slide. No harm, no foul, as we used to say back on Earth."

"No harm?" Rayob protested. "What of your patient? You would abandon the *Yiyova* so readily?"

His words pricked McCoy's conscience. "Look, I never said I

was going to forget her case altogether. Let me examine her scans back on the *Enterprise*, review the relevant medical literature, and so on; if I come up with any fresh insights or suggestions, I'll be sure to transmit them to you." Other options occurred to him as well. "And I'm hardly the only doctor in the Federation. If you like, we can certainly arrange for additional physicians and specialists to visit Ozalor on your princess's behalf, without any need for ambushes or abductions."

Who knows? McCoy thought. Perhaps Avomora's agonies, as grueling as they were, could open up a new era of improved relations between Ozalor and the Federation. It would be comforting if some good came from her ordeal.

"Keep your alien doctors and nostrums to yourself," Vumri said, her lip curling in contempt. "The *Yiyova* doesn't need strangers experimenting on her. Our ways are best for her. My gifts alone can ease her affliction."

McCoy's hackles rose. That sounded more like ego than empathy to him. "What's the matter? Worried about competition?"

"Hardly," she scoffed before appealing directly to her ruler. "Please, Your Excellency, pay no attention to an ignorant foreigner who knows nothing of our ways or your daughter, and who never wanted to tend to Avomora in the first place. Send him back where he belongs, far from here."

McCoy started to object, then realized that Vumri was actually lobbying to return him to the *Enterprise*. Did he really want to contradict her?

Whose side am I on?

"If only it were that simple," Salokonos said. "Despite the doctor's assurances, neither Starfleet nor the Federation can be expected to overlook the forcible abduction of one of their own, particularly in light of the painful history between our peoples. And the fact that the ambush took place on Braco of all planets complicates matters considerably; the last thing we need is for Ozalor to be accused of infringing on Braco's sovereignty at the very time that Vok grows more aggressive in asserting its claims to the Birth World."

McCoy recalled that Braco was a hot issue in the election on Vok.

"So?" Vumri said. "What do we care what foreign powers think of our actions? The Federation is no friend of Ozalor, as proven by their affinity with our ancestral enemies on Vok. We have no diplomatic relations with the Federation, so our relations with them cannot be harmed by this incident, and as for Braco . . . who are Vok or Starfleet to dictate what we can or cannot do on the world that spawned our race? Braco is our native soil. We have as much right to it as the greedy Vokites!"

"That goes without saying," Salokonos said, "but there's a difference between asserting our rights and inviting trouble. We may keep our distance from the Federation, but I have no desire to provoke them either."

"Your prudence does you credit, sire," Vumri argued, "but the Federation already set themselves against Ozalor when they sided with Vok. Why worry about offending those who have no love for us to begin with? We are already at odds."

"Whoa there," McCoy said. "Just because the Federation enjoys peaceful relations with Vok doesn't mean that we've taken sides with them against your people. We pursue peace with every advanced world we encounter, not all of whom like each other very much."

He realized that he was hurting his own chances of getting back to the *Enterprise* by challenging Vumri on this point, but he couldn't keep silent while Vumri painted the Federation as an inveterate foe of Ozalor to the planet's supreme ruler. He felt compelled to defend the Federation's neutrality, even against his own interests.

"The friend of our enemy is not our friend," Vumri insisted, "and does not belong on our world. Send him back where he came from."

"And give the Federation an excuse to take action against us?" Salokonos asked. "Or another reason to side with Vok when it comes to dominion over Braco?" He stroked his beard thoughtfully. "These are treacherous waters. We must be careful how we navigate them."

"I just told you," McCoy said. "You don't have to worry about Starfleet retaliating against you, at least as long as you don't make a habit of kidnapping our people. This doesn't have to spark a crisis. We can move past this."

"So you say," Salokonos said, sounding doubtful, "but I wonder if you can truly speak for your superiors . . . or for our adversaries on Vok. Even if the Federation chooses to look the other way, the Vokites are sure to use this incident against us, portraying us as villains and aggressors who cannot be trusted on Braco or any other world."

McCoy didn't have a ready rebuttal. Kidnapping a foreign national on somebody else's planet wasn't exactly a good look for anyone and was bound to get some people's noses out of joint. He couldn't guarantee that it *wouldn't* be used against Ozalor, diplomatically or politically.

"Maybe this doesn't have to become a big controversy," he suggested. "Perhaps we can still handle things quietly."

If it wasn't already too late for that. For all he knew, the ambush on Braco was headline news by now. Unless Kirk and Commissioner Dare were keeping the whole thing hushed up for the duration.

"There is another issue to consider, Your Excellency," Rayob said, joining the debate. "We cannot risk knowledge of the *Yiyova*'s affliction spreading beyond the palace walls. If the people were to know of her condition, if other worlds become aware that the Heir is unwell, then the very future and stability of the monarchy is cast into doubt." He spoke softly but firmly. "Regrettably, the good doctor knows too much to be allowed to return to the Federation."

"And whose fault is that?" McCoy snapped. "And give me some

credit for respecting my patient's confidentiality. I'm not going to go blabbing about her medical condition all over the quadrant."

"Perhaps not, Doctor," Salokonos said, "but how do you expect to explain your abduction to your superiors if and when you return to them? You are not to blame for learning of my daughter's malady, we understand that, but the majordomo is not mistaken; we cannot risk Avomora's condition becoming known to Starfleet and the rest of the quadrant. To do so endangers the dynasty, and thereby the security of our planet."

McCoy glared at Rayob. *Thanks for nothing.*

"Just so, sire," the older man said. "But let me qualify my remarks. Doctor McCoy cannot be allowed to return to the Federation . . . until or unless he has cured your daughter."

McCoy's jaw dropped. The wily majordomo was boxing him in good and tight. "Now hold on there. I never promised I could do anything for her."

The word "cure" caught Salokonos's attention. "But is it possible?"

"I don't know," McCoy said. "I'd only just begun to—"

"Your Excellency!" Vumri interrupted. "Don't you see what Rayob is doing? He's trying to trick you into putting your daughter in the care of a stranger!"

"No trickery," Rayob said. "I'm merely suggesting that Doctor McCoy be given a chance to help Avomora, which would be in the best interests of all concerned."

"The child does not need a captive Earthman toying with her royal personage, or giving her false hopes of a cure," Vumri said. "Her condition is under control."

"*Your* control, you mean," Rayob countered. "That is what this is truly all about, isn't it?"

"I care only about the child! I alone have eased her suffering!"

The increasingly heated exchange left McCoy not entirely sure whom to root for: Vumri, who wanted to send him home for all the wrong reasons, or Rayob, who wanted to keep him prisoner for the best of reasons?

"How many people know of this?" Salokonos asked. "How many are aware that the doctor ever came to Ozalor?"

McCoy was troubled by this line of questioning. It occurred to him that there was a third alternative to releasing him or continuing to hold him captive. What if the worried monarch concluded that it would be simpler and safer just to make this thorny problem disappear without a trace? McCoy gulped, suddenly realizing how precarious his position was. Salokonos wouldn't be the first ruler in history to try to bury an inconvenient embarrassment six feet deep. McCoy wanted to think that Ozalor was more advanced and civilized than that, but when the future of the monarchy was at stake . . . ?

"Not many," Rayob attempted to assure his ruler. "Only a trusted few."

"Which is far too many," Vumri said. "And you have the audacity to speak of trust, after going behind the *Yovode's* back as you did?" She laughed scornfully. "Please, Your Excellency, do not heed the words of this reckless fool, particularly where your beloved daughter is concerned. Who knows better how to care for the child than I?"

Salokonos weighed her words. "It is true, *Lossu*, that you have proven your value to my daughter more times than I can count. I do not take your counsel lightly. Perhaps—"

The door to the sanctum sublimed and Avo strode into the room, walking confidently on her own two feet. The guards posted at the door started at the *Yiyova's* unexpected arrival, but, understandably, made no effort to obstruct her.

"Pardon my tardiness," she said brightly. "I trust I'm not too late to take part in this conversation."

"Your Highness!" Vumri exclaimed, all fluttery solicitousness. "You mustn't be here. You should be resting."

"To the contrary," Avo said. "I feel quite restored, thanks to your diligent efforts."

She *did* look better, McCoy observed. There was more color in her cheeks, and her body language was less strained. No longer confined to her chair, she marched boldly through the assemblage, which parted to let her pass, and approached Salokonos, who appeared pleasantly surprised by his daughter's arrival. She paused directly before her sire.

"Father," she addressed him.

"Daughter." He gazed at her with obvious affection. "It pleases me to see you up and about, but are you quite certain you are well enough to do so?"

"For the time being." She glanced around at the impromptu conclave. "So, what have I missed?"

"There's some debate," McCoy said, "as to whether you require my professional services."

"Is that so?" She raised a substantial eyebrow. "And shouldn't that be my decision?"

You'd think, McCoy thought.

"It is rather more complex than that," her father said. "There are serious political ramifications to be taken into account. Issues of foreign policy and planetary security."

"No doubt," she said, "but, ultimately, it is my health and my care that is being decided. I should have some say in the matter, don't you think?"

Salokonos nodded.

"Spoken like one born to rule," he said approvingly. "Very well, Avomora, what is your preference?"

She smiled at McCoy. "With all due respect to *Lossu* Vumri, I see no harm in letting Doctor McCoy apply his knowledge and expertise to finding new remedies for my condition. Ozalorian medicine has done all it can for me; why not look beyond our world for a fresh approach?"

This was not what Vumri wanted to hear. "But, child, please reconsider—"

"I am *not* a child," Avo corrected her. "I'm Heir to the throne of Ozalor, and if I want to give the doctor the opportunity to help me, then I believe my wishes should be honored." She bowed her head respectfully to her father. "With your generous permission, of course."

Salokonos mulled over her request a moment or two before reaching a decision.

"So be it." He fixed his gaze on McCoy. "If my daughter believes you may be able to relieve her of her affliction, who am I to deny her?"

Good for Avo, McCoy thought, *I guess.*

He was proud of her for standing up for herself, and appreciated her vote of confidence, even as he realized that he might have reason to regret winning her trust. His odds of making an easy exit from Ozalor were shrinking by the moment. *No good deed goes unpunished.*

"Tell me, Doctor," Salokonos said, "can you truly cure my daughter?"

McCoy heard the father speaking, not the sovereign. He was tempted to lie, to say that her case was hopeless and beyond his abilities to treat, just in case there was still a chance of him being quietly returned to the *Enterprise,* but when he looked at Avo, bravely taking control of her own treatment in hopes of finally overcoming her affliction, he couldn't bring himself to let her down by dissembling. It was his duty as a doctor to answer Salokonos as honestly as he could.

"I can't make any promises, but, in my experience, it seldom hurts to get a second opinion."

"My thoughts exactly, Doctor," Rayob said. A thin smile indicated his satisfaction at how matters were shaking out. "All we can ask is that you do your best for our courageous *Yiyova.*"

Vumri gave him a look that would have peeled the scales off a Gorn. She appealed once more to Salokonos.

"You will not reconsider, Your Excellency?"

"My daughter has spoken. We will respect her wishes."

"As you command, sire," Vumri said, her face and voice downcast. "If my gifts are no longer required, I shall take my leave of the palace forthwith."

"What?" Salokonos sat up straight in his chair. "Who said anything about you leaving? What if Avomora suffers another of her spells?"

Vumri sighed, playing the martyr. "Surely, that is the Earthman's province now."

"Nonsense," Salokonos decreed. "You are needed here as well. Doctor McCoy may or may not be able to cure my daughter, but under no circumstances will I allow her suffering to go unrelieved in the meantime. You will remain on call to tend to her pains as you always have."

"Of course, Your Excellency." Vumri turned toward Avo. "And is that acceptable to you as well, child . . . that is, Your Highness?"

Avo hesitated before answering. For the first time since making her entrance into the sanctum, her nerve seemed to falter. McCoy couldn't blame her for wavering; for better or for worse, Vumri was still the only one who could relieve her symptoms when her spells hit. The prospect of doing without the healer's special gifts had to be a terrifying one.

"Yes, *Lossu*," the princess said glumly. Her gaze dropped to the floor, unable to look Vumri in the eyes. "Do stay."

The healer smirked triumphantly.

"Naturally, *Yiyova*. You had only to ask."

"It's settled, then." Salokonos relaxed into his seat. "I regret the confusion, *Lossu*. Rest assured that your place in my household is secure for as long as my daughter is in need of your care."

"Thank you, sire." She shifted her gaze to Rayob. "But what of the traitor's place?"

Rayob stiffened as though slapped across the face. "Traitor?"

"Do you deny it?" She wheeled about to confront him. "By your own admission, you conspired behind the *Yovode*'s back to recklessly risk Starfleet's wrath and Ozalor's good name. You yourself declared Avomora's affliction to be a state secret that must be kept hidden for the sake of the dynasty, yet you revealed it to a Starfleet officer allied to our enemies on Vok? What would you call that but treason of the highest order?"

"What I did I did for Avomora," Rayob said, "and Ozalor."

"And are you the *Yovode* to make such decisions?"

McCoy didn't envy Rayob. Vumri was clearly out to make her foe pay for plotting against her. Even if she had failed to remove McCoy from the palace, she could still strike back at Rayob and get some of her own back.

"Your Excellency, surely the majordomo's transgressions cannot go unpunished? Never mind your daughter and the doctor; Rayob brazenly usurped your authority. Will he pay no price for that?"

Jemo stalked toward Vumri, her fists clenched. "And how is that your business, healer?"

Vumri flinched at the angry bodyguard's advance. Guards stationed around the sanctum started forward, ready to shut down any altercation before it started, but Rayob beat them to it by placing a restraining hand on Jemo's shoulder.

"Back down, brave one. Do not forget yourself on my account." He waited to make certain that Jemo was not going to get herself into more trouble than she already was before releasing her shoulder. "Save your fire for another day."

Jemo nodded, still fuming.

"You should keep your accomplice on a leash," Vumri said, regaining her composure and her attitude. "See what comes of encouraging insurrection?"

"I believe you have made your opinion clear," Rayob said, "but this is between the *Yovode* and myself." He turned his back on Vumri to face his sovereign head-on. "Forgive my friend her eagerness to defend my honor. I will gladly accept whatever judgment you deem fit."

Salokonos contemplated the older man.

"It grieves me to be placed in this position. Your many years of service and loyalty to the dynasty are indisputable and deserve recognition. Still, the *Lossu* is correct: your unsanctioned actions far exceeded your authority and betrayed my trust. There must be consequences, if only to ensure that you can never abuse your position again."

"I understand, Your Excellency," Rayob said. "I throw myself upon the mercy of the throne."

Vumri sneered. "Mercy? Traitors deserve no mercy."

"But a lifetime devoted to duty cannot be dismissed," Salokonos said. "You have served long and well, majordomo, but I think the time has come for you to retire at last . . . with a full pension."

Is that all? McCoy thought. *Seems like he's getting off easy.*

Vumri definitely thought so.

"Retire?" she echoed in disbelief. "But, Your Excellency, an offense of such magnitude must warrant more punishment than that."

"I disagree, Father," Avo said. "Is this truly necessary? Rayob was only doing what he thought was best."

"I have made my judgment," Salokonos declared in a tone that brooked no further debate. "Is that understood?"

"Yes, Your Excellency." Rayob removed his sash and presented it to Avomora, who accepted it with obvious reluctance, visibly fighting back tears. The cashiered advisor bowed stiffly to her father. "It has been an honor and a privilege to serve the throne these many years. I have no regrets."

McCoy felt a twinge of sympathy. He had his own ax to grind with the now-former majordomo, but it couldn't be easy being put out to pasture this way, ending a long and distinguished career under a cloud. Rayob was maintaining a tight upper lip, but McCoy had to wonder what he was feeling inside: relief, sorrow, some combination thereof?

Did he have anything else in his life besides duty?

Yet, despite Rayob's forced retirement, Vumri remained unsatisfied.

"And what of his co-conspirator?" She pointed an accusing finger at Jemo. "She was party to this intrigue as well."

"Father!" Avo spoke up. "Don't listen to her. Jemo is a true friend and loyal subject. I won't have her punished simply for following the majordomo's instructions!"

"That, however, is not solely your decision," Salokonos said. "I know how fond you are of her, but it appears as though she *did* assist in covertly bringing Doctor McCoy into our lives."

"Only on my orders," Rayob said.

"You no longer have any standing here," Salokonos reminded him curtly. "Keep your counsel to yourself." He peered at the accused bodyguard. "Come forward, Jemo."

She took her place before him. Her insouciant posture displayed a conspicuous lack of contrition, although she refrained from whittling in the ruler's presence.

"Well, Jemo, what do you have to say for yourself?"

"I'm not one for making speeches, but I can tell you this: I will always do everything I can for Avomora."

This was perhaps less of an apology than Salokonos was expecting. His expression hardened behind his beard.

"And what of Ozalor?"

Jemo shrugged. "Avo is the future of Ozalor."

Salokonos frowned, as though he wasn't quite sure how to take that.

"Your loyalty to my daughter is duly noted, but what of your duty to your sovereign?"

"How can I possibly serve you better than by doing what is best for your own flesh and blood?"

Touché, McCoy thought. If Jemo was as good at actual combat as she was at verbal jujitsu, he wouldn't want to get on her bad side. *The question is, how is her cockiness playing with Salokonos?*

The *Yovode* glanced back and forth between Jemo and Avo. The princess looked back at him, her anxious eyes pleading on behalf of her friend. A low chuckle escaped him.

"Plainly spoken," he granted Jemo. "I suppose my daughter is entitled to one stalwart defender who places her interests above all others. Certainly, I cannot find it in myself to fault you for your loyalty to Avomora." His voice grew sterner. "But understand this: Doctor McCoy is fully your responsibility now. His actions reflect on you and you will be held accountable if he transgresses against the throne in any way. Watch him like a Pryglarian hawk. Ensure that he is confined to the secure regions of the palace and, at all costs, see that he cannot communicate with Starfleet. I want no trouble with the Federation."

"I fear we cannot avoid that eventuality," Vumri said, "so long as the Federation remains allied with the bloodstained savages of Vok."

"Perhaps so," Salokonos said, "but I would prefer to choose my battles where the Federation is concerned." He returned his attention to Jemo. "Have I made myself clear?"

"Very much so, Your Excellency." Jemo smirked at McCoy. "You can count on me to make sure our guest doesn't get into any trouble."

McCoy bit his tongue.

"See that you do," the *Yovode* said. "Please escort the doctor back to his guest quarters." His decisive gaze swept over the assemblage. "I pronounce this audience concluded."

That's that, McCoy thought glumly. *I'm not going anywhere soon.*

"Daughter," Salokonos said, his voice softening, "please linger so I may enjoy your company for a time."

"Of course, Father. I would be happy to."

"The rest of you are dismissed," he said. "Leave us."

The various parties dispersed toward the exit, Vumri keeping her distance from the others. Jemo took McCoy by the arm.

"You heard the man, Doctor. I'm sticking to you like glue."

"Oh, joy," McCoy said.

As they passed out of the sanctum, leaving father and daughter to enjoy some family time, Rayob approached McCoy and Jemo with a grim expression on his gaunt face. He glanced around warily before speaking to Jemo *sotto voce.*

"Watch over McCoy closely. Keep him safe."

McCoy could guess from whom. Vumri had her knives out. "Why do I feel like I'm more in the crosshairs than ever?"

"Because you are, Doctor. We all are."

Twelve

Braco

The trooper looked uncomfortable. "I'm not sure the chief inspector would approve, miss."

"Please," Chapel entreated as Deputy Tyly blocked the exit from the hotel suite, standing between her and the hallway beyond. "Mister Spock and I just want to take a stroll around the neighborhood, get a bit of fresh air, that's all. I'm going stir-crazy cooped up here with nothing to do but worry about Doctor McCoy."

Her plea had the ring of sincerity, Spock noted. He hoped the trooper thought the same.

"Perhaps we should check with headquarters first?" the trooper hedged.

"Excuse me, Deputy," Spock said, "but I was under the impression that we were guests, not prisoners. If we are indeed under house arrest, please confirm this so I can promptly notify the Federation of our incarceration."

"No, no," Tyly said hastily. "Please don't misunderstand. You are definitely not under arrest."

"In which case, logically, we are free to leave our lodgings as we please," Spock said. "Is that not correct?"

"I suppose," Tyly replied hesitantly, "but—"

"Thank you for the clarification," Spock said. "Nurse Chapel and I will take our constitutional now."

Backed into a figurative corner, Tyly grudgingly conceded the point. "In that case, I must insist on accompanying you . . . for your own safety."

"Your dedication to duty is to be commended," Spock stated,

having anticipated the trooper's response. He and Chapel donned heavy civilian overcoats and caps, obtained through the hotel's hospitality department, over their Starfleet uniforms. "Shall we?"

Levine and Godwin hung back. "Still wish I was going with you," Levine said, scowling.

"Another time," Spock said. "As discussed, it is best that you and Lieutenant Godwin stand ready in case there is urgent news from the inspector."

That was not the only reason the security officers were staying behind, but it was the one most suitable for Tyly's consumption.

"Understood," Levine said. "We'll contact you immediately if we learn anything."

Likewise, Spock thought silently.

He and Chapel departed the suite, accompanied by Tyly, who glanced suspiciously at the medkit Chapel slung over her shoulder.

"What are you bringing that for?"

"I'm a nurse," she said. "Never go anywhere without it."

The answer mollified the deputy, who escorted them out of the hotel, bypassing the Bureau troopers and hotel security posted in the lobby and immediately outside the building. It was midafternoon and although the precipitation had abated somewhat since they had first arrived at the hotel, the weather was still gray and damp. Heavy clouds dimmed the daylight while a clammy fog enveloped the streets and sidewalks. Spock was grateful for their outerwear, which provided protection from the elements as well as concealing their Starfleet attire, allowing them to blend more easily with the populace. He and Chapel had no desire to attract any unwanted attention. Ground vehicles cruised past them, while the inclement weather appeared to have driven most other pedestrians indoors. Spock glimpsed only the occasional blurry figure treading through the mists.

"Not really a good day for a stroll," Tyly said a little too eagerly. "Perhaps we ought to turn back."

"Oh, not so soon," Chapel said. "We've barely begun to see the sights."

Glancing about, she started forward, only to trip over a partially filled crater in the pavement. She stumbled to the ground, yelping slightly as she did so.

"Crud," Tyly muttered, looking dismayed. He hurried toward her. "Are you all right, miss?"

"I'm not sure," she answered, wincing. "I think I might have twisted my ankle." She extended an arm. "Mind helping me up?"

"Certainly, miss." Tyly bent over to assist her, presenting his back to Spock, who took advantage of the opportunity to administer a nerve pinch to the unsuspecting trooper, who went limp immediately. Spock caught the unconscious man before he fell and gently deposited him on the stoop of an adjacent building, leaving him slumped against the doorway. Chapel sprang to her feet.

"That worked out nicely," she said.

"Indeed," Spock said. "I congratulate you on your performance. You were quite convincing."

"Well, I'm no Lenore Karidian, but I can fake a decent pratfall if I have to." She spared Tyly a sympathetic look. "The poor deputy never saw it coming."

"As was always our intention." Spock relieved the trooper of his disruptor and Bureau communicator, which he concealed in the pockets of his overcoat. "It is for the best, however. I suspect the deputy would not be welcome where we are going."

"You realize we've just assaulted a police officer," Chapel said. "Chief Inspector Wibb is not going to be happy about that."

"I expect not," Spock said, "but we can face the consequences of his displeasure *after* we discover what has become of Doctor McCoy." Spock was confident in his course of action. "If the inspector did not wish us to interfere with his troopers, he should not have directed them to obstruct our rescue mission."

Chapel smiled at Spock. "Pretty sure Captain Kirk would agree."

Spock reviewed Kirk's own history of taking action against the wishes of local authorities when the safety of his ship and crew were at stake. Kirk had never been one to sit by idly when ordered to do so by politicians or bureaucrats.

"The record supports that conclusion," he said. "Let us continue to emulate the captain's example."

Contrary to what they had told the unfortunate deputy, he and Chapel were not simply out to enjoy some healthy exercise. D'Ran Colc had indeed managed to broker a clandestine meeting with one of his confidential sources, a civilian named F'lun who had unspecified ties to the United Bracon Front. After some negotiating, employing Colc as a go-between, F'lun had agreed to meet with Spock and Chapel at a location of his choosing, elsewhere in the city. Unsurprisingly, he had insisted they come alone, unaccompanied by either Bureau troopers or Starfleet security. Spock had agreed to these terms, albeit with some reservations. He had not forgotten Colc's warnings regarding ulterior motives.

We are taking a calculated risk, he acknowledged.

Leaving the insensate deputy behind, they made their way through foggy streets and alleys, following directions passed along by Colc, which Spock had diligently committed to memory. The circuitous route detoured around inconvenient security checkpoints, sometimes taking them through abandoned buildings and crumbling rear courtyards. They moved briskly but confidently, doing their best to avoid behaving suspiciously. The overcast sky grew darker, threatening rain. Chill breezes rustled scattered litter.

The farther they got from the Capital Hotel, the less salubrious the neighborhoods became. The drifting mist failed to entirely veil the debris and damage marking the war-scarred slums and tenements, which reminded Spock of the more disreputable districts of certain Orion trading outposts. Filmy water filled unpaved craters. Avian, mammalian, and insectoid vermin picked at uncollected heaps of rubbish. Offensive odors assailed his nostrils. Raucous laughter and angry curses escaped the run-down structures.

"Is it just me," Chapel said quietly, "or are we heading into the bad part of town?"

"One can hardly expect to confer with suspected terrorists in the most secure of environments," Spock replied. "Or the most sanitary, it appears."

"I know." She stepped carefully to avoid an oily puddle of uncertain depth. "Just wish Levine or Godwin could have joined us."

"That would have been preferable," Spock agreed, "but our elusive contact was quite explicit in his demands." In fact, it had required some effort and persuasion to include Chapel in the meeting, despite her insistence on coming along. "And there are strategic advantages to not risking additional crew members on this outing, thereby leaving more reinforcements in wait."

"In case we need rescuing as well?" Chapel translated.

"Precisely."

He was glad to have claimed the deputy's disruptor and was ready to hail the shuttlecrafts at the spaceport if necessary, but he was also aware that merely being prepared was no guarantee of safety, as the ambush at the mining camp had demonstrated. He wondered briefly if allowing Chapel to join him on this expedition was the wisest choice, although she had certainly faced danger before and was deeply invested in finding Doctor McCoy.

Both the weather and milieu grew more dismal as they ventured into a shabbily maintained plaza whose shattered fountain had clearly seen better days. Stagnant green water filled the basin, beneath a sculpted stone nymph whose head lay semi-submerged at her feet. Broken metal pipes were strewn among the debris. A shirtless Bracon male sat on the lip of the fountain, smoking a pipe and sipping from a half-empty bottle of spirits. He glared belligerently at Spock and Chapel as they entered the plaza.

"Hey, you!" he challenged them. "What are you looking at?"

Spock could smell the alcohol on his breath from several meters away. "Nothing in particular," he replied evenly. "Pay us no heed."

"Who you calling nothing?" The man lurched to his feet, plucking a rusty length of metal pipe from the rubble. He lumbered toward them, manifestly looking for trouble. "I'll 'heed' whatever and whoever I want!"

Spock felt obliged to attempt to reason with the man, although he deemed it unlikely that the effort would succeed. "We have no conflict with you. We are simply passing through."

"That's what you think!"

He swung the pipe at Spock's head, but his attack, dulled by inebriation, was no match for Spock's reflexes or training. The Vulcan easily grasped the pipe, halting its progress, and wrenched it from the drunkard's grasp. Taking hold of the pipe with both hands, he calmly bent it in two before the man's eyes before casually flinging the warped implement away.

"Perhaps you should reconsider your intentions," Spock said.

The crude demonstration of physical strength was rather beneath his Vulcan intellect and heritage, yet achieved the desired effect. The bellicose stranger swallowed hard and backed away from his targets.

"Eh, you're not worth my time," he said in a transparent attempt to save face. He staggered back toward his bottle, waving them away. "Go on. Get out of my sight."

"Affirmative."

Spock led Chapel across the plaza, his borrowed weapon still resting in his coat pocket. He had been reluctant to draw the weapon since disruptor fire might have attracted the attention of the authorities. Chapel let out a sigh of relief as they put the unpleasant episode behind them.

"Mister Spock," she said. "I sometimes forget how strong you are."

"Merely a byproduct of my Vulcan ancestry," he stated. "Nothing I ordinarily care to advertise, but it does prove useful at times."

Thankfully, they endured no further incidents on their way to their destination: a reputed drinking establishment located in the basement of a dilapidated brick building whose upper stories appeared to be derelict. They descended a short flight of concrete steps to an entrance located just below ground level. Bracon script was scrawled above the doorway in faded paint.

"The Dreaming Oasis," Spock translated.

A scuffed metal door slid open to admit them. A staticky chime announced their arrival.

They entered the smoky neighborhood watering hole. A motley assortment of patrons lounged on cushions around a variety of tables, indulging in liquid refreshments and games of chance, the most popular of which seemed to involve marked rubber tiles and beads. Bracon folk music, relying heavily on what sounded like flutes and zithers, issued from loudspeakers. The noxious fumes and grating trills were not to Spock's taste, but he had endured worse environments in his explorations. Chapel sidled closer to him and whispered softly.

"An 'oasis,' you said?"

"That does appear to be somewhat of a misnomer," he replied, just as quietly. "Perhaps it gains something in translation."

The general hubbub ceased abruptly on their entrance. All heads turned toward the newcomers, who found themselves objects of scrutiny. The expressions of the patrons, all of whom appeared to be native Bracons, ranged from wary to hostile. Spock discreetly gripped the disruptor in his pocket.

A hefty, heavy-muscled woman came out from behind the bar and strode up to the Starfleet visitors. She wore a stained apron over a black tank top and trousers, the former showing off her formidable biceps. A purple turban was bound around her hair with only a stray auburn tress escaping the wrappings. A pungent floral perfume combatted the pervasive smokiness, while contributing to the noisome atmosphere. Her face and manner were no more hospitable than those of her customers. Narrowed eyes sized up Spock and Chapel.

"You lost?" she asked.

"I do not believe so." Spock surveyed the bar, looking for F'lun, whose image had been provided to them. He did not immediately spot the man. "We are here to see an individual named F'lun."

Recognition dawned on the woman's face. She scowled at the curious eyes and ears around them.

"Keep your voice down," she said tersely. "Follow me."

She led them through a vinyl curtain at the rear of the public area, where they found two equally imposing Bracons stationed before a closed door. Their sullen expressions and imposing musculature hinted that they were most likely employed as guards or enforcers. Spock understood "bouncers" was generally the term employed in such establishments, not that he often had occasion to frequent them. It was possible Chapel, being human, was more experienced in that respect.

"My name's Ummu," the barkeep said. "The party you're looking for is through there."

"We are grateful for your assistance, madam," Spock said.

They started toward the door, but Ummu placed her palm against Spock's chest, halting him. "Slow down," she said. "We need to search you first."

Spock could not be too surprised by this precaution. Exchanging a glance with Chapel, he bowed to the inevitable and surrendered his disruptor to Ummu.

"As a show of good faith," he stated.

Ummu examined the pistol. "This is Bureau issue. Where'd you get this?"

"I 'borrowed' it from a deputy who was in no position to object, purely for purposes of self-defense." Spock removed his cap to expose the tapered tips of his ears. "As you can see, I am obviously not a Bracon police officer."

"And neither am I." Chapel opened her coat to reveal her blue Starfleet uniform. "I'm a nurse looking for a missing doctor."

Ummu held on to the weapon as she looked them over. "Still going to need to frisk you anyway," she said.

"If you must," Spock said.

He and Chapel submitted to the tactile inspections, losing their communicators in the process. His tricorder and her medkit were also confiscated.

"They're clean," a bouncer reported.

"All right," Ummu said, nodding. "Let 'em through."

The door slid open, admitting Spock, Chapel, and their escorts to a dingy back room lined with shelves and cupboards, where F'lun and several other rough-looking Bracons awaited them, most of whom appeared to be armed with batons, blades, or sidearms. Spock immediately suspected that he and Chapel had walked into a trap; surely F'lun did not need so large a contingent for a private conversation? The Starfleet pair were outnumbered and outgunned. The door slid shut behind them.

"Damn," Chapel murmured, also grasping the situation.

Spock sought to take control of events. His eyes singled out F'lun: an individual of average height and weight distinguished by sallow skin, greasy black bangs, and a drooping mustache. Spock knew better than to judge sentient beings purely by their appearance, but F'lun certainly fit the part of a shady underworld informer. Rumpled work clothes denoted his social status, while his expression could best be described as "vulpine." A missing tooth struck Spock as unusual in this day and age. The overpowering aroma of the man's aftershave was potent. Only his Vulcan self-control kept his nose from wrinkling in distaste.

"Mister F'lun, I believe. As our mutual acquaintance has already informed you, I wish to question you on an important matter."

F'lun sneered at him. "And what makes you think we like Starfleet digging around in our business? From what I hear, you're working with the Bureau to track us down . . . and pin a kidnapping on us."

"Reports of our collaboration with the Tranquility Bureau have been greatly exaggerated," Spock said dryly. "Nurse Chapel and I are interested in the United Bracon Front only as far as they may or may not be holding one of our colleagues from the *Enterprise*."

"And what if we are?" F'lun asked. "What do you mean to do about it?"

"That depends," Spock said. "*Are* you holding Doctor McCoy?"

"Wouldn't you like to know," F'lun said, snickering. He claimed Spock's tricorder from a bouncer and directed it at Spock and Chapel. "Let's see what else you may be hiding."

"We already searched them," Ummu said.

"Not like this, you haven't." He fiddled with the sensor controls while squinting at the display panel. His eyes bulged in surprise. "Son of a smoke weasel."

Ummu looked at him. "What is it?"

"You didn't search beneath their skin." F'lun pointed to the visual display. "They both have subdermal transponders hidden in their forearms, so they can be tracked from orbit." He snarled at the captives. "What exactly were you trying to pull?"

"Merely a reasonable precaution," Spock said. "Standard procedure when venturing on a potentially hazardous mission to an unaligned world."

In truth, he was slightly overstating the case. Although subcutaneous transponders were occasionally employed on certain missions, it was not standard practice because of long-term health concerns associated with overuse of the measure. Spock had judged the precaution worth taking in this instance, but it seemed he had underestimated F'lun's suspicious nature . . . to a degree.

Ummu drew a knife from her belt. "Guess we're going to have to cut those out of you."

"Wait!" Chapel protested. "Let me have my medkit back. I can do it painlessly . . . and with a lot less mess."

Ummu paused and looked at F'lun. "Less mess would be bet-ter. Easier to clean up after, and less evidence to dispose of."

"All right," F'lun said, "but no tricks."

Chapel held up empty hands, as though to demonstrate she had nothing up her sleeve. "I'm a nurse, not a magician."

A bouncer returned the medkit to her and she got to work. Spock shed his coat and rolled up his sleeve. Working with skill and efficiency, she applied a topical anesthetic to the site with a spray applicator, then deftly extracted the capsule-sized transpon-der with a finely tuned laser scalpel. A spray-on dermal patch completed the procedure, which was indeed painless. Spock of-fered to return the favor, but she politely declined.

"No offense, Spock, but I'd rather do it myself." She grimaced slightly as she sliced into her flesh after numbing it. "I'm just glad we injected the transponder into my *left* arm."

Once done, a pair of bloody transponders, one smeared with green and the other red, rested in her palm. She held them out to F'lun.

"Satisfied?"

"Drop 'em," he instructed.

"If you say so."

She let the devices fall to the dusty cement floor. F'lun targeted them with the twice-stolen disruptor. A crimson beam disinte-grated the transponders. He smirked at Spock as the glow of the atomized capsules faded away.

"So much for that. Bet you thought you could outsmart us."

"It seemed worth the effort," Spock replied.

"So now what?" Chapel asked, rolling down her sleeve. A bouncer reclaimed the medkit, laser scalpel and all.

"Now we talk, but not here," F'lun said. "You have questions, we have questions, so you're coming with us."

His gaze darted to a trapdoor at the rear of the room. Evidence of a lower level, Spock speculated, or an underground escape route leading to another location? He considered whether to

resist or not. With his Vulcan strength and Starfleet combat training, he might be able to subdue their foes, despite their greater
numbers, but there was no guarantee that neither he nor Chapel
would be harmed in the melee, and even if they should make
their escape unscathed, it would not bring them any closer to the
answers they sought.

"Will we find Doctor McCoy where we are going?" he asked.

"You're asking the wrong person." F'lun adjusted the disruptor,
switching it to the lowest setting.

"Seriously?" Chapel said. "Again?"

F'lun aimed the weapon at them. "See you on the other side."

The blast ended Spock's cogitations for a time.

Thirteen

Vok

"It is a fake, obviously," General Gogg stated.

His campaign headquarters was located in a former government armory, a site presumably chosen for its symbolic and historic significance. Kirk and Tanaka had beamed down to a closed-door meeting with Gogg in his personal suite. Campaign posters displaying the General's stern, unyielding visage adorned the walls. His face also appeared, rather more ignominiously, on a viewscreen displaying the recording provided by Lom during his interrogation aboard the *Enterprise*. The recording was paused at a point right after Gogg could be seen and heard ordering the attempt on Doctor Ceff's life.

"I want to believe that, General," Kirk said carefully, "but the recording has held up to examination so far."

Gogg sat behind a spartan steel desk, his stiff posture rendering him almost as immobile as a granite statue. His habitual scowl deepened.

"I give you my word that this recording is a fabrication," he said. "I never authorized the attack on my opponent. I never uttered the words on that tape."

"And yet the recording exists," Kirk said. "I can't ignore that."

Gogg bristled. "Are you questioning my word?"

"That's not for me to say," Kirk said. "I'm simply doing my duty in sharing evidence that has come into my possession."

"How convenient for you . . . and the Federation," Sozz said, his voice dripping with contempt. The General's aide-de-camp stood behind and to one side of Gogg. "We all know which candidate you are rooting for. How do we know you didn't fake that so-called assassination attempt?"

Kirk took offense at the suggestion. "Commissioner Dare is in our sickbay now, recuperating from a near-mortal wound. Would you care to see her medical records?"

"Perhaps," Sozz said, not backing down.

"That will not be necessary." Gogg overruled his subordinate. "I regret that the commissioner became a casualty in this conflict. I trust she will recover?"

"So it appears," Kirk said. "Thank you for asking. At the risk of pushing my luck, however, I can't help noticing that you often frame this election as a literal battle for Vok's future. A diligent prosecutor might ask why *wouldn't* you resort to violence to achieve victory? All's fair in war, correct?"

Gogg did not mince words. "If I wanted Doctor Ceff dead, she would be dead, and I would certainly not enlist some . . . mountebank . . . to carry off the operation instead of a properly trained soldier. Moreover, I am not so oblivious to the political realities of this new democratic era as to think that there would not be repercussions, electoral and otherwise, to disposing of Ceff in such a manner. For better or for worse, we live in a time that frowns on naked displays of force. Assassinating Ceff would be poor . . . public relations."

He uttered that last term as though it left a bad taste in his mouth.

"But if you truly believed you might lose the election," Kirk pressed, determined to get to the truth, "what then?"

"I have no intention of losing," Gogg answered. "I am entirely certain we can and will win this war without shedding a drop of Vokite blood."

"Lom thinks so, too," Kirk said, "yet he still claims you ordered him to assassinate Doctor Ceff."

"I do not know this Lom." Gogg turned toward Sozz. "Do we know this performer? Is he one of ours?"

"Not that I know of, General."

"No matter," Gogg said. "He is obviously a liar, intent on slandering me."

He spoke as though that settled the matter. *If only,* Kirk thought.

"I'm afraid it's more complicated than that, General. While aboard the *Enterprise,* Lom voluntarily submitted to a psycho-tricorder test, which confirmed that he's telling the truth as far as he knows it."

Gogg harrumphed. "Your test results are in error."

"Unlikely," Kirk said. "When properly operated by a trained technician, as it was in this circumstance, the tricorder scans the subject's brain waves to detect any signs of hypnosis, amnesia, or deliberate deception. Lom passed the test with flying colors as it were." Kirk had sat in on the session personally to make certain it was administered according to protocol. He nodded at Tanaka, who handed him a data disk. "I'll spare you a long lecture on the science involved, which is not my field of expertise to begin with, but all the technical details and readings are contained on this disk. You're free to have your own scientists examine the test re-sults in depth. In fact, I encourage you to do so."

He laid the disk down on the desk in front of Gogg, who point-edly ignored it. "I don't need any scientists to know this man is lying."

"It's not just his word against yours." Kirk glanced at the view-screen, which still held the incriminating shot of Gogg. "There's also the recording."

"I told you before," Gogg said impatiently. "It's a fake."

"Again, that's not what the science says." Kirk could tell he was on thin ice with Gogg, but this might be his only opportunity to have a frank, face-to-face exchange with the man regarding the charges leveled against him. Kirk wasn't about to waste that chance, not where an assassination plot was concerned. "We con-sidered the possibility that the recording might be a hoax and ran an in-depth voiceprint analysis on the audio component of the footage, comparing the voice on the recording to existing voice samples from your public speeches and interviews. I regret to say that our computer concluded that the voice on the tape belongs to you, with only a five percent margin of error."

Spock would have been more precise, Kirk knew, but unlike his absent first officer, the captain was not inclined to quibble over decimal points. He also declined to mention that Uhura was personally reviewing the voiceprint data, just in case the computer missed something. No need to open that door unless Uhura found something worth passing along.

"Five percent," Gogg echoed. "I see."

"We can probably get even more precise results," Tanaka said, "if you would agree to submit a fresh voice sample, reciting the text from the recording to eliminate certain variables. Of course, we can't compel you to provide such a sample, but—"

"Don't waste your breath." Gogg rose from his chair, standing tall before them. "Brain scans, voiceprints. Enough with all this talk of computerized tests and readings." He looked Kirk in the eye. "Stop hiding behind your bloodless technology, Kirk. What does your gut tell you? Do you believe me or your machines?"

In truth, Kirk wasn't sure what he believed. Despite the evidence, something about this whole scandal still felt too pat to him. Why would Gogg deny what he freely confessed on the recording—and vice versa? Spock would no doubt urge him to rely on the science, to a degree, but McCoy would surely urge him to trust his feelings instead. As usual, Kirk felt stuck in the middle.

"What I think doesn't matter," he said. "That's up to the voters and your own authorities to decide. My priority is simply to ensure that the election is a fair and peaceful one, which means not sitting on any evidence regarding threats of violence, no matter who it may or may not implicate."

"In other words," Gogg said, "you're perfectly ready to spill this poison into every ear, but you refuse to take responsibility for your actions." He gazed contemptuously at Kirk. "And to think I once judged you an honorable soldier."

"I'm sorry you feel that way," Kirk replied. "I'm doing you a courtesy by informing you of the tape's contents in advance, before the news goes—"

His communicator chimed urgently, demanding his attention. He flipped the device open.

"Kirk here. What is it?"

"Sorry to interrupt, Captain," Uhura said, *"but you should know that Lom's story and the recording have been leaked to the press. The footage is all over the planet's news and social communication networks."*

"Damn it," Kirk muttered. So much for getting out ahead of the story. "I appreciate the heads-up, Lieutenant. Kirk out."

He put away his communicator while bracing for the storm ahead. The news had been bound to break eventually, but he'd hoped for more time to manage the situation—and perhaps confirm Gogg's involvement in the assassination attempt—before the accusation went public.

Tanaka gulped. "Did I just overhear what I thought?"

"I'm afraid so," Kirk said. "The cat is out of the bag."

There was no need to inform Gogg and his aide of the development. Other campaign staffers were already bursting into the suite to alert Gogg to the news. Alarmed, Sozz employed a control panel to switch the display on the viewscreen to various planetary news sources. Multiple windows opened up on the screen, proliferating at a geometric rate, so that they kept shrinking in size in order to accommodate yet more outlets. Every window displayed the damning footage, which was obviously fast on its way to becoming ubiquitous.

Gogg clenched his fists at his sides. A vein pulsed at his temple. "You were saying something about courtesy, Kirk?"

"This leak was not of my doing," Kirk said, wondering who had spilled the beans prematurely. "But it *was* inevitable. You're going to have to address these charges and soon."

"I don't need advice from you," Gogg said, visibly fuming, albeit in a characteristically clamped-down way. His jawline was so tight that it was a wonder that he could spit out any words at all. "This meeting is over."

"Please, General," Tanaka began, "you have to understand—"

"I said, this meeting is *over*."

Kirk couldn't blame Tanaka for trying to unruffle Gogg's feathers, but he knew a losing battle when he saw one. It was time for a strategic retreat. He flipped open his communicator again.

"Kirk to *Enterprise*. Two to beam up."

Fourteen

"How long is this going to take?" Jemo asked.

"Long enough to get it right," McCoy said. "Now sit still while I run these scans."

Jemo sat impatiently on a stool as he scanned her with his medical tricorder, seeking a baseline against which he could compare Avomora's readings. A study nook in the guest suite had been converted to a makeshift clinical laboratory, complete with a computer terminal and other equipment supplied by the palace at McCoy's request. The setup was no match for the lab back in his own sickbay, and the technology was at least a generation behind Federation standards, but it would have to do. Ozalor was modern enough, even if his tricorder was probably the most sophisticated diagnostic tool on the planet.

"All right," Jemo said. "If this will help you help Avo, I'm game."

"You and the princess go back a ways, I gather," McCoy said, making conversation as he worked. "What's the story there, if you don't mind me asking?"

"Your basic rags to slightly better rags story," she quipped. "Never knew my father, but my mom worked as a servant in this very palace and I used to tag along after her. One afternoon, out on the south lawn, Avo choked on a piece of hard candy while having a picnic lunch. Everybody else stood around like dummies, afraid to lay hands on her royal personage, but I was only eight years old and didn't know any better, so I just ran over and whacked her hard on the back, dislodging the half-eaten candy, which went flying from her lips." Jemo grinned at the memory. "My bold move impressed Count Rayob, who saw potential in me, I guess. He took me under his wing, trained me, fashioned me into an instrument to protect the *Yiyova*. If we're being honest here, he's the father I never had."

"And Avomora?" McCoy asked.

"She was six at the time I smacked that candy out of her, but we've been friends ever since. She's more than just the Heir to me. She's like my kid sister."

"Sounds like she's lucky to have a friend like you in her life," McCoy said, warming to his unwanted babysitter. "Can't be easy being the Heir to the throne, even without having serious health issues."

McCoy thought of his own daughter, Joanna. It was one of his lasting regrets that he had not been there as she was growing up. Like Avo, Joanna was an only child. He wanted to think that she'd had friends and confidantes like Jemo when she needed them.

She could do worse, he thought.

His hand scanner whirred as he took some up-close readings of Jemo's eyes, optic nerves, and frontal lobes. Looking the bodyguard in the face, he noted again the diagonal scar marring her features.

"You know," he said delicately, "I don't mean to offend, but I could easily fix that scar of yours. It would be a very simple procedure."

"Don't you dare," she said. "That scar is a badge of honor. I won it fair and square."

"In defense of the throne?" he guessed.

"Nah. In a fight over a girl." She flashed him a wicked grin. "Won the girl too."

"I don't doubt it," McCoy said. "Forget I said anything."

"Said what?" she replied.

He didn't press the point. This was hardly the first time he'd encountered this kind of resistance to cosmetic surgery, or even to a more serious wound. A Capellan warrior was apt to challenge you to a duel if you even suggested stitching him up, as McCoy knew from painful experience, and then there was the time he'd made the mistake of offering an anesthetic to a Gorn.

Nearly bit my head off . . . literally.

He wrapped up his scans and traded the tricorder for a hypospray. He inserted an empty ampule into the device and set it for extraction. "If you don't mind, I'd like to take a physical sample of your blood as well."

He approached her with the hypospray, but she hopped off the stool and raised her arm defensively.

"Not so fast! How do I know you're not trying to drug me so you can make a break for it?"

"Oh, ye of little faith." He handed the device to her, with the business end pointed toward him. "But feel free to examine it first."

"Like you wouldn't try to get away if you had the chance."

"And where the devil would I go?"

"You tell me. You Starfleet types are supposed to be clever." She gave the hypospray a thorough inspection before returning it to him. "This looks legit, though." She rolled up her sleeve, which wasn't strictly necessary, then held out her arm. "Try not to drain me dry, okay?"

"Do I look like a bloodsucker? All I need are a few cc's." He pressed the head of the hypospray against the crook of her arm. "You may feel a slight pinch."

The device hissed and the ampule filled in a heartbeat. McCoy noted that Ozalorian blood was a lighter shade of red than the stuff in his own veins. Closer to orange, really.

"There we go. That wasn't so bad, was it?"

Jemo shrugged. "I've had worse sneezes." She examined the extraction site. "Hmm. No scar."

She sounded mildly disappointed.

"Sorry about that," he said.

"I'll live," she said. "Now what?"

"Now I get down to work, comparing your results to Avo-mora's." He sat down at his workstation, only to glance at the nearest food dispenser, which was on the other side of the adjacent living room. "But first some coffee, I think."

"Let me." She crossed the suite to the slot. "You should eat something, too, to keep your strength up."

She wasn't wrong there. McCoy's stomach grumbled at the thought of food. He was starting to develop a taste for Ozalorian cuisine. She returned moments later with a steaming cup of coffee and a plate of spiced fruit biscuits, which she insisted on sampling first.

"You're really going to keep tasting my food?" he groused.

"Can't be too careful," she said with her mouth full. "You're a threat to Vumri's power and position. I wouldn't put it past her to have one of her bootlickers tamper with the food processors."

McCoy looked longingly at the biscuits. "I could just scan it first."

"But would you know what to scan for?" She took a long draw of coffee, then checked her pulse for any adverse side effects. "You don't know our world, our recipes, or our native poisons. Trust me, you're safer this way."

She had a point, he conceded. "What about your safety? That doesn't concern you?"

"You end up poisoned on my watch, I'm going to wish I went first."

She finally placed the food and coffee on McCoy's desk, away from his medkit and other equipment, before retreating to a nearby sofa from which she could keep an eye on him. She unsheathed her ionic blade and fished a fresh chunk of agate from a pocket to whittle on.

Enough talk, McCoy thought. *Let's get to this.*

He started uploading the tricorder's readings into the computer terminal before him. He had argued for and received access to a computer console so he could consult Ozalor's medical databases as well as run computerized simulations and analyses. The access had come with severe limitations, however; the desk viewer had been disabled to keep him from communicating with anyone outside the palace.

Including the *Enterprise*.

So he was startled when a dialogue box suddenly appeared on the terminal's display screen:

Do you want to leave Ozalor?

"What the—?"

Jemo looked up from her carving. "Something the matter?"

"No, no," McCoy fibbed. "Just trying to get my tricorder to work with your computer. They're about as compatible as you and Vumri."

"That bad?" she asked.

McCoy's body blocked her view of the screen, at least as long as she stayed over on the sofa. He feigned nonchalance to keep her there.

"Well, maybe not quite," he said. "I'm just grumbling. It's my way."

"You don't say."

She went back to whittling, apparently none the wiser, and McCoy suppressed a sigh of relief. He didn't know what this was about, but he already suspected that he didn't want his babysitter to know about it. Doing his best to play it cool, he called up a virtual keyboard in order to reply to the mystery message.

Who is this? he typed.

The response came instantly, replacing the original box.

A friend.

That wasn't good enough for McCoy. At the risk of looking a possible rescuer in the mouth, he knew better than to take an anonymous offer of friendship at face value. He wasn't born yesterday.

A name?

Too risky. But I can help you.

Why?

We want the same thing: to get you back where you belong.

McCoy stared at the screen. An obvious suspect came to mind.

Vumri?

No. But her interests are also mine.

He pondered that. Both Rayob and Jemo had warned him that Vumri had allies and agents within the palace. It occurred to him that there might also be other individuals who simply shared the healer's hardline views regarding Vok and Braco and who therefore appreciated her growing influence over the *Yovode*. Such individuals would also have a vested interest in seeing McCoy returned to the *Enterprise* sooner rather than later.

How are you doing this? he asked.

We have our ways.

His mysterious correspondent's cryptic responses did not engender trust, yet McCoy could hardly ignore the opportunity being offered here. That the *Enterprise* had yet to come warping to his rescue suggested that Rayob had done a good job of covering his tracks when he'd had McCoy snatched off Braco. For all McCoy knew, Kirk and the others were scouring the wrong system looking for him, having no idea he was on Ozalor.

This could be my best chance, he thought.

Do you wish to return to the *Enterprise*?

McCoy glanced furtively over his shoulder at Jemo, who remained oblivious to the covert dialogue being conducted only meters away from her. Guilt pricked his conscience; he didn't want to abandon Avo or get Jemo in trouble, but he *was* being held against his will with no end in sight. He had other obligations as well, to Starfleet, to the *Enterprise*, to people who cared about him.

Jim and the others have no idea if I'm alive or dead.

Do you wish to escape?

McCoy thought again of Joanna. They weren't as close as he would have liked, through no fault but his own, but the prospect of vanishing from her life without a trace, leaving her with nothing but unanswered questions, was too ghastly to contemplate. He had his own daughter to think of.

He typed his response.

I'm listening.

Fifteen

Braco

"Wakey, wakey."

The hiss of a hypospray roused Spock, who found himself lying in an open cargo container roughly the size of a photon torpedo casing. F'lun leaned over him, gripping a Starfleet hypospray he had presumably liberated from Nurse Chapel's medkit. Sitting up, Spock looked for Chapel and was relieved to see her rising from an adjacent container, looking understandably confused and disoriented. The containers rested in what appeared to be the storage compartment of some manner of vehicle, which had apparently been used to smuggle them from one location to another. Some of F'lun's confederates clustered behind him; Spock recognized them from the back room at the Dreaming Oasis.

"C'mon, get moving." F'lun brandished the stolen disruptor. "Don't want to keep the boss lady waiting."

Boss lady?

The description piqued Spock's curiosity. He rose fully from the container and assisted Chapel to her feet.

"Thank you, Mister Spock," she said. "I still feel a little wobbly."

"That is to be expected," Spock said before turning to F'lun. "Please lead the way. I am eager to meet with your leader."

They departed the vehicle, which Spock discovered to be a streamlined, stripped-down commercial delivery transport whose scuffed aerodynamic contours suggested that it was designed for atmospheric flight. Surveying his surroundings, however, he saw that it had apparently been repurposed to travel through an underground tunnel. Limestone walls, reinforced with metal scaffolding and buttresses, indicated that he and

Chapel had been conveyed from the smoky bar to a subterranean lair or bunker.

The hidden base of the United Bracon Front?

Most likely, Spock thought. He noted that Ummu was nowhere to be seen; he assumed she had remained at the Oasis, tending to her bar. He didn't particularly regret her absence.

Leaving the platform where the flyer was docked, they navigated a network of caverns connected by branching galleries and shafts. Paved pathways eased their trek through the tunnels, while overhead lights provided illumination. The lights flickered erratically, drawing irritated looks from F'lun and his accomplices; Spock gathered the power fluctuations were not deliberate. A susurrus of voices, coming from ahead, echoed through the cramped corridors.

"How long do you think we were out, Mister Spock?" Chapel asked, walking beside him.

Spock stroked his face. A minute degree of stubble, along with the degree of his hunger and thirst, provided clues to the duration of their journey.

"Approximately four to five hours." His eyes studied the cave walls. "In addition, the presence of what appears to be fossilized coral in the composition of our surroundings suggests that these caverns were once part of a seabed in the far distant past."

"The Sea of Glass!" she blurted. "It's several hours from the capital. That must be where we are."

Spock recalled the post-atomic wasteland in question from his studies of Braco. "Or, more precisely, we are beneath it."

Their deductions elicited a surly look from F'lun.

"Well, aren't you too clever for your own good?" he grumbled. "Kinda defeats the whole point of stunning you."

Spock took his objection as confirmation of their location. "I agree that firing upon us was unnecessary."

The tunnel opened up onto a large grotto, comparable in size to the *Enterprise*'s shuttlebay, packed with active people and machinery, the latter looking distinctly well worn and cobbled together in ways that would surely not meet with Mister Scott's approval. The base was abuzz with activity, with Bracons of various ages scurrying about, intent on their respective tasks. In some ways, the grotto reminded Spock of the *Enterprise* during a yellow alert, albeit with much more ramshackle and improvised resources. Stalactites, hanging from the ceiling, testified to the cavern's natural origins.

"The United Bracon Front, I take it?"

"Got it in one, genius," F'lun replied. "Need your Vulcan smarts to figure that out?"

The lights sputtered again. A technician at a computer terminal reacted angrily as her screen crashed. She slapped its casing in a manner unlikely to restore its proper functions. "Freaking piece of junk!"

"I take it your infrastructure leaves something to be desired," Spock observed.

"Stop dawdling," F'lun said. "This isn't a sightseeing tour."

A wide, sweeping ramp led up to a stone ledge overlooking the bustling grotto. A metal guardrail prevented anyone from tumbling off the natural mezzanine, which looked to be a command center of sorts. An array of viewscreens, of varying sizes and models, monitored other sections of the caverns: dormitories, a mess hall, an infirmary, storerooms, generators, a mechanic's shop, and an armory. The latter appeared to be worryingly well stocked with a wide variety of weaponry. Spock did not immediately spy McCoy anywhere in the sprawling underground complex.

Troubling, he thought. *I hope this expedition is not in vain.*

They approached a woman whose back was turned toward them as she stood at the far end of a low calcite shelf that had been drafted into service as a table. Maps, charts, slates, and microtapes littered the tabletop. An impatient voice barked orders into a headset.

"You heard me. If there's even a chance that cell has been compromised, we need to pull our people out before the Bureau swoops in. I want that address stripped clean by oh-seven-hundred. Not a bit of evidence or intel left behind, you got that? Good."

She took off the headset and flung it onto the table. She plucked a cigarette from behind her ear and lit it up with a ring on her left hand, which briefly flared red at its center. She took a deep draw on the cigarette.

F'lun cleared his throat. "Ahem."

The woman turned toward them, revealing the face of Hynn V'sta, whom Spock recognized from the image Wibb had shown them at Bureau headquarters. Her skin was more orange than Wibb's, indicating a slightly different ethnicity. Graying brown hair formed a widow's peak atop her brow. Despite the precarious circumstances, Spock considered it progress that they were finally face-to-face with the elusive leader of the UBF. Perhaps they could get some definitive answers at last.

"Ah, Commander Spock, Nurse Chapel," she said, exhaling a puff of smoke. "Welcome to our humble abode. Not nearly as slick as the *Enterprise,* I'm sure, but we make do."

"I'm pleased to make your acquaintance," Spock said. "It is my hope you can clear up certain outstanding mysteries concerning a missing colleague."

Chapel was more direct. "Do you have Doctor McCoy? Is he here?"

"I'm afraid not," V'sta said, shaking her head. "Contrary to what you may have heard, we had nothing to do with kidnapping your doctor, not that that's stopping the Bureau from busting down doors and interrogating people about it, trying to get them to admit that the Front is responsible." Anger tightened her expression. "Frankly, I don't appreciate being blamed for a crime we didn't commit."

"And yet you abducted us," Spock pointed out.

She took another puff on her cigarette. "The way I see it, if we're going to take the heat, we might as well do the crime. Who knows, maybe we can exchange you for some political prisoners, or maybe get the Federation to exert some leverage on the Provisional Government to recognize us as a legitimate protest movement, uncontaminated by archaic loyalties to Vok or Ozalor?"

"I understand that you have issues regarding Braco's current political situation," Spock said, seeking common ground.

"Nothing too complicated," she said. "Just want Vok and Ozalor to abandon all 'ancestral' claims to our world . . . and to leave us alone to settle our differences on our own."

Spock recalled that Colc regarded the latter prospect with skepticism. "Is that a probable outcome?"

"Maybe," she said, "if we can finally get past the idea that Braco is some sort of holy relic. I swear, the worst thing that ever happened to our world was getting anointed as the sacred 'Birth World.' Who wants to live on a shrine everyone keeps fighting over? Bracons deserve a chance to just live and progress like any other people."

"Easier said than done," Chapel said. "Old ideas die hard."

"So the sooner we get started, the better," V'sta said. "The coalition is just dragging out our misery by trying to appease both Vok and Ozalor. Honestly, even if we *are* the mother to their respective races, it's past time they cut the cord, you know?"

Spock suspected that V'sta had delivered this particular oration many times before.

"We have no vested interest in your world's internal politics," he stressed. "Only in Doctor McCoy."

"Tough to be you, then," V'sta said. "Like I said, we don't have him. We never did."

"I have to ask," Chapel said, "how do we know you're telling the truth? Sorry to be rude, but getting stunned—again—takes a toll on my manners."

V'sta chuckled, more amused than offended. "You're just going to have to take my word for it, I guess, not that it really matters to me what you think."

"Unless you wish our help proving your innocence," Spock said. "Do you have any notion who *did* abduct McCoy?"

"We're looking into that," she admitted, "but—"

A small creature abruptly dropped onto the table from above. Chapel gasped in surprise, while Spock immediately took note of the creature's fuzzy orange trunk, triplicate lower limbs, and rotating eyestalk. Seemingly unharmed by its fall, the animal scuttled toward V'sta, who took its startling arrival in stride.

"Hi there, Troxy," she greeted it. "Where have you been?"

The creature leaped into her arms. A lime-green tongue licked her face.

"What is . . . that?" Chapel asked, her hand to her chest as though to still a racing heart.

"Nothing to worry about." V'sta cuddled the creature. "Meet Troxy, our self-appointed mascot. He's perfectly harmless . . . unless you're scared of wet, sloppy kisses."

Spock took a closer look at the specimen. "Troxy" had an ovate trunk supported by three multiply jointed limbs. The orange fuzz coating its exterior was somewhere between fur and moss. Along with its triple legs, it also possessed a trio of identical mouths positioned evenly along its equator, punctuated by three pairs of nasal slits located between the triple maws. A single eyestalk rose approximately ten centimeters above its trunk. Green veins, matching the color of the creature's three tongues and mouths, streaked its solitary eye, which also boasted a bright chartreuse iris. Overall, it was roughly the size of a domestic cat or monkey and, aside from the vertical eyestalk, resembled a miniature stool topped by a round, melon-shaped cushion. Spock did not recall reading about any such life-forms while familiarizing himself with Braco. Then again, he *had* been focused primarily on the planet's politics and security issues.

"Fascinating," he said. "What creature is this?"

"We call them trivets," V'sta said. "As far as we can tell, they're native to these caverns and nowhere else on the planet. We found them when we moved in and, since they were here first, we've made our peace with them. Like I said, they're harmless, if occasionally underfoot. They also feed on certain unpleasant molds that could pose a problem if not for the trivets keeping them in check."

"Curious," he noted. "Their trilateral symmetry is not consistent with other Bracon life-forms such as yourself. I am hardly an authority on Bracon taxonomy, but they strike me as an anomaly when it comes to the fauna of your world. It is unclear at a glance how they fit into the evolutionary development of life on Braco or even this sector. One would almost suspect alien origins were they not apparently adapted to survive in this singular environment."

Troxy rotated its eye toward Spock. Wriggling free of V'sta's embrace, it scuttled across the table to inspect the Vulcan. Hopping onto Spock's shoulder, Troxy sniffed him curiously.

"Hah!" V'sta laughed. "Troxy seems to like you, Mister Spock. That's one point in your favor."

"It is evidently a discriminating creature," Spock said, "not to mention—"

"V'sta!" A random aide ran into the command center. "Sorry to barge in, but you need to see this! It's all over the big news services!"

"What is?" V'sta demanded. "What's this about, Ohop?"

Without pausing to elaborate, the aide raced to a control panel and flicked a series of switches. All at once, the security footage on the viewscreens was replaced by a general broadcast featuring Chief Inspector Wibb. The police detective stood at a podium in front of a tricolor Bracon flag. Ohop dialed up the volume so that Wibb's voice rang out over the nerve center.

"... *regret to confirm that a Starfleet medical officer, one Doctor Leonard McCoy of the* Starship Enterprise, *was captured by ter-*

rorists during an unprovoked attack on a Starfleet landing party in the hills outside the capital. Since then, two more Enterprise crew members have gone missing while recklessly searching for their doctor. The Tranquility Bureau is actively investigating these crimes and has every reason to believe that the radical organization calling itself the United Bracon Front"—Wibb uttered the name with palpable disdain—"is responsible for these heinous attacks on our Federation visitors. Rest assured that the Bureau will use every means at its disposal to bring these cowardly terrorists to justice and, if possible, to return the hostages safely to their ship . . ."

"That lying clot of mucus!" V'sta snapped. "He's found us guilty already!"

Chapel looked at Spock. "What do you think prompted this? Our heading off on our own to look for Doctor McCoy?"

"If I were to hazard a guess," Spock replied, "I would surmise that the inspector is attempting to get out ahead of the story, to 'control the narrative,' as our journalistic ally predicted. He knew that Colc was ready to take the news public, so he wants to get the Bureau's side of the story on record first." Spock gently lifted Troxy off his shoulder and cradled it in his arms. "Granted, our own sudden disappearances, after neutralizing his security officer, may have also provoked him to this action."

"Whatever," V'sta said bitterly. "The whole world thinks we kidnapped you two and McCoy. Might as well milk that if we can."

"There is an alternative strategy," Spock said. "You can release us so that we can clear your name."

V'sta shook her head. "Too late for that." She nodded at Ohop. "Let me see that shameless load of propaganda again."

"Yes, ma'am." He operated the control panel, restarting Wibb's announcement from the beginning.

"My fellow citizens," Wibb said gravely, "on behalf of the Bracon Tranquility Bureau, it is my sad duty to report . . ." zzzz, crackle, zzzz.

Static drowned out Wibb's voice, only seconds before flurries of visual snow obscured the images on all the screens.

"Are you kidding me?" V'sta said. "Get it back!"

"Sorry." Ohop looked up from the console sheepishly. "Working on it."

Spock watched with interest as the aide removed the cover from the control panel to get at the apparatus beneath. Clearly under pressure, the man wiped perspiration from his brow as he applied a microspanner to the balky circuitry. Spock considered offering his assistance, but he was unsure if the gesture would be appreciated.

"Hang on," Ohop said. "I think I've almost got it . . ."

A sudden eruption of sparks belied his assurances. Electricity hissed and Ohop stumbled backward, holding up his hands, which had clearly received second-degree burns. The spanner clanked to the floor. Wisps of white smoke rose from the exposed wiring. The acrid smell of burnt circuitry assailed Spock's nostrils. Frightened by the commotion, Troxy sprang from the Vulcan's arms and scuttled away. Another Bracon rushed toward the console with a compact fire extinguisher: a narrow-beam force field cut the circuitry off from oxygen, suffocating any remaining combustion.

Chapel hurried toward the injured man. "My medkit, hurry!"

V'sta nodded at F'lun, who returned the kit to the nurse, who promptly got to work treating Ohop's burns. Spock knew the injured aide was in good hands. A hissing hypospray numbed Ohop's pain, prior to Chapel applying an antiseptic spray to the burns to prevent infection.

"Feeling better?" she asked Ohop.

"Yes, miss." He winced at the sight of his scorched hands. "Thanks so much for the quality first aid."

Chapel turned to V'sta. "I've done what I could, but this man needs to be taken to an infirmary."

"Sounds like good medical advice." V'sta gave Chapel an approving look. "You handled yourself well here. You report to the infirmary too. We can use your skills there, I think, and not just for poor Ohop."

Chapel glanced worriedly at Spock, no doubt reluctant to have them split up, but her professional ethics won out. "If you have patients in need of care, I can hardly say no."

"I was hoping you'd feel that way," V'sta said. "I'm seeing at least one silver lining to this situation already."

"Forgive me if I'm not quite as enthusiastic." Chapel looked over her shoulder as two nameless subordinates escorted her away from the command ledge. She looked back over her shoulder at Spock. "Be careful, Mister Spock."

"I trust you to do the same," he replied.

He watched with some misgiving as she descended to the ground floor of the grotto and then disappeared into a tunnel. Left to his own devices, he resolved to make himself useful, at least partially in hopes of earning V'sta's trust.

"It seems you are in need of technical assistance as well," he said. "May I volunteer my services?"

"Forget it," she said without a moment's reflection. "No way am I letting a Starfleet science officer, and a Vulcan to boot, get anywhere near our hardware. I wouldn't put it past you to secretly transmit a distress signal or hack into our confidential files and communications. Maybe even sabotage our systems."

"That was not my intent," Spock said, while privately conceding that he might do so if the opportunity arose, purely in the interest of completing his mission. "I was merely offering you the benefit of my expertise."

"Sorry," she said. "From where I'm standing, the risks outweigh the advantages."

More men and women rushed into the command center, anxious about Wibb's broadcast and its possible consequences. V'sta was besieged by worried people wanting to know what she thought of the news, how she intended to respond to it, and what it meant for their movement. She spared a moment to address Spock.

"Seems we'll have to continue our chat later. Thanks to your friend the chief inspector, I've suddenly got my hands full." She nodded at Wibb and his cohorts. "Take him to the Pit."

The Pit?

Spock found that label less than encouraging.

Sixteen

Vok

If only there were two of me, Kirk thought.

The word from Braco was not good. According to Lieutenant Levine, both Spock and Chapel had gone missing after attempting to make contact with an alleged terrorist group who might have been responsible for McCoy's abduction, which meant that three of his crew were now unaccounted for and mostly likely in the hands of hostile parties. Levine had assured Kirk that a search was already underway for them, and Kirk had no reason to doubt that every effort was being expended to that end, but his first instinct was to immediately set course for Braco to take charge of any possible rescue operation. Spock and McCoy and Chapel were in danger; they needed their captain on the case.

And yet . . .

Down on Vok, equally urgent matters demanded his attention. Election Day was bearing down on them inexorably, one presidential candidate had been credibly accused of trying to have the other assassinated, Commissioner Dare remained in sickbay, and Braco was days away at maximum warp. He couldn't just abandon his mission on Vok to go warping off to another planet in another system . . . could he?

"You found something, Lieutenant?" Kirk entered the briefing room, where Uhura had requested a meeting with him.

She was already seated at the conference table, while Lieutenant Palmer occupied her post on the bridge. A data slate, accompanied by a pile of microtapes, rested on the table before her, alongside a cup of herbal tea; Kirk had assigned her to personally review the voiceprint analysis of the recording in which the General could be heard ordering the assassination attempt. Uhura's expertise in audio transmissions and universal translation programs, among other things, rendered her particularly well suited to the task.

"Possibly, Captain. Nothing conclusive, mind you, but there is something odd about these results."

Kirk sat down at the table. "How so?"

"Well, it's funny, Captain. Overall, the computer calculates a roughly ninety-five percent probability that the voice on the recording belongs to General Gogg, based on comparisons between the incriminating tape and other records of his voice, but here's the odd part: that percentage varies significantly depending on which prior recordings you compare the Lom tape to, sometimes by as much as two percent."

Kirk nodded. "Elaborate."

"It's like this. With *some* one-on-one comparisons, the correlation is almost exact, but with others . . . not so much. The computer averaged the results to achieve its final calculation, but when you take the analysis apart, piece by piece, comparison by comparison, the range of results is . . . unexpected."

The possible implications of what she was saying, with regard to Gogg's alleged involvement in the attack on Ceff, set Kirk's mind racing, but he was careful not to get ahead of himself.

"I don't pretend to be an expert on voice analysis," he said, "but isn't a certain amount of variation to be expected? I'm sure I'm raspier on some occasions than on others and may sound different on a tape depending on the acoustics, my age, my mood, and whether I've had my morning coffee yet."

Uhura shook her head. "Not to this degree, Captain, and the computer is programmed to compensate for any such variables."

That's true, Kirk thought. As he understood it, even a deliberate attempt to disguise one's voice could be detected by the computer. "So how do you explain this?"

"I'm not sure, Captain. It makes no sense. You shouldn't find this much variation when comparing voiceprints of the same individual."

Kirk understood what she was saying. His brow furrowed as he pondered the conundrum. "Unless . . . they're *not* all from the same individual."

She gave him a quizzical look. "Captain?"

"Lieutenant, it's not unknown for public figures to sometimes employ doubles and decoys, either to foil their enemies or perhaps simply to manage an overcrowded schedule. Take Zefram Cochrane, for example. It's believed that, after he achieved worldwide fame, many of his public appearances were made by doubles to free up the real Cochrane's time so that he could concentrate on his research and experiments. Or look at Dame Ruklew of Motnos, who famously sent her clones into battle to bolster her reputation for bravery while she stayed safely out of the line of fire."

Uhura grasped where he was going. "You're thinking the 'Gogg' on the tape is a double, an impersonator?"

"That's right," Kirk said confidently, "and a damn good one." The more he thought about it, the more plausible the scenario seemed. "That would account for the variations you detected. Presumably some, but not all, of the test recordings are of the impostor, not the General, and those are the ones that matched up exactly."

"Now *that* makes sense," Uhura agreed. "Well done, sir."

"Well done yourself, Lieutenant. Please prepare a report summarizing your findings. I suspect I'm going to need it."

"Aye, sir." She looked over at him. "If I may ask, Captain, what are you planning to do with this information?"

Kirk rose from his seat, already thinking ahead.

"I believe I need to have another talk with General Gogg . . . about his alter ego."

Seventeen

Ozalor

"Thank you for coming so promptly, Doctor," Avomora said weakly. "I admit I was hoping not to require your attention quite so soon."

The drapes were already drawn in the princess's study, where she had retreated to her mobile comfy chair. Subdued lighting from the chamber's incandescent crown molding illuminated her wan features, which were notably strained. The healthy vigor she had displayed in her father's sanctum only the day before was just a memory.

"How are you doing?" McCoy asked as he and Jemo called on Avo. He scratched irritably at his fake beard, which he was still required to sport. "Or do I need to ask?"

"I feel another spell coming on." She winced, only partly in anticipation. "A bad one, I think."

"So soon?" Jemo asked. "Is it just me or are these spells becoming more frequent?"

"I wish it was just you," Avo said, "but you're not wrong." She looked hopefully at McCoy. "Can you help me, Doctor Bones?"

"Possibly."

Comparing her scans to Jemo's, on top of a coffee-fueled crash course in Ozalorian biology, had actually yielded a breakthrough.

"From what I can tell, the root cause of your issues is a chemical imbalance in your brain, caused by a shortage of certain crucial neurotransmitters. Your brain tries to overcompensate by producing more of other chemicals, leading to a subtle disorder in your spinal fluid, aggravating your nervous system and triggering a cascade effect as one symptom leads to another." He figured she didn't need an entire treatise, complete with charts and footnotes. "Bottom line, it's an ugly chain reaction, kicked off by a slight irregularity in your brain chemistry."

Avo listened intently. "So why couldn't our own doctors detect this?"

"Well, not to brag," McCoy said, "but it's hard to beat Federation sensors. Plus, in your doctors' defense, it's a tricky sequence of events, in that there are several steps between the low neurotransmitter levels and your actual symptoms, obscuring the diagnosis. One leads to the other, but only indirectly."

Avo nodded. "So what can be done about it?"

He opened his medkit. "I've prepared a compound that should counter the faulty enzymes inhibiting production of the neurotransmitters in question. In theory, it will allow your brain to generate the chemicals it needs."

"An interesting theory, Earthman, but only a theory."

Vumri entered the study unannounced, accompanied by Bilis. McCoy could guess who had alerted the healer to the situation.

"What is she doing here?" Jemo protested.

"The *Yovode* thought it best that I be on hand for any experimental medical procedures, simply as a precaution should his daughter's faith in you prove misplaced." She smirked at McCoy. "You have already had the opportunity to observe me at my work. I trust you have no objection to returning the favor?"

"None whatsoever," he said. "I have nothing to hide."

Avomora shivered under her blanket, pulling it up to her shoulders. That simple movement made her flinch. A sharp intake of breath betrayed her pain.

"Please, Doctor," she said, "can we proceed? I'm anxious to try your new remedy."

Jemo sidled up to McCoy, looking rather more apprehensive than Avomora. "I have to ask," she said in a low voice, "but are we sure about this? Maybe you should do more testing first?"

"I would if I thought it was necessary," McCoy assured her.

He had run numerous simulations on the computer to eliminate any possible risk factors, so he was confident of his conclusions within a negligible margin for error. "Ultimately, I'm just helping her brain produce enough of what it's already supposed to have. I'm not adding anything to her gray matter that you don't already have in yours."

"Like that's supposed to make me feel any better."

Jemo looked on warily as he readied a hypospray, which was already preloaded with the compound he had synthesized in his temporary laboratory back in his suite. Jemo had secured the necessary raw materials at his request.

"So we're not worried about any nasty side effects?"

"I'm not anticipating any." He tilted his head at Vumri. "Besides, we have a healer on hand, don't we? Just in case."

"You had to remind me."

"I trust you, Doctor Bones." Avo eyed the hypospray hopefully. "Please hurry, before this spell gets any worse."

Little did she know, McCoy reflected, that the clock was ticking in more ways than one. He and his mystery pen pal had been surreptitiously working out the details of his upcoming escape from house arrest. With any luck, he'd be out of the Summer Palace and off Ozalor soon. He would feel better knowing he'd cured Avomora before skipping town.

"No time like the present," he agreed.

The hypospray hissed as it introduced the compound into her bloodstream. Avomora, in obvious discomfort, sank into her chair, closing her eyes. Trembling hands gripped the armrests.

"How long before it works?" she asked.

"The effect should be rapid. The imbalance is slight, if significant, so you can expect some relief soon."

Avo mustered a smile. "Thank you, Doctor."

"Don't thank me yet. But I'll be happy to take a bow once you're back on your feet again."

Minutes passed, however, and rather than abating, Avo's

symptoms grew steadily worse. She curled up into herself, trying to keep as still as possible, despite the involuntary tremors and spasms racking her form. Her eyes were squeezed shut against even the faint glow of the molding. A tear leaked from one eye, wetting her cheek. Clenched jaws held back any cries or whimpers.

"What's the matter?" Jemo asked. "Why isn't it working?"

"I don't know," McCoy said, confused and frustrated. He scanned Avo with his medical tricorder, which confirmed that her physical distress was increasing, despite the formula he had administered. By now, the cells of her neurons should have already started synthesizing certain key peptides and nucleotides in sufficient quantities to make a difference. He didn't understand. *It should be working, damn it.*

"This has gone on long enough." Vumri strode forward. "We cannot allow the *Yiyova* to suffer any longer."

"N-no," Avo said, despite her anguish. "Give it more time."

Her stubborn determination to stick it out for as long as it took testified to just how much she resented being so dependent on Vumri. Was that just a matter of pride and personal autonomy, McCoy wondered, or did Avo also have serious reservations about the healer's influence over her father? McCoy had never discussed interstellar politics with the young Heir, but he couldn't imagine that her enthusiastic curiosity about the galaxy beyond Ozalor meshed with Vumri's hostile attitude regarding other worlds and ways. Certainly, Avo had seemed much more positively disposed toward visitors from beyond than Vumri was, by a country mile.

Still, he couldn't watch her go through agony for no reason.

"It's no use, Your Highness," he said gently. "If it was going to work, it would have done so by now." He stepped aside to let Vumri approach the stricken princess. "Let your healer help you."

Avo opened her eyes, cringing as she did so. She gazed at the waiting healer with naked dismay. "But . . . the cure?"

"I'm sorry, Your Highness," McCoy said. "Seems I spoke too soon."

"Your bravery does you credit, *Yiyova,* but your 'cure' is merely a dream." Vumri held out her palms. "Give me your hands."

Avo persevered a few moments more before reluctantly grasping the healer's hands. McCoy watched glumly as Vumri's soothing touch once again eased the princess's discomfort. A discreet tricorder scan verified that Avo's vital signs were stabilizing. She sighed in relief as she slipped into what appeared to be a genuinely peaceful slumber. Vumri released her charge's hands, which dropped limply into the princess's lap. The healer tucked the blanket securely around Avo, then turned to face McCoy and the others. A compassionate façade barely masked her satisfaction at succeeding where McCoy had failed. Her upraised chin was practically aimed at the ceiling.

"It is done," she said quietly, so as not to wake Avo. "Her torment has been banished once again."

McCoy couldn't regret that. "Good thing you were standing by, I suppose."

"You need not worry about that, Earthman. I will always be there for Avomora." She peered down her nose at McCoy. "Unlike some, perhaps."

What did she mean by that? he wondered. Just a snarky dig at his prospects at the palace, or was she aware of his imminent escape from Ozalor? It troubled him to think she was in on the plan, even though he knew she had no reason to interfere. To the contrary, it was in her own best interests for him to vacate the planet as soon as humanly possible.

"We should let the poor child rest," Vumri said. "Bilis, please see the doctor and his ill-bred watchdog out. There is nothing more he can do here."

McCoy scowled. "Nice of you to rub that in."

"No need to take offense, Doctor," she replied. "I'm sure you did your very best. A pity it wasn't enough."

"For now," Jemo insisted. "This isn't over, you leech."

Vumri's smug expression curdled. "Don't think you can count on Avomora's friendship forever. When she's inevitably forced to choose between you and me, do you really think she'll choose the one who *can't* take away her pain?"

"Point taken." McCoy decided to break up this face-off before it escalated any further. He started toward the exit, knowing Jemo was obliged to keep close to him. "We'll show ourselves out."

Jemo hesitated, visibly torn between her babysitting duties and her manifest desire to clean the healer's clock. She compromised by giving the healer one last scorching look of contempt before exiting Avo's quarters with McCoy. She waited until they were in the hallway outside the archway, well out of earshot of Vumri and Bilis, before confronting him.

"What went wrong? Why didn't your potion fix her?"

"I wish I knew," said McCoy. "I can't explain it."

All the evidence supported his diagnosis. He knew what was causing Avo's affliction and he knew how to fix it. Or so he'd thought.

It *should* have worked.

What am I missing?

Eighteen

Braco

"The Pit" was quite literally a deep underground shaft, approximately six meters deep, which was now employed as a jail by the United Bracon Front. The circular wall of the Pit had been polished smooth, then coated with a hard enamel glaze, to prevent it from being scaled. In lieu of a force field, a retractable metal grille sealed off the top of the Pit; given the base's erratic power supply, this struck Spock as a highly sensible measure. His prison, which was comparable in size to a cell in the *Enterprise*'s brig, was simple but effective, much to his inconvenience. Hours had passed since he had last seen Nurse Chapel. He hoped she'd been provided with less primitive accommodations.

Granted, his cell was reasonably comfortable, furnished as it was with a cot, blankets, lamp, a short stool, and other modest amenities. The temperature was cooler than Spock preferred, but that was the case with most Class-M environments. A tray bearing the remains of a somewhat brown salad respected his vegetarian leanings. He had even been provided with mental stimulation in the form of a data slate loaded with generous amounts of political literature supporting the UBF's cause: manifestos, speeches, videos, exposés, and so on. Many of the rhetorical arguments relied too heavily on emotion, but he appreciated the courtesy even as he pondered his captors' underlying motives. Did V'sta genuinely hope to convert him to her cause—or did she merely wish to keep his mind occupied on matters other than escape?

A relatively canny strategy, he reflected, sitting silently on the edge of the cot, although he was certainly capable of analyzing more than one problem simultaneously. Meditation also provided a highly effective means of passing the time, along with isometric exercises to maintain his physical fitness. *I would not object to a shower, though.*

"Heads up!" F'lun barked from above. The untrustworthy informant had ended up as Spock's interim jailkeeper, relieved on occasion by one or two of his associates. "You've got company."

Spock looked up, briefly wondering if Chapel had been allowed to check on him. A familiar hooting alerted him to the actual identity of his visitor.

Troxy scuttled onto the metal grille overhead. The gaps in the grating, which were too small for most humanoids to pass through, posed no obstacle to the trivet, which dropped onto the cot, then jumped into Spock's lap. An inquisitive eyestalk peered at the Vulcan, who allowed the creature to sniff his open palm with all three sets of nostrils. Hoots, whistles, and chirps escaped Troxy's triple mouths, respectively. It folded its legs, settling in.

"Looks like you've got an admirer," F'lun jeered. "No accounting for taste, I guess."

Spock declined to respond with a dry riposte; baiting one's jailer tended to have negative consequences. Examining the peculiar life-form was undoubtedly a better use of his time. Troxy extended its eyestalk to look Spock directly in the face; it seemed to be studying Spock just as intently as he was examining it. He considered that the trivet's evident fascination with him posed an intriguing puzzle in its own right.

What is it about me that intrigues this animal? Spock wondered. *How do I differ from the other humanoids now occupying its territory?*

One possibility came immediately to mind. Contemplating the trivet, he took special note of its green veins as well as the equally verdant coloration of Troxy's tongues and inner mouths. Spock's own veins pulsed with green blood. Was this merely a superficial similarity or did the comparison go deeper?

He longed for a tricorder or medical scanner, but doubted that F'lun would oblige him if asked. Scientific curiosity tempted him to try to collect a blood sample anyway, yet he quickly discarded the idea. Troxy was a mascot, not a lab specimen; Spock suspected that injuring the trivet in even an inconsequential way would not be well received by V'sta and the others, so he conceived of another experiment instead.

The results could be illuminating, he thought.

Not allowed sharp objects, he turned to the only implements at hand: his own canine teeth, inherited from more carnivorous ancestors on both his human and Vulcan sides. He bit down on the tip of his little finger just enough to break the skin. A stoic expression masked any momentary discomfort as he squeezed a bead of jade-colored venous blood from the fingertip and presented it to Troxy, curious to see if and how the animal would react.

He was not disappointed.

The dark green droplet provoked an excited response from the trivet. It capered energetically, vocalizing loudly in three different registers. Its eyestalk bent sharply in the middle, the better to inspect the blood. One tongue after another tasted the cut, as though to confirm one another's findings. Springing from Spock's lap onto his shoulder, it hugged the Vulcan enthusiastically in what definitely seemed to be an embrace rather than an attack.

Fascinating, Spock thought.

His interest was more than purely intellectual. He had a theory about what had so excited the trivet, and if what he surmised was correct, the discovery could have meaningful political ramifications as well as scientific ones. Assuming he could verify his theory should the opportunity arise.

"Come again?" F'lun said, speaking into a communicator. "What just happened?"

Despite his acute hearing, Spock was unable to make out the other side of the conversation over Troxy's three-part cacophony.

"Shush," Spock instructed the giddy animal, adopting a soothing tone. He stroked Troxy's velvety orange fuzz to quiet it. "Softly, if you please."

"Got it," F'lun replied. "Good to know." He switched off his communicator and peered down at Spock through the grating. "Tough luck, Vulcan. The Bureau just announced to the whole planet that they're *not* going to trade anything for the release of you and the nurse . . . or that doctor they claim we have. They 'refuse to negotiate with terrorists' and all that. They're talking tough, promising 'severe retribution,' not rescue."

Spock accepted the news with his usual equanimity. If F'lun was expecting an emotional reaction, he clearly underestimated Vulcan self-discipline.

"Thank you for keeping me informed," Spock said.

"My pleasure. Better make yourself at home in the Pit, 'cause it doesn't look like you're going anywhere." He smirked at the captive. "Bet you wish we hadn't found those transponders you hid under your hide."

"That was a setback," Spock admitted.

Which rendered it all the more fortunate that the subcutaneous units were not the *only* precautions he had taken.

Nineteen

Vok

"Well, General, what do you think of my theory?"

Kirk addressed Gogg and his aide via the viewscreen in the briefing room, several hours after Kirk's meeting with Uhura in the same chamber. It had not been easy arranging even a long-distance conference with Gogg, given how acrimoniously their last encounter had ended, but Commissioner Dare had managed to make it happen from her sickbed, with the able assistance of Tanaka, who was now in attendance along with Uhura. Dangling a chance to clear the General's name had surely helped expedite this meeting as well, or so Kirk assumed.

Gogg took a deep breath before answering.

"You are correct, Kirk. I have in the past employed a double named Huss to take my place at various public appearances. Not out of any fears for my personal safety," he stressed, "but merely because I had better uses for my time than posing for cameras and reciting my stump speech over and over again. I had a campaign to run, debates to prepare for, strategies to plan."

Kirk could believe it. Gogg had made his distaste for politicking clear from the start.

"No need to defend your use of a double, General. We simply wish to know whether it's possible this Huss person could be the individual seen on the tape incriminating you."

Gogg replied carefully, as though weighing every word.

"That possibility cannot be ruled out."

I knew it, Kirk thought. "I have to ask, General, why didn't you mention this earlier when the tape first surfaced?"

A pause, along with Gogg's stony expression, caused Kirk to

briefly wonder if there was a lag in the transmission, but then Gogg spoke again.

"Pride, Kirk, and loyalty. We did not wish to divulge the deception, nor accuse a faithful operative, before we could conduct our own investigation into the matter." Gogg's face and voice conveyed a touch of embarrassment. "I will not deny that my ego played a part in my silence. I was not eager to admit to being party to a hoax."

Kirk wasn't sure he bought that explanation. "As opposed to being accused of plotting Doctor Ceff's assassination?"

"Some of my followers might find that preferable to being deceived," he said dryly. "Moreover, I had my image as a steadfast leader to protect. I feared that, without any solid proof of Huss's involvement, any hasty attempt to throw the blame at another would be seen as weak . . . and unworthy. Better to be suspected of being ruthless than to whine 'it wasn't me' like a coward or child." He shrugged. "I freely admit this may have been a miscalculation on my part."

"You think?" Tanaka murmured from the sidelines. "Lom's accusation is killing you in the polls, at least among independents and undecideds."

Which means it's in his best interests to cooperate with us, Kirk thought, *even if it damages his pride.*

"You mentioned that you were conducting your own investigation. What, if anything, have you learned so far, and where can we find Huss?"

Gogg glanced at his faithful aide-de-camp, who was, as ever, standing by the General's side. "Sozz, report on your progress."

Now it was Sozz's turn to look slightly abashed, although his rigid posture and bearing indicated a desire to maintain his dignity.

"I regret to inform you, Captain Kirk, that we have . . . lost track of Huss. He has not been seen or heard from since, well, shortly before the incident at Doctor Ceff's rally. We have made

every effort to locate him, but this has proved rather more difficult than anticipated."

"I see." Kirk wondered how hard Sozz had looked or whether
the man could be trusted at all; certainly, he had made no secret of his distrust of the Federation. What if he was protecting
Huss . . . or even Gogg? Kirk still had no idea how far or deep the
conspiracy to kill Ceff went. "That's disappointing."

"My apologies, Kirk," Gogg said. "We had hoped to settle this
matter, one way or another, before now."

Then again, Kirk reflected, it was possible that both Gogg and
Sozz were telling the truth about Huss dropping off their sensors.
He could wish that they had chosen to be more forthcoming
about Gogg's double earlier, but, honestly, he wasn't too surprised
that the campaign had chosen to circle the wagons instead. He
could easily imagine McCoy saying something wry and pithy
about the universal tendency of politicians to close ranks and
cover their tracks rather than come clean about any impropri-
eties. Perhaps General Gogg had become more of a politician
than he wanted to admit.

"In any event," Kirk said, "finding Huss and getting his story
is a top priority if we want to get to the truth before the election."
Which was only days away, Kirk reminded himself. "I'm going to
need whatever information you have on Huss."

"That's confidential data," Sozz said, balking at the request.
"Need I remind you, Captain Kirk, that you and the *Enterprise* are
here strictly as observers and have no legal authority or jurisdiction to make any such demand."

Kirk frowned. Gogg's campaign had been withholding vital information long enough; he was in no mood to tolerate any more
runarounds.

"My job is to make sure this election is legitimate, so it is
certainly within my purview to try to find out whether one candidate attempted to murder the other. Now, if you insist, we can
waste time while Commissioner Dare and myself enlist your own

planetary authorities to get you to cooperate, or we can get on with the business of possibly clearing the General's name." Kirk stared at Sozz across three hundred kilometers or so. "Unless there's a reason you want to obstruct our investigation?"

"No reason at all," Gogg said firmly. "We will see to it you receive all relevant files on Huss. Is that understood, Sozz?"

"Yes, General."

"Good," Gogg said. "Now then, Kirk, is there anything else you require from us?"

Uhura cleared her throat. Kirk nodded at her, remembering something they'd discussed earlier.

"We're going to need an accurate listing of which voice samples belong to Huss and which are actually your own voice. My communications officer has compiled a complete list of all relevant voice files, which is contained in the report we transmitted to you before."

Gogg glanced at a data slate resting on his desk.

"That can be arranged," he said.

Kirk appreciated his belated cooperation. Even with Huss apparently in the wind, Kirk felt like they were zeroing in on the truth at last. Lom's story about receiving his orders directly from Gogg had always struck Kirk as fishy, although it now appeared that Lom had sincerely believed that Huss was Gogg, thus allowing him to pass the psycho-tricorder test.

"Thank you," Kirk said. "Now we just need to find Huss with all due speed."

"Ahem," Tanaka said, raising his hand. "I might be able to help with that."

Twenty

Ozalor

"Maybe you should call it a night," Jemo said. "That puzzle's not going anywhere."

That's what you think, McCoy thought.

It was well past the Ozalorian equivalent of midnight. McCoy was burning the figurative oil as he pored over the data on his desktop viewer, while keeping one eye on its chronometer. What Jemo didn't realize was that this was possibly the doctor's last night in the palace, his best chance to get off Ozalor, and his final opportunity to find a solution to Avomora's illness before he escaped back to the *Enterprise,* assuming all went as planned, that was.

Be nice to wrap up this case before I leave.

The failure of his curative compound still baffled him. All the evidence supported his original diagnosis: that low levels of certain vital neurotransmitters were responsible for Avo's condition. The remedy he'd developed would have corrected the imbalance, so why had her symptoms actually gotten worse? Had he missed something, some additional factor contributing to her affliction? Or was he off base altogether? He stared at the data for the umpteenth time, hoping that an answer would leap off the screen, but inspiration eluded him.

"Think I want to work a little longer," he said. "Feel free to turn in if you like."

"You'd like that, wouldn't you?" She was camped out on the sofa in the living room, whittling as usual. She stretched out along the couch's length, with her boots resting upon an armrest. "Who knows what trouble you'd get into if I wasn't keeping tabs on you?"

That's what I'm hoping to find out, McCoy thought. *Soon.*

He returned to his research, but found it hard to concentrate. His gaze kept drifting to the chronometer as the minutes and seconds ticked by. He waited anxiously for the right moment to put his plan into action. He just needed Jemo to give him a few moments alone.

"Be right back," she said finally, taking a bathroom break. "Don't miss me too much."

"I'll manage."

About time, he thought. He was starting to think nature would never call. If worst came to worst, he could have tried to manufacture a distraction to occupy Jemo long enough for him to do what he had to, but this was simpler and less likely to raise her suspicions. *Thank goodness for the basics of humanoid biology.*

Now he just needed to move quickly.

Only moments later, Jemo emerged from the bathroom to find McCoy away from his desk. Her eyes widened as she spotted him over by the food slot, extracting a steaming mug of black coffee from the processor.

"Needed to stretch my legs," he explained. "Figured I could use a jolt of java, too."

He started to lift the mug to his lips.

"Uh-uh," she said, shaking her head. "Don't even think of sipping that yet." She strode across the suite and wagged her finger at him. "You know the rules."

McCoy gave her an exasperated look. "We're still doing this?"

"Having this same conversation again? I hope not." She reached for the mug. "Hand it over."

"Yes, Mother," he grumbled. "Just try to save me a gulp or two."

"Don't I always?" She took a deep swig of the coffee, then licked her lips approvingly. "Yeah, that's what the doctor ordered all right."

"Literally," he pointed out. "Now if you don't mind . . ."

He didn't need to feign impatience as he watched her take

another sip, probably just to tweak him, then deigned to hand him the mug. "You this cranky with your nurses back on the *Enterprise*?"

"I can't remember back that far," he said archly.

"Well, you know what they say, the memory is the first thing to . . ."

Her voice trailed off as she reeled unsteadily, struggling to keep her balance. Her head swayed woozily. She blinked in confusion before realization dawned in her eyes. She slurred her syllables.

"Whadya dozz me wiff . . . ?"

The look of betrayal on her face stung McCoy more than he expected it to, considering the circumstances. He palmed the hypospray hidden beneath his sleeve.

"Nothing you can't sleep off, I promise."

Tottering, she managed to draw the ionic knife at her hip, but it slipped from her fingers before she could even charge it, thudding harmlessly onto the carpet. Her eyelids drooped, along with the rest of her, and he rushed forward to guide her onto the sofa before she collapsed to the floor. She was out cold before her head hit the cushions.

"Sorry, Jemo. You should have gotten your own coffee."

Salokonos was not going to be happy about this. McCoy felt bad about getting Jemo in trouble, but he reminded himself that he was the injured party here. You don't want to get in hot water, don't kidnap people and keep them locked up, even in a palace. With any luck, Avomora could dissuade her dad from punishing Jemo too harshly. Didn't she say that the palace didn't even have dungeons anymore?

I refuse to feel guilty about getting my jailer fired.

In theory, the sedative in the coffee would knock Jemo out for hours, but McCoy didn't waste a moment mounting his escape. He claimed the fallen knife, then gathered his medkit and tricorder as planned. He had already loaded all of the info related to Avo's medical issues into the tricorder, as well as onto a backup microtape tucked into the medkit, so he could keep working her case once he was back aboard the *Enterprise*. One way or another, he was bound and determined to find a way to help the princess, and get her out from under Vumri's thumb, even if it meant finding a way to transmit a cure to Ozalor via back channels.

I don't give up on my patients until they're six feet under.

He swung by the computer terminal long enough to fire off a text message to his mystery pen pal:

On my way.

The exit from the suite was not a fancy mirror portal like the one guarding the princess's quarters. It was a simple, wood-paneled steel door that had been programmed not to respond to McCoy's voice commands. Firing up the ionic blade, he performed surgery on the door's locking mechanism, then applied enough elbow grease to slide it open a crack. He peered through to make sure the coast was clear; an empty corridor encouraged him. Grunting, he slid the door open enough to squeeze through, glancing back at Jemo on his way out.

Thanks for the hospitality, he thought.

He slipped into the hall, his medkit slung over his shoulder by a strap. He tucked the uncharged knife under his belt just in case he ran into trouble. To say that he didn't entirely trust his anonymous benefactor was an understatement; he preferred to be safe rather than sorry when it came to strangers bearing jailbreaks as gifts. He would have done anything for a phaser, but he supposed Jemo's blade would have to do.

Moving stealthily, he navigated the sleeping palace via his tricorder, which now contained a downloaded escape route. His fake beard itched more than ever; he couldn't wait to peel it off at last.

Low voices and laughter, coming from just around the corner, complicated his plans. Peering around the corner, he spotted a frisky pair of servants fooling around against the wall only a few meters ahead. He bit back an exasperated snort. From the look of things, the couple were in no hurry to be on their way.

Just my luck, he groused silently.

He considered trying to take a detour around the inconvenient couple, but worried about losing his way in the sprawling palace or stumbling into an even more public area. Waiting them out was not an option; the clock was ticking. His only choice was to brazen his way past them. He took a deep breath before rounding the corner and striding down the hall with far more confidence than he actually possessed. The startled couple reacted to his footsteps, coming up for air. Embarrassment pinked their faces.

"Don't mind me," McCoy muttered. "Don't see a thing."

Praying they'd return the favor, he hurried past them, not really relaxing until he'd left them well and truly behind him. *As you were,* he thought, feeling as though he'd just lost a year of his life or at least a layer of stomach lining. With a sigh of relief, he made his way to a spiral staircase that grew narrower and more antiquated-looking as he climbed it; weathered stone and mortar suggested that this portion of the stairway dated back to the palace's original construction. His leg muscles protested the climb, having been spoiled by turbolifts. He reminded himself to spend more time at the gym if and when he got back to the *Enterprise*.

Doctor, exercise thyself.

He emerged from the stairwell onto the top deck of a cylindrical watchtower overlooking the nocturnal countryside beyond the palace walls. A glowing, waist-high rail provided both illumination and safety, while a low bench ran along a portion of the rail. A solitary guard, wearing a waterproof slicker over his uniform, faced McCoy, who gulped at the sight. His heart sank. Was the jig up already? Had his supposed benefactor always wanted him to get caught trying to escape?

"Excuse me, I seem to have made a wrong turn . . ."

"To the contrary, Doctor McCoy. You're exactly where you're supposed to be."

McCoy squinted at the sentry, who was tall and blond and burly. "My nameless 'friend,' I take it?"

Truth to tell, he had half expected to find Vumri or maybe even Bilis waiting for him atop the tower. Then again, this was a big palace, housing lots of people, so it stood to reason that the list of suspects was bigger than just the few individuals he had encountered so far. McCoy peered more closely at the sentry. An impressive gold beard carpeted the man's features, but McCoy thought he looked vaguely familiar, sort of. One of the guards stationed at *Yovode*'s sanctum earlier, perhaps, or elsewhere on the premises?

"Good to meet you in person, Doctor."

McCoy relaxed a little and took a moment to survey his surroundings. It was a dark, cloudy night, not to mention uncomfortably hot and humid. A summer storm could be seen approaching from the west. Thunder rumbled not too far away, accompanied by flashes of heat lightning. A translucent deflector screen protected the rooftop from the elements, but McCoy could still hear the wind whipping up.

"So who the devil are you anyway?"

"Call me Guhai."

"That your real name?"

He snickered. "What do you think?"

For all McCoy knew, "Guhai" was the Ozalorian equivalent of "Smith," but he chose not to press the point. He needed the man's help to get away from the palace. That he had turned out to be a palace guard might not be a bad thing, even as McCoy could see why the man had not risked divulging that earlier. "I think that's none of my business, as long as this plan of yours is on the level."

"That it is, Doctor, but we shouldn't waste time. My shift on the tower still has a few hours on it, so we should be uninterrupted, but why tempt fate? Are you ready to take your leave of the Summer Palace?"

"And then some." McCoy felt a twinge of remorse regarding the sick princess, but he also had a duty to return to the *Enterprise* and its captain and crew. "I don't object to the occasional house call, but I've got other places to go and people to see."

"Let me help you with that." Guhai opened a storage locker under the bench and extracted a pair of levitation boots, similar to those found in the Federation. He dropped them at McCoy's feet. "Get going."

The plan was for McCoy to jet away from the palace under cover of night to a rendezvous point in the countryside where Guhai's partners in crime would hustle McCoy into hiding and shelter him until they could arrange to smuggle him off the planet.

"I'm going to be able to contact my captain, right?" McCoy asked, wanting to confirm that detail. "So I can let him know what's become of me?"

A rendezvous in a neutral sector would be preferable to Kirk having to violate Ozalor's sovereignty to extract McCoy, but the doctor wanted to make sure the *Enterprise* knew where he was as soon as possible, partly just to put their minds at rest, but also in case getting off the planet proved trickier than anticipated.

The best-laid plans of mice and medics . . .

"Naturally," Guhai said, "but first things first. We need to get you out of here." He used a control panel on the railing to lower the dome-shaped deflector screen. "Put on those boots."

McCoy regarded the boots uneasily. He'd been obliged to take part in some Starfleet drills involving their use in emergencies, but he'd always regarded them as a damn foolhardy way to risk life and limb. As a means of getting from one point to another, he actually preferred transporters—which was saying something. A clap of thunder, coming from far too close for comfort, drew McCoy's gaze to the approaching storm. Lightning strobed the horizon.

"Not to throw a wrench into things at the last minute, but are we sure this is a good idea? Doesn't exactly seem like an ideal night for zipping through the air."

"The storm will cover your flight," Guhai said. "It'll hide you from sight and confuse the security sensors. Granted, there's an element of difficulty and even danger, but did you really expect to escape the palace without any risk? Where's that bold Starfleet derring-do one hears about?"

"I'm usually the one patching people up after that derring-do," McCoy said, "but you have a point. Nobody ever said a prison break was going to be a cakewalk."

"That's the spirit." Guhai looked McCoy over. "You have the coordinates for the rendezvous point loaded into your tricorder?"

"Absolutely," McCoy said. "Not planning on flying blind."

Guhai held out his hand. "Let me see."

On the surface, it seemed a reasonable request, but something about the man's tone put McCoy on guard. He found himself reluctant to surrender the device, which held all of Avomora's medical records as well.

"I double-checked earlier." McCoy slung the tricorder over his shoulder. "We're good."

"Don't be foolish," Guhai said. "Hand it over."

The sentry's persistence did nothing to assuage McCoy's suspicions. Why was he so dead set on getting his hands on the tricorder?

"Frankly, I'm more concerned with whether these boots are in proper working order." McCoy picked up one of the boots and examined it, not entirely sure what he was looking for. "I assume they're fully charged?"

"They're fine. Put them on already."

McCoy eyed Guhai warily, still unsure whose side he was really on. Was the sentry simply suffering from a bad case of nerves, or was there something fishy going on here?

"Anything bothering you, friend?"

"Stop asking so many questions," Guhai said impatiently. "You need to trust me, Doctor."

"Trust you? I barely know you."

"Shards!" the sentry swore. He reached beneath his slicker and drew a sidearm that looked unnervingly like a disruptor. "I don't have time for this. Give me that tricorder."

McCoy wished he could be surprised.

"This was a setup all along, wasn't it? Let me guess. We're going with the old 'killed while escaping' routine?"

"More or less," Guhai said, "except it's going to look like you got yourself killed without any help from anyone else." He pointed at the boot in McCoy's hand. "Bad luck for you, it turns out those boots are defective. They've barely got enough juice to get you off this tower before sputtering out. Gravity will take care of the rest."

McCoy could visualize that too easily, considering how high up they were. The prospect of plunging to his doom did not appeal to him. "How are you planning to explain how I got my hands on these boots?"

"You're Starfleet, you're clever. People will figure you managed somehow." Guhai didn't seem worried about any future inquiries. "But this time you were a little too clever for your own good and your luck ran out. Pity that."

"Sounds a bit far-fetched to me," McCoy said. "Here's a better idea: Why not just let me escape like we planned? You don't have to kill me to get rid of me. I'll be happy to get gone."

Guhai shook his head.

"That doesn't work for us. Your fate, when it's ultimately revealed, will drive an even deeper wedge between the Federation and Ozalor, thwarting any chance of our people trading away our vengeance for some false promise of peace. Some of us still remember what Vok did to our world in the Before Time, how they all but destroyed our civilization, forcing us to waste millennia clawing our way back from the wreckage. If not for Vok, we'd be more advanced than your Federation by now, or the Klingons or the Romulans. We can never forget or forgive that great wrong, even if the Federation thinks nothing of allying itself with the fiends who laid waste to our world."

"Good God, man," McCoy protested, "that was thousands of years ago. Everyone involved in that war, on both sides, has been dead for ages. Don't you think it's past time you buried the hatchet so both your peoples can move on?"

"Never! Some crimes can never be washed away. Our butchered ancestors, and lost glory, cry out for vengeance, even across generations."

Talk about holding a grudge, McCoy thought. "You people really love your old scars, don't you?"

"Those scars define us," Guhai said. "Beyond that, though, we also can't take the chance that you'll eventually find a cure for the *Yiyova.* We're counting on *Lossu* Vumri to hold sway over the court for decades to come, particularly once Avomora inherits the throne . . . and will be unable to refuse the only person who can relieve her suffering."

"So that's your long game," McCoy said. "Keep Avo dependent on Vumri so that she can become the power behind the throne."

"Precisely, so you can see why we can't risk your tricorder surviving the crash. We need to make sure all your medical scans of Avomora are lost forever."

McCoy recalled the backup tape in his medkit, as well as the files remaining on the computer terminal in the guest suite. Unfortunately, he imagined that it would be all too easy for Vumri and her agents to quietly eradicate any copies of his research, especially after Jemo was dismissed for negligence.

"Seems you've thought of everything."

"You bet we have," Guhai said. "And I'm going to need your medkit as well."

"What for?"

"Need to knock myself out with your hypospray," Guhai said, "to explain how you got past me. *After* you crash, of course."

"Won't that look bad on your record?" McCoy asked, stalling.

"The *Lossu* will protect me and see that I'm rewarded when the time comes."

Lightning flashed nearby, followed almost immediately by a boom of thunder. The storm was almost upon them.

"Just one thing," McCoy said. "What makes you think I'm going to make it easy for you? You want to kill me, you're going to have to shoot me. Going to be hard to explain a disruptor blast to my chest."

"Harder, but not impossible. Maybe I claim self-defense, say you came at me with that knife." Guhai glanced at the approaching tempest. "Or maybe we just say you were struck by lightning. Who's going to contradict me?"

The wind was howling more loudly by the moment, buffeting the two men. A thunderbolt streaked the sky. Guhai shouted over the gale.

"Now put on the boots."

"Like hell," McCoy said. "I'm not going to help cover up my own murder."

"You're a stubborn man, Doctor."

"So I've been told . . . by better people than you."

His defiant words masked the genuine chill running down his spine, as well as his anger and dismay at how things had shaken out. As a doctor, he understood better than most how fragile life could be, but that didn't make facing his own end any easier. Getting blasted to death far from friends and family, because of political intrigues on a planet he'd barely heard of before a few weeks ago, was not how he wanted to cash in his chips, and knowing that his untimely demise was going to be exploited by schemers and warmongers galled him even more. He'd spent much of his adult life saving lives; he didn't want anyone dying to avenge him.

"Have it your way." Guhai kept the pistol aimed squarely at McCoy's chest. "I'd ask if you had any last words, but I think I've heard quite enough from—"

"Eat glass, you shard-cracking piece of glint!"

Jemo came charging onto the tower top. McCoy couldn't believe it; the drug he'd spiked the coffee with should have put her out for hours, but she seemed none the worse for wear as she charged headlong at Guhai, distracting the startled sentry, who spun around and fired wildly at his attacker. A crimson beam flared brighter than the lightning, scoring a glancing blow to Jemo's side. It wasn't a direct hit, but it was still enough to send her tumbling to the tiled stone floor, clutching her side. Thunder drowned out any cries or gasps from the wounded bodyguard. It was hard to tell how badly she'd been injured.

No! McCoy thought. *Nobody else was supposed to get hurt!*

Her failed charge, however, distracted Guhai long enough for McCoy to make his own desperate move. Crouching down below the level of the safety rail, he manually triggered the booster rocket in the heel of the levitation boot, aiming it upward at Guhai, who was caught by surprise. A vaporous blue blast slammed into the sentry, propelling him across the tower top and over the railing, even as the same blast sent McCoy flying backward into the bench with bone-jarring force. The impact knocked the wind out of McCoy, but he was still better off than Guhai, who screamed all the way down as he met the same end he'd intended for McCoy, who was not too stunned to appreciate the poetic justice involved. He regretted the man's death, but he found it hard to feel too guilty about it.

Told you to let me get away like we planned.

As warned, the boot malfunctioned before McCoy could even manage to switch it off. The booster rocket sputtered and died, bright yellow sparks spraying alarmingly from the jets. McCoy hurled the sabotaged footwear away from him, then staggered to his feet to see to Jemo. Ignoring his own bruises, he hurried over to the injured bodyguard, who was sprawled on the floor, cursing and moaning in equal measures. Still conscious, if probably not for long, she managed to gripe at McCoy as he knelt at her side.

"Of all the idiotic, suicidal stunts . . ."

"Right back at you." His throat tightened as he realized that she had taken a high-energy weapon blast for him. "Now let me get a look at you."

Her injuries were as bad as he'd feared. The right side of her torso was badly burned, while a rapid tricorder scan indicated both organ damage and internal bleeding. He could only imagine how much pain she was in. He hurriedly administered an anesthetic along with a finely calibrated dose of cordrazine to stabilize her, taking care to allow for the sedative already in her system.

"How'd you find me?" he asked to distract her until the analgesic took effect.

She found the strength to tug on his phony beard. "Viridium filaments in the whiskers. To track you with . . ."

"Sneaky." McCoy was suddenly glad he hadn't torn the annoying disguise off yet. "There's probably a 'close shave' joke to be made here, but I can't quite find it."

"Lucky me," she said. "Anybody ever tell you your bedside manner—?"

A ragged cough cut off whatever quip she'd been going for. Bright arterial blood trickled from the corner of her lip as her eyelids sagged and she lost consciousness, going limp upon the cold stone floor. Despite the medications McCoy had already employed, she needed major medical intervention . . . stat.

So much for my Great Escape, he thought.

Rapid footsteps sounded on the steps leading up to the tower. Guhai's fatal plunge had apparently not gone unnoticed. McCoy shouted at the newcomers.

"Hurry up! I need help here!"

Twenty-One

Braco

"Anything?" Levine asked.

The security officer piloted *Copernicus* as the shuttlecraft scanned the planet from orbit. Godwin occupied the copilot's seat to his right, monitoring the long-range sensors.

"Nothing yet." She peered intently at the globe-shaped monitor before her. A silver earpiece aided her concentration.

Levine scowled. They had been at this for hours without getting a hit on the display screens. He consulted the built-in astrogator as well as their flight plan. "That's it for loop nine-seven-seven-K. Moving on to the next longitude."

"Acknowledged," she said. "Commencing new sensor sweep."

Along with *Galileo,* which was methodically scanning the southern hemisphere, they were trying to pick up a signal from one of the hidden transponders Spock and Chapel had taken with them when they snuck off to meet that alleged informant, a fact-finding mission that had clearly gone south in a big way. Levine kicked himself again for not accompanying them, even though that had been Commander Spock's call. He should have known better than to let them head off on their own after what happened to Doctor McCoy.

"I certainly hope you're not wasting my time," Chief Inspector Wibb said from behind and between them. He stood in the cockpit, gripping the back of their seats, instead of sitting in the passenger compartment with the pair of Bureau troopers he had insisted on bringing along. It seemed he intended to breathe down their necks the whole flight. "Despite your promises, I have yet to see any results."

"Nobody insisted you come along," Godwin muttered. Hours stuck in a cramped shuttlecraft with the inspector were obviously wearing on her nerves. Levine knew just how she felt.

"Don't be ridiculous," Wibb replied. "After what happened the last time you people set out unsupervised, against my express advice, I might add, I'm keeping a close watch on you from now on." The armed troopers seated in the rear, one of whom was the very deputy Spock had nerve-pinched, were presumably there to keep them in line. "Consider yourself fortunate that I sanctioned this operation at all."

Tell me about it, Levine thought. Persuading Wibb to let them do these orbital flybys had taken more effort and time than Levine would have liked. Fortunately, the Bureau had a strong interest in locating the terrorists' hideouts, which had given him and Godwin a certain amount of much-needed leverage. "We all have the same goal here: finding Mister Spock and Nurse Chapel."

"Not to mention your Doctor McCoy," Wibb said.

"Hopefully," Godwin said, "although we still don't know for sure that he's being held in the same place . . . or even by the same people."

"You needn't trouble yourself about that," Wibb said confidently. "Mark my words, the UBF has all three of your missing comrades. Chances are, you find the last two kidnapping victims, you'll find the first."

"I hope you're right," Levine said. That would definitely up their odds of safely returning all three crew members to the *Enterprise.* Godwin had a point, though: they still didn't know for sure that the United Bracon Front had snatched Doctor McCoy in the first place. Ironically, that was what Spock and Chapel had been trying to find out when they were taken hostage. So far the UBF had only claimed responsibility for holding Spock and Chapel.

"Count on it, Lieutenant," Wibb said. "I know what I'm talking about."

Keeping one hand on the pilot's seat to maintain his balance, the inspector extracted his pipe from his vest pocket and placed it between his teeth before moving to light it with his ring.

"Uh-uh," Godwin said, keeping one eye on her monitor. "We talked about this. No smoking aboard the *Copernicus*. You may be overseeing this operation, but this is still a Starfleet vessel. Our shuttle, our rules."

Wibb glowered at her, but removed the pipe from his lips.

"We wouldn't need to use your shuttlecrafts," he said sourly, "if you simply shared your transponder codes with the Bureau as I requested."

"Sorry," Levine said, "but those are classified. Regulations. You of all people must appreciate that."

He took a certain degree of satisfaction in turning the tables on the inspector, but tried not to be too obvious about it. Godwin gave him a conspiratorial smirk nonetheless. And, of course, he had no intention of surrendering what little leverage they had. If the Bureau wanted to find the kidnappers via those transponders, they were going to have to work with the Starfleet teams.

Wibb harrumphed mightily. "Let us hope your insistence on Starfleet protocol doesn't doom your search by denying us your full cooperation."

Me too, Levine thought. The *Enterprise*'s sensors could probably search larger areas faster, but even a *Constitution*-class starship would need time to scan an entire planet. Not that the *Enterprise* could take a detour to Braco anyway; from what Levine had heard, Captain Kirk had his hands full with assassins and political conspiracies and an election only a few days away. There was no way the ship could get to Braco, take time out to search for Spock, Chapel, *and* McCoy, and return to Vok before Election Day.

Ignoring Wibb, he hailed *Galileo* to check on their progress. Deep down, he figured they would have already alerted *Copernicus* if they'd detected the signals, but it beat squabbling with

Wibb. *And who knows? Maybe they're too busy tracing the signals to notify us right away?*

"*Copernicus* to *Galileo*," he said, setting the helm on autopilot. "What is your status?"

"*Galileo here*," replied Lieutenant Nguyen, who had arrived on Braco with Spock and the rest of his security team. "*We're striking out so far. How about you?*"

"The same," Levine admitted. "Continuing search loops."

"*Acknowledged*," Nguyen said. "*We'll keep you posted.*"

The other shuttlecraft signed off. Godwin sighed in disappointment. "I have to admit I'm getting worried. What if they're not even on Braco anymore?"

"We'll cross that sector when we come to it," Levine said.

"Perhaps your persistence is misguided." Wibb fiddled impatiently with his pipe. "We should consider turning back."

"You can't be serious," Levine said. "We can't give up until we've scanned every square centimeter of this planet, no matter how long it takes."

"Easy for you and your cohorts to say," Wibb said, "but I'm a busy man with many responsibilities. Yours is hardly the only case open at the Bureau, nor is this our sole line of investigation." He shrugged. "Perhaps we can resume your search later after we've paused to regroup and reassess the viability of this strategy."

Levine bit his tongue to keep from informing Wibb that his continuing presence was unneeded and unwanted, choosing to argue the merits of the search instead.

"We can't assess anything until we complete our passes. For all we know, we could pick up the signals any moment now."

"Or we could waste more hours pointlessly circling the globe when I could be making more productive use of my time back at—"

"Hold on!" Godwin interrupted. "I think I'm getting something!"

Levine sat up straight. Wibb shut up and stopped grumbling. "What is it?" the pilot asked urgently.

"It's faint," she reported, adjusting her earpiece. "Almost as though it's coming from *beneath* the surface of the planet."

"Can you pinpoint its origin?" Levine asked.

"Not yet." She squinted at the monitor globe. "It's too indistinct. Maybe if we descend lower . . . into the atmosphere?"

Levine looked at Wibb. "Well, Chief Inspector?"

"I'll have to clear it with the proper authorities," Wibb said. "As you can well imagine, we frown on alien vessels traversing our airspace without permission."

"But . . . ?" Levine pressed.

"I suppose I can obtain the necessary clearances," the inspector said, "if it means locating the terrorists."

"And the hostages," Godwin stressed.

"Naturally," Wibb said. "Find one, we'll find the other."

The two security officers exchanged a worried glance. Levine feared that Wibb and his troopers were more intent on apprehending the UBF than retrieving the hostages. He and Godwin had very different priorities.

We may need to keep reminding the Bureau of that.

Wibb contacted the relevant authorities via his personal communicator. Long minutes passed before he finally got the go-ahead to proceed. *Copernicus* descended into Braco's cloudy atmosphere, forcing Levine to compensate for the wind and weather as Godwin zeroed in on the origin of the signal, feeding him the proper vectors and coordinates as she determined them. A chronometer indicated that it was midafternoon in this time zone, while the weather was typically bleak. Braco was never going to challenge Risa as a vacation destination.

"Yes! It's working," Godwin said. "The signal is getting stronger the lower we go."

Levine glanced at his own globe monitor, where a faint yellow blip was rapidly gaining in intensity and coherence. Consulting the coordinates, he experienced an unnerving sense of déjà vu.

"We're heading for the Sea of Glass," he said.

"That Prime-forsaken wasteland?" Wibb responded. "It's entirely uninhabitable."

"Where better to hide out, then?" Godwin said. "I'm getting a good feeling about this. Seems like we're finally on the right track."

"Affirmative," Levine said. It worried him, however, that they only seemed to be picking up *one* signal. "Which transponder is it?"

"The *third* one," she said. "In the medkit."

Both Spock and Chapel had been implanted with subcutaneous transponders, but, as an added precaution, they had also hidden a third transponder inside a spare heartbeat reader in Chapel's medkit, just in case they underwent some sort of body scan or inspection. It appeared that extra measure had paid off . . . possibly.

"What does that mean?" Wibb asked.

"It means we're getting a lock on their equipment, but not necessarily the hostages." Levine considered the implications. "It could mean Chapel and Spock are being kept elsewhere. Or it could just mean that their transponders were detected and neutralized somehow."

He didn't want to think about how the terrorists might have removed the hostages' transponders. Filling his head with gruesome images wasn't going to help anybody. He needed to stay sharp.

Copernicus came in low above the Sea of Glass. "How we doing tracking that signal?" Levine asked Godwin.

"Pretty good." She deftly operated the sensor controls. "I'm reading a fairly extensive cave system approximately fourteen hundred meters beneath the surface."

Levine's pulse raced. "Life-forms?"

"Seems like it." Godwin recalibrated the sensors. "I'm getting some interference from the Sea of Glass. Possibly residual radiation left over from the old atomic war, but, yes, there *are* indications of multiple life-forms. Humanoids, no less."

"By the Prime, we have them!" Wibb gleefully slammed a fist into his palm before taking out his communicator. "We need to alert the Bureau immediately. Prep for a full-scale assault."

"Whoa there!" Levine protested. "We can't just storm in, phasers blazing. Too much chance of the hostages getting hurt or killed in the fighting."

Wibb frowned, unhappy at having his jubilation spoiled. "And what exactly do you suggest, Lieutenant?"

"A surgical strike," Levine said. "We go in, get the hostages, and get out, preferably before the kidnappers even know what's happening. You can always raid the place afterward," he added, throwing the inspector a bone.

Wibb appeared dubious about Levine's proposal.

"And how exactly do you intend to slip quietly into those caverns without a massive show of force?" the inspector asked. "Pretend you're on a harmless spelunking expedition?"

Levine didn't have an immediate answer. "We're going to need to work that out, develop contingency plans, before rushing into anything. This type of rescue operation requires careful preparation and precision."

"The transporter room back at Bureau Headquarters," Godwin suggested. "Now that we have the exact coordinates, based on the transponder signal, we can beam in a strike force." She pivoted away from her monitor to face Wibb. "You need to let us use your transporter."

"I don't know," Wibb said. "I don't want to risk losing the element of surprise. We know where the terrorists are now. I'm not about to let them scurry away into the shadows by waiting too long."

"Do you want dead Federation citizens on your hands? Does your government want that?" Levine pleaded with Wibb. "Just give us time to get our people out, then you can go in, full force, and round up as many hostiles as you want. That's your business. But at least give us a chance to rescue our people first."

Wibb didn't answer right away. Clearly conflicted, he gnawed on the stem of his unlit pipe as he paced the length of the shuttlecraft and back. He peered through the forward portholes at the glittering expanse below.

"How much time do you need?"

Twenty-Two

Vok

"Welcome to Paranoia Arms," Tanaka quipped.

They had tracked General Gogg's missing double to a luxury apartment complex that boasted the latest in state-of-the-art security measures for its tenants, including insulation suffused with magnesite to keep unwanted visitors from beaming in. An automated doorway barred Kirk's entry to the garishly painted skyscraper, which was located in a ritzy, rather exclusive part of the city. A robotic voice issued from an armored security kiosk situated next to the entrance.

"Present proof of occupancy . . . or request admission from oc-cupant."

Kirk and his companions, which included Tanaka, Ensign Pavel Chekov, and a pair of security officers from the *Enterprise*, clustered on the sidewalk outside the building. A cool spring evening made waiting outdoors comfortable enough, but Kirk wasn't here to enjoy the fresh air. He turned toward the sixth member of their party: a uniformed Vokite police officer.

"Sergeant?" Kirk asked. "If you could lend a hand here?"

"My pleasure."

A lanky young woman with a freckled face and dyed turquoise hair, Sergeant Myp was the official police liaison to the Federation embassy. Kirk had met her briefly at the reception welcoming him and Commissioner Dare to Vok, but apparently Tanaka had been working with her for months. Indeed, judging from their easy familiarity, Kirk got the distinct impression that they had become very good friends, and possibly more than that, not that

that was any of Kirk's business. He was just grateful to have Myp on hand to assist in this operation.

She approached the security kiosk, casually easing past Tanaka as she did so, and held her palm up to the biometric scanner. An elaborate tattoo on her palm served as the Vokite equivalent of a badge. Kirk understood that special viridium inks, exclusive to the planet's civic security force, made such tattoos all but impossible to counterfeit.

"Police business," she said. "Please allow admittance."

It took the security program only a moment to recognize and confirm her credentials.

"Admittance granted. Enter at will."

A pair of thick transparent aluminum doors retracted, permitting access to the lobby beyond. Kirk started through the doorway only to be blocked by an invisible force field. A warning buzzer sounded, followed by another computerized announcement.

"Energy weapon detected. No firearms permitted on premises."

Kirk couldn't fault the building's security sensors. His hand went to the phaser beneath his uniform, which he'd brought just in case Huss strenuously objected to being questioned. Kirk sighed impatiently, reluctant to surrender his weapon.

"Sergeant?"

"On it," she said.

While Myp pulled rank to get their phasers past the sensors, Kirk wondered if Huss had sought out such high-security lodgings on purpose. It was probably not too surprising that a man involved in an assassination plot would be fearful of his safety, but who exactly was Huss seeking protection from? General Gogg? His aide Sozz? Starfleet? The police? Angry Ceff supporters, seeking revenge?

Kirk hoped to get some answers straight from Huss before long.

"We're clear," Myp announced. "Phasers and all."

They entered the lobby, where a lift took them to the fourteenth floor. Vokite numerals guided them to a sturdy steel door on one side of a tiled corridor. A tinted viewer and intercom unit was embedded in the door at eye level. The arcane numerals meant nothing to Kirk, whose universal translator was of little use when it came to the embossed alien glyphs.

"This the right address?" he asked.

"Yep," Tanaka said, "according to Vok Populi."

The orbiting supercomputer had a database of every eligible voter on the planet, including their current addresses and electoral districts, the better to ensure that everyone was voting where they were supposed to. Few could access its memory banks, but Tanaka, as one of the primary architects of the system, had not been above using his special privileges to do what Gogg and his people could not: locate Huss's current address.

"Good thing he made the effort to update his voter info even while lying low," Tanaka added.

"Well," Kirk said, "he went so far as to order Lom to attack Doctor Ceff, so it stands to reason that he has strong feelings regarding the election, and wasn't going to risk not being able to take part in it."

"Good point," Tanaka said. "I suppose we should applaud his sense of civic duty."

"Only to a degree," Kirk said, recalling the javelin striking Dare. He contemplated the closed door. "You care to do the honors, Sergeant?"

"Don't mind if I do." She pressed the intercom button, but received no response. "Hello? This is an official police call. Please come to the door."

The ensuing silence prompted an apologetic shrug from Myp, who switched to a more aggressive approach. She raised her voice and rapped her knuckles against the door.

"Vok Civic Security! Open up!"

It occurred to Kirk that a coconspirator to an assassination attempt might well want to pretend not to be home when the police came calling, but he couldn't blame Myp for following proper protocol. Waiting restlessly in the hallway, Kirk glanced at the door across from Huss's apartment. He wondered what Huss's neighbors thought of the ruckus. *Might be worth questioning them later,* he thought, *if we can't get our hands on the man himself.*

"No luck," Myp reported.

"Maybe he's out?" Chekov speculated.

Kirk wasn't inclined to leave a note and come back later. Thanks to data grudgingly supplied by Sozz, which had meticulously itemized which voice films belonged to the real Gogg and which could be attributed to his double, Uhura had confirmed that the "General" who had ordered Lom to attack Ceff was indeed Huss. As far as Kirk was concerned, that gave them probable cause to enter the apartment, by both Vokite and Federation standards.

He nodded at Myp. "Only one way to find out."

"Attention! We're coming in," the sergeant announced via the intercom to whoever might be inside the apartment. "Your cooperation is expected and appreciated." She used her official tattoo to unlock the door, which slid open to offer a view of Huss's living quarters. "All yours, Captain."

"Thank you, Sergeant." Kirk took a moment to address his team. "On your guard, everyone. If Huss is present, we have no way of knowing how desperate or violent he might become. Stay alert, watch each other's backs, and don't take any unnecessary risks. If he's here, he's not going anywhere, so we don't need to rush in recklessly." He drew his phaser. "Let's keep our eyes open and our heads in the game."

"Aye, sir." Chekov had his phaser ready. "Understood."

Kirk trusted the young Russian to handle himself if things got dicey, but what about Tanaka? He doubted if the up-and-coming civil servant had much in the way of combat training or experience.

"Mister Tanaka, please keep back until we've cleared the premises and determined that there's no immediate threat. No offense,
but I don't want any harm coming to you."

"None taken, Captain. This is your wheelhouse, not mine."

"Don't worry, Captain Kirk," Myp said. "I won't let anything
happen to Steve."

Kirk took her at her word, while quietly noting that she and
Tanaka were on a first-name basis. *Good for them,* he thought.

Phasers in hand, the Starfleet personnel swept in and across
the apartment, encountering no immediate resistance. Kirk called
out to its apparently absent occupant.

"Mister Huss? This is Captain James T. Kirk of the Federation
Starship Enterprise. You are wanted for questioning. If you're here,
show yourself."

His eyes surveyed the apartment. At first inspection, it appeared to be somewhat larger than his quarters back on the
Enterprise, consisting of a main living room, kitchen, dining
nook, workstation, and bedroom. The furnishings looked both
new and comfortable, congruent with the fact that Huss had only
recently taken up occupancy here. Personal touches were few and
far between, although some old-fashioned codex books suggested
that Huss was a reader or an antiquarian or both. A shoebox-
sized housekeeping robot was docked in its port, accounting for
the apartment's cleanliness. Conspicuously missing: any windows
looking outdoors.

Paranoia Arms indeed, Kirk thought.

He lowered his phaser as it increasingly looked as though Huss
was not at home. The rush of adrenaline Kirk had felt on entering
began to subside, replaced by an unpalatable blend of disappointment and frustration. He was already thinking ahead to his next
move when Chekov called out from the kitchen.

"Captain! We found him . . . but I don't think he's going to be
answering any questions."

Kirk feared he knew what that meant. He hurried over to the

kitchen, where Chekov and another crew member were grimly contemplating the contents of a large walk-in pantry. Stuffed in amidst shelves of fresh produce and other groceries was the lifeless body of a middle-aged male Vokite who, despite having shaved his head, bore a striking resemblance to a certain dour presidential candidate. If Kirk didn't know better, he might easily think that it was General Gogg's body awkwardly wedged in among the fruits and vegetables.

Damn, Kirk thought.

McCoy was not on hand to pronounce the man dead, but that was hardly necessary. The corpse's still form and slack features betrayed no sign of animation. Glassy eyes stared blindly into oblivion. It was unclear, at a glance, whether rigor mortis had set in.

"Holy Triton!" Tanaka exclaimed as he and Myp rushed in from the hallway, anxious to see for themselves what Chekov had discovered. "Is that really Huss? What happened to him?"

Kirk didn't object to Tanaka joining them. Clearly, Huss was not going to be putting up a fight.

"More like *who* happened to him," Kirk said. "Somehow I doubt he died of natural causes."

"No one touch anything," Myp said. "This is a crime scene."

That much was evident, although Kirk could not immediately discern an obvious cause of death. He requisitioned a tricorder from Chekov and scanned the body from outside the pantry. The device confirmed the total absence of life signs, but also failed to determine how exactly Huss had been killed. Kirk hoped that a more comprehensive forensic examination would yield more fruitful results.

"How long you think he's been like this?" Tanaka asked.

"Good question." Kirk observed the freshness of the produce and tentatively stuck his bandaged hand into the pantry. A slight numbing sensation confirmed his suspicion. He withdrew his hand. "Stasis field, to keep the groceries fresh. Handy way to preserve a body, too."

"Why bother?" Tanaka asked.

"Best guess?" Kirk answered. "Someone—or someones—didn't want the corpse found right away because that might raise too many unwelcome questions right before the election. Better that his death go quietly undetected for a while."

"I suppose," Tanaka said. "But why was he killed in the first place?"

"Tying up loose ends," Kirk guessed, "which suggests that Huss was not acting alone when he tricked Lom into attacking Doctor Ceff, and that he may not have been the instigator of the plot. He might well have been just another pawn, now conveniently removed from the board."

"Unless somebody is simply trying to cover up the whole thing after the fact," Myp speculated. "Merely as damage control."

"Possible," Kirk said, "but I suspect Huss was deemed expendable after he served his purpose by impersonating Gogg. Chances are, someone anticipated that we'd come looking for him, particularly after that recording went public."

"You think he was killed before or after the tape was leaked?" Tanaka asked.

"Another good question," Kirk said. "With any luck, a more thorough examination of the body will shed some light on that, although that stasis field complicates matters."

Kirk wished that McCoy was available to conduct the autopsy. He was debating whether he should order the body beamed up to the *Enterprise,* as opposed to turning it over to the Vokite authorities, when he heard raised voices coming from the hallway outside the apartment.

"Please, ma'am. I need you to let us handle this."

"This is my home. I have a right to know what's happening!"

Intrigued, Kirk crossed the apartment to investigate. He found Lieutenant Enrique Tovar dealing with a petite older woman who was apparently curious about the commotion. Silvery hair was done up in a bun, while a brightly colored caftan gave her a flamboyant air. She peered past Tovar, trying to catch a glimpse of the goings-on in Huss's quarters. Kirk noted that her left eye was obviously artificial. Concentric metal rings, of alternating bronze and electrum, served as irises, circling a glowing electronic pupil, while also matching her gleaming hoop earrings. Arcane symbols, whose meaning eluded Kirk, were etched into the rings.

"Is there a problem, Lieutenant?" Kirk asked.

"Just a neighbor from across the hall, Captain," Tovar said. "Says her name is Zell."

"That's Madame Zell to you." She turned away from Tovar to address Kirk directly. "Are you in charge here?"

"More or less." Kirk saw no need to parse the finer points of the jurisdictional issues involved. "How can I help you?"

"I just want to know what's going on here," she said. "Did something happen to Mister Pukk? Is he in some kind of trouble?"

"Pukk?"

"That's his name, or so he said." She eyed Kirk suspiciously. "Why don't you know that?"

Kirk assumed Huss had adopted an alias, at least as far as his neighbors were concerned, in hopes of maintaining a low profile.

"We're still gathering the facts, ma'am. You'll have to bear with us."

"Facts about what?" Zell demanded. "Should I be concerned for my own safety?"

"You're quite safe," Kirk assured her, "but I'm afraid that there *has* been an incident regarding your neighbor. I regret to inform you that he's been found dead in his apartment."

Zell gasped at the news. Her hand went to her chest.

"How did he die? And what does this have to do with Starfleet?"

"That's what we're trying to determine, ma'am." It occurred to Kirk that Zell was a potentially valuable source of information. "How well did you know Mister . . . Pukk?"

"Not well at all, truth be told." She shrugged her bony shoulders. "People in this building, we value our privacy. Mister Pukk and I nodded at each other in passing, exchanged a few casual pleasantries on occasion, but he largely kept to himself."

Kirk was not surprised to hear that. He glanced back into the apartment, where Sergeant Myp was busy securing the crime scene.

"I see," he said. "Even still, I'd like to ask you some more questions about your neighbor if that's all right with you. Is there someplace more comfortable we can continue this conversation?"

She looked Kirk over as though gauging his trustworthiness. Her metal irises rotated at varying rates, with the inner rings spinning faster than the outer. "Hmm. Your aura looks sincere enough. I suppose I can trust you that far. Come along."

My aura? Kirk raised an eyebrow, but he wasn't about to challenge her assessment. He followed Zell into her apartment, whose door automatically opened to admit her. The basic layout resembled Huff's residence, but the colorful décor gave the residence its own character. Twinkling strings of crystalline lights crisscrossed the ceiling, their glow reflected by sequined curtains and wall hangings. A round theatrical poster, at least two meters in diameter, dominated the main living area. The dynamic artwork depicted a much younger Zell communing with the cosmos, surrounded by holographic stars and swirling nebulae as she lifted her gaze to infinity. A spotlight highlighted her artificial eye.

"A personal memento, I take it?" Kirk remarked of the poster. "You were in show business?"

She feigned dismay. "You've never heard of Madame Zell and her All-Seeing Zodiac Eye?"

"You'll have to forgive my ignorance," Kirk said. "I'm not exactly from these parts."

"True enough. You're excused, then." She settled into a plush armchair facing a low coffee table and gestured for Kirk to make himself comfortable on a nearby ottoman. She looked up at the circular poster. "Headlined a cyber-seeress act for years before I retired. I saw all, knew all, peered beyond the space-time continuum into the eighth dimension." She chuckled at her own ballyhoo. "Between you and me, I was just good at reading people, with a little help from my prosthetic peeper." She lightly tapped her optical implant. "Didn't hurt to be able to view people's electromagnetic fields up and down the spectrum."

"I can imagine."

"Oh, you should've seen me back in my prime," Zell said. "I drew crowds every night, with matinees on weekends and holidays. Had the audience in the palm of my hand, hanging on my every utterance." She sighed wistfully before looking away from her past glory. "But that's not what you want to talk about, is it?"

"I'm afraid not." Kirk got down to business. "When was the last time you saw your neighbor?"

"Yesterday," she said. "Not that I pry, mind you, but I try to keep my eyes open when it comes to what's going on around me, as one should. From what I've seen, Pukk hasn't come or gone from his rooms since late last night."

Kirk did the math in his head. If what Zell was saying was true, then Huss had been killed sometime after the rally, only hours after Lom had been apprehended.

"I don't suppose you know if he received any visitors around that time?"

"Just the one," Zell said, frowning at the memory. "I knew there was something shifty about that stranger. I can tell such things, you know."

Kirk's pulse sped up, as though he'd just caught a glimmer of a cloaked ship on the sensors. "Tell me about this visitor."

Before Zell could answer, there was a buzz at the door. Sergeant Myp's voice issued from an intercom:

"Captain Kirk? Lieutenant Tovar said you were interviewing a possible witness?"

Kirk applauded her timing. "That's one of your own peace officers," he explained to Zell. "She should probably hear this."

"Very well." Zell raised her voice. "Admit visitors."

The door slid open, allowing Myp and Tanaka to join them. Kirk quickly made the necessary introductions as the newcomers found a cozy spot on a loveseat.

"Please go on, Madame Zell," Kirk urged. "You were saying something about a visitor across the hall?"

"So I was," she said grandly, clearly enjoying the attention. Kirk guessed this was probably the most attentive audience she'd had since she'd retired from performing. "It was late last night, the very day that scoundrel tried to spear Doctor Ceff, when I heard footsteps in the hall outside. As it happened, I'd been meaning to ask Mister Pukk about some small matter, so I took advantage of the opportunity to step outside to greet him . . . and his guest."

Kirk couldn't help wondering if perhaps Zell was snoopier than she wanted to let on. She'd made a career, after all, of ferreting out hidden secrets for fame and fortune.

"What about this guest?" he prompted.

"I got a bad impression from him straightaway," Zell said. "Pukk didn't even try to introduce me to his friend, who kept his face turned away from me, not letting me get a decent look at him. Didn't say a word either. His whole manner was, well, *furtive* . . . that's the word. It was none of my business, of course, but you can't fool Madame Zell. I can tell when someone doesn't want to be seen."

Kirk found himself ever more interested in this secretive visitor. "Can you describe him at all?"

"Adult, male, about your height, plus or minus a few centimeters. He had on a hooded jacket, obscuring his face, but I caught a glimpse of pale, pinkish skin. And, oh yes, he was clutching a bottle of spirits."

Kirk didn't recall seeing a bottle, empty or otherwise, in Huss's apartment, not that he had been looking out for one. He would have preferred a more detailed description of the mystery caller, but he felt they were making progress nonetheless.

"Anyway, I barely had a chance to say hello before Pukk and his friend vanished into his apartment, leaving me alone in the corridor." Zell tsked in disapproval. "They were quite brusque about it, really."

"I don't suppose you have any idea how long this guest stayed?" Kirk asked.

"Not long. An hour, maybe less."

Kirk was struck by how confidently she replied. "Are you certain?"

"I may have just happened to be watching the hall through the door viewer when he left," she said, only a wee bit defensively. "Call it a premonition, call it intuition, but something was not sitting right with me. I saw him slip out of the apartment not too long after he and Pukk went inside, still keeping his head down and looking, if anything, even more furtive than before. I didn't need to scan his aura to know that he was hiding something. His guilty body language came across loud and clear." She paused for dramatic effect. "And that night was the last time I ever saw my neighbor alive."

Myp scowled. "And you didn't think to report this to the authorities?"

"What can I say?" Zell said. "I mind my own business."

Right, Kirk thought. He had to feel sorry for the nameless visitor, who was almost surely Huss's killer. All that intrigue and manipulation and conspiracy, only to run afoul of a nosy neighbor. Kirk appreciated the irony even as he resolved to take full advantage of it.

"Is it possible our suspect's face was caught by a security camera?" he asked.

"Don't get your hopes up," Myp said. "If this guest arrived with Huss, he wouldn't have needed to check in at the security kiosk."

"Huss?" Zell asked, confused.

"Your Mister Pukk went by another name," Kirk explained. "Too bad there's no video. We could use a good look at him."

Zell chuckled. "You're forgetting my eye, Captain. It sees all *and* records all. I just need to access the right file."

———

The old poster of Madame Zell turned out to be an image on a circular viewscreen. Kirk and his colleagues waited, facing the screen, as Zell called up a video file from the day before. Her optical implant could only hold so much data in its memory, so she routinely uploaded her daily visual records to her apartment's computer banks. Kirk understood that this was a common limitation of many cybernetic prosthetics even throughout the Federation; he'd known a crew member aboard the *Farragut* who'd needed to prune and download his memories on a regular basis.

"Here we go," Zell said. "Fortunately, this was only yesterday, so I didn't have to go rummaging through all my old files. I'm a bit of an optical hoarder, if you must know. My apologies for lack of audio, since I still have my original, flesh-and-blood ears. No depth perception either, I'm afraid." She winked at Kirk. "Just the one 'special' eye, you know."

Kirk briefly wondered how Zell had lost her original left eye, but that was neither here nor there at the moment. He watched intently as the playback replaced the old poster on the screen. A hooded figure could be seen exiting Huss's apartment in what indeed could be described as a "furtive" manner. He glanced up and down the corridor as though worried about being seen. A gloved hand clutched an open bottle, which the figure was apparently intent on taking with him. Kirk made a mental note to have Huss's remains tested for poison.

Zell wasn't wrong, Kirk thought. Even with his face obscured, the man in the video gave off a distinctly guilty vibe. *Not a professional killer,* Kirk surmised; a more experienced assassin wouldn't appear so conspicuously ill at ease. *He's not a natural at this.*

The man in the video looked back at the door, possibly concerned that he'd left some incriminating evidence behind. He extracted a handkerchief from a pocket and nervously dabbed at his hidden face. The mannerism struck a chord in Kirk's memory.

Hold on, he thought, leaning forward. *Could it be—?*

Twenty-Three

Ozalor

"Your Excellency, surely you can't believe that I would conspire to have the Earth doctor killed?" Vumri acted shocked, shocked at the very suggestion. "I swear by my gifts that I knew nothing of this alleged plot."

"In a pig's eye," McCoy said.

His blunt response lacked diplomacy, but he was too tired and cranky to watch his words. It was the morning after his near-fatal confrontation on the tower and he was dead on his feet. Between the bogus escape attempt, his close brush with death, and hours of emergency surgery on Jemo to save her life, McCoy felt like he'd been put through the wringer. He was badly in need of sleep, black coffee, a stiff drink, or possibly all of the above. What he didn't need was a command appearance before Salokonos in the *Yovode*'s private sanctum, but when the planet's supreme ruler demanded answers regarding last night's turbulent events, McCoy could hardly say no, nor truly blame Salokonos for wanting to get to the bottom of the matter without delay.

At least he let me finish operating on Jemo first.

"Excuse me?" Vumri said in response to his remark.

"You heard me," McCoy said. "I was there," he reminded Salokonos, having already provided an honest account of what had transpired earlier, up to and including his deliberate attempt to escape the palace, which he hadn't bothered trying to conceal for fear of insulting the sovereign's intelligence. "That double-crossing sentry told me to my face that he and others wanted to get rid of me because they saw me as a threat to Vumri's position in the palace."

This time he did choose his words carefully, despite his grumpy disposition. He didn't want to go so far as to imply that the healer already had too much influence over Salokonos, who might bristle at the suggestion that his authority and judgment had been compromised. Better to tread delicately around that nuance, even if diplomacy had never exactly been the doctor's forte.

"Nonsense," Vumri protested. "Sheer hearsay, nothing more."

"I don't know. Makes perfect sense to me." McCoy glowered at the healer. "You really expect us to believe that you had no idea what was being done on your behalf? Or that you wouldn't love to see my 'alien' brains splattered all over the landscape?"

"Your Excellency!" Vumri waxed indignant. "Am I to be slandered by a foreign prisoner who, by his own admission, killed one of your own guards while attempting to escape?"

"A guard who apparently betrayed my trust," Salokonos said.

To McCoy's relief, the *Yovode* seemed more concerned by the plot against McCoy's life than by the doctor's attempted escape. At least for the moment, that was.

"Still, I must ask you, Doctor," the ruler continued, "what proof do you have of the *Lossu*'s involvement in the scheme? Did the sentry name her as the instigator of the plot?"

"Not in so many words," McCoy admitted, "but it stands to reason. Who else benefits from getting rid of me?"

"You flatter yourself, Doctor," Vumri said. "You pose no threat to me, nor offer any true help for the *Yiyova* as far as I can tell."

The princess herself was not present at the conference, preferring to sit by Jemo's bedside as her friend recovered from surgery. It was Avomora who had explained to McCoy that Jemo had shook off the sedative because her training as a bodyguard and food taster had involved deliberately building up a tolerance to ordinary drugs and toxins. Small wonder she'd recovered from the spiked coffee faster than any ordinary humanoid would.

"That remains to be seen," McCoy said.

"In any event," Salokonos said, "we cannot condemn *Lossu*

Vumri simply on the basis of your suspicions, which are themselves based on the claims of a dead miscreant who cannot be
interrogated. If the *Lossu* says she is blameless, we must take her
at her word."

You must maybe, McCoy fumed, *but I sure as blazes don't
have to.*

He was convinced that Vumri was up to her tattooed dome in
the conspiracy, but he had to concede that he couldn't prove it. He
wondered, however, whether Salokonos's decision to give Vumri
the benefit of the doubt was based solely on the lack of hard evidence against her, or was there more to it than that? Was he also
reluctant to take action against the healer because she remained
his daughter's only source of relief from her recurrent agonies?

All the more reason to find a cure for Avo's condition.

"I'm honored by your faith in me." Vumri bowed her head
respectfully. "But what of the Earthman's crimes? His heinous accusations may be mere figments of his imagination, but there is
no question of his own guilt. He defied your will by attempting to
flee the castle without your permission. He killed an Ozalorian."

"In self-defense!" McCoy said. "And after he shot Jemo!"

She sneered at him. "So you say, at least."

"What are you implying?" McCoy said. "That I shot Jemo and
then worked till dawn to save her?" He turned toward Salokonos.
"Examine Guhai's weapon. Chances are, you'll only find his
fingerprints and DNA on it."

Turned out Guhai was actually the sentry's real name after all,
despite what he had led McCoy to believe while pretending to
help him escape. In reality, he hadn't bothered with a fake name
because he'd assumed that McCoy would be dead in a few minutes anyway.

"Our forensic investigators have already determined that the
physical evidence supports your account of what happened on
the tower, even if there is no way of knowing who, if anyone,
the sentry might have been conspiring with." Salokonos looked

solemnly at McCoy. "You say he said he had accomplices, but can you say for certain that he was not working alone?"

"No," McCoy confessed. "I never actually saw or heard anyone else."

In retrospect, there had obviously been no coconspirators waiting for McCoy at the supposed rendezvous point since he was never intended to survive his flight for freedom.

"Guhai talked as though he wasn't alone, but I'll grant he wasn't the most trustworthy of guys."

"He was a liar and a traitor," Salokonos said bluntly. "Yet I am confident, Doctor McCoy, that you are not a murderer."

"I appreciate that, Your Excellency, sincerely." He realized he should be grateful that he wasn't being charged with homicide. "As a doctor, I regret taking any life."

Salokonos nodded. "No doubt Jemo will also corroborate your story once she is well enough to be questioned."

The bodyguard's injuries were severe, but McCoy had every reason to believe that she would fully recover in time, possibly with some nifty new scars to show off. He doubted, however, that her job was all that secure after letting him get past her.

"Regardless," Vumri persisted, "the Earthman still attempted to escape. Will he face no consequences for that perfidy?"

I'll say this for Ozalorians, McCoy thought. *They sure know how to hold a grudge.*

Salokonos waved her righteous ire aside.

"McCoy was merely doing his duty as a Starfleet officer in attempting to return to his ship, unlike Guhai, who betrayed his duty to the throne. I cannot fault the doctor for attempting to escape, even if stronger measures are clearly required to keep him from doing so again."

Uh-oh, McCoy thought. *What does that mean?*

Salokonos stroked his beard as he contemplated the captive doctor. "All of which raises the pressing issue of who is to guard you, in both capacities, now that Jemo can no longer do so."

"I don't suppose the honor system is an option?" McCoy drawled.

"This is no laughing matter, Doctor. New guards must be assigned to you."

McCoy scowled. "With all due respect, Your Excellency, you'll forgive me if I'm reluctant to trust my safety to some palace guards, given the example set by the late, unlamented Guhai."

"I will personally select your guards this time and will vouch for their loyalty and devotion to their duty." His gaze swept over the guards posted around the sanctum before making his selection. "Sergeant Halbo, I place you in charge of Doctor McCoy's security and confinement. Corporal Mitoe, you will report to Halbo in this matter. Am I understood?"

The guards stepped forward. Granite expressions offered little hint of their personalities or dispositions, aside from the fact that they were probably not to be messed with. Everything about them shouted on-duty.

"Absolutely, Your Excellency," Halbo said. "You may rely on us."

"I would not have chosen you otherwise," Salokonos said. "Rest assured, Doctor, these handpicked guards will watch over you as Jemo was meant to do."

McCoy felt obliged to stick up for his former bodyguard, considering. "She did a damn good job of keeping me alive, even after I did my best to shake her."

"True," Salokonos acknowledged, "but do not expect that you will be able to elude my own guards so easily."

You call that easy? McCoy thought, although obviously he was going to think twice before accepting any more unsolicited offers of assistance when it came to an unauthorized exit from the palace. He glumly inspected his rather forbidding new babysitters; he wasn't entirely confident about this arrangement, but supposed it was the best he could expect under the circumstances. He could only hope that Salokonos was indeed a good judge of character where his personal guards were concerned and pray that Vumri hadn't gotten to these two yet. Not for a moment did he think that the ambitious healer had given up on trying to eliminate him. *Remind me to sleep with one eye open.*

Whoever thought he'd end up missing Jemo watching his back?

"Your Excellency," Vumri said, "must we continue with this dubious initiative? Look at the endless turmoil the Earth doctor's presence at the court has already generated. Cannot he at least be confined somewhere far from the palace until, in your wisdom, you choose the best course of action regarding him?"

"The only 'turmoil' seems to be coming from your direction," McCoy said. "It's almost as though you don't want me to find a cure for Avomora."

"I care only for the *Yiyova*'s welfare," she insisted.

McCoy snorted. "I'm sure."

"How goes your work regarding my daughter's affliction?" Salokonos inquired.

"Honestly? It's proving more challenging than I anticipated. I thought I had the answer, but it appears her condition is more complicated and requires further study."

"In short," Vumri said, "you have achieved nothing."

McCoy glared at her. "I wouldn't say that. Medical science doesn't always yield instant results. A certain amount of trial and error is part of the process, so even failures can bring you closer to a solution. I'm not giving up," he promised. "I can tell you that."

"Is that simply your pride speaking, Earthman?" Vumri said. "Perhaps you are merely unable to admit that—" A chime from her belt interrupted her and she retrieved a compact personal communication device from a small pouch. "If you will excuse me, Your Excellency, this appears to be urgent." She consulted the device, then sighed heavily. "I regret to inform you, sire, that the *Yiyova* has taken ill and requires my attention."

"Again?" Salokonos said, visibly chagrined. "So soon?"

"Her affliction is a cruel one, sire, and remains so despite any false hopes to the contrary."

McCoy assumed that last bit was directed at him.

"If I may take my leave, Your Excellency?" she asked.

"Go," he said. "Without delay."

"As ever." She bowed her head respectfully before swiftly exiting the chamber, leaving McCoy alone before the dismayed ruler, who looked understandably distressed by his daughter's latest episode. His shoulders slumped, revealing the anguished father beneath the monarch.

"Is there nothing you can do for her, Doctor?" he asked. "Even with the *Lossu*'s help, Avomora's spells are growing ever more frequent and severe. How do you explain this?"

"I'm not certain," McCoy said. "I wish I could explain, but I'm still trying to figure it out."

All the evidence pointed to a chemical imbalance in her brain, so it remained unclear why correcting that via his compound had not cured her. By rights, her condition should be improving, not deteriorating. And even if his cure was ineffective, why were her episodes coming more and more often? It was possible, he supposed, that she was building up an immunity to whatever Vumri did for her, so that the healings were growing less effective, resulting in shorter periods of recovery and harsher relapses, or could it be that Avo had grown so dependent on Vumri's gifts that . . . ?

A theory suddenly beamed into his brain as though from orbit.

Could that be it? The reason she's getting worse, not better?

Excitement dispelled the fatigue weighing him down.

"Your Excellency, with your permission, I'd like to observe *Lossu* Vumri as she heals your daughter again. It may help me understand what is happening to her."

"Very well," Salokonos said, "if you truly think it will aid you in your quest."

"I do, Your Excellency."

"Then I will not keep you from your work." Salokonos looked to McCoy's newly appointed guards. "Escort the doctor to my daughter's chambers. See that no harm comes to him—and that he goes nowhere on his own."

"Yes, sire," Halbo said. "We will not let him out of our sight."

"Come on, then," McCoy said impatiently, already halfway to the door. "I haven't got all day."

Twenty-Four

Vok

"Good to see you again, Captain," Doctor Ceff said. "Please tell me the commissioner is recovering as quickly as can be expected."

"I'm happy to say she's on the mend," Kirk replied, "and sends her compliments."

Kirk had beamed down to Ceff's campaign headquarters along with Tanaka, Sergeant Myp, and a small complement of security officers from the *Enterprise*. Heightened security measures, instituted in the wake of the assassination attempt, had necessitated the headquarters lowering its shields long enough to allow the landing party to drop in. Given what he had to say, Kirk wasn't counting on their warm welcome staying that way.

"You have no idea how pleased I am to hear that." Ceff came out from behind a cluttered desk littered with campaign paraphernalia. Her warm attitude and hospitality seemed none the worse for the attack at the rally. "I literally owe my life to her, and to you as well, Captain. Indeed, I feel terrible about the fact that I haven't managed to visit your sickbay to express my gratitude to Commissioner Dare in person, although we did speak briefly via viewscreen."

"I'm sure she understands that a candidate's time is not their own," Kirk said, "and was grateful for your call."

"That's all very well and good," Div said indignantly, "but why hasn't Gogg been arrested yet, after being caught on tape ordering the attack on my sister? It's an outrage that he's not behind bars already, let alone still campaigning for president. Ceff was almost killed!"

The campaign manager was among the top staff members taking part in the meeting, which Kirk has asked to keep relatively private. Prup was also on hand, multitasking on her ubiquitous data slate, but closed doors kept the bulk of Ceff's volunteers from listening in, while also insulating Kirk and company from the hubbub and commotion of a campaign in the final days of a heated election. Calendars and to-do lists competed with political posters for wall space.

"That *was* a close call," Kirk agreed. "Why, if you hadn't spotted Lom in time and called out a warning, who knows what could have happened?"

"Luck was with us that day," Div said, humbly enough. "I just happened to glance in the right direction at the right time." He shuddered. "When I think about how close we came to losing Ceff . . ."

"But that didn't happen." She gave her brother a reassuring pat on the back. "We survived to keep on fighting for Vok's future."

"No thanks to General Gogg and his henchmen." Prup uttered Gogg's name with naked disgust. "Div makes a good point. Why isn't Gogg being prosecuted yet? Granted, he's already being vigorously tried in the press, but that's not good enough. When did it become okay to order an attack on your opponent's life?"

Here we go, Kirk thought. "I'm afraid the situation is not as clear-cut as that." He quickly outlined what they had learned regarding Gogg's double, as well as the discovery of said double's body. "A thorough forensic examination confirmed the presence of cyalodin in Huss's remains. He was obviously poisoned by someone trying to cover their tracks with regard to the assassination attempt."

"Oh my." Ceff appeared stunned by the revelations. "I think I need to sit down." She dropped into a folding chair resting by a round conference table. "I had no idea matters had gotten so complicated."

Div remained on his feet. "Why weren't we informed of these developments?"

"I'm informing you now," Kirk said. "And we thought it best to keep the details of our investigation confidential until we had a clearer picture of what kind of conspiracy we were really dealing with."

"Which is?" Ceff asked.

"For starters, we know now that Huss posed as Gogg to trick Lom into attacking you. And Huss's subsequent murder clearly indicates that he was not working alone. Someone apparently put him up to deceiving Lom, then eliminated him afterward."

Prup's brow furrowed. "'Someone,' you say. But who else would want to assassinate Doctor Ceff except Gogg and his people?"

"Are you suggesting," Ceff asked, "that perhaps one of Gogg's supporters was acting on their own accord, without the General's knowledge?"

Kirk shook his head. "I'm thinking the intent was never to actually harm you, Doctor, but to frame General Gogg for the attempt."

Div scoffed. "Not *that* ridiculous conspiracy theory!"

"Maybe not so ridiculous," Tanaka said, stepping forward. "You've surely seen the latest public-opinion polls. These accusations are not helping Gogg. To the contrary, they seem to be reminding a significant percentage of the electorate of just how draconian the old regime could be when it came to suppressing dissent and making its opponents disappear. Your own numbers have seen a measurable bounce since the attack at the rally."

Ceff sat up straight in the chair. "I hope you and the captain are not accusing me or my people of being behind this alleged conspiracy."

"I doubt you volunteered to have a spear hurled at you," Kirk said, "but as for who actually might have staged that incident . . ." He turned his gaze on Div. "Refresh my memory, Mister Div, who was it who arranged for Lom's troupe to perform at the rally? I remember you saying they came highly recommended."

Div tensed up. "I can't immediately recall."

"Well, do you remember who recommended them to you?" Kirk asked.

"Not at the moment," Div said testily. "Do you have any idea how many balls I'm juggling at any given moment, how many moving parts a global political campaign involves? I can't be expected to remember every minor detail."

Kirk turned the heat up. "Even when that detail almost cost your sister her life?"

"Hold on a moment." Div's eyes narrowed; he regarded Kirk warily. "What's happening here? Are you seriously implying that I would risk my own sister just to get a bump in the polls?"

"And thereby ensure her election?" Kirk said. "Why not? You knew there was plenty of security on hand, that you could sound an alarm in time."

"Don't be absurd! The very idea is insane."

Sweat beaded on his brow. He plucked a handkerchief from his pocket and wiped his brow, just as Kirk had anticipated.

"You're prone to perspiration, aren't you, Mister Div?" he observed. "I imagine whoever poisoned Huss must have worked up a sweat that night, lugging his body over to the pantry and cramming it in with the groceries. Probably seemed like a clever idea at the time, using the pantry's built-in stasis field to keep the body 'on ice' as it were, so that it wouldn't be detected before the election. Funny thing about stasis fields, though; they're also pretty good at preserving evidence . . . like the genetic material found in perspiration."

Div swallowed hard. "What exactly are you saying?"

"You must know where this is going," Tanaka said. "Vok Populi has the genome of every eligible voter in its memory banks, so it can confirm their identity on Election Day when they report to their designated polling places. The idea was to guarantee against fraud, but apparently it helps identify assassins too."

Div tugged at his collar. His eyes darted to the nearest exit as though weighing his odds of getting away. Starfleet security officers quietly moved to block any escape routes. Sergeant Myp was all business.

"Well, Mister Div?" Kirk said. "Care to explain how your DNA ended up dripping onto Huss's skin and clothing . . . after you poisoned him? Let me guess, you met up with him after the rally and brought a celebratory bottle of spirits, supposedly to toast the success of your hoax. I'm curious: Did you simply avoid taking a sip yourself, or had you consumed an antidote in advance?"

Div backed away from Kirk, looking more and more like a trapped animal. "I, that is, I . . . there must be some mistake . . ."

"Brother?" Ceff rose from her seat, visibly disturbed. "Is this true?"

He flinched at her words. He averted his face from her in a way that reminded Kirk of the furtive figure Madame Zell had recorded via her optical implant. Ceff approached her sibling, even as he continued to avoid her gaze.

"Please, Div," she said softly. "Look at me. Talk to me. Please don't lie to me."

Kirk watched tensely, his hand on his phaser, just in case Div reacted violently, but instead the man's shoulders sagged in defeat. He lifted his eyes to face Ceff. His voice was ragged.

"I did it for you, Ceff. The polls, the projections, were turning against us. There was still too much lingering support for the old regime and the stability it represented; people were afraid of change, of going too far too fast. Victory was slipping away from us. We needed to do something drastic to turn things around."

"Oh, Div," she said, more in sorrow than anger. "How could you?"

"I swear, there was never any chance that you would be harmed," Div said, pleading for her understanding. "I made sure that Captain Kirk and his security officers were on hand to intervene. Hell, I was ready to tackle Lom myself if the commissioner hadn't dived to your rescue first."

Kirk scowled. Whatever sympathy he felt for the man's distress was mitigated by the memory of Dare taking a spear in the back. Div's manufactured stunt had nearly cost Dare her life. The commissioner's spilled blood was on his hands.

"I don't believe this!" Prup stepped away from Div, physically distancing herself from him. She clutched her data slate to her chest. "What on Vok were you thinking?"

Ceff turned toward her protégé. "Please tell me you weren't in on this too."

"Of course not!" Prup said. "I would never be party to something like this. Our whole movement is based on peace and integrity, not murders and deception. I would *never* betray our cause this way."

Ceff gazed at her mournfully. "I want to believe that."

So do I, Kirk thought. *And that you're truly innocent as well.*

"You can," Div said. "This was all me, no one else. I kept my plans to myself to avoid compromising the campaign." He looked anxiously at Kirk. "You have to believe me, Captain. My sister knew nothing about my scheme, and neither did Prup or any others. Please don't let them be tarred by my crimes. I'll make a full confession, take a psycho-tricorder test, do whatever's necessary to clear my sister's name!"

Kirk's gut told him Div was telling the truth, although the Vokite authorities were surely going to want more confirmation than that.

"I may take you up on that," he said. "One thing still puzzles me, however. How did you convince Huss to take part in your scheme to frame General Gogg? Bribery, blackmail, or did Huss truly believe you were out to assassinate your own sister?"

"Hardly." Div chuckled bleakly. "You think he would have agreed to let that damning tape of him as Gogg be recorded if he actually wanted the General elected? The truth of the matter is that he'd had a change of heart, politically and morally. Running around as Gogg, giving all those belligerent, warmongering speeches, seeing firsthand the anger he was stirring up against both Ozalor and his fellow Vokites . . . Seems his conscience got the better of him. He couldn't face the possibility of being responsible, at least in part, for another interstellar war, so he quietly approached me about switching sides." Div chuckled again. "At first, he simply wanted to come clean about doubling for Gogg, in hopes of embarrassing the General, but he wasn't thinking big enough. That would be a minor scandal at best; it certainly wouldn't be enough to sway the election. I saw an opportunity to do something bigger, more decisive. Something that would turn the whole election around."

"And you took it." Ceff shook her head sadly. "Oh, brother, you always did put image over the issues, and look where it's brought us."

"I'm afraid your plan may backfire on you," Tanaka said. "This news isn't going to help your cause, not once the truth gets out."

"It doesn't have to." Div perked up, as though spying a way out at last. "Let's be honest. None of us want Gogg to be elected. That would be a disaster for the entire sector. We can keep this to ourselves, let the world keep thinking that Gogg wanted my sister dead, and save Vok from making a cataclysmic mistake. And I'm not just saying that to get myself out of trouble. We need to look at the big picture here."

Tanaka glanced around the room, from Kirk to Myp and back again. He shuffled his feet uncomfortably. "I hate to say it, but he's not entirely wrong. Maybe we need to think about what we do next?"

"Nothing wrong with thinking before acting." Kirk couldn't blame Tanaka for wanting to contemplate the consequences of exposing Div. Politics often involved weighing pragmatism versus principle in hopes of achieving the greater good; that was the nature of the beast. Kirk had occasionally kept certain details out of his official logs in the interests of discretion, as when he'd kept his promise to Zefram Cochrane by hiding his continued existence. Kirk understood what was at stake here: revealing the truth about the staged assassination attempt, and Huss's subsequent murder, could well throw the election to General Gogg, increasing the chances of, among other things, a bloody civil war on Braco.

Nevertheless, he shook his head.

"We can consult Commissioner Dare if you wish, but I'm pretty sure I know what she'd say. For better or for worse, we're here to be impartial observers. We start putting our fingers on the scale, trying to tip the election one way or another, then we've compromised our mission beyond recognition."

"But haven't you already interfered," Div argued, "just by sticking your noses in where you didn't belong? You didn't have to play detective!"

"Maybe you shouldn't have gotten a Federation citizen speared in the back?" Tanaka retorted. "Did you really think we were going to just overlook that?"

Div wavered. "I . . . I was just thinking of Vok's future."

"In any event," Myp chimed in, "Captain Kirk conducted his investigation with the full support and cooperation of myself and the rest of our Civic Security agencies. We appreciate his efforts to expose the conspiracy in our midst."

"Thank you, Sergeant." He valued her vote of confidence yet felt obliged to address Div's accusation directly. "To the contrary, Mister Div, our mission was to ensure a fair election. We're not interfering by making certain that the candidates aren't trying to kill each other . . . or by letting the truth be known. The best way we can stay neutral is to put the facts before your people, as accurately as possible, so they can choose for themselves, no matter where those facts point or who they may favor."

"Easy for you to say," Div said sourly. "You're just going to fly away when this election is over. You're not going to have to face the consequences." His face twisted in contempt. "I hope you can live with that, Kirk."

Me too, Kirk thought.

"You're mistaken, brother." Ceff squared her shoulders. "This isn't his decision, or the commissioner's, or anyone else's." Her voice was firm and resolute as though she'd reached a decision. "It's mine."

Twenty-Five

Braco

The grate above the Pit slid back. A metal ladder extended until it reached the floor of the cell. Spock looked up from his cot to see Nurse Chapel descend into the Pit. The ladder contracted after she reached the bottom and the grille slid back into place. F'lun shouted down through the grating.

"You have twenty minutes, tops. Better make the most of them."

Chapel ignored the jailer, turning toward Spock instead. "I'm so sorry, Mister Spock. I wanted to come earlier, but they wouldn't let me."

"No need to apologize." He rose to greet her. "Neither of us are free to come and go as we please at present." He offered her the stool. "Please make yourself comfortable."

He inspected the nurse, whom he had not seen for several hours. Although showing signs of fatigue and worry, she appeared in relatively functional condition despite their captivity. He noted that she was not in uniform, having changed into a faded yellow coverall, no doubt provided by their captors. Troxy, who was nibbling on the remains of Spock's most recent salad, rotated a curious eyestalk toward the new arrival. Spock had placed the tray with the leftovers on the floor earlier.

"How go your labors in the infirmary?" he asked.

"Keeping me busy." She sat down on the stool. "Nothing too serious. Mostly minor injuries: cuts, sprains, a dislocated shoulder, plus some headaches, upset stomachs, and such, much of them stress related. Delivered a baby late last night, which is probably the highlight of my stint here. Took me a while to earn enough brownie points before V'sta would let me visit you." She eyed him with concern. "How are *you* doing, Mister Spock?"

"I have not been mistreated," he assured her. "The United Bracon Front are humane in their handling of prisoners."

"I'm very glad to hear that," she said. "I've been worried."

"I appreciate your concern, Nurse, as well as you calling on me."

Chapel glanced up at the grate overhead. She lowered her voice. "How long do you think they'll keep holding us?"

"That remains to be seen."

"But it doesn't make any sense," she protested, venting her frustration. "The Bracon authorities have already declared that they're not going to negotiate for our release, so what is the point of keeping us?"

Spock refrained from pointing out that Chapel had already demonstrated her value through her services in the infirmary since he could hardly expect her to abstain from treating patients in need for strategic reasons. That would be against both her character and her professional ethics.

"Perhaps," he speculated, "they hope that the Federation can eventually exert enough pressure on the Bracon government to achieve a face-saving compromise of some variety, although I am uncertain how probable that scenario is. In any event, the UBF have committed themselves to this action. To release us now, without extracting any concessions, would undermine any future negotiations."

"I can't argue with your logic, Mister Spock, unfortunately," she said, sighing. "I suppose we should be thankful they're not threatening our lives yet . . . or sending pieces of us back to the capital, if you'll pardon the grisly image."

"Vulcans have strong stomachs," he replied. "We are not easily nauseated by hypothetical dismemberment."

"I almost envy you," she said. "I could use a little of that unflappable Vulcan stoicism right now."

"You appear to be bearing up in a most exemplary manner, Nurse Chapel."

"Thank you, Mister Spock. That means a lot coming from you."

He glanced upward. F'lun was not immediately visible, but Spock could hear the jailer pacing impatiently above them, along with at least one other confederate. Their presence inhibited his conversation with Chapel; because he and the nurse could not count on not being overheard, they were unable to freely discuss the possibility of being rescued by their fellow Starfleet personnel, forcing Spock to approach the topic obliquely.

"You are out of uniform, Miss Chapel."

"It's being cleaned," she said. "Nursing can get messy, you know."

"And your medkit?" he asked casually, feigning mere curiosity. "You do not appear to have it on your person."

The significance of his question was surely not lost on her. As long as the hidden transponder remained undetected, the greater the odds that their comrades would be able to locate them, even deep beneath the glassy sea.

"My minder is holding it for me." She pointed upward. "Think they're afraid I'll slip you a laser scalpel or something."

Spock was reassured to hear that the concealed transponder was still in their proximity.

"A pity." He stroked his chin, which was rather bristlier than he preferred. "I could use a shave."

Chapel smiled. "You might look good with a beard."

"I experimented with one in my youth," he confessed. "It was not universally well received."

"Now you've got me curious," she joked. "Seriously, though, I feel terrible about you being locked up in solitary confinement all this time."

"Unlike humans, I do not fear solitude," he said. "Nor, for that matter, am I truly alone."

He indicated Troxy, who scuttled over to be petted.

"I see," Chapel said. "Good to see your new friend is keeping you company."

An opportunity presented itself to Spock.

"Perhaps we can prevail upon our captors to let me borrow your medical scanner for a few moments. I have a theory about these creatures that I am eager to verify."

Chapel looked intrigued. "What sort of theory?"

Before he could explain, a high-pitched whine came from above, followed almost immediately by the sound of weapons fire. A pair of bodies thumped loudly onto the paved concrete floor above. Troxy issued a puzzled chirp. Chapel looked to Spock in excitement.

"Mister Spock! Do you think—?"

Her hopes were quickly confirmed by the appearance of Lieutenant Levine, peering down through the grate. "Spock, Christine, good to see you!"

"You have no idea." Chapel sprang off the stool. "Talk about a sight for sore eyes."

"It is indeed gratifying to be found, Lieutenant," Spock said. "I believe you will find an extendable ladder near you."

"Sit tight," Levine said. "We'll get you right out of there."

A crimson phaser beam dissolved the metal grate. Moments later, the ladder expanded to reach the bottom of the Pit. Spock chivalrously gestured at the ladder.

"After you, Nurse."

"Don't mind if I do."

She scrambled nimbly up the ladder. He followed her up to the floor above the Pit, where they found a four-person rescue team consisting of Lieutenants Levine, Godwin, Nguyen, and Yoder. F'lun and his associate lay stunned upon the floor. Nguyen and Yoder had already staked out defensive positions at the only entrance to the small grotto, where a solitary tunnel connected the jail to the rest of the cave system. Not wanting to be left behind, Troxy hurried up the ladder after Spock, eliciting a bemused look from Godwin.

"What or who is that?" she asked.

"A harmless local life-form of notable scientific interest," Spock stated. "You tracked the transponder in the medkit, I assume?"

"Got it in one, Mister Spock." Levine provided a fresh communicator and phaser to Spock, while Godwin returned the medkit to Chapel. "Where is Doctor McCoy?"

"The UBF doesn't have him," Chapel said. "They never did."

"Damn," Godwin said. "That's a letdown."

"Succinctly put," Spock agreed.

"No point in sticking around, then," Levine said. "The sooner we beam out, the better." He flipped open his communicator. "Rescue team to Bureau HQ. Six to beam—"

A piercing siren interrupted him. A steel door slammed into place, sealing the entrance. Troxy vocalized loudly in triplicate.

"I believe a rapid extraction is in order," Spock said.

"I can't get through!" Levine said. Static emanated from his communicator. "They're jamming us!"

The shrill alarm pained Spock's ears, so it came as no small relief when the siren was cut abruptly, replaced by the amplified voice of Hynn V'sta:

"Having troubles, gentlemen, ladies?"

Spock gathered they were being monitored. "I take it you are responsible?"

"Naturally," she replied over a concealed public-address system. *"Did you truly think we wouldn't detect your people beaming in . . . or phasers discharging in a secure area? We may have stuck you in a convenient hole for economy's sake, but that doesn't mean we're actually in the Stone Age or that we aren't prepared for any eventuality, up to and including an attempted jailbreak. We've raised the base's deflector screens. Nobody is beaming in or out anytime soon."*

"Great," Godwin said sarcastically. "We're screwed."

"Looks like we're going to have to fight our way out," Levine said. "Yoder, Nguyen, open fire on that door. Phasers on full."

"*Don't waste your batteries,*" V'sta said. "*You're not going to be upright long enough to disintegrate that barrier.*"

Thick white fumes jetted into the sealed cavern through cracks in the ceiling. Spock targeted the vents with his newly acquired phaser, trying to disable them, but the gas spread too fast and too potently, filling the grotto. Troxy succumbed to the fumes first, collapsing onto the floor, while the bipeds struggled to stay on their feet, coughing and covering their mouths with their hands in a doomed attempt to avoid inhaling the gas, which Spock immediately identified as a highly concentrated variant of anesthezine. Levine tottered unsteadily near the lip of the Pit and Spock grabbed his arm to keep the young security officer from toppling over the edge.

"Keep clear of the Pit," Spock shouted over the hissing of the jets. "Don't fall in."

The effort forced him to inhale even more of the gas. Dizziness assailed him and his legs grew more unreliable. His inner eyelids drooped as he fought a losing battle to remain conscious. One by one, the rescue team passed out. Through the choking white fog, Spock registered them falling to the ground until he was the last person standing. He turned the full force of his phaser on the door, hoping to bore a hole in it through which the fumes could escape, but the solid steel barrier was just as dense as one would logically expect a prison gate to be. He attempted to concentrate the beam on one small spot even as his arm grew subjectively heavier and heavier, making it ever more difficult to maintain his aim. The beam drifted and wavered despite his best efforts. His thoughts grew muddy, his vision blurrier.

"*I admire your persistence, Mister Spock,*" V'sta's voice taunted him, "*although I question your logic in not surrendering to the inevitable.*"

"You need not add insult to injury," Spock replied, coughing as he did so. "My compliments on your prison facilities, however.

They are clearly more sophisticated—and effective—than they first appear."

"*Why, thank you,*" she replied. "*You're too kind.*"

He kept on firing at the door for as long as he could, yet calculated that he was losing his race with time. A tiny spot on the door began to glow red.

Just as his world turned black.

Twenty-Six

Vok

The presidential debate, scheduled long in advance, took place in the very amphitheater where the staged assassination attempt had taken place, amplifying the charged atmosphere onstage and in the audience. Partisans on both sides packed the tiered seats of the ancient crater, each in their own sections, while trading angry glares and taunts with each other. Silver epaulets identified Gogg's base, while Ceff's followers had taken to wearing flowing, brightly colored scarves in emulation of their idol. What few undecideds were present looked both outnumbered and uncomfortable.

I can sympathize, Kirk thought. *I'm feeling rather caught in the middle myself.*

For better or for worse, he had been drafted to serve as the moderator of the debate after the original moderator, a respected Vokite jurist, had dropped out after receiving death threats in the wake of the assassination attempt and subsequent revelations thereof. Kirk had been reluctant to assume such a prominent role in the proceedings, which struck him as going rather beyond the bounds of simply observing the election, but as apparently he was one of the few individuals whom both sides regarded as sufficiently "neutral" and could agree on, he had grudgingly consented to emcee the event. He hoped that this would entail nothing more than occasionally playing referee or timekeeper if one or the other candidate overstepped the established rules of the debate. Certainly, he had no intention of trying to steal the spotlight from either Ceff or Gogg.

I'm just here to keep the proceedings on track.

With that in mind, Kirk sat at a low table at the rear of the stage, behind the candidates, which also had the advantage of offering him a good view of the audience. In light of recent events and controversies, security was tighter than at a Federation summit, with an excess amount of both *Enterprise* personnel and Vokite peace officers on hand to maintain order and protect the polarized audience from itself. Needless to say, no spear-swallowers or plasma-breathers were performing tonight, nor any other entertainment for that matter. This crowd didn't need to be warmed up; if anything, they were already on the verge of boiling over.

Tonight was all about the candidates.

Appropriately, Ceff and Gogg entered from opposite sides of the stage to take their places behind twin podiums. A concert-sized viewscreen, at least twenty meters high, magnified their images and voices for the folks in the cheap seats, as well as for Vokites watching the live transmission all across the globe. Cheers and jeers greeted the candidates, who were separated by a few meters of stage, not to mention vast ideological differences. Ceff attempted to bridge that gap by approaching Gogg, her hand extended, but received only an icy glare from the General, who was apparently not quite over being framed for conspiracy to commit murder by his opponent's brother.

No surprise there, Kirk thought. *Gogg has reason to be angry.*

Her sportsmanlike overture rebuffed, Ceff retreated to her podium on Kirk's right. Applause and catcalls persisted, forcing Kirk to call for silence. A public-address system amplified his voice so that it rang out over the crater.

"Quiet, everyone, please. We're all here to hear the candidates speak. Let's give them the opportunity to do so."

The hubbub died down, much to the relief of Kirk, who kept his remarks and introductions brief in the interest of getting the debate underway.

"Both candidates will begin by making their opening statements," he said. "As determined by a random drawing, Doctor Ceff will go first."

"Thank you, Captain Kirk."

She waited for another wave of cheers and hisses to subside. This was her first public appearance or statement since the news of Div's crimes had spread across the planet. Kirk had some knowledge of how she intended to address the scandal, so he waited expectantly for the fireworks to come.

"Brothers, sisters, elders, children, you have all heard the troubling reports and rumors concerning a scandal at the heart of my campaign. It is my sad duty to inform you that much of what you have heard is true. My own brother, Div, whom I still love dearly, staged the shocking attempt on my life that took place on this very stage only days ago. He also conspired to falsely blame General Gogg for the attack and even committed murder to cover up his crimes."

The stark admission provoked an uproar in the audience. People leaped to their feet, shouting furiously. Gogg's supporters appeared both outraged and vindicated, while Ceff's fans reacted with visible dismay. Many of them, Kirk suspected, had been hoping that the charges against Div were false and that Ceff would vigorously dispute them. That she had just done the opposite had thrown them for a loop.

"You hear!" Gogg thundered from his podium. He cast an accusing finger at Ceff. "She admits that I have been wrongly slandered . . . and by her own kin no less!"

"General," Kirk said firmly. "Please wait your turn. You will have your opportunity to speak, I assure you, but let's allow Doctor Ceff to finish her remarks without interruption."

Gogg scowled, but he fell silent long enough for Ceff to continue.

"That my brother acted out of a tragic excess of loyalty to me and my campaign does not excuse his crimes. Know that he has made a full confession to the proper authorities and will be prosecuted to the full extent of the law, regardless of the outcome of the election. Justice *will* be served."

"And what of the damage to my name and honor?" Gogg challenged her. "Where is the justice there?"

Kirk chose to overlook the interruption so that Ceff could respond directly.

"Let me take this opportunity, General, to extend my sincere apologies for my brother's efforts to implicate you in a crime you played no part in."

"And you think a mere apology is enough?" he said, unmoved.

Ceff shook her head. "No, I realize it is far from sufficient. Although I promise you and all of Vok that I had no knowledge of my brother's crimes, I recognize that his heinous acts have irrevocably damaged the credibility of my campaign and my candidacy, so that while I may hope for your collective trust in my innocence, I cannot realistically expect it. Our world's next leader must be above suspicion." She took a deep breath. "It is for that reason that I am formally withdrawing from the race."

There it is, Kirk thought.

As he'd expected, the announcement triggered an explosive reaction among the audience. Gogg's side erupted in jubilation, whooping in victory, while Ceff's defenders looked as though they had just been stunned by a wide-angle phaser burst. Many of the latter sobbed openly, tears streaming down their faces, to the delight of the crowing Gogg partisans. The General himself merely nodded in satisfaction, even as his aide, Sozz, rushed from the wings to congratulate him.

"Wait!" Ceff shouted over the tumult. She raised her hands to quiet the crowd. "Let me make one thing clear: although I am stepping down as a candidate, we are *not* surrendering the election to General Gogg. The future of our planet is too important for that. It is for that reason that I urge you to vote instead for my esteemed and abundantly qualified friend and colleague, the remarkable Ms. Prup!"

She beckoned to her protégée, who strode out onto the stage. Kirk admired Prup's poise under the circumstances. If the passionate young activist was at all nervous about stepping into the spotlight, she didn't show it.

"Objection!" Gogg boomed, his deep voice reverberating above the startled reactions of the crowd, many of whom were still on their feet. He stared contemptuously at Ceff. "Your seditious campaign has been proven corrupt and illegitimate. You and your fellow radicals have relinquished any right to vie for the leadership of our precious world. Do not think you can thrust your handpicked puppet upon us while you pretend to step aside. We see through this fraud just as we saw through your libelous plot to defame me, just as we saw through your brazen attempt to deceive the people!"

Prup took Ceff's place at the podium as the prior candidate retreated toward the wings, ceding the floor to her successor.

"I am no puppet, General, and our people deserve a choice, despite everything. I am ready and willing to debate you before our world."

"Save your breath," Gogg said. "I shall not legitimize this fraud by taking part in a debate with a puppet candidate backed by a criminal conspiracy." He turned away from Prup to address the audience instead. "I call upon all true Vokites, to all who still believe in honor and courage and patriotism, to stand up against this fraud and those who would perpetuate it. Never forget how this supposedly 'fair' election was almost stolen by liars and murderers." He shook his fist in the air. "We must fight back against those who will clearly stop at nothing to seize control of our glorious world . . . and all who stand with them!"

Angry shouts and raised fists answered Gogg's call to arms. Kirk feared the General was coming dangerously close to inciting violence. He felt obliged to speak up via the public-address system.

"Excuse me, General. At the risk of interrupting, I want to give you a chance to clarify your remarks. I assume you are merely exhorting your fellow citizens to 'fight' back at the polls, correct?"

"You may assume whatever you wish, Captain," the General said, seemingly undaunted by Kirk's attempt to dial down his inflammatory rhetoric. "I am grateful for your role in clearing my name, but do not presume to put words in my mouth." He stepped away from the podium, even as his imposing figure loomed upon the giant viewscreen behind him. "We are done with this farce. I will not be party to a hoax."

He started to march off the stage.

"General!" Kirk rose from the moderator's chair. "Don't do this. There is still an election before us."

"That's right!" Prup called out. "Please, General, Vok deserves to hear from both of us!"

Gogg paused only long enough to fire off a closing shot. "I have said my piece . . . and have nothing more to say to Ceff's puppet."

He stormed off the stage, vanishing into the wings. Kirk considered pursuing him, but he could tell that Gogg was in no mood to reconsider. Kirk contemplated the audience, wondering whether he should tell them to go home, but this proved unnecessary. His heart sank as Gogg's supporters followed the General's example by heading for the exits *en masse*. Within minutes, a good half of the audience had cleared out, leaving Ceff's dispirited followers behind. Prup stood stiffly at her podium without an opponent to debate. She shared a worried look with Kirk, who switched off his mic.

"Well, that could have gone better," he murmured.

Twenty-Seven

Braco

"I want answers and I want them now."

In the wake of the failed rescue mission, Spock and the others, now including the four security officers, had been disarmed and brought before V'sta in her elevated command center overlooking the larger grotto below. They were lined up on the mezzanine, under heavy guard by F'lun and other scowling members of the United Bracon Front. Spock still felt slightly groggy from being gassed, but his head was clearing. He noted that a few of his human comrades were still blinking and massaging their brows and temples, as though suffering from headaches. V'sta did not appear particularly sympathetic.

"That is quite understandable," Spock said.

A full evacuation was already in progress now that the underground base's location had obviously been compromised. From his vantage point upon the ledge, Spock witnessed scores of Bracons dashing about, packing up what equipment they could and destroying the rest to keep it from falling into the hands of the Tranquility Bureau. Technicians hastily downloaded data from computer terminals before blasting the hardware with black-market phasers and disruptors. The array of monitors in the nerve center displayed equally urgent activities throughout the subterranean complex as the base's occupants fled through a variety of secret tunnels and escape routes. Despite its haste, Spock was impressed by the efficiency and organization of the evacuation, which implied much prior planning and drilling. The UBF was clearly prepared to pull out of the caverns expeditiously if the need arose.

"How did you find us?" V'sta demanded. "How much does the Bureau know? Did you share your intel with them or not?"

Excellent questions, Spock thought, *which we would be foolish to answer.*

"Why don't you just let us go?" Chapel said. "There's no need to risk anyone getting hurt or killed. As long as you're holding us prisoner, you're always going to be a target."

"Like we weren't already," V'sta snapped. She stepped up to Levine. "Again, how did you find us?"

Spock refrained from glancing at Chapel's medkit, which was now in the hands of a UBF soldier standing nearby. It was imperative that they not divulge the existence of the hidden transponder, particularly if they were on the verge of being relocated. It might be necessary for Starfleet to track the transponder's signal again.

"Well?" V'sta shoved the muzzle of a disruptor up against the underside of Levine's chin. "I asked you a question. How did you locate us?"

Levine clamped his jaws shut, refusing to cooperate.

"Perhaps," Spock suggested, "your sensors locked onto my unique copper-based blood?"

"Copper blood?" V'sta pivoted away from Levine, lowering her weapon.

"It is a matter of common knowledge that Vulcan blood is copper-based, as opposed to iron-based like many other humanoid species, including your own. Given that I am quite possibly the only Vulcan on Braco at present, it would not be impossible for a skilled operator to use Starfleet-quality sensors to isolate my life-signs from the rest of the general population."

In fact, he was severely minimizing the technical challenges; to zero in on the blood chemistry of a single individual amidst a population of billions was beyond the capability of even a starship's sensors. It was necessary, however, to provide V'sta with an alternative explanation to divert her from the correct one.

She eyed him skeptically.

"How do I know you're not making this up?"

"Vulcans do not lie," he lied. "And if you have any doubts regarding the particulars of Vulcan biology, this data is easily accessible." He glanced at Troxy, who was currently recuperating from the knockout gas atop a nearby computer console; the groggy mascot had been carted from the Pit chamber by a worried UBF member. Spock discerned a convenient opportunity to change the subject. "Meanwhile, with regard to copper-based blood, I have reason to believe—"

A sudden tremor shook the base. Dust and bits of limestone rained from the ceiling. Startled people gasped and cried out in alarm. The overhead lights flickered worryingly. Along with everyone else, Spock struggled to keep his balance. F'lun staggered, bumping into a computer console. V'sta grabbed her planning table to steady herself, even as muted explosions boomed from somewhere far above. Roused from its stupor, Troxy hooted, squealed, and squawked, leaping from its perch and scurrying away.

"Report!" V'sta barked.

"We're under attack!" a technician shouted from a console. "Fusion missiles bombarding us from the air!"

V'sta's face hardened, her expression reminding Spock of Captain Kirk's tense resolve whenever the Enterprise came under fire. "Shields?"

"Holding," the man said, "but not for long, not under this kind of punishment. They're pummeling us, trying to overpower our screens through sheer force and attrition." He gulped. "Once the deflectors start breaking down, you can bet they'll be beaming in troopers."

"Keep them up as long as we can," V'sta ordered. "We have to finish getting our people out of here."

More detonations rocked the caverns, sending people tumbling to the floor. Frightened men and women dove for cover as stalactites broke loose from the ceiling, crashing down onto the floor below. The monitor array revealed similar scenes of turbulence and destruction throughout the base. The lights went out entirely, throwing the nerve center into darkness, until a battery of emergency lights kicked in. Wailing sirens echoed through the tunnels. Fleeing UBF members helped injured confederates keep moving. Spock glimpsed a handful of adolescents and small children mixed among the evacuees; he recalled the infant Chapel had delivered not too long ago.

"Wibb's going too far here," Levine said, aghast. "This isn't a police raid; this is a major military assault."

"No wonder he caved so easily when we insisted on handling the rescue op ourselves," Godwin said. "He had bigger plans . . . and different priorities."

"You think?" V'sta said sarcastically. "How naïve are you Starfleet types? They want to crush us utterly, even if it means sacrificing you lot." She wheeled angrily on Levine. "You led them here! You brought this on us!"

"To the contrary," Spock said, "you brought this on yourselves by taking us hostage in the first place." He held up his hand to forestall any indignant rebuttal on V'sta's part. "Nevertheless, it is apparent that the situation is escalating rapidly. Perhaps if I am allowed to communicate with Chief Inspector Wibb, I can persuade him to stand down before we accrue significant casualties?"

The beleaguered technician looked anxiously at V'sta. "Our screens are crumbling, Hynn. We're running out of options."

"Fine." She thrust a confiscated Starfleet communicator at Spock. "Knock yourself out, for all the good it will do." She nodded at the tech. "Unjam their frequencies, but keep the screens up so they can't beam out."

"You got it." The tech flicked a switch. "Frequencies unjammed."

Spock flipped open the communicator and attempted to contact Chief Inspector Wibb. "This is Commander Spock of the *U.S.S. Enterprise*, hailing the Bracon Tranquility Bureau."

"You have reached the Bureau," an unfamiliar voice responded. *"This is Assistant Deputy R'Far speaking. How may I assist you?"*

"There is little time to explain," Spock said. "I need to speak to Chief Inspector Wibb at once."

"I'm sorry, sir, but the chief inspector is occupied at the moment, overseeing a major offensive against a terrorist stronghold."

"I am quite aware of that, Deputy, as I and several other hostages are currently in the middle of the bombardment. You need to stand down so we can resolve this situation without serious loss of life, on either our part or that of those you seek to apprehend. We are prepared to seek a more peaceful resolution to this crisis."

"I'm sorry, Commander Spock, but I'm afraid you have no authority in these matters. You are advised to seek whatever shelter you can find and await rescue by our strike forces."

"Provided we survive the attack," Spock said, "which is hardly guaranteed."

"The Bureau is doing what is necessary. Please remain on hold while I notify my superiors of your status."

Bracon folk music emanated from the communicator.

"No luck, Mister Spock?" V'sta asked sardonically. "I could have told you that—"

A massive explosion, the most tremendous yet, shook the command center, throwing people across the wide stone ledge. The impact hurled V'sta over a railing and she plummeted to the floor of the grotto, more than five and a half meters below. Shouts and explosions all but drowned out the sound of her body hitting the cement floor.

"Hynn!" F'lun shouted.

Falling debris pelted Spock and the others as he scrambled to his feet and staggered over to the rail, with Chapel already several paces ahead of him. Peering over the edge, they saw V'sta sprawled on the lower level, amidst a scene of increasing chaos and confusion. She writhed in pain, the movements indicating that she had survived the fall, although the full extent of her injuries could not be determined from the quaking mezzanine.

Chapel took immediate action. "Give me that!" she said, snatching her medkit out of the hands of an unresistant UBF guard and racing for the ramp down to the lower level. "Out of my way! Medical emergency!"

Spock sprinted after her, weaving through the tumult. They quickly reached V'sta's side, where Chapel examined the injured woman, who appeared to be barely conscious. A handheld scanner hummed as Chapel inspected the visual readouts on her medical tricorder. Her intent expression indicated both concentration and concern.

"How is she, Nurse?" Spock asked.

"Not good, Mister Spock. I'm registering a hairline skull fracture." A hypospray hissed and she placed a blinking osteostasis unit on V'sta's brow to reinforce the skull's structural integrity for the time being. "I'm doing what I can to stabilize her, but she needs care, preferably not in the middle of a target range."

The injection revived V'sta to a degree. Her eyelids fluttered before opening entirely. She looked about groggily, then tried to sit up. Chapel gently restrained her.

"Please, you need to stay still. You had a bad fall."

"But . . . the attack . . . I need to handle this . . ."

"What you need," Chapel said firmly, "is to lie back and let me treat you." She looked meaningfully at Spock, who was fully prepared to render V'sta unconscious again if the patient failed to cooperate. "You're no good to anyone unless you survive your injuries."

V'sta tried to get up anyway, only to swoon and clutch her head. "You may have a point, Nurse."

By now, a mixed crowd of Starfleet and UBF personnel surrounded Chapel and V'sta even as the assault on the base continued. Explosions and aftershocks inflicted more damage on the grotto. Sputtering lights created a strobe effect. Swirling clouds of dust and smoke further impaired visibility. Flames burst from damaged machinery and broken conduits. Pounding footsteps reverberated through the caverns as the UBF ran for safety. Random trivets scurried for cover as well.

It occurred to Spock that the turmoil provided an excellent opportunity to elude their captors. Many of their guards had already abandoned their posts or were occupied dealing with the immediate effects of attacks—putting out fires, clearing debris, herding their confederates, and other vital tasks—while F'lun and a few others were distracted by V'sta's accident.

We may never get a better chance to make our escape, Spock thought.

Levine apparently reached the same conclusion. He drew a phaser, which he must have surreptitiously obtained during the confusion, and snatched F'lun's weapon from the jailer's holster while the other man was focused on his injured leader. F'lun spun around in surprise.

"Hey there! Don't you even think of—"

"Quiet." Levine brandished the phaser. He lobbed the extra weapon over to Godwin, who caught it easily. "We're getting out of here . . . on our terms. Anyone have a problem with that?"

"I do, Lieutenant," Chapel said. "This woman needs my help. You can do what you have to, but I'm not going to abandon her."

Levine looked to Spock for guidance. "Mister Spock?"

Spock contemplated the nurse and her patient. He could safely predict how McCoy would react in this instance, and he doubted that Nurse Chapel would be any easier to dissuade.

"Our mission to Braco began in response to a medical emergency, albeit a fictitious one," he stated. "Now that we are faced with a genuine medical emergency, I am inclined to defer to Nurse Chapel's judgment."

"Your call, Mister Spock," Levine said. "Just the same, I'm not surrendering my weapon again."

"Nor do I expect you to," Spock said. "I fully expect you and your fellow security officers to see to our safety for the duration of this crisis."

Levine nodded. "We have your backs, sir."

Despite some grumbling, F'lun and the remaining UBF members did not seem overly eager to clash with the former hostages. Spock recalled the venerable Klingon adage about not fighting in a burning house; that would certainly apply in this case. Shrugging off the loss of his weapon, F'lun looked anxiously at Chapel.

"Can you help her, miss?"

"I'll do my best," Chapel said, "but we need to get somewhere safe, where I can treat her without bombs dropping on our heads."

"Maybe it would be better to surrender to the troopers?" Godwin suggested. "Let them beam in and take her into custody? At least she could get properly treated."

"Not a chance," F'lun snarled. "I wouldn't trust those Bureau bastards to remove a splinter from my big toe."

"Just an idea," Godwin said. "This isn't exactly sickbay, you know."

Concussive blasts brought more powdered limestone and calcite onto their heads, punctuating her observations. Ohop, the technician Chapel had treated earlier, consulted a data slate. "Our screens are shredding, especially around the fringes. I'm getting reports of Bureau strike teams beaming into the upper levels. They're making their way toward us. They'll be here in no time." He looked about nervously, as though he expected troopers in body armor to come bursting into the central grotto at any moment. "We need to get her out of here, pronto."

"I . . . I know a place," V'sta said, stirring. She pointed through the smoke and dust. "That way!"

"What place?" F'lun was visibly puzzled. "What are you talking about?"

"Top secret," she managed. "Need to know . . ." She tried to rise. "Help me up."

Chapel nodded at Spock, who bent down and effortlessly lifted the injured woman from the floor, striving to avoid any jarring motions. His Vulcan strength more than sufficient to the task, he cradled her in his arms as she guided him and the others to what seemed to be an unremarkable alcove just off the main grotto. A flowstone curtain at the rear of the alcove appeared to be a dead end.

"Authorization V'sta tetra-mono-icosa," V'sta said to the wall. "Let us in."

"Authorization recognized," an electronic voice answered. *"Entry granted."*

The dead end proved to be a camouflaged door, which opened to reveal a cylindrical compartment that, on first impression, struck Spock as looking rather less ramshackle than the rest of the underground compound. Gleaming enamel walls seemed better suited to a modern starship than a refurbished cavern. Unusual hieroglyphics, emblazoned on panels, bore little resemblance to modern Bracon script. Although Spock was hardly well versed in the topic, he believed the markings corresponded to an ancient Bracon language dating back to an earlier civilization that had thrived before the cataclysmic war millennia ago. Was this chamber also a vestige of that bygone era?

"Squeeze in, everyone," V'sta said. "Hurry."

Spock curbed his curiosity due to the urgency of the situation; ideally, there would be time enough to inquire as to the provenance of the compartment after the party saw to their immediate safety. He carried V'sta into the chamber, where the rest of their party, including both Starfleet personnel and a few UBF soldiers as well, quickly joined them. It was indeed a tight squeeze, but the space managed to contain them all. The door was starting to slide shut again when an urgent chorus of hoots and squawks assailed his ears. Spock spied Troxy sprinting toward the closing doorway, its triple legs pistoning.

"Lieutenant," he addressed Godwin, "kindly hold the door."

She gave him a bemused look, but raised no objection. "If you say so, Mister Spock."

His own hands were occupied, but Godwin stuck out her arm to keep the door from closing until the frantic trivet darted into the compartment with them, finding room for itself between people's ankles. Godwin withdrew her hand and the door slid shut completely.

"Down," V'sta ordered.

"Acknowledged," the chamber responded. *"Descending."*

The compartment proved to be an elevator or turbolift of some variety. Spock experienced only a minor lurch as it descended smoothly for 5.38 minutes. With no landmarks to chart their progress by, Spock could not reliably calculate their velocity, but the length of their descent suggested that their destination was located far below the cavern they had just departed. He hoped that V'sta was correct in judging that they would find sanctuary at this greater depth—and that there would soon be an opportunity to satisfy his curiosity.

"Descent complete," the compartment announced. *"You may exit the lift."*

The door retracted, accompanied by an electronic chime, and they emerged into what appeared to be a highly advanced bunker or command center that, like the lift, struck Spock as both sophisticated and well preserved. Lights came on automatically, while technology hummed in the background. Compared to the smoke-filled chaos they had just fled, the environmental conditions were clear and comfortable. Levine and his security team glanced around warily, appropriately leery of a trap or ambush, but the location appeared to be unoccupied.

"Fascinating," Spock said. "What is this place?"

"A forgotten bunker that survived the war," V'sta explained, still resting in Spock's arms. "Thousands of years old, or so they tell me . . ."

Her voice faltered. She grimaced in pain.

"Is there someplace we can put you?" Chapel asked, appropriately focused on more practical questions.

"Over there." V'sta waved weakly toward an adjacent chamber. Her eyelids sagged as though she was on the verge of losing consciousness again. She moaned softly. "Is it just me or is it getting dark in here?"

"There is no evident loss in illumination," Spock said. "You need rest and care."

"I was afraid of that," she whispered. "Crap."

Following her directions, they proceeded into the indicated room. Overhead lights switched on, revealing a modest infirmary perhaps a quarter of the size of the *Enterprise*'s sickbay. Cabinets and counters lined the walls. Handwritten labels, in modern Bracon, had been taped over the original labels, which were presumably printed in a far older tongue. Modern medical supplies were mixed with exotic equipment of undetermined purpose. Spock gently laid V'sta down on what appeared to be a biobed of sorts; a display screen built into the headboard failed to activate.

"This will do." Chapel nodded in approval. "I don't know what some of this gear is for, but at least this place is clean and quiet, compared to upstairs."

Spock noted that no tremors or loud explosions disturbed the age-old bunker. The relative silence provided further evidence that they were currently hidden deep beneath the surface of the planet.

"Do you think we're safe here?" Levine asked.

"Given that this bunker survived a war that destroyed entire civilizations, it is probable that it will endure the Bureau's assault as well," Spock replied.

"I like your logic, Mister Spock," Godwin said.

"As well you should." He turned to Chapel. "How may we assist you, Nurse?"

"I need one security officer with medic training," she said.

"Then I need the rest of you to clear out and let me work on my patient." She opened her medkit and laid it out on a counter, pausing only to catch her breath and wipe her brow. "I'll be honest, though. I really wish Doctor McCoy was holed up here with us."

"As do I, Nurse," Spock said. "As do I."

Twenty-Eight

Braco

The mosaic had survived the ages surprisingly well. Only a few random tiles had flaked off the artwork, which adorned one wall of a common room in the ancient bunker deep beneath the Sea of Glass. The mosaic depicted a collection of hardy Bracon pioneers working the fields while playful trivets capered around the edges of the scene. Spock scanned the art with his tricorder, recording it for posterity, as he had the varied hieroglyphics and equipment throughout the site. Given the age and historical value of the bunker, he would be remiss not to take advantage of the opportunity.

Hours had passed since he and his companions had escaped the assault on the UBF's caverns. While V'sta recovered from her injuries, and Nurse Chapel attended to her patient, Spock had made good use of the time, exploring and analyzing the well-preserved bunker, which promised considerable insight into Braco's pre-apocalyptic past. Many questions demanded further study, but Spock judged that he had made significant progress already, particularly when it came to translating key portions of the arcane hieroglyphics. The remainder of the refugees, both Starfleet and the UBF, were scattered throughout the bunker, occupying themselves as best they could. The Starfleet security officers kept watch, to ensure that the *Enterprise* crew remained safe and in control of the situation. So far there had been no serious conflict between the two factions sheltering in the bunker, yet Lieutenant Levine was wisely not taking any chances. Spock appreciated his assiduousness; the Vulcan had no desire to be taken hostage again.

Troxy tagged along after him, its solitary eye currently fixed on the stylized representations of its ancestors. Spock wondered if the mosaic was evidence that the early Bracons were well acquainted with trivets before the cataclysm drove the tri-legged creatures underground, or if the long-dead artist or artists had merely been inspired by the presence of the trivets in the caverns above the bunker. At present, Spock could not rule out either possibility, although the question certainly seemed worthy of future investigation, particularly in light of what he had finally determined regarding the trivets' singular biology.

"Finding enough to interest you, Mister Spock?"

V'sta came up behind him, assisted by Chapel, who had hold of her patient's arm. The Front's leader moved slowly and with care, but she appeared to be in substantially better condition than she had been when they first arrived in the bunker. Spock credited her recovery to Chapel's expert care.

"Greetings, Hynn V'sta," he said, uncertain of her actual rank or title. "Should you be up and about?"

"Christine gave me the go-ahead to stretch my legs a bit."

"Within reason," Chapel cautioned. "Don't expect to run a marathon anytime soon. Just a short stroll, then it's straight back to the bed for you."

"Yes, Nurse." V'sta rolled her eyes. "Are all Starfleet medics so stubborn?"

"Compared to Doctor McCoy," Spock said, "Nurse Chapel is a paragon of reason."

"Why, Mister Spock." Chapel placed her free hand above her heart. "I'm flattered."

"I'll have to take your word for it regarding McCoy," V'sta said. "So what *do* you think of this bunker, Mister Spock?"

"As accommodations go, it is certainly preferable to the Pit," he said honestly.

V'sta looked slightly abashed by the remark. "Sorry about that, but you have to remember: that was *before* you folks patched me up." She shrugged. "Anything I can do to make it up to you?"

"Perhaps you can answer some questions about this site?" Spock said. "Your compatriots, alas, seem to be in the dark on the subject."

"No surprise there," she said. "It was a deeply guarded secret." She settled down onto a bench in anticipation of a longer discussion. "What do you want to know?"

"To begin with," Spock said, "how did you come upon this place?"

"We stumbled onto it shortly after we set up shop in the caverns above. One of my right-hand people at the time, a brilliant tactician named D'Relle, was a former archaeologist; she deciphered some old inscriptions, which, along with her general knowledge of the lost times before The Leveling, led her to that ancient elevator, which we managed to get operational again." A look of sorrow passed over V'sta's face. "Tragically, however, D'Relle was killed in a political demonstration turned riot before she had a chance to truly study this bunker the way she wanted to. A damn shame."

"A true waste," Spock agreed. "My condolences."

V'sta's face hardened. "Hers wasn't the first life lost in our struggle. She won't be the last."

"It was a loss nevertheless," Spock said. "May I ask why the UBF did not make more use of this facility prior to the assault?"

F'lun, who had been sitting sullenly on a couch nearby, joined the conversation. "Been kinda wondering about that myself, to be honest."

"For one thing, it seemed like a good emergency shelter," V'sta said. "More importantly, I felt I owed it to D'Relle to preserve this priceless historical site as much as possible, so that someday it can be studied the way it should be . . . after the current strife is over and done with. Braco has been scarred enough by violence. I just wanted to keep one piece of our past untouched for future generations."

Chapel sat down beside her. "I thought you were all about Braco letting go of the past?"

"I want to let go of the notion that Braco is holy ground to be fought over," V'sta said. "Doesn't mean I don't care about our history or want to sweep it under the rug. Knowing the past is one thing; worshipping it is another. And call me crazy, but I'm still optimistic enough to hope that someday sites like this can simply be appreciated for what they tell us about our ancestors, as opposed to being exploited to push one agenda or another. Best to keep it hidden, until a united Braco can delve into its secrets." She looked at Chapel. "Does that seem hypocritical to you?"

"No," Chapel said. "Not when you put it that way."

"Plus," V'sta admitted, "most of this antique hardware is so old we barely know what it does or how to operate it." She chuckled wryly. "It's not like I've got volunteers who can read ancient Braconic, let alone technicians trained to work with equipment that's been forgotten for thousands of years."

"How long are we planning to hide out in this museum?" F'lun asked impatiently. "I'm starting to feel like I've been buried forever as well."

"I'm not sure," V'sta said. "There is no way to know what's going on up there. We need to wait long enough for the heat to die down, then try to slip away from the caverns after the Bureau has packed up and cleared out."

"That could be a while," Chapel said. "Chief Inspector Wibb strikes me as a very driven investigator, if more than a little bull-headed. Chances are he's going to want to thoroughly scour your old base for incriminating evidence and clues. In fact, I wouldn't be surprised if he leaves some troopers posted in the caverns indefinitely, to snag any stragglers like us."

"That's no good." Godwin leaned against a doorway, a disruptor at her hip. "We can't stick around in this mausoleum forever, no matter how historic it is. We need to get back in touch with the *Enterprise*."

"And keep looking for Doctor McCoy," Chapel said.

"So there's no way out of here besides that old elevator?" Levine asked. "No secret escape tunnels?"

"Not that we've ever discovered," V'sta said. "And that elevator takes us right back up into the Bureau's clutches. We have to assume they're in full control of the base by now." She glanced worriedly in the direction of the lift entrance. "Possibly only a matter of time before they stumble onto that camouflaged lift and figure out how to get past our newly installed security codes."

"Sounds to me like another good reason not to stick around," F'lun said, "now that you're feeling better, that is."

"I'm open to suggestions," V'sta said.

Spock finished recording the mosaic. "I may have a possible solution if you'll follow me."

"If you know a safe way out of here, I'll follow you on my hands and knees if I have to," V'sta said.

"That will not be necessary," Spock said.

Chapel carefully assisted V'sta to her feet and Spock led the entire party down a side corridor into an unattended chamber dominated by a large triangular platform, raised 10.32 centimeters above the floor. Computers and control panels faced the platform. Hieroglyphics, similar to those seen elsewhere in the bunker, were printed on the machinery and walls. The markings were more than merely decorative; Spock identified them as labels, instructions, and safety warnings.

"Correct me if I'm wrong," Spock said, "but this appears to be a transporter room, some many thousands of years old."

V'sta nodded. "That's what D'Relle thought too. She was an archaeologist, not an engineer, though, so she was only just beginning to investigate that platform when she was killed. I've had a few very discreet technicians look it over, after swearing them to secrecy, but they made no progress when it came to discovering whether it was still operational. For all we know, it's been broken for millennia." She supported herself against an inactive console, showing signs of overexertion. "I always hoped to get it up and running again, but, deep down, I suspected that was just a pipe dream."

"Perhaps not," Spock said. "Granted, the task of reactivating this device after hundreds of centuries is indeed a daunting one, considering the immense passage of time, the loss of scientific expertise, the necessity for secrecy, and the language barrier. I cannot fault your technicians for failing to achieve success under such circumstances."

"However?" V'sta prompted.

"Our enforced leisure has given me the opportunity to decipher these hieroglyphs, which appear to be written in a regional variant of Early High Braconic," Spock explained. "Furthermore, a thorough scan of the operating mechanisms indicates that the primary energizers simply need to be recharged after lying dormant, and that a few loose or corroded connections need to be restored. None of which obstacles strike me as insurmountable."

"Hold on," V'sta said, excitement warring with exhaustion. "You actually think you can get this prehistoric transporter working again, after all this time?"

"I believe I just stated as much," Spock said. "Do I have your permission to proceed?"

"Permission granted! Get on it, Mister Spock!"

Twenty-Nine

Vok

Prup's youthful visage looked boldly toward the future, then disintegrated before Kirk's eyes. Stray photons lingered like after-images before fading into the nothingness.

"Damn," Kirk muttered. "I don't like seeing that."

Thankfully, the image occupying the *Enterprise*'s main viewer was not actually the candidate but merely a hastily erected 3-D billboard that had been incinerated by an energy blast from a moving vehicle on a busy thoroughfare in Vok's southern hemisphere. Kirk grimly observed the recorded footage from his chair upon the bridge. A steaming cup of black coffee helped to keep his wits sharp, despite the long hours he'd been putting in both on the ship and the planet below, but did little to improve his mood.

"*You said it,*" Sergeant Myp replied from the scene. Her head and shoulders replaced the disintegrating billboard on the viewscreen. She looked as though she could use some coffee too. Kirk was tempted to have some beamed down to her with his compliments. "*I thought things would get better after we cracked that bogus assassination scheme, but I guess I was just fooling myself.*"

Emotions were running hotter and higher after Div's confession and the aborted debate. Every day brought new reports of voter intimidation, vandalism, and even attacks on regional campaign offices all across the planet. Most of the aggression seemed to be coming from General Gogg's supporters, incensed over the attempt to frame the General, but there had been reprisals from Prup's followers as well. Physical brawls between the rival factions were erupting all over Vok; according to Myp, she and her fellow peace officers were running ragged trying to keep a lid on things, even with whatever backup the *Enterprise* was able to supply.

"But no casualties this time?" Kirk asked, looking for a bright side.

"*Only symbolically,*" Myp replied. "*However—*"

"Excuse me, Captain," Uhura interrupted from her station, "but I'm receiving an urgent transmission from Braco."

Kirk's pulse sped up. At last report, Lieutenant Levine and his team on Braco were planning a stealth raid to rescue Spock, Chapel, and possibly McCoy as well. Kirk allowed himself to hope that his friends were safe at last.

"Forgive me, Sergeant," he addressed Myp, "but I'm being hailed on a vital matter. Please stand by."

"*No problem,*" she replied.

Kirk nodded at Uhura. "Put it through."

"Aye, sir."

To Kirk's surprise, Ensign Dom Amirpour appeared on the screen. Kirk recalled that the young Iranian officer had been assigned to Spock's mission searching for McCoy. Kirk had hoped to see Spock, but he concealed his disappointment, while noting that the ensign's taut expression did not portend welcome news.

"Kirk here. What do you have to report, Ensign?"

"*It's not good, sir. We've lost contact with Lieutenant Levine and his team, who have missed two check-ins. We have to assume that the operation has . . . encountered difficulties, Captain.*"

Kirk's heart sank. While he was stuck here on Vok, more and more of his crew were going missing. "Anything else, Ensign?"

"*I'm afraid so, sir. The Bracons have reportedly launched a major military assault on the site where Commander Spock and Nurse Chapel were possibly being held.*" Amirpour did his best to maintain his professional composure despite the pressure he was under. "*We . . . we can't be sure of their safety, sir.*"

The dire news provoked anxious looks across the bridge. Kirk shared his crew's worries. Had he sent Spock and the others to their deaths?

"What do the planetary authorities have to say?" he asked.

"*Not much, Captain. To be honest, they're pretty much keeping us out of the loop.*"

Kirk wished that came as a surprise, but it jibed with what the landing party had reported earlier. Frustrated, he would have given a year's salary to be able to bang some Bracon heads together, figuratively or otherwise. Too bad they were dozens of light-years away.

"Understood, Ensign. Keep me posted."

"*Aye, sir. You'll be the first to know if we hear something.*"

"I expect nothing less. Kirk out." He glanced at Uhura. "Is Sergeant Myp still standing by?"

"Affirmative, Captain. Shall I switch back to her?"

"Please do so, Lieutenant."

Kirk gazed steadily at the main viewscreen. Vok was still spinning below. He couldn't put his mission on hold just because his crew was in danger a system away. He put down his coffee as Myp returned to the screen.

"Sorry to keep you waiting, Sergeant."

"*Actually, as it happens, I'm going to have to sign off,*" she replied. "*Just got word that an unmanned drone canvassing for General Gogg has been shot down near the equator. Initial reports are that its mangled remains were then hurled through the window of a voter registration center, largely staffed by volunteers working for the Prup campaign.*"

Kirk felt a headache coming on. "Retaliation for the vandalized billboard?"

"*Probably just more of the same craziness.*" Myp shook her head in dismay. "*As far as I'm concerned, this election can't be over soon enough.*"

"You and me both, Sergeant."

Thirty

Braco

"Are we certain this is a good idea?" Chapel asked Spock. "I'm not sure I want to trust my atoms to an ancient transporter that hasn't been operational since the pyramids were young." She eyed the Bracon platform with an understandable degree of apprehension, despite Spock's meticulous efforts to restore the pre-apocalyptic mechanism to full functionality. "I'm pretty sure I know what Doctor McCoy would have to say about this."

"It is perhaps just as well, then, that he is not present," Spock replied. "If all goes as planned, however, this test run should allay your concerns."

Most of the bunker's current inhabitants were crammed into the forgotten transporter room, or peering in from the doorway, as Spock prepared to test whether the device could be safely employed following his repairs. Lighted control panels and humming machinery provided positive indications that the transporter was working, but prudence dictated that he first test the device on an inanimate object before attempting to beam a living being from one location to another. Transporter malfunctions could yield grievous results.

"If you can pull this off, Spock," V'sta said, "we're all going to owe you big-time."

The UBF's leader had insisted on being present for the test even though she was still recovering from her accident. At Nurse Chapel's insistence, a small chair had been relocated to the transporter chamber so V'sta wouldn't have to stand. Troxy napped in her lap, apparently bored by Spock's careful preparations. The Vulcan refrained from pointing out that, not too long ago, V'sta had strongly opposed him being allowed to inspect and repair any of the UBF's equipment, but the contrast between then and now was not lost on him. Circumstances had indeed changed since he and Chapel had first been taken hostage.

"Lieutenant Godwin," he said. "Would you please do the honors?"

"Certainly, Mister Spock." She placed her communicator on a triangular transporter pad, then stepped away from the platform. "I regret that I have but one communicator to give for the cause."

"I have every expectation that it will be returned to you," Spock said. "If it is not, then we have more work before us."

"Enough jawing," F'lun said from the doorway. "Let's get on it."

"I quite concur." Spock performed one last diagnostic on all crucial systems, quadruple-checked to make certain that the pattern buffers were empty of any residual data, synched the targeting scanners with the Doppler compensation monitor, and entered the preselected destination coordinates. "Energizing."

Unlike on Starfleet transporter consoles, the energizers were controlled by dials, not sliders. Spock methodically turned the appropriate dials counterclockwise while silently hoping that he had translated the hieroglyphic instructions correctly, considering that there was in fact a certain ambiguity about the precise meaning of a particular glyph that arguably referred to either the direction of sunrise *or* sunset. Judging from his scans of the relevant circuitry, he was 97.2 percent confident that the symbol meant "sunset" in this context; nevertheless, he experienced a moment of relief as the transporter performed as anticipated.

"I'll be damned!" V'sta exclaimed, startling Troxy. "It's working!"

The transporter effect varied in appearance from what Spock was accustomed to. Instead of dissolving into a shimmering column of energized particles, the communicator acquired a purplish glow, then rippled like hot air above a parched desert floor before fading from sight like a mirage. A low bass rumble accompanied the dematerialization process, as opposed to the usual high-pitched whine, but the ultimate effect was the same: the communicator vanished before their eyes.

"I knew you could do it!" Chapel said, her evident excitement somewhat belying her statement. "I should have never doubted you!"

"Let us not celebrate prematurely," he advised. "Disintegrating a solid object is a relatively simple task. Successfully reintegrating it at the desired location is the more challenging feat."

The status display on the control panel indicated that the transport had been completed successfully, at least as far as he was able to interpret the unfamiliar readouts. He flipped open his own communicator to confirm the results.

"Lieutenant Levine, can you read me?"

"Affirmative, Mister Spock. The communicator arrived safe and sound . . . and obviously in working order."

For this initial test, they had opted to simply beam an object from one end of the bunker to another, where Levine had been stationed to observe the communicator's arrival. That the device had reached its destination intact, while remaining functional, was encouraging.

"Acknowledged," Spock replied. "Does the communicator appear damaged or distorted in any way? Is it unusually hot or cold to the touch?"

"Negative to all of the above, sir. Do you want to try beaming me back with the communicator?"

"I appreciate your confidence, Lieutenant, along with your eagerness to resume our mission, but there is no need to risk a humanoid trial just yet. Please stand by as I attempt to reverse the transport."

"Aye, sir."

Spock locked onto the communicator—and *only* the communicator. "Reenergizing."

Turning the dials clockwise this time, toward the sunrise, he watched with satisfaction as the communicator rematerialized upon the transporter platform. Godwin retrieved the item and conveyed it to Spock, who examined it intently. As Levine had reported, the communicator appeared none the worse for wear for its round trip, although Spock fully intended to scrutinize it more carefully before reaching any final conclusions. Placing the device on the console, he scanned it with his tricorder, but failed to detect any worrisome quantum irregularities or reversed polarities. The communicator had been accurately re-created right down to the atomic level. A full subatomic analysis would require additional time and concentration later.

"Well, Mister Spock," Chapel asked, "did it come back okay?"

"Early indications are promising," he answered.

"So that's it?" F'lun squeezed his way into the room, as though anxious to secure his place in line before the transporter platform. "We can beam ourselves out of here?"

"Not yet," Spock said. "Further tests are in order before I can confidently declare this device safe for organic life-forms."

In particular, he intended to expand the range of the transporter beam by increments to determine the maximum safe distance objects could be transported across. Logic suggested that the transporter had been designed to beam Bracons to and from the underground bunker, but he was not inclined to trust the lives and bodies of himself and his companions to mere supposition.

"How many 'tests' do you have in mind?" F'lun asked irritably. "This isn't the Vulcan Science Academy, you know. The Bureau could come busting in here anytime now!"

"I am aware of the urgency of our situation," Spock said, "as well as the need to balance caution with expediency. The transportation of organic matter is not to be undertaken lightly when employing archaic and unfamiliar equipment. I have witnessed the results of severe transportation mishaps, so I know better than to take unnecessary risks."

"Easy for you to say," F'lun said. "You're not being hunted as a terrorist." He nodded at Troxy, who was still resting in V'sta's lap.

"What about that critter? Why not use it to test the transporter, see if it's safe for living things?"

Troxy peered back at the man and let out an anxious chirp. It was doubtful that the trivet comprehended F'lun's words, but the man's tone was enough to cause Troxy to cling tightly to V'sta with its three legs.

"Don't even think about it," she said. "Troxy is a pet, not a lab specimen."

"Just a suggestion," F'lun said, rather defensively. "I mean, it beats testing the machine out on one of us."

There was a certain logic to the man's suggestion, Spock conceded. In ideal circumstances, he would prefer to risk a test animal before a sentient being; still, he also found himself reluctant to endanger Troxy if it could be avoided, and thus he was in no hurry to challenge V'sta on this point. It was not logical, but it was how he felt.

"Troxy *is* one of us," she insisted. "Case closed."

"I believe that an efficient, if accelerated, sequence of tests will allow us to determine the transporter's safety within a reasonable margin of error," Spock said, "so that we can be confident of its abilities before using it on *any* living creature."

"Works for me," V'sta said, "but F'lun has a point, too. How many tests *are* we talking about?"

"No more than necessary," he said.

As it happened, the additional tests required no more than 29.3 minutes; this was longer than Spock had calculated, but the time had been well spent familiarizing himself with the finer points of operating the ancient transporter as well as making a few last adjustments to the long-neglected equipment.

"Spock to *Copernicus* and *Galileo*," he said into his communicator. "Prepare to receive landing party shortly."

"*Galileo* standing by."

"Copernicus *standing by*."

Communicators had been beamed successfully to both shuttle-crafts, which remained parked at the spaceport outside the capital. Now that the bunker's transporter had been determined to be reliable, the plan was to beam the stranded Starfleet personnel back to the shuttles.

But first there was the matter of V'sta and her people.

"Do you agree?" Spock turned away from the console to address the leader of the Bracon dissidents. "I will beam you and your associates to a UBF safe house of your choice, using the coordinates you provided?"

She nodded. "That will do just fine."

"Not so fast," F'lun objected. "How do we know you won't just beam us straight into Bureau headquarters? Seems to me you have plenty of reasons to turn us over to the troopers the first chance you get."

"Vulcans do not hold grudges," Spock said, "nor do Starfleet officers take sides in the internal conflicts of independent worlds. I assume you no longer aspire to hold us hostage?"

"No," V'sta said emphatically. Her hand drifted toward her recently fractured skull, which Nurse Chapel had succeeded in mending. "Not after all you've done for us . . . after what we did to you."

"Then we are no longer at odds," Spock stated. "Your dispute with the Provisional Government and its Tranquility Bureau are none of our concern. Let me suggest, however, that you think twice before continuing kidnapping as a political tactic. Even if the Bureau brands you as terrorists, you are not obliged to live up to that characterization."

"Easier said than done," V'sta said. "You don't know our world, Mister Spock. We're not going to be able to unite Braco without getting our hands dirty."

"Amen," F'lun said, nodding. "The coalition isn't going to step down voluntarily."

"Perhaps," Spock said diplomatically, "but achieving unity through conflict strikes me as counterintuitive. Violent actions tend to provoke equally violent counterreactions, begetting yet more conflict. It may serve you better to heal old wounds than open new ones, as I'm sure Nurse Chapel would agree."

"I couldn't put it any better, Mister Spock," the nurse said. "Braco has been scarred enough by old wars and hatreds. Maybe it's time to start building instead of bombing?"

"Tell that to the Bureau and its troopers," V'sta said bitterly. "Still, this is our struggle, not yours. It was a mistake to drag you into it."

Spock wanted to believe that he'd given V'sta something to think about, but it was up to her and her followers to chart their future course. Binding Braco's deep and enduring divisions was beyond Starfleet's purview.

"On that we can agree," he said. "From the beginning, our mission was only to locate and recover Doctor McCoy."

"We may be able to help you with that," V'sta said.

Spock arched an eyebrow. "How so?"

"I thought you had nothing to do with his disappearance?" Chapel said.

"We didn't," V'sta said. "But since we were taking the blame for it, I thought it best to look into the matter, quietly of course. Never got to the bottom of it, but our investigation *did* turn up one interesting detail: a diplomatic courier ship from Ozalor hastily departed Braco mere hours after your doctor was snatched." She shrugged. "I can't say for certain that the one has to do with the other, but the timing seemed . . . provocative."

"Indeed," Spock said.

"Ozalor?" Chapel's face betrayed her puzzlement. "What would Ozalor want with Doctor McCoy?"

"That remains to be determined," Spock said, "assuming that the Ozalorian ship's departure is in fact related to McCoy's abduction." He considered the information V'sta had just shared with them. "If nothing else, this intelligence opens up a possible new avenue of investigation. Thank you for sharing it with us."

"No problem," V'sta said. "Hope you find your friend."

Spock had no reason to doubt her sincerity. "In the meantime, we should get you and yours to a more secure location with all due speed."

"About time," F'lun muttered. He took his place upon the transporter platform.

"Think you need to say goodbye to somebody first." V'sta carried Troxy over to Spock. The trivet's eyestalk tilted toward Spock. "Troxy's going to miss you."

Spock experienced a twinge of regret at the parting, not that he would ever admit it. "I did not come to Braco in search of a pet, nor do I believe this creature would be happy removed from its native environment. I trust you to take good care of your mascot."

"Count on it," V'sta said.

Spock reached out and gave the friendly animal a final pat on the head, then raised his hand in a Vulcan salute.

"Live long and prosper, Troxy. I have valued your company."

The trivet hooted in reply.

Chapel chuckled nearby. Spock observed her hiding a smile behind her hand.

"Do you find something amusing, Nurse?"

"No, Mister Spock," she said unconvincingly. "Not at all."

Thirty-One

Braco

"For what it's worth, Mister Spock," the reporter said, *"I wasn't in on the plan to kidnap you and the nurse. I negotiated that meeting with F'lun in good faith. I never intended for you to be taken hostage."*

D'Ran Colc's visage filled a globe monitor in *Copernicus's* cockpit. Spock occupied the copilot's seat as Levine prepped the shuttlecraft for takeoff. Chapel and Godwin had beamed aboard *Copernicus* as well, and were now resting in the passenger compartment, while Nguyen and Yoder had returned to *Galileo*, which was also preparing to depart the spaceport, whose open tarmac was visible through *Copernicus's* forward ports. The early-morning sky was typically overcast. Falling rain streaked the transparent aluminum windows. Spock was not going to miss Braco's perpetually dreary weather.

"I will take you at your word," he replied. Certainly, none of their captors had ever indicated that Colc was party to the scheme; furthermore, Spock recalled that the reporter had indeed warned him in advance that the meeting contained an element of risk. "In any event, what's done is done. All concerned have escaped captivity unharmed."

Spock had contacted Colc via a secure frequency per their earlier agreement to share whatever information they acquired regarding McCoy's disappearance. He concisely apprised the reporter of his experiences in the hands of the UBF, omitting only a few confidential details. Colc listened intently, seeming especially interested in Spock's eyewitness account of the military assault on the caverns.

"That's great stuff," Colc enthused. *"Good to get something besides the official version of that so-called raid. The Bureau just keeps bragging that they have a few dozen terrorists in custody, awaiting trial, without giving the press access to the prisoners. Wibb's claiming total victory over the UBF . . . even though Hynn V'sta seems to have escaped his grasp."* Colc eyed Spock through the monitor. *"I don't suppose you know anything about that?"*

After some consideration, Spock had neglected to inform Colc of certain particulars: namely the existence of the ancient bunker, that V'sta and her associates had beamed to a safe house, and the exact manner in which the Starfleet personnel had escaped captivity. He had merely informed Colc that they'd managed to free themselves during the confusion engendered by the assault, which was accurate enough . . . in a broad sense. The omissions were perhaps not entirely in the spirit of his original pact with the reporter, but Spock reasoned that larger concerns took precedence. Ultimately, the discovery of the bunker—and the location of the safe house—were not his secrets to share. And as for his newly acquired insights into the trivets and their unique biology, he thought it best to redact that information as well, at least for the time being, due to their potentially explosive political ramifications.

"I can only confirm that V'sta is unlikely to be in the hands of the authorities."

"Why do I get the distinct impression you're not telling me everything, Mister Spock?"

"Perhaps because it is the nature of your profession to seldom take anything at face value?" Spock said, deflecting. "It occurs to me, however, that I should also inform you that the UBF *did* provide me with a possible clue to Doctor McCoy's whereabouts."

"Now we're talking," Colc said, his curiosity visibly piqued. *"Don't hold out on me, Spock. Give."*

Spock shared V'sta's revelation that an Ozalorian courier ship had departed Braco in approximately the same timeframe as McCoy's disappearance.

"*A diplomatic vessel, you say?*" Colc grinned wolfishly. "*Consider me intrigued. Let me do a little digging and see what else I can come up with.*"

Spock had anticipated that Colc would find the clue tantalizing. He hoped to benefit from the reporter's investigative talents and contacts.

"Any additional intelligence you can provide will be appreciated," Spock said. "In exchange, I *may* be able to facilitate a one-on-one interview with a certain fugitive UBF leader, who has good reason to get her own side of the story out to the general populace."

Colc's brows shot upward. He took a moment to process Spock's offer, as well as its implications. His eyes narrowed as he chuckled knowingly.

"*Remind me not to play tiles against you, Mister Spock. Tell me, are all Vulcans so crafty?*"

"I'm quite certain I don't know what you mean," Spock said.

"*Sure you don't.*" Colc winked at him. "*Anyway, I've got to go run down that new lead of ours. Be talking to you.*"

"Affirmative," Spock said.

Colc's face vanished from the globe as the transmission ended. Levine glanced over at Spock.

"You sure we can trust him to get back to us?" the security officer asked.

"It is in his best interests to do so," Spock said. Although reluctant to interfere in Braco's affairs, he saw no harm, and possibly only benefits, in promoting a peaceful dialogue between the UBF and the public via the free press, in lieu of an endless cycle of violence. And if the prospect of landing an exclusive interview with V'sta provided Colc with an additional incentive to remain in contact with Spock, so much the better. "Let us hope that Mister Colc's journalistic acumen can build on the data we acquired from Hynn V'sta."

"You said it, Mister Spock," Levine agreed. "Guess it can't hurt to milk every connection we have on this planet." He peered through a porthole at the cheerless gray sky outside. "You really think Ozalor had something to do with kidnapping Doctor McCoy?"

"We cannot eliminate that possibility," Spock said carefully, "particularly in light of this new information. Are we fully prepared for takeoff?"

Levine nodded. "Awaiting permission from Flight Control now."

"Very good, Lieutenant."

By Spock's calculations, Ozalor was 46.8 hours away, so he wanted to get underway as promptly as possible. He turned back toward the passenger compartment to inform Nurse Chapel and the rest of the shuttle's crew of their imminent departure, only to be interrupted by an urgent chime from the shuttlecraft's comm unit.

"We're being hailed, sir," Levine said redundantly.

"So it appears, Lieutenant."

Consulting the instrument panel, Spock saw that the hail was on a priority channel and coming directly from the Bracon Tranquility Bureau. He answered the hail, quietly bracing himself for the discussion ahead. He did not anticipate it being a particularly congenial one.

"Spock here," he said. "How may I assist you, Chief Inspector?"

Wibb's face occupied the globe. *"Mister Spock. I am pleased to see you well and at liberty. We feared for your safety after your Starfleet rescue operation failed to report back to the Bureau in a timely fashion."*

"There were . . . complications," Spock replied, "but we succeeded in liberating ourselves without any casualties."

Despite the bombardment Wibb had ordered.

"Glad to hear it," the inspector said. *"And Doctor McCoy?"*

"The UBF denied responsibility for his capture."

"*Well, they would, wouldn't they?*" Wibb retorted, none too logically.

"I am relatively convinced of their veracity. Moreover, we now have reason to believe that McCoy may no longer be on Braco at all."

"*I see,*" Wibb said skeptically. "*Is that why your shuttlecrafts have requested permission to exit our world?*"

The Bureau was clearly in touch with the spaceport and monitoring the status of the Starfleet vessels. Spock had assumed nothing less.

"That is correct," he said. "Our gratitude for your hospitality and cooperation."

Listening in, Levine snorted.

If Wibb overheard the less-than-diplomatic response, he chose to ignore it. "*What's this about, Mister Spock? What have you discovered?*"

Spock preferred not to implicate Ozalor on such slender evidence. The politics of the sector were too fraught to make unfounded accusations, or even raise dire suspicions, without more solid proof. At the moment, Ozalor was merely a planet of interest as far as the search for McCoy was concerned.

"Nothing conclusive, Chief Inspector," he said honestly. "We merely seek to pursue other avenues of investigation beyond Braco's environs."

"*You need to revise your plans,*" Wibb declared. "*I'm afraid I cannot allow you and your associates to depart Braco at this time. If nothing else, you need to be thoroughly debriefed on your encounters with the UBF. We must review everything you saw and heard while you were in the hands of the terrorists. As long as Hynn V'sta and other key figures remain at large, this case remains open.*"

"For you perhaps," Spock said, "but our purpose on Braco is concluded for now. Our mission calls us elsewhere . . . and without delay."

"*Need I remind you, Mister Spock, that your doctor was abducted, your people ambushed, on Bracon soil?*" Wibb puffed on his pipe as though to assert the primacy of Bracon ways over Starfleet preferences. "*That makes this very much a Bureau matter, which means you are not going anywhere until I'm satisfied that you have cooperated fully.*"

Spock repressed a sigh. He had expected this response. He was also prepared for it.

"Am I to understand that *you* now intend to hold us hostage?"

"*Don't try playing games with me, Spock. Hostages are kept by criminals. I represent the government.*"

"The Provisional Government, to be exact."

"*That is immaterial,*" Wibb said, scowling. "*Do you wish me to file a formal complaint with the Federation, informing them that you have defied the lawful orders of our world's recognized authorities?*"

"That depends," Spock replied. "Do you wish me to report, quite accurately, that you endangered the lives of Federation citizens by launching fusion missiles at a location where you had every reason to believe that we were being held, and that the bombardment continued even after the Bureau received an explicit message from me alerting you to the fact that I and the other hostages were in immediate danger from your assault?"

Spock had naturally kept a recording of his urgent transmission to Bureau headquarters during the attack on the underground base.

"You may consult your own communication logs to verify that last point."

"*That was a strategic decision,*" Wibb said stiffly. "*After your rescue operation failed to check in, I had no choice but to assume that Lieutenant Levine and his team had been killed or captured by the enemy. Stealth had failed, so extreme force was called for instead.*" His pipe jutted from one corner of his mouth as he paused to draw on it, then exhaled a puff of smoke that was mercifully confined to his end of the transmission. *"It was a hard choice, a regrettable choice, but I stand by it."*

Spock privately questioned just how difficult the decision to launch the assault had truly been for Wibb, but he saw nothing to be gained by expressing such doubts out loud.

"That is your prerogative," he said, "but I cannot guarantee that the Federation will see it quite the same way, depending on how I frame the incident in my report. The facts are not in dispute, but how they are interpreted may well determine whether or not your 'strategic' decision sparks an unpleasant interstellar incident, which I am certain your superiors would prefer to avoid . . . if possible."

Wibb's face flushed. *"You wouldn't dare!"*

"Do not test me, Chief Inspector. You have already risked one awkward rift between Braco and the Federation. Do you truly wish to compound that by grounding Starfleet vessels against our will?"

Wibb's bravado faltered. He put down his pipe and licked his lips nervously, as though worrying about how he was going to explain this to Braco's ruling coalition.

"Now, now, Mister Spock," he said in a notably more conciliatory tone. *"It doesn't have to come to that. We're both reasonable men after all."*

"I would hope so, Chief Inspector, in which case you will do the reasonable thing and let us go on our way." Having gained the upper hand, Spock offered Wibb a carrot along with the stick. "If it is any consolation, it may be that we will be able to prove that Braco and its people had little or nothing to do with Doctor McCoy's abduction. Surely that is an outcome to be desired . . . from your government's point of view."

"I suppose," Wibb said, wavering, *"when you put it that way . . ."*

"Be thankful that we are departing unharmed and that Doctor McCoy was not, in fact, found captive on your planet." Spock let that sink in. "To employ a germane human expression, Chief Inspector, take the win."

Wibb peered unhappily from the globe. His jaw clenched for no less than forty-seven seconds before he finally brought himself to say:

"On consideration, I will inform Flight Control that you are free to go. Good hunting, sir."

Spock considered wishing the inspector a long life and prosperity, but found he had little inclination to do so.

"Acknowledged. Spock out."

Thirty-Two

Braco System

"You may be onto something, Mister Spock."

D'Ran Colc's voice emanated from *Copernicus*'s comm unit. Although the shuttlecraft was still within Braco's solar system, it was out of range for anything except audio transmission, and even that was growing steadily weaker the farther they traveled from the planet, forcing Spock to dial up the volume. He considered it fortunate that the reporter had managed to contact *Copernicus* before it exited the system entirely. As it was, a time lag of approximately 2.56 seconds prolonged the dialogue to a mildly irritating degree.

"How so, Mister Colc?" Spock asked from the copilot's seat. The forward ports offered him a clear view of empty space, which was a pleasing change from Braco's dismal weather and dank, clammy caverns.

"I did some digging, called in some favors, and get this. That diplomatic courier that left here the same night McCoy vanished? Seems it was carrying none other than Count Rayob, majordomo to His Excellency, Salokonos, Yovode *of Ozalor."*

Spock naturally recognized the name of Ozalor's current monarch, but he was unfamiliar with the other individual cited. "I gather this Rayob is a figure of some importance?"

"And then some," Colc said. *"Longtime advisor to the royal family and very much part of the* Yovode's *inner circle, or so it's said. I don't claim to be an expert on Ozalorian royal gossip and palace intrigues, but he's supposed to be a fixture at the court. Been close to the royals for decades now."*

Spock trusted Colc to be better informed on such matters than he was. Given the long, contentious history linking Braco to both Vok and Ozalor, it stood to reason that the savvy reporter would pay attention to the politics of the rival planets, each of which claimed Braco as the cradle of their race . . . despite certain evidence to the contrary.

"Interesting," Spock observed.

"You can say that again," Colc replied. *"The question is, what was an Ozalorian big wheel doing on Braco the same time your doctor got snatched? And who else, besides the majordomo, was on that sudden flight back to Ozalor?"*

Not wanting to leap to conclusions, Spock played devil's advocate. "Was there any particular occasion to account for Rayob's visit to Braco?"

"That's the thing, Mister Spock. As far as I can tell, there was no official reason for his visit: no diplomatic conference, trade negotiations, state dinner, funeral, video op, or any of the usual pomp and circumstance. If anything, his recent trip to Braco was surprisingly, maybe even suspiciously, low profile. I like to think I stay on top of these things, but even I hadn't known he'd been here until I started asking the right people the right questions. He slipped on and off the planet with no fanfare . . . almost as though he went out of his way to avoid attracting attention, if you know what I mean."

"I do indeed," Spock said.

Granted, as the son of an ambassador, Spock was well aware that interstellar diplomacy sometimes needed to be conducted discreetly out of the public eye. Sarek could often be rigorously closemouthed about his work; Spock recalled more than a few occasions when not even he nor his mother knew precisely where and what Sarek was doing while away on assignment. That being said, Spock also knew that such *sub rosa* negotiations were more usually conducted via intermediaries or lower-level representatives, at least in their preliminary stages. What could be so important, or so potentially explosive, as to require Rayob's personal supervision on Braco?

The abduction of a Starfleet medical officer, perhaps?

Spock's familiarity with diplomatic protocols prompted another thought. "I assume, as is the norm, that a diplomatic
courier ship from Ozalor would have been exempt from any customary inspections?"

"*That's right, Mister Spock. Diplomatic vessels are generally off-
limits to that sort of thing.*" Colc quickly grasped the implications
of this fact. "*Wouldn't have been too hard to smuggle McCoy off-
planet in that courier.*"

"And with judicious speed," Spock added.

The courier's hasty departure, along with the whirlwind nature
of Rayob's visit to Braco, certainly fit the scenario under discussion. If Ozalor was behind McCoy's kidnapping, they would
surely want to get him off Braco as quickly as possible.

"*In and out . . . just like the majordomo.*" The glee in the reporter's voice was unmistakable, despite the long-distance transmission. "*This story is getting juicier by the moment. A possible link to
the royal family, maybe even to the* Yovode *himself? This is big, as
in seriously big. The headlines practically write themselves.*"

His enthusiasm concerned Spock, who did not need to confer
with Commissioner Dare to understand that merely *suggesting* that the hereditary ruler of Ozalor might have sanctioned
McCoy's abduction could have severe political ramifications
throughout the entire sector and beyond. In particular, the accusation might have a decisive effect on the presidential election
on Vok by lending support to the hardliners' position that Ozalor
could not be trusted—on Braco and elsewhere. Spock could too
easily imagine General Gogg and his supporters making the most
of a high-ranking Ozalorian official being implicated in such a
crime on the disputed world, with the news possibly turning the
election in Gogg's favor.

"I caution you not to release your story before the facts are in,"
Spock said. "If there is even a possibility that responsibility for
the abduction reaches all the way to the throne of Ozalor, then it
behooves us to tread carefully."

"*What are you asking me, Mister Spock? To sit tight on the story of the sector, possibly the biggest scoop since the imperial sex scandal on Tybalt Prime?*" Colc's voice alone conveyed his resistance to the idea. "*We've talked about this before. I'm a reporter, not a big-picture guy. My job is to spread the news as I uncover it, and let the tiles fall where they may.*"

"I would argue that the bigger the story, the greater your responsibility to ascertain the truth before breaking the news. Putting aside any potential consequences for the moment, I assume you take pride in the accuracy of your reporting?"

"*I'm a reporter, not a fabulist,*" Colc maintained. "*I don't make up my stories.*"

"Then I would urge you to refrain from reporting until you are certain of your facts. We are presently en route to Ozalor to investigate this very matter. Allow us time to provide you with more than mere uncorroborated speculation."

"*Assuming you don't disappear like McCoy,*" Colc said. "*Last I heard, you Federation types are* persona non grata *on Ozalor. What's your plan anyway? To just drop in on the royals uninvited and ask His Excellency if he ordered your doctor kidnapped?*"

"Our strategy is a work in progress," Spock admitted, "but I believe you have already benefited from our agreement to share information regarding this matter. Give us the opportunity to find out what we can rather than risk airing a misleading story . . . if only for your own credibility's sake."

"*That's what follow-up stories and corrections are for,*" Colc said. "*Still, I'll concede that our arrangement has paid off so far. My in-depth report on the bombing of the UBF base, citing you as an anonymous source, is causing a sensation. Everyone is talking about it.*"

"And it may be that we will be able to provide you with additional information, perhaps even definitive answers regarding McCoy's disappearance. Is that not worth waiting for?"

"*Are you promising me another exclusive? I don't know, Mister*

Spock. You're asking a lot. I'm not the only investigative reporter on Braco, you know. What if one of my competitors gets wind of the Ozalor connection and beats me to the scoop?"

Spock was less concerned with who got the "scoop" than with any number of more important concerns.

"That would be unfortunate, but there is another vital issue to be considered. If you reveal this lead prematurely, you may alert Rayob and his confederates to our suspicions and thereby compromise our mission to rescue Doctor McCoy. Indeed, it is even possible that fear of exposure might spur McCoy's captors to go to greater lengths to conceal him . . . or perhaps even to dispose of him."

Spock did not relish hypothesizing about McCoy being killed, but the possibility could not be discounted. Who knew how far the kidnappers might go to avoid being exposed, particularly if Ozalor's royal family was in danger of being implicated?

"Do you wish that on your conscience, Mister Colc?"

"That's not fair, Spock! Since when do Vulcans resort to emotional blackmail?"

"To the contrary, I am simply pointing out the logical consequences of alerting McCoy's kidnappers to our efforts before we have safely recovered him. If you reveal in advance that we are aware of Rayob's possible involvement in the scheme, then you might as well warn the kidnappers that we are heading to Ozalor in search of McCoy."

The ensuing pause lasted long enough that Spock checked to make sure the connection had not been lost. Indicator lights confirmed that the transmission was still operational, even if it was growing weaker as *Copernicus* neared the outer borders of the solar system.

"All right, Spock," the reporter said finally. *"You win . . . for the time being. I'll give you the chance to confirm that McCoy is on Ozalor, but understand that I'm not going to sit on this story indefinitely."*

"Acknowledged," Spock said. "I can hardly expect you to."

The lag between their exchanges was now at least three seconds long. Static impaired communication, and Spock was forced to boost the signal simply to respond.

"We are exiting communication range," he informed Colc. "We will contact you again on this frequency after the completion of our mission."

"If *you complete your mission*," Colc said, his voice fading out. *"And don't forget, you still owe me that interview with V'sta—"*

Any further words were lost to static.

Levine looked at Spock from the helm of the shuttlecraft. "Do you want me to turn back so you can try to pick up the signal again?"

"That will not be necessary, Lieutenant." Spock switched off the speaker, his business with Colc concluded for the present. "Continue on course to Ozalor."

"Aye, aye, sir."

Copernicus left Braco's system behind, accelerating across the void toward Ozalor. The shuttlecraft crossed the dark alone; on Spock's orders, *Galileo* was headed back to the *Enterprise* to report on the status of the search. Spock judged it imperative that Captain Kirk be made aware of recent developments. If *Copernicus* and its crew did disappear, along with McCoy, at least Kirk would know where and why.

"That reporter was right about one thing," Levine said. "We can't expect Ozalor to roll out the red carpet for us. What are we going to do when we get there?"

Spock consulted the astrogator.

"By my calculations, we have approximately forty-five hours to figure that out."

Thirty-Three

Vok

Kirk was impressed by the turnout.

It was election eve and throngs of Vokites were already lining up by the hundreds to vote in the state-of-the-art polling center now occupying a vast public square in the middle of the capital city. Floodlights mounted to the surrounding buildings illuminated the crowded plaza. Harmless red laser beams cordoned the teeming voters into discrete lines that wound back and forth in front of rows of voting booths waiting to be activated at dawn. Tanaka had demonstrated the voting process to Kirk the day before, during a final round of inspections. Fully automated, the two-step procedure first confirmed the voter's identity via a genetic scan before admitting each individual, one at a time, into a private booth whose tinted walls protected the secrecy of their vote, which was transmitted directly to the master satellite orbiting high above Vok via secure emitters built into the roof of each booth. The voter then exited out the back of the booth, freeing it up for the next citizen. This particular center featured roughly four dozen booths; similar complexes had been set up all across the planet.

"Looks like a busy day ahead," Kirk observed.

"You can say that again," Lieutenant Hikaru Sulu said. "Haven't seen lines like this since the Narzan Combo's farewell concert."

Their vantage point was an empty marble pedestal that had once belonged to a toppled statue of a hero of the old regime. Roughly two meters tall, the pedestal offered the two men an elevated view of the proceedings. Kirk had drafted Sulu to oversee operations at this site; with the *Enterprise* locked in a standard orbit overhead, no fancy piloting was required, so Kirk had judged Sulu's talents were better put to use on the planet's surface for the duration of the election. Beyond being a first-rate helmsman, Sulu's natural leadership abilities made him one to watch—and rely on.

"They've been waiting a generation to be heard," Kirk said. "Small wonder they've been queuing up for hours, even though the polls don't open until sunrise."

Sulu surveyed the crowd. "What do you think, Captain? Should we anticipate trouble?"

"Nothing we can't handle, I hope."

Given the rising tensions engendered by the election, and particularly after the tumultuous events triggered by the staged assassination attempt, Kirk was taking no chances. Both Starfleet security and Vokite peace officers were out in force. Every building overlooking the plaza was on lockdown for the next twenty-two hours, which was the length of a Vokite day. Marksmen equipped with phaser rifles were stationed on rooftops and balconies just in case things got hairy. Kirk hoped they wouldn't be needed, that Election Day would not be marred by violence, but better safe than sorry. Borrowing a compact pair of Starfleet-issue binoculars from Sulu, Kirk glanced up at a fifth-floor balcony across the way, where he spied Chekov carefully keeping watch over the square. The high-powered phaser rifle gripped by the vigilant young Russian was possibly overkill, but part of Kirk still worried that such strenuous measures might not be enough. Even with his security teams supplemented by the likes of Sulu and Chekov, a single starship could not police an entire planet.

If only, he thought.

Speaking of police, it occurred to him that he had no idea where Sergeant Myp was stationed at present, since it had been some time since they had last touched base. He could only assume that wherever on Vok she was this election eve, she had her hands full, as did Tanaka, whom Kirk had last seen fussing over some last-minute computer run-throughs. Kirk suspected they were all going to need plenty of coffee before this contest was decided.

"FRAUD ELECTION! FRAUD CANDIDATE!"

Loud chanting disturbed the cool spring night. Turning the binoculars toward the clamor, Kirk spotted a group of trouble-makers raising a ruckus in line. Telltale silver epaulets marked them as Gogg supporters, as if their bellicose slogans didn't make that clear.

"PRUP IS A PUPPET! PRUP IS A PUPPET!"

Sulu gave Kirk a worried look. "Captain?"

Kirk debated his options. The chanters' obstreperous display was surely making the other voters in line uncomfortable and approached active intimidation, but intervening too aggressively might ignite an even more serious disturbance. This warranted judicious handling lest he make a volatile situation worse. He re-moved a handheld loudspeaker from his belt.

Figured I was going to need this.

"Attention," he addressed the assembled voters. "I'm going to have to ask some of you to be less vocal when it comes to express-ing your views. I realize many of you have strong opinions about this election, but this is neither the time nor the place for rallies and demonstrations. Please be considerate of your fellow citizens and keep your voices down."

"You can't silence us, Starfleet!" another Gogg partisan shouted back only a few meters away. "Mind your own filthy Federation business!" He started up another chant: "Ceff surrendered! Gogg won! Ceff surrendered! Gogg won!"

His cohorts took up the chant, even louder than the other group.

"CEFF SURRENDERED! GOGG WON!"

"Pipe down!" Kirk adopted a sterner tone. "You're all here to vote in the morning. I don't want to have to remove anyone from the line, but I'm not going to allow anyone to create a distur-bance. Am I understood?"

"Understand this!"

The same loudmouth reached beneath his jacket and pulled out a translucent globe similar to the one thrown at the force field at Doctor Ceff's rally. Kirk had since learned that this was in fact a commonplace agricultural product used to fertilize fields. He drew back his arm as though to hurl it at Kirk—who didn't give him a chance.

You just crossed the line, mister.

Kirk drew his personal phaser. An azure beam stunned the would-be globe thrower with pinpoint accuracy. He slumped against his cohorts, who barely caught him in time to keep him from crashing to the tiled floor of the plaza. The fertilizer globe slipped from his fingers to splatter against his boots. Gasps erupted from startled Vokites on both sides of the electoral divide.

"Like I said, no disturbances." Kirk seized the opportunity to lay down the law. "If you're here to exercise your lawful right to vote, that's one thing, but if you're here to cause trouble and discourage your fellow citizens from voting, think again. We're not going to tolerate that. No exceptions."

His stern words drew some dirty looks and grumbling, but no one seemed inclined to test his patience any further. The stunned Vokite remained propped up by his allies, who tried to rouse him.

Give it an hour or so, Kirk thought. *Chances are, he'll regain consciousness in time to vote. Here's hoping he has a better attitude by then.*

Sulu whistled in appreciation. "I think they got the message, sir."

"Time will tell." Kirk lowered his weapon. He wondered if he should wait a bit longer before beaming back to the *Enterprise* to monitor the global situation from the bridge. He had wanted to get a firsthand look at the situation on the ground, and had gotten an eyeful, but he still hoped to leave this particular site under Sulu's watch. He was needed elsewhere as well. "You've got this under control, Lieutenant?"

"As much as it can be, Captain," Sulu said honestly. "Hard to say how long your lesson will linger with this crowd, considering the—"

Shouts of alarm, coming from the far end of the plaza, cut Sulu off. Crashing noises, along with the roar of a powerful engine, alerted Kirk to the source of the commotion: a speeding hover truck that had just smashed through the traffic barricades at an entrance to the square and was now accelerating toward the lines of voters and the polling booths beyond. Panicked citizens scrambled to get out of the vehicle's way. Security officers shouted at the unseen driver, but the truck kept on coming.

It's not out of control, Kirk assumed. *It's heading for the voters on purpose.*

Phaser beams targeted the vehicle, although the frantic crowd surely obstructed the officers' line of fire, whether they were on the ground or overlooking the scene from above. Crimson beams strafed the truck's exterior, burning holes through its roof and hood, but failed to halt its momentum as it dipped onto the floor of the spacious plaza, tearing up the tiles as it barreled forward, a tinted windshield obscuring any glimpses of the driver, assuming the vehicle even had one; for all Kirk knew, the truck could be self-driving or operated by remote control.

Neatly organized queues dissolved into chaos as terrified Vokites scattered, ignoring the incandescent red cordons in order to keep from being run over by the oncoming truck. Most moved fast enough to make it, but Kirk saw one older gentleman freeze in the path of the threat as though stunned by the very sight. The man gaped helplessly at his impending doom.

"Move it!"

Without hesitation, Kirk sprang from the pedestal and dashed toward the transfixed Vokite, racing to get to him before the truck did. Kirk was closer, though, so there was just time enough to grab the older man and fling him forcefully out of the way of the scarred and smoking vehicle, which was now less than ten meters away and eating up the distance at a rapid clip. Kirk found himself standing between the truck and the endangered polling booths, which were quite possibly the truck's true target. He reached for his phaser, which struck him as woefully inadequate to halt the motorized juggernaut bearing down on him. Armored plating could be glimpsed through gaps in its seared plastiform exterior; at best, his hand phaser could only turn the truck into a red-hot chunk of molten material before it plowed through him on its way to the voting complex.

Where's a photon torpedo when you need one?

"Captain!" Chekov's voice, artificially amplified, came from a nearby balcony. "Catch!"

Kirk looked up to see a phaser rifle arcing through the air toward him. Gravity delivered the weapon to his hands. He hastily switched the rifle to its highest setting and opened fire on the truck barreling toward him. A white-hot beam sliced the already-compromised vehicle straight down the middle from front to back, splitting it in two. The halves of the bisected truck broke apart, screeching past Kirk on his left and right, missing him by centimeters before skidding and sparking to a stop just short of the first row of booths.

Kirk gasped out loud, somewhat amazed that neither piece had grazed him. He took his finger off the trigger as Sulu rushed toward him.

"Captain! Are you all right?"

"Can't complain." Kirk lowered the rifle, his heart still racing like a runaway shuttlecraft. "Thanks to Chekov's quick thinking." He looked up at the balcony and gave the ensign a sincere thumbs-up. Chekov beamed back at him, looking both relieved and pleased with himself. "Remind me to cite him for thinking fast under pressure."

"I'll do that," Sulu said, "and buy him a drink too." He shook his head at what he had just witnessed. "What kind of maniac pulls a stunt like that?"

"See for yourself."

They looked on as uniformed peace officers dragged a burly woman from the driver's side of the halved hover truck. Silvery blond dreadlocks fell to her shoulders. Shining epaulets proclaimed her political allegiance unless this was yet another false-flag operation, which struck Kirk as unlikely now that Div was in custody awaiting trial. A tool belt jangling from her waist was swiftly confiscated by the officers. Although she appeared somewhat battered and disheveled, the driver remained defiant.

"No votes for the Puppet! Fight for the General!"

She kept shouting as the officers escorted her away. Kirk scanned the plaza, grateful not to see any actual carnage. Things could have gone a lot worse.

"Any casualties?" he asked Sulu. "Or reports of similar incidents?"

"Not that I'm aware of." Sulu consulted his communicator, as did Kirk. No urgent hails demanded their attention.

Not a coordinated attack, then, Kirk thought. *Good.*

Dozens of frightened Vokites were still fleeing the violated plaza, swarming the exits, while others hesitated at the periphery of the square, stalled by confusion and uncertainty. It seemed at first glance that nobody had been seriously hurt, only scared. Kirk was genuinely heartened by that, yet he feared that the incident had inflicted serious damage anyway. If the anonymous driver's goal was to scare voters away from the polls, she may have already succeeded.

No, Kirk resolved. *Not on my watch.*

He handed the rifle to Sulu, trading the weapon for the compact loudspeaker he had employed earlier. He raised the device to his lips.

"Attention! Listen to me, everyone. This is Captain James Kirk of the *U.S.S. Enterprise.* I know you must be frightened by what just happened, but our security measures worked. The threat has been neutralized and the polling center is undamaged. You can safely return to your places in line. Don't let this one upsetting incident deter you from voting. You have the right to take part in this election. I repeat: the threat has been neutralized. Your safety is being protected."

Kirk wondered if his words would be enough with the charred halves of the hover truck still in plain view. Could mere oratory overcome fear and intimidation? He wanted to think so, but he wasn't so arrogant as to think he could turn the tide single-handedly.

"The Starfleet captain is right!" a voice called out. "Don't be afraid!"

The old man Kirk had rescued came forward, joining Kirk before the voting booths. His close brush with death had apparently not dampened his civic spirit. Kirk offered him the loudspeaker, hoping that the voice of an actual Vokite would carry more weight than that of a foreign starship captain.

"We can't let anyone scare us away from voting," the man exhorted his fellow citizens. "We've fought too long and too hard for this moment. If we falter now, if we let the bullies win, we might as well give up our rights for good!"

His passionate appeal did the trick. Murmurs of agreement rose from those remaining at the edges of the plaza, the voices swiftly growing in volume and intensity. Slowly, hesitantly, but in increasing numbers, people began to file back into the square, taking their chances for the opportunity to vote. Young people, old people, men and women, started lining up again.

How about that? Kirk thought, deeply moved by the sight. He was impressed and encouraged by the resolve of the would-be voters. Perhaps this contest of principles would not be decided by fear and deception after all. He turned toward the old man whose life he had saved—and who had possibly just helped save Vokite democracy as a result.

"Looks like they heard you loud and clear," Kirk said, smiling. "I can't thank you enough, Mister . . . ?"

"Bloj," the man said. "You can call me Bloj."

Kirk offered the man his hand. "Pleased to meet you, Mister Bloj."

"Likewise," Bloj said. "And let me say, on behalf of my people, that I appreciate everything you and the Federation have done to ensure this election is a fair one."

"We're not done yet," Kirk promised, freshly inspired to do his part. "If you'll excuse me, Mister Bloj, I have duties to carry out."

"Understood, Captain. Don't let me detain you."

Kirk glanced at the wreckage of the hover truck. "Mister Sulu," he began.

"Already on it, Captain," Sulu said. "We'll have those unsightly reminders carted away before the hour is out."

"Very good, Lieutenant." He knew he could count on Sulu to get the job done; the sooner the bisected truck was removed from sight, the better. He stepped away from Bloj and flipped open his communicator.

"Kirk to *Enterprise*. New orders. We're tripling security at as many major polling centers as we can manage. Beam down every hand on every shift available; the *Enterprise* can get by on a skeleton crew for the duration of Election Day if it has to."

"*Aye, Captain*," Mister Scott replied promptly; Kirk had left the engineer in command of the ship. "*It may take some creative shuffling, but we'll muster as many able bodies as we can spare, even if it means double shifts for all concerned. What's a little overtime when there's a world at stake?*"

"My thoughts exactly, Mister Scott." Kirk was going to owe his crew some serious shore leave when this mission was over, but that was a debt to be paid another day. "Meanwhile, Lieutenant Uhura, can you please get the word out, through every planetary media and on every emergency channel, that the situation here has been contained, that security at the polls has been reinforced, and that we and the local authorities are doing everything possible—and then some—to ensure the safety of all eligible voters."

"*Understood, Captain,*" Uhura responded. "*Consider all frequencies opened. We'll do what we can to get the message across.*"

"Thank you, Lieutenant." Kirk wondered if it was worth delivering a global address himself or if it would be better to enlist Vokite dignitaries to assure the population that voting remained safe across the planet. Perhaps Dare could draft a high-ranking member of the executive committee? Or Sergeant Myp could speak on behalf of the Civic Security forces? If she wasn't too busy keeping the peace, that was.

"*Excuse me, Captain,*" Uhura said. "*Commissioner Dare just hailed me from sickbay. She says she needs to speak to you . . . urgently.*"

Uh-oh, Kirk thought. *This can't be good.*

"Patch her through, Lieutenant."

"*Aye, sir. Over to you.*"

Only a moment passed before Dare's voice replaced Uhura's. Her anxious tone instantly brought Kirk to red alert.

"*Kirk? We have a big problem . . . with VP-One.*"

Thirty-Four

Ozalor

"Attention, Starfleet vessel! You are violating Ozalorian space! Turn back immediately!"

The command issued from the shuttlecraft's control panel as *Copernicus* sped toward Ozalor, ignoring all warnings from the planet, which was the only Class-M world in the sparsely populated system. Ozalor's sister planets and their moons were inhospitable to humanoid life, so *Copernicus* had passed only a handful of scattered planetary habitats and space stations on its approach to Ozalor, which was nevertheless guarded by an impressive array of security satellites and scanners. Absent a cloaking device, which were off-limits to Starfleet vessels, there was no way to arrive at the planet undetected, forcing Spock to resort to another form of subterfuge.

"This is the Starfleet shuttlecraft *Copernicus*," he responded, "making an emergency landing. We were thrown off course by a pulsar compression wave and are rapidly losing power and life-support. Requesting landing coordinates."

In truth, any damage to the shuttlecraft was mostly simulated or cosmetic. A controlled fuel leak, along with deliberately random fluctuations in their ion trail and power signatures, produced the *appearance* of distress to standard scans. A brief detour through the corrosive outer atmosphere of a gas giant had also yielded a degree of decorative scoring to *Copernicus*'s outer hull to provide visual corroboration to their claim.

"Attention, Copernicus," a harsh voice replied. *"Permission to land is denied. Reverse course and come no closer to Ozalor."*

"We're getting company, Mister Spock," Godwin shouted from the passenger compartment, where her seat was rotated toward an auxiliary instrumentation panel, which was patched into the shuttlecraft's sensors. "I'm picking up three Ozalorian fighters on an intercept course for us."

Spock sensed an increased tension in the atmosphere aboard the shuttlecraft. He could not fault his human companions for their anxiety; they were all in very real danger.

"This is *Copernicus*," Spock said. "We do not have sufficient power to reach any other safe haven. We must land or perish."

A fighter ship became visible through the forward ports. Its streamlined contours were designed for rapid atmospheric ascents into space. All three fighters registered on the shuttlecraft's sensor display as well. Preliminary scans detected fully armed weapon batteries. Spock considered raising the shuttlecraft's blast shutters, but feared that might be taken as girding for combat.

"Weapons locked on us," Godwin reported.

Levine swallowed hard. "Mister Spock?"

"Stay on course, Lieutenant."

Spock was gambling that the Ozalorians would not fire upon *Copernicus* and thereby risk war with the Federation. Keeping their distance from the UFP was one thing; shooting down a ship in distress was rather a more drastic response. It was difficult to calculate the probabilities involved with any degree of accuracy, due to the scarcity of data, but the fact that Chapel and Levine had not been killed by the original ambushers factored into Spock's considerations. If Ozalorian officials were indeed behind McCoy's abduction, they appeared to have avoided killing any Federation citizens to date. Spock hoped they would show similar restraint now.

Then again, there *had* been fatalities several years ago, the last time Starfleet had attempted to make contact with Ozalor . . .

"*Copernicus* to Ozalorian defense forces," he said. "Please scan our vessel. You will see that our shields and weapons are inoperative. We pose no threat to your world or people. This is strictly an emergency situation. I repeat: this is an emergency. Our lives are in immediate jeopardy."

Silence ensued as the fighters remained in formation, poised to fire upon the shuttlecraft from above, below, and behind. Spock waited tensely for Ozalor to respond to his urgent appeal.

"Maybe they think that's not their problem," Levine worried aloud.

"Possibly," Spock said, "but I prefer to think that high-level discussions are being conducted in great haste at this very moment."

Scanning all standard frequencies, he attempted to pick up any transmissions between the fighters and the planet, but found himself unable to eavesdrop on any relevant exchanges. All military communications were heavily encrypted, as was to be expected. He made the effort anyway, if only to occupy his mind as they awaited the Ozalorians' next move.

"*Attention,* Copernicus. *You are ordered to land at the designated coordinates, where you will immediately surrender your crew and vessel. Our Defense interceptors will escort you down. Any deviation from the prescribed fight path will result in the immediate destruction of your ship.*"

"Acknowledged," Spock said, "and affirmative."

Levine sighed in relief, his reaction echoed by similar responses in the passenger compartment. He wiped his brow as he adjusted his heading to comply with the landing coordinates transmitted by the Ozalorian authorities.

"Looks like they blinked after all, Mister Spock."

"I prefer to think that they made the logical choice," Spock replied. "An encouraging development."

"Well, don't feel too encouraged," Levine said. "Let's not forget that these same 'logical' folks very possibly kidnapped Doctor McCoy, and stunned Christine and me while they were at it."

"I am unlikely to overlook that," Spock assured him, "although they may have had what they deemed logical reasons for doing so, at least from their perspective. That does not excuse their actions, but, given a choice, I would prefer to deal with rational adversaries rather than the alternative."

"Can't argue with that," Levine said.

In any event, all was proceeding according to the plan they had devised en route to the system. Even if they had been able to somehow touch down on Ozalor undetected, they could hardly search an entire planet for McCoy with only one slim lead to go on. Given that said lead pointed to McCoy being held by a member of the royal court, Spock had concluded that their best chance of locating him was to be taken into custody by the Ozalorian government as well. The challenge now was to ensure that they weren't simply put on the next ship back to Braco . . . or confined elsewhere.

"Time to beat ourselves up a bit more?" Levine asked. "To support our sob story?"

"Affirmative." Spock had been reluctant to inflict significant damage on *Copernicus* before receiving the go-ahead to land, but it was now necessary to ensure that their cover story stood up to a close inspection of the shuttlecraft by the authorities on the ground. Operating the instrument panel, he increased the fuel leak so that they would retain just enough power to land safely, then deliberately induced power surges to burn out select circuits and systems, including the phasers, deflectors, and air-filtration mechanisms. Warning lights flashed as gauges tipped into red zones. The smell of burning circuitry confirmed that any Ozalorian investigators would indeed find evidence of damage. Acrid white fumes polluted their air supply, which remained sufficient to sustain them until they reached the surface. Spock's stomach experienced an acceptable level of nausea as the artificial gravity shorted out. Unhappy noises from the passenger compartment made their way to the cockpit.

"Careful there, Mister Spock," the pilot said. "We don't want to overdo it." He coughed on the smoke. "We still have to land this bird."

"I assure you, Lieutenant, our systems are degrading at a calculated rate. Despite any temporary discomfort, we will reach our destination before our situation becomes critical."

"Good to know, sir, as long as we don't cut it too close."

Flanked by its military escort, *Copernicus* touched down at a military base on the very continent said to house the *Yovode*'s primary residences. This was not a lucky accident; Spock had deliberately seen to it that their initial approach vector was directed toward the hemisphere and landmass where McCoy was most likely to be found. Daylight shone through the ports as armed soldiers in tan uniforms swarmed the grounded shuttlecraft, their disruptor rifles aimed at *Copernicus*.

"*Exit the shuttle with your hands up!*" an amplified voice blared from outside. "*Surrender yourself to custody without delay!*"

"Welcome to Ozalor," Levine muttered. He shut down what little power remained to their engines. "Now what, Mister Spock?"

"One step at a time, Lieutenant. We have successfully arrived at our destination. Let us now discover the lay of the land."

They exited the shuttle, possibly for the last time, into warm summer weather. Taciturn soldiers confiscated their communicators and other gear, while other soldiers rushed into *Copernicus* to secure it. Glancing up, Spock spied the interceptors returning to base. He wondered if their pilots were as relieved as he was that *Copernicus* had not been fired upon.

Unlikely, he estimated.

A ground vehicle conveyed the landing party to a nearby compound, where they were escorted at disruptor-point to an office where a uniformed officer scowled at them from behind a large wooden desk. A clerk sat off to one side, transcribing the meeting. A framed portrait of the *Yovode* was displayed prominently on one wall. The officer did not rise to greet them.

"I am Colonel Jaresi, the commander of this base, and I was having a perfectly decent morning before you decided to make my day a lot more complicated." She swept her disapproving gaze over Spock and his companions. "Which of you is in charge?"

Spock stepped forward. "I am in command of this mission and take full responsibility for our arrival here."

The colonel nodded. "Go on."

"I am Commander Spock, first officer of the *Starship Enterprise*. We were on a routine scientific mission, observing a previously unrecorded micropulsar, when we were thrown off course by an unexpected gravimetric burst and found ourselves in a dire situation. We appreciate your hospitality in allowing us to make an emergency landing."

"You're welcome," she said dryly, "but you might want to temper your gratitude. You're prisoners, not guests. Just because we chose not to blow you to atoms doesn't mean we appreciate the Federation dropping in on us out of the blue."

"Understood," Spock said. "We are grateful nonetheless."

She snickered at the sentiment. "Just out of curiosity, what kind of treatment are you expecting?"

"That remains to be seen," Spock said. "I am naturally aware that the Federation has no formal relations with your world, but I would hope that you would find a way to notify Starfleet of our whereabouts and condition."

"Don't get your hopes up," she warned. "Anyway, that's not my call. You bunch are a political hot potato that I intend to hand off as soon as possible. It's up to the diplomats and bigwigs to figure out what to do with you."

"I see," Spock said. "In that case, perhaps we can take the matter up with a certain Count Rayob? I believe he is your monarch's personal majordomo?"

Dropping Rayob's name was a calculated risk, but Spock deemed it worth taking as long as he stopped short of actually accusing the majordomo of kidnapping McCoy. Rayob was their only lead after all, so Spock desired to make contact with the man sooner rather than later.

The name certainly caught Jaresi off guard, although she maintained her professional composure. "As it happens, Count Rayob is retired."

Spock raised an eyebrow. It seemed that Colc's intelligence was out of date.

"Recently retired?"

"Very recently." She regarded him suspiciously. "How is it you know of Rayob?"

"My father is Sarek, a Vulcan ambassador of considerable experience. He has spoken of Rayob in the past."

The latter was an utter fabrication, but Spock hoped it was a plausible one. Considering their strained relationship, he was uncomfortable invoking his father's name and reputation, yet locating McCoy necessitated working their way up Ozalor's political food chain to the royal court, and Spock suspected, albeit reluctantly, that the son of a prominent ambassador might carry more weight, and pose more of a diplomatic challenge, than a mere Starfleet officer, particularly in a hierarchical monarchy. Ironically enough, he concluded, their covert mission required them to attract as much attention as possible from the planet's ruling class. This was counterintuitive, but true regardless.

"Your dad's an ambassador?" Jaresi sighed. "Terrific. Could this day get any more delightful?"

"My apologies for the inconvenience," Spock said.

Although far weightier matters were at stake, he could not help hoping, purely on a personal level, that word of his ploy would not reach his father. That would be . . . unfortunate.

Let us hope McCoy appreciates the lengths I'm willing to go on his behalf.

"Inconvenience is an understatement." Jaresi rose from her chair and started toward a side door marked "Private" in Ozalorian script. "Wait here while I knock this upstairs . . . way upstairs." She nodded at the guards and clerk. "Keep a close watch on them and get their full names and ranks."

She exited the office, leaving Spock and the others standing. Chapel quietly turned toward Spock. "I take it . . . your father . . . was unaware that Rayob had retired?"

"So it seems," Spock stated. He wondered if the majordomo's retirement was related to his recent visit to Braco.

"Quiet!" a guard ordered, curbing any further discussion. "Speak only when spoken to."

Spock complied with the guard's request. He waited patiently for 45.37 minutes before Jaresi returned. "Good news," she announced, "for me, that is. You're being taken off my hands and none too soon." She addressed her soldiers. "We have our orders. Ship them off to the Summer Palace and be quick about it."

Spock took note of their destination. "Palace?"

"You heard me," the colonel said. "The *Yovode* wants to see you . . . personally."

"We are honored."

She shrugged. "Better hope he feels the same way."

Thirty-Five

Ozalor

Their audience with Salokonos, *Yovode* of Ozalor, was a private one, with only a handful of the monarch's advisors in attendance, along with a number of vigilant guards. Count Rayob, whose image Spock had previously familiarized himself with, was not present, confirming what they had heard at the Ozalorian military base about his retirement. Spock regretted that their chief suspect in McCoy's kidnapping was absent, but he could hardly complain about meeting with Salokonos himself. The question was, how much did the planet's ruler know about the abduction?

"As we were losing power rapidly, we had no choice but to make an emergency landing on your world," Spock said, repeating their cover story yet again. He refrained from mentioning McCoy to avoid revealing their true agenda prematurely. The faked emergency had gotten them to the royal court; Spock now intended to "play it by ear," as Captain Kirk might say, until he had a better sense of how to proceed. Years of serving under Kirk had taught Spock the value of improvisation. He hoped this lesson would serve them well on Ozalor.

Salokonos regarded the prisoners from an elevated seat. He stroked his beard thoughtfully. A series of quartz bands girded his arm; Spock understood from his studies that each ring signified the sovereigns who had come before Salokonos, along with one band for the present ruler himself, so that the *Yovode* wore an entire dynasty on his person. *Not unlike the way a tree's age can be gauged by the rings of its trunk,* Spock reflected.

"I am not aware of a micropulsar in our proximity," Salokonos said, "nor are my scientists."

"With all due respect," Spock answered, "our Starfleet scanners are a generation more sophisticated than those available to your scientists. Moreover, the pulsar was merely passing through an adjacent region of deep space; it was not a permanent fixture in this sector, which is precisely why we seized the opportunity to study it once we detected it."

Along with his comrades, Spock had been forced to trade his Starfleet uniform for local garb to avoid attracting undue attention. A cap masked his Vulcan ears, although his and Levine's clean-shaven features still distinguished them from the average Ozalorian male, who appeared prone to displaying their facial hair. Chapel and Godwin blended in rather more easily.

"So you say," Salokonos said. "And yet I wonder about your alleged 'emergency.' How convenient that you were observing a transitory phenomenon that we are unable to verify."

"Facts are neither convenient nor inconvenient," Spock replied. "They simply are."

"Send them back where they came from, Your Excellency," a robed woman urged Salokonos. Her bald head, which was adorned with curious tattoos, seemed hardly in keeping with the appearance of other Ozalorian women, such as Colonel Jaresi back at the military base. Unusual white eyes, all but lacking irises, held little sympathy for Spock and his fellow prisoners. "We want no part of the Federation and its spies."

"If we are spies, we are exceedingly poor ones," Spock replied, "considering how easily you detected our arrival." He turned toward the woman. "I do not believe we have been introduced."

"This is *Lossu* Vumri," the monarch declared. "A healer of renown, as well as a valued member of my court."

"I am pleased to make your acquaintance, madam," Spock said.

"Don't be," she replied. "I am no friend of the Federation."

Duly noted, Spock thought.

"Nor am I," Salokonos said. "To be frank, Commander Spock, I find your chance arrival on my world rather too coincidental for my tastes, in light of recent other disturbances."

Spock raised an eyebrow. "And those would be?"

Was their arrival, immediately following McCoy's abduction, the coincidence to which Salokonos referred? Spock could see how the "accidental" arrival of a Starfleet landing party would seem extremely suspicious—if McCoy was indeed being held on Ozalor.

"None of your concern," Salokonos said, "if your landing was as unplanned as you profess. I remain unconvinced of this, however. Therefore, I am reluctant to send you on your way until I am confident that you had no ulterior motive for violating our borders."

"I regret that you doubt our motives," Spock said, not entirely sincerely. As a matter of fact, Salokonos's suspicions served Spock's own interests; he was in no hurry to leave Ozalor before determining whether McCoy had indeed been abducted by Count Rayob and brought to the planet. "In any event, I believe our damaged vessel requires considerable repair and refueling before we can even attempt to depart your world."

This was an exaggeration of sorts. Given the opportunity, Spock expected he could restore *Copernicus* to working order in no time.

"You need not concern yourself with that shuttlecraft, which is now the property of Ozalor," Salokonos decreed, dismissing the matter with a wave of his hand. "If and when you are allowed to leave us, you will be taken to neutral territory, such as Braco, where your people may recover you."

Spock felt obliged to feign a desire to return to the *Enterprise*. "And when might that occur?"

"*If* and when I so choose," Salokonos said, "and no sooner."

"But why delay, Your Excellency?" Vumri asked. "Why harbor these Federation vipers in our midst any longer than necessary?

Let us not forget that, even now, the Federation is consorting with Vok, our primal enemy."

"All the more reason not to proceed rashly," Salokonos said. "Make no mistake, Commander Spock, I am well aware of the *Enterprise*'s current assignment to Vok, and of the heated presidential election being waged there as we speak. Vok's politics are their own affair, of course, but I would be a fool not to monitor what goes on there and what is being said by the various candidates about Ozalor and Braco. Given a choice, I would prefer not to fan the flames of war at this critical juncture, which makes your ill-timed presence here all the more delicate a matter."

"I sympathize with your position," Spock said, watching his words carefully. He had to avoid persuading Salokonos to release them while not making it too apparent that they wished to remain on Ozalor for the time being. "You may rest assured, however, that the *Enterprise*'s mission to Vok is simply to observe the election there and see to it that the planet's president is elected fairly. We had no mandate to involve ourselves in Ozalor's affairs at all."

That much was true. Had Doctor McCoy not been abducted, and had the clues not pointed toward Ozalor, they would have had no reason to approach the planet at all, let alone force a landing here. Nor did he intend for his mission to influence the election on Vok if that could be avoided.

"I wish I could believe you, Commander," Salokonos said. He looked past Spock to address the security detail that brought the Starfleet captives from the base. "How many individuals know of this incident?"

"Only those directly involved in the capture and transport of the prisoners," the captain of the detail reported. "All such personnel have been informed that the subject is not to be discussed, upon penalty of court-martial."

"Good," Salokonos said. "I want this entire incident, including the existence of the prisoners, kept strictly classified." He looked over Spock and the others. "Have them confined to a secure location in the palace until I decide how best to handle this. And do so discreetly. I want this kept off the books, understood?"

"Yes, Your Excellency."

Salokonos fixed his gaze back on Spock and the others. "I would apologize for not being more hospitable, but you are hardly invited guests. We will see to your comfort and safety, to a degree, but are under no obligation to do any more than that. Be grateful that we allowed your vessel to touch down on our planet in the first place."

"You may rely on that, sir," Spock said.

He was not looking forward to being held captive again, nor was he entirely certain how to continue searching for McCoy from a position of confinement; nevertheless, he felt they were making progress in their investigation—and were perhaps one step closer to finding the missing doctor.

First, we made it onto Ozalor. Now we are in the Yovode's *palace.*

But where was McCoy?

Thirty-Six

Ozalor

Spock was becoming a connoisseur of captivity.

The rescue party found themselves confined to a well-equipped gymnasium beneath the Summer Palace. Medieval-looking shackles and oubliettes, preserved as décor, suggested that the subterranean vaults had been employed as dungeons in bygone days before being converted to less barbaric purposes. Compared to his other recent prisons, the accommodations were more comfortable than the Pit but less so than the luxury hotel suites on Braco. The amenities included showers, lavatories, padded mats, exercise equipment, temperature controls, and even a handful of virtual-reality booths for entertainment. Spock contented himself with simply resting on a workout bench, while his companions occupied themselves as best they could. He imagined that they were being confined to the gym, instead of a formal containment facility, in order to keep their captivity out of any official records. Or perhaps Salokonos simply wanted to avoid treating them too harshly for the present?

"How long do you think he intends to hold us?" Chapel asked. She paced restlessly about the room.

"Perhaps only until the election is over on Vok?" Spock speculated. By his calculations, the balloting was already underway on that other world. "So that the news will not influence the results?"

"Or maybe it depends on *who* gets elected." Godwin worked out on a weight machine; Spock had noted earlier that any individual free weights had been removed, no doubt to prevent them from being employed as weapons. "What if Salokonos is waiting to see who ends up in charge on Vok?"

"That's no good." Levine was on his back, exercising his legs via a wall-mounted treadmill similar to the one used for physical examinations in the *Enterprise*'s sickbay. "We've got things to do, if you know what I mean. We can't just cool our heels here indefinitely."

"I quite agree, Lieutenant," Spock said.

The possibility that they were being monitored hampered their ability to speak freely. Granted, the gymnasium was not designed to be as secure as an actual prison, but Spock preferred to err toward caution anyway. He discreetly eyed the entrance to the shower room; it was likely it lacked any security cameras for reasons of privacy, which presented definite possibilities should they need to conspire with less fear of being overheard.

"All right, up against the wall, away from the door!"

The command issued from an intercom unit on the wall near the entrance. Spock and the others complied, lining up at the opposite end of the gym. A barred door, with transparent aluminum panels between the antique metal bars, slid open to admit a uniformed jailer.

"You have a visitor," the man stated, sounding none too pleased about it. He patted the disruptor holstered at his hip, as though there was any chance of them overlooking it. "Mind your manners and don't even think about trying anything."

"Acknowledged," Spock said, curious as to who their visitor might be.

The guard took a deep breath and assumed a more formal tone.

"Announcing Her Highness, Avomora, *Yiyova* of Ozalor."

A young woman glided into the gym upon a mobile chair. Spock recognized Avomora from her official portraits, while recalling that *Yiyova* was roughly equivalent to crown princess, although the palace's automatic translators clearly preferred the local term. He noted the agate bracelet on her wrist, which would someday be joined by her predecessors' bands when she eventually took the throne. More mysterious was why she was apparently confined to the chair. A quilted blanket covered her lower body, making it difficult to determine whether there was any obvious defect with her legs. A half-dozen armed guards accompanied her. Their expressions ranged from wary to hostile.

"Are all these soldiers truly necessary, Sergeant Muzla?" she asked, indicating the guards. "These are Starfleet officers, not Orion pirates."

"I'm sorry, Your Highness. I can't deny you access to the prisoners, not if you command it, but I'm not going to take any chances with your safety." He scowled at the gym's unwilling inmates. "Keep your distance. No sudden moves. There will be no warnings if you even *appear* to pose a threat to the *Yiyova*."

"We would not think of it," Spock said.

"See that you don't," Muzla said redundantly.

"We are honored by your visit," Spock said to the royal. He noted her familial resemblance to her father, but remained puzzled by her seeming infirmity, which he did not believe to be a matter of public knowledge. Certainly, Spock had noted no reference to her being disabled when prepping for their arrival on Ozalor. It seemed the royal palace guarded its secrets well.

"I heard through the grapevine of your presence in the palace and could hardly stay away," she said. "I could pretend I am simply extending a courtesy to travelers from afar, but I'll confess to a healthy amount of curiosity as well. We don't get many visitors from the Federation."

Interesting, Spock observed. She had not said they *never* received such visitors. "Few at all, I imagine."

Avomora opened her mouth, as though to reply, then glanced cautiously at the guards surrounding her, who were paying close attention to all that transpired. Spock got the distinct impression there was more she wished to say, but that she was inhibited from doing so.

"So one would think," she said cryptically.

Muzla cleared his throat. "Pardon me, Your Highness, but we should watch what we say to these prisoners. They may well be Federation spies, operating in collaboration with our enemies on Vok."

"Have no fear, Sergeant," she said breezily, laughing off his concerns. "I'm not about to give away any state secrets or royal scandals." She smiled at the landing party. "You must forgive the sergeant. He's afraid that I'll carelessly reveal—what is the expression?—the 'bones in the cupboard.'"

"Skeletons in the closet?" Chapel suggested.

"Ah, we obviously need to adjust our automatic translators," the princess said. "Funny, though, I could have sworn the phrase was '*bones*,' not skeletons, as in heaven forbid I should tell you where the *bones* are hidden."

The stress she placed on the word "bones" was not lost on Spock, although he easily concealed any obvious interest or reaction. Was she indeed confirming that she had encountered McCoy—and that he was being kept in some secluded corner of the palace?

"I take your meaning," he replied. "A venerable edifice such as this palace must inevitably have its fair share of bones tucked away out of sight. Figuratively speaking, that is."

She nodded. "I see Vulcans are as perceptive as they say." She peered at the exposed points of his ears. "You are a Vulcan, correct, and not a Romulan?"

"Romulans are unlikely to serve in Starfleet," he said.

"So I understand," she replied. "Despite my rather cloistered existence, I make it a point to learn a great many valuable things."

"That much is clear," Spock replied. "I applaud your curiosity. It was, in fact, the pursuit of knowledge that led us to your world, albeit indirectly."

"Ah, yes," she said. "A scientific survey gone amiss, I believe?"

"Something like that," Chapel said. "Speaking of bones and such, I'm a nurse by profession. I'd be happy to volunteer my services at whatever infirmary or medical facility you might have on the premises."

"That's very gracious of you," Avomora said. "I can't make any promises, but let me see what I can do about—"

"Excuse me, Your Highness," Muzla interrupted, "but that's probably enough for now. You mustn't tire yourself."

"Let me be the judge of that, Sergeant," she said, frowning.

"I wish I could, Your Highness, but I answer to your father as well, and he's not going to be happy about this visit as it is."

"You were acting on my orders," she said.

"Yes, Your Highness, but even still . . ."

". . . I'm only the Heir, not the *Yovode*." Avomora sighed. "Very well, Sergeant. I have no desire to get you or your guards in trouble with my father. I will not linger much longer." She turned toward the landing party. "Before I go, is there anything I can do to make your stay more comfortable? More blankets and pillows, perhaps?" She shivered theatrically. "Even with modern climate controls, these old vaults can get drafty, I know."

"That would be most kind," Chapel said. "Thank you."

"You're welcome." She tugged on the quilt covering her lap and legs. "Here. This will make a good start."

"Your Highness," Muzla protested. "Is this wise? You didn't say anything about passing objects to the prisoners."

"It's just a blanket, Sergeant," she said, visibly exasperated. "Stop being so paranoid. You're embarrassing me."

Muzla blanched. He was young enough, Spock noted, that he could reasonably expect to serve under Avomora someday, when she finally ascended to the throne.

"My apologies, Your Highness, but please allow me to personally transfer your gift to the prisoners . . . for security's sake."

"If you must."

She carefully folded the quilt into a square and handed it to the jailer, who crossed the gym to give it to Chapel, before returning to the princess's side.

"Now then, Your Highness," he prompted, "if we're quite finished . . ."

"Yes, yes, Sergeant, I get the message. Just let me bid farewell
to our guests . . . for now." She looked at the prisoners. "Have a
pleasant evening. I regret we cannot talk longer. Perhaps we will
speak again, sooner than one might think."

She winked at Spock.

"This way, Your Highness, if you please."

"Lead the way, Sergeant."

Rotating her chair, she exited the gym, taking the guards with
her. The transparent door slid shut behind them, leaving the
prisoners alone in the vault. Spock waited a brief interval, to be
certain that their jailers would not return, before turning toward
Chapel.

"Excuse me, Nurse. May I borrow that quilt for a short
period?"

"Of course, Mister Spock. Are you chilled?"

"To a degree, but I also find myself interested in studying the
local textiles."

Avomora had demonstrated an interest in communicating
more than the guards might allow. Spock pondered what lengths
she might go to achieve that end.

"I don't blame you," Chapel said, playing along. It was evident
she realized Spock's interest was more than merely academic. She
eyed him quizzically as she handed him the blanket. "It's lovely
work."

He quietly retreated to a corner of the gym, betraying no unusual eagerness or curiosity. Chapel casually positioned herself
between him and the transparent door, shielding him from view.
Levine and Godwin followed her lead by engaging in vigorous
calisthenics in front of him as he methodically palpated the quilt
in search of . . . what?

It was possible that he was overestimating the *Yiyova*'s devi-
ousness, yet he preferred to think that her parting wink had been

a signal. Such hopes were rewarded when his probing fingers detected a small, solid object within one of the quilt's corner panels. He deftly tore open the panel at its seam and reached within, extracting a compact metal earpiece minute enough to be detectable only by a close physical inspection. Glancing about warily, he activated the device by pressing a button at one end, then swiftly inserted it into his right ear. That both Ozalorian and Vulcan ear canals conformed to basic humanoid design meant it fit snugly enough to remain in place.

"*Hello?*" Avomora's voice sounded. "*Can you hear me?*"

"Affirmative," Spock whispered. "Are you reading me as well?"

"*Yes! Is that you, Mister Spock? You don't have to speak aloud. Just subvocalize and I'll hear you.*"

"Understood," he said almost silently. "My compliments on the sophistication of this device."

"*I can't take the credit. It was devised for my own safety, so I can secretly summon help if ever I'm taken hostage. Mind you, I've never had occasion to do so, but it occurred to me that the earpiece could just as easily be put to another use as well.*" Her excitement was audible. "*I was hoping you would find it, but I couldn't be sure!*"

"I'm pleased we lived up to your expectations," Spock said. "I gather there is information you wish to convey to us, perhaps concerning a certain Doctor Leonard McCoy?"

"*That's it exactly. Your friend 'Bones' is right here in this very palace, only a few floors away from where you are now. I'm embarrassed to admit that he was commandeered against his will to assist me in a medical capacity.*"

Spock listened carefully as she explained how Count Rayob had abducted McCoy in hopes of treating the princess and thereby weakening *Lossu* Vumri's influence at the royal court. Avomora did not dwell on the details of her illness, but Spock gathered that it was debilitating enough to warrant extreme measures.

"*Please don't judge Rayob too harshly,*" she urged. "*He was only thinking of my welfare, as well as the future of the monarchy. Alas, I fear that Doctor McCoy is not safe on Ozalor as long as he poses a threat to Vumri's power. There's already been one attempt on his life.*"

Spock was troubled to hear this.

"I appreciate your candor. Is there any way you can help us recover him, perhaps by facilitating our release?"

"*If only I could. I may be the Heir to the throne, but even I don't have the authority to overrule my father with regard to your situation. I was able to bully the sergeant into letting me see you, but that alone was pushing my luck. I can tell you where to find Doctor McCoy, but I have no idea how to get you out of that dungeon. I'm sorry.*"

"No need to apologize," Spock said. "As it happens, I may already have some ideas of my own."

Thirty-Seven

Ozalor

"So what do you think the *Yovode* is going to do with these Starfleet intruders?"

Junior Private Hakoo cocked his head toward the entrance to the once and present dungeon, to the annoyance of Senior Private Zezly, who was trying to concentrate on a tablet of math puzzles he had brought to occupy his time during the long graveyard shift ahead. The two guards were seated at a small portable table outside the underground gymnasium. A pot of strong tea rested on the table to help keep their eyes open until dawn. Zezly prayed that the younger guard wasn't planning to chitchat through their entire shift.

"No idea," he answered tersely. "Our job is to just make sure they stay put. Anything else is above our pay grade."

Two guards struck Zezly as overkill, to be honest, given that the prisoners were already locked up tight, but he supposed Sergeant Muzla was taking no chances. Zezly focused on his tablet, hoping that Hakoo would take the hint and leave off jabbering.

No such luck.

"You want to know what I'd do with them, if I was in charge?"

"Not particularly."

A loud crash from inside the gym cut off the already tedious conversation. Frantic shouts and commotion accompanied the crash, causing the guards to spring to their feet and rush to the door, where they found one of the prisoners, the blond nurse named Chapel, pounding frantically on the other side of the door's transparent aluminum panels.

"Help us!" she shouted through the locked door. "He's out of control!"

Peering past her, Zezly glimpsed some sort of fight going on in the main exercise room. He and Hakoo traded anxious looks.

So much for a quiet shift, he thought.

"Cover me." Zezly drew his disruptor. "Watch the door."

Hakoo nodded, proving he did know when to shut up after all. He readied his weapon as well.

"Hurry, please!" the nurse pleaded. "We can't manage him on our own!"

Zezly keyed in the command code and the door slid open. He half expected the woman to try to make a break for it, along with the other prisoners, but she simply scooted out of the way to let them charge into the gym, where a chaotic scene confronted them.

"Let go of me! I'll kill you all!"

The Vulcan, Spock, had gone berserk. His eyes bulged from their sockets as the other two humans struggled to restrain him. Overturned exercise equipment explained the crash heard moments ago. Spittle sprayed from the Vulcan's lip as he fought to free himself. "Unhand me, humans. My blood burns! My eyes are flame!"

Zezly looked in confusion to the nurse. "What the splinter is the matter with him?"

"It's the blood fever!" Chapel said. "It comes over Vulcans sometimes. All their repressed emotions just . . . explode. Ordinarily, it can be controlled with medication, but you took my medkit away . . ."

Zezly got the idea. He set his disruptor on stun and took aim at the crazed Vulcan, none too concerned with accidentally stunning the other two prisoners as well. He could sort them out after order was restored.

"No!" Chapel darted between the guards and the fracas, shielding Spock with her body. "In this agitated state, his metabolism is under severe stress . . . even a stun blast could kill him!"

Zezly hesitated, uncertain whether to believe her or not. He was just an ordinary grunt who had never set foot off-planet; what he didn't know about Vulcan physiology would fill the Royal Library. He was pretty sure, though, that the *Yovode* didn't want any of his Federation prisoners to die in custody.

"Senior Private?" Hakoo asked, looking equally at a loss.

"Help us!" the human male named Levine shouted. "He's too strong! We can't hold him much longer!"

"It is the Red Hour!" Spock roared. "I will not be caged!"

With a burst of strength, he hurled Levine across the room, so that only the woman, Godwin, remained to grapple with him, her arm locked around his neck in an effort to keep him from running amok.

"Don't just stand there!" she called to the dumbfounded guards. "Help me!"

Zezly didn't have any better ideas, so he holstered his weapon and dashed past Chapel to assist Godwin. "Come on!" he shouted to Hakoo. "We need to shut this down!"

Spock shook loose Godwin, who went stumbling backward even as the guards each seized one of the Vulcan's flailing arms. Between the two of them, Zezly figured they could wrestle Spock to the ground, but he had underestimated just how strong the Vulcan was. It was all he could do to just hold on to Spock's arm, let alone subdue him. He could tell Hakoo was struggling as well. The younger guard grunted with exertion, barely keeping Spock from tossing him aside the way he had Levine.

"Shards!" Hakoo exclaimed. "How strong is this madman?"

"Don't ask!" Godwin said, scrambling to her feet.

"Please!" Chapel shouted over the commotion. "Don't hurt him! He doesn't know what he's doing!"

Hurt him? Zezly reconsidered his decision to holster his disruptor. The *Yovode* wouldn't be happy to have a dead Vulcan on his hands, but they couldn't let Spock injure anyone else either. *Especially Hakoo and me!*

"Senior Private?" Hakoo asked anxiously. "I'm not sure this is working out so well."

"Tell me something I don't know—"

A sharp blow to his neck resolved his dilemma abruptly.

The Ozalorian guards dropped to the floor, rendered unconscious by karate chops delivered by Levine and Godwin, one each per guard. Spock admired the effectiveness of the security officers' blows. Not quite as elegant as a nerve pinch, perhaps, but efficient nonetheless.

"Well done, Lieutenants." He discarded his assumed madness with relief. "And my compliments to you as well, Miss Chapel. You were quite convincing."

"No more than you," she replied.

"Maybe a little too convincing." Levine massaged his shoulder. "Did you have to toss me quite so forcefully?"

"My apologies, Lieutenant. It was necessary to persuade our captors of my apparent insanity." He grimaced at the memory. "Rest assured that I found the performance entirely distasteful, albeit necessary."

Levine shrugged, then winced as a result. "Hey, anything that gets us out of this glorified dungeon."

"Ditto," Godwin said.

Spock appreciated their attitudes, which were commendably logical. He moved on to the next stage of their plan, which they had relayed to one another during overlapping visits to the showers.

"Godwin, Levine, help yourself to the guards' weapons and uniforms. Bind them also so that they will be unable to sound an alarm when they regain consciousness."

That there were only two guards to contend with was a mixed blessing; for better or for worse, he and Chapel would have to rely on their Ozalorian civilian garb to disguise them. Spock found a cloth sweatband, retrieved from a gym locker, to hide the points of his ears. The fact that he and Levine were clean-shaven on a planet where facial hair was the masculine norm was less than ideal as far as camouflage went, but Spock was not inclined to let time remedy that difficulty. Doctor McCoy was waiting, as was their royal accomplice.

He cupped his hand around his ear. "Your Highness, the way is clear."

"We're ready for you, Mister Spock," Avomora replied via the hidden earpiece. A trace of anxiety entered her voice. *"You didn't have to hurt anyone, did you?"*

Spock glanced at the fallen guards. "No lasting damage was inflicted."

"I'm glad to hear that," she confessed. *"They* are *my father's soldiers after all."*

"They are merely incapacitated." Spock spoke aloud so his companions could hear his side of the dialogue. "Your promised guide is standing by, as planned?"

"Not standing by, Mister Spock," a voice intruded. "I'm right here."

A young woman slipped into the exercise room. Her short black hair and scarred face matched the description Avomora had provided of her agent, who was to guide them to McCoy. A knife was sheathed at her hip.

"Jemo, I take it?"

"Right the first time," she said. "What took you so long?"

Her insouciant attitude suggested either confidence or recklessness; it remained to be seen which predominated. In any event, Spock and his team were in no position to be picky when it came to allies within the palace; Avomora had vouched for Jemo's trustworthiness. That would have to suffice.

"Haste is indeed called for." Spock glanced at Levine and Godwin to confirm that they'd finished changing into the guards' uniforms, which fit them adequately if not perfectly. He nodded at Jemo. "Lead the way."

She poked her head out of the gym to ensure the coast was clear, then gestured for them to follow her out into the corridor beyond. "Keep your voices down," she cautioned. "Most everybody should be asleep now, but your Federation accents pretty much scream that you're not from these parts."

"Noted." Spock modulated the volume of his voice accordingly. By his calculations, they were indeed in the early hours of the morning in this time zone. In theory, that reduced the probability of any further violence being required between here and their destination. Sealing the gymnasium door behind them, they made their way through the lower levels of the palace. The women walked ahead of the men, the better to hide the smooth faces of the latter, who were prepared to turn their faces down if they encountered any stray residents embarked on late-night errands. Jemo guided them with assurance, evidently quite familiar with the various halls and stairways.

"Thanks so much for your help," Chapel whispered. "We wouldn't have wanted to navigate this maze on our own."

"Save your thanks," Jemo said curtly. "This wasn't my idea. Frankly, I can't believe I'm actually doing this."

Chapel examined the other woman's face. "Then why are you?"

"It's what Avo wants. And who else can she trust to do it?"

Spock took her word for it, while wishing that he had a fuller grasp of the palace's intrigues and politics. Ascending from the dungeons, they encountered no obstacles until they reached an archway holding a large silver mirror, which proved to be a portal to the chambers beyond, guarded by a matron wearing a night coat and a severe expression.

"Really, Jemo?" she challenged their guide. "At this hour?"

"Good to see you, too, Bilis," Jemo replied. "The *Yiyova* is expecting me . . . and my friends."

The older woman eyed the rest of the party dubiously. "She's with the doctor now. It's not a good time."

"That's what you think," Jemo said. "You going to let us in or not?"

"I'm not sure why you think you still have privileges here," Bilis said scornfully, her manner reminiscent of a haughty Ardanan aristocrat. "As I recall, you were dismissed from duty."

"It's called friendship," Jemo shot back. "Sorry you've never heard of it. Pretty sure Avomora still gets to pick her friends, or do you want to tell her otherwise?"

That was apparently further than Bilis wished to go, as she grudgingly relented and admitted them to the princess's personal chambers. They passed through the silver portal even as the indignant matron continued to protest.

"I certainly hope you're not planning to disturb the *Yiyova* while—"

Jemo ignored her. "This way," she told her charges.

A wood-paneled antechamber branched off into three short hallways, impressing Spock with the size of the princess's personal quarters. Jemo led them down a short hall to another archway. A pair of guards were stationed before the door. They sprang to their feet at the sight of the visitors.

"Hold on, what's all this?" one blurted. He squinted at Godwin and Levine. "I don't know you—"

Twin disruptor beams stunned the guards before they had a chance to see through the security officers' disguises. They slumped to the floor.

"Nice," Jemo said approvingly. "Serves them right for taking my job."

Bilis gasped in shock. "Wha-what's happening?"

"Just a late-night social call," Jemo said, smirking. "And don't even think about raising a fuss unless you want to get the same treatment."

"You wouldn't dare!" A quaver in Bilis's voice belied her certainty on that count. Her frightened gaze fixed on the stolen disruptors in the Starfleet officers' hands. Awareness dawned on her face. "By the Throne, you're the spies from Starfleet! You can't be here! You can't!"

Agitation raised her voice an octave. Spock determined she was on the verge of panic.

"Forgive me, madam," he stated before applying a nerve pinch to quiet her, "but I fear your emotions are getting the better of you."

He started to lower the woman to the floor when a familiar voice drawled from the doorway.

"Haven't heard that cold-blooded Vulcan logic for a while," McCoy said.

Thirty-Eight

Vok

"What's wrong with Vok Populi?" Kirk asked.

Only minutes had passed since he'd stopped the hover truck from slamming into the voting booths in the crowded plaza. Now Commissioner Dare's voice issued from his communicator as she reached out to him from the *Enterprise*, more than a thousand kilometers overhead. No pain or weakness could be heard in the recovering diplomat's voice, only urgency.

"It's trying to commit suicide, basically."

"Come again?" Kirk stepped behind the looming marble pedestal, out of sight and earshot of the courageous Vokites lining up to vote in the morning. If there was another threat to the rapidly approaching election, he wanted it kept quiet until he had a better idea of what was what. "I don't understand."

"I've been monitoring VP-One from my bed," she said, *"making certain everything was ready to go, or at least as much as I could while I'm laid up in sickbay. Everything seemed in order until I got a sudden notification that Vok Populi had gone into self-destruct mode and was counting down to total disintegration. We've got only seventeen minutes until high-intensity photon charges reduce the entire satellite to atoms!"*

"What?"

Kirk recalled Steve Tanaka mentioning that Vok Populi was programmed to self-destruct if ever its automated integrity was irretrievably compromised, but Tanaka had also assured Kirk that such an eventuality was all but inconceivable due to the sophistication of the supercomputer's firewalls and other cybernetic defenses. The self-destruct function, which went so far as to ensure the actual physical destruction of the satellite, had been included simply to assure nervous Vokites that the election results could not be tampered with and, just as importantly, that the secrecy of their votes would remain so.

"How is that even possible?" he asked.

"*I have no idea,*" Dare said. "*But the clock is ticking . . . and I don't know how we're going to stop it.*"

Kirk glanced up at the sky. It was not lightening yet, but he knew that dawn was only a couple hours away on this part of the planet, where the voting was scheduled to begin.

"Have you contacted Tanaka?"

"*I've been trying to, but he's not responding.*"

Kirk scowled. Tanaka knew Vok Populi as well as or better than probably anyone else on the planet or the *Enterprise*. His going silent at the same time that VP-One was going buggy couldn't be a coincidence. Had something happened to Steve?

"Uhura, can you hail Tanaka for me?"

He assumed correctly that she'd been monitoring the transmission. "*I've been attempting that for Commissioner Dare,*" she replied, "*but, as she said, he's not answering my hails.*"

"Can you pinpoint his location via his communicator?" Kirk asked.

"*Aye, Captain. His communicator has not been switched off. He's just not responding.*"

"Because he can't or won't?" Kirk wondered aloud. His course was clear to him. "Contact the transporter room. Prepare to transport Chekov, Bradley, and me to his current location."

"*Acknowledged, sir,*" Uhura replied. "*Stand by.*"

Kirk stepped out from behind the pedestal and signaled Sulu, who came over to join him. "I'm needed elsewhere, and I'm taking Chekov and Bradley for backup." Ensign Lisa Bradley was also assigned to this voting center; Kirk judged one or two fewer

officers on the site were unlikely to make a difference, especially
if VP-One disintegrated. "I'm leaving this location in your hands.
Hold down the fort."

"Absolutely, Captain." Sulu was perceptive enough to pick up
on his captain's mood. "Is there a problem, sir?"

There was no time to fully brief Sulu on the crisis, nor did Kirk
have much in the way of real information. "That's what I need
to find out. Keep watch here and await further instructions as
needed."

"Understood, Captain." The helmsman was surely curious, but
he kept any additional questions to himself. He nodded at Kirk.
"Good luck, sir."

"Thank you, Sulu." Kirk recruited a security detail via his communicator. "Kirk to Chekov and Bradley. We need to deal with a
possible issue involving computer security. Prepare for transport."

"*Aye, Captain,*" Chekov replied from the balcony.

"*Acknowledged, sir,*" Bradley responded as well. She was not in
Kirk's line of vision, but he knew she was posted in and about the
plaza. "*May I ask where we're going, sir?*"

"To round up some missing technical support." Kirk figured he
could brief them on site. "Assuming nothing's happened to him."

"*Captain,*" Uhura broke in. "*The transporter room is ready to
beam you to the requested coordinates.*"

"Which is where, exactly?"

"*An administrative building on the other side of the city. It's the
same location where you and Commissioner Dare first beamed
down to the planet.*"

Kirk remembered that initial meeting with the candidates and
their aides. He also recalled Tanaka showing off a sophisticated
computer station linked to Vok Populi. Was Tanaka already cop-
ing with the crisis on his own? If he was frantically trying to abort
the self-destruct sequence, that might explain why he was too
busy or distracted to answer Uhura's hails.

"Acknowledged, Lieutenant. Three to beam over. Energize."

A familiar tingle enveloped him. In the split second before he dematerialized entirely, he glimpsed the dazzling sparkle of the transporter effect flashing up on the balcony where Chekov was posted. In the plaza, the men were several meters apart, both horizontally and vertically, with Bradley occupying yet another position, but a heartbeat later all three Starfleet officers were standing beside one another in the garishly painted parlor Kirk had visited before. He briefly admired the smoothness of the site-to-site transport, which displayed the steady hand and skill of Lieutenant John Kyle, who had previously beamed Kirk down to the voting center while Mister Scott commanded the bridge. *Nicely done,* Kirk thought.

"Stay where you are! I mean it, don't move a muscle!"

Kirk found himself facing the business end of a disruptor improbably gripped by an agitated Steve Tanaka, who stood between the new arrivals and the exposed computer station. A digital display on the large circular viewscreen counted down to VP-One's demise . . . in less than thirteen minutes.

"You too, Ensigns," Tanaka said. "Raise your hands above your heads, all of you. Don't even think of reaching for your phasers. I can't let you stop me!"

"Stop you?" Kirk put the pieces together even if the picture was still pretty blurry. He got the distinct impression that Tanaka was not, in fact, working to fix the problem at hand, but apparently *was* the problem. "What have you done, Steve?"

"Hands up!" Tanaka repeated.

Kirk slowly raised his hands and indicated that Chekov and Bradley should do the same. They outnumbered Tanaka three to one, but Kirk wanted facts more than he wanted a fracas, at least for now.

"What's this about?" he asked.

"I had no choice!" Tanaka insisted, guilt all over his face. He looked and sounded more anxious than Kirk had ever seen him. He ran his free hand through his unkempt hair; one foot tapped nervously against the floor. "It wasn't easy, but I managed to do it. I'm probably the only person who could, knowing Vok Populi the way I do . . ."

Kirk eyed the countdown with concern, but he kept his voice calm and made no sudden movement. "Do what, Steve?"

"Convince VP-One that it's been compromised." A pained smile lacked any semblance of mirth. "It's funny, really. I don't actually have to hack VP-One and take control of its programming; I just had to trick it into *thinking* that it's been successfully breached. Its own automated self-destruct measures will take care of the rest. Goodbye, Vok Populi. No more election."

Clever, Kirk thought. "But why, Steve. Who got to you . . . and how?"

Anguish contorted Tanaka's features.

"It's Myp," he confessed. "They're holding her hostage. They promised they'd release her, that she wouldn't be harmed if I destroyed VP-One so Prup can't possibly be elected . . ."

So that's why I haven't seen or heard from her for a while, Kirk realized. "Who? Who has her?"

"Some of her fellow peace officers, I think, who are still loyal to the old regime. We underestimated Gogg's support among the Civic Security forces." His voice caught in his throat, choking on a sob. "She trusted them, damn them! They were her comrades-in-arms. That's the only way they could have caught her off guard!"

Kirk could believe it. Sometimes it wasn't the Klingon in front of you that you needed to watch out for; it was the friend or companion you thought you could trust with your life. Like Gary Mitchell, or Ben Finney, or Janice Lester . . .

"It's not too late, Steve. Halt the countdown. We'll find a way to rescue Myp, I promise. You can rely on me, on my crew. We can get her back without sacrificing Vok's first real election in a generation, everything you and Dare and Sergeant Myp have worked so hard for."

Tanaka shook his head. "I can't take that risk."

The countdown on the viewscreen ticked down mercilessly. Only ten minutes remained before Vok Populi disintegrated. A certain irony was not lost on Kirk, who had been known to talk rogue computers and androids into self-destructing for the greater good. Now here he was, racing time to stop a one-of-a-kind supercomputer from destroying itself.

"And I can't let you do that," Kirk said. "You know that."

Lowering his arms, he started toward Tanaka.

"Captain?" Bradley asked.

"Stay back!" Tanaka blurted. "I'm warning you!"

His eyes darted back and forth between Kirk and the other two officers as he kept the phaser aimed squarely at Kirk, who wondered why Tanaka hadn't simply stunned his unwanted visitors by now. Did he doubt his ability to take down all three of them before Chekov or Bradley could draw their weapons? Not an unreasonable worry, Kirk deemed; it might be worth getting stunned if it distracted Tanaka long enough for the other officers to take action.

But perhaps that wouldn't be necessary. *If I can just get through to him before it's too late.*

"Think, Steve. Don't let this go any further."

He displayed open palms. He took another step forward.

"Stop! Don't come any closer!" Steve said; it sounded more like a plea than a command. He backed away from Kirk, toward the computer station behind him, and hastily switched the setting on his pistol. "I'm not joking, Kirk! This phaser is set on kill." He shot glances at Chekov and Bradley. "You hear me? Is this election worth your captain's life?"

"That's for me to decide," Kirk said.

Knowing that Tanaka's phaser was now set on kill gave Kirk pause, but he also saw an opportunity of sorts. Tanaka had just raised the stakes in a big way; perhaps, Kirk strategized, he could take advantage of that by going all in—and gambling on the fact that Tanaka was a Federation diplomat after all.

"You're no killer, Steve. You believe in everything the UFP stands for, which is why I don't believe you'll fire the weapon." Kirk slowly approached the armed man. "I'm calling your bluff because I'm certain that your conscience—and sense of duty—will prevail."

His bold words and resolute expression conveyed more confidence than he felt. Tanaka was not a member of his crew, was not Starfleet. The young man had Dare's confidence, but Kirk had only known him for a short time. Did he truly want to risk his life on the brief impression he'd formed of Tanaka's character?

"Captain," Chekov said, "are you sure this is wise?"

Not entirely, Kirk thought, but it wasn't as though he had any choice. Time was running out—for Vok Populi and the planet's fledgling democracy—and they were probably going to need Tanaka's help to undo the damage he'd done, which meant making him part of the solution again.

"Give me that phaser, Steve." Kirk held out his hand. "You and I both know you don't want to do this. Myp would never want you to do this."

Tanaka flinched at her name. Distraught, he again ran his free hand through his dark hair, mussing it further. Kirk feared he was on the verge of breaking down.

"It's just an election," Tanaka said. "It's not worth Myp's life. Don't ask me to throw that away over politics."

Kirk shared his concern for Myp's safety, but he had to force Tanaka to face the truth and look past his rationalizations.

"Politics matter. This election matters. We're not talking about an abstraction here; this election could have major consequences for this entire sector and beyond. You know that as well as anyone."

He was only a few paces away from Tanaka, within reach of the phaser. It was tempting to make a grab for it. Tempting, but potentially fatal.

"Please don't make me do this!" Tanaka begged. His other

hand was tangled in his hair as though trying to get at his tormented brain. "I don't want to hurt you. I don't want to hurt anyone!"

Kirk paused, even as he remained acutely aware of the countdown to VP-One's immolation. He felt torn between the urgency of the situation and the need to not make any sudden moves that might push Tanaka over the edge. He had to settle this while there was still time to save the crucial satellite.

"I know that, Steve," he said gently, "which is how I know I'm not in any danger here. We're on the same side."

Tanaka's face crumpled. The arm holding the phaser trembled. He shook like a lunar willow in the moonlight. His voice quavered.

"You're right," he said weakly. "I can't do it. I can't kill you just to keep her safe."

I knew it, Kirk thought, relaxing slightly.

"But I can do this!"

Tanaka surprised Kirk by spinning around and blasting the computer station. Sparks erupted from the control panel, which glowed blue-hot before melting into slag. The viewscreen went blank, erasing the digital countdown at five minutes and counting. Smoke and steam billowed from the dissolving terminal.

"No!" Kirk lunged forward, tackling Tanaka from behind. He seized the other man's arm, twisting his wrist until Tanaka let go of the phaser, which fell to the floor. The destructive beam vanished as soon as Tanaka released the trigger, but the deed was done. The advanced computer station was a smoldering ruin, visibly beyond all repair. Kirk stared at the wreckage in dismay. "You didn't need to do that!"

"Agree to disagree." Tanaka put up no resistance. "It's done. You can't stop it now."

Kirk let go of Tanaka, turning him over to Chekov and Bradley, who came forward to take him into custody. The smell of burning plastiform and circuitry permeated the previously pristine atmosphere of the chamber. The discarded phaser rested on the floor, its destructive work completed. Kirk almost wished that Tanaka *had* shot him instead. His mind raced to find another path to saving Vok Populi.

"But . . . there must be other terminals, other interfaces, other ways to contact VP-One."

"Naturally," Tanaka said, calmer now that he no longer had Kirk at gunpoint. "But you've almost run out of time, Kirk. Honestly, I'm not certain I could halt the self-destruct sequence now even if I had access to Vok Populi . . . or wanted to."

The viewscreen was dead, but Kirk estimated that they only had four minutes left before the photon charges went off, disintegrating the satellite. He looked again at the cooling ruins of the computer station. Clearly, there was nothing more that could be done from this location. Not even Spock could turn the wreckage back into a working control panel in time.

He flipped open his communicator.

"Kirk to *Enterprise.* Four to beam up, pronto."

He wasn't sure what could be done from the ship, but that's where his resources were. Scotty and Uhura had both studied Vok Populi at his orders; he could use their input and expertise, even though the problem with VP-One wasn't actually an engineering or communication issue. This was an advanced programming challenge, better suited to Spock—and Spock was at least a solar system away.

"Give it up, Kirk," Tanaka said. "What's done is done."

"We'll see about that, mister."

The transporter beam captured them, beaming them back aboard *Enterprise.* An express turbolift and a brisk march brought them to the bridge. Chekov and Bradley escorted Tanaka, on the off chance that he might still prove useful in averting VP-One's imminent destruction. Mister Scott surrendered the captain's chair, relocating to his accustomed place at the engineering station, as Kirk moved quickly to direct operations from the bridge.

Glancing around, he couldn't help lamenting the absence of both Sulu and Spock. Yeoman Zahra operated the helm in Sulu's stead.

"Time to self-destruct?" Kirk demanded.

"Three minutes," Scott reported. His doleful expression offered little hope that they could pull a rabbit out of a hat this time. "Those charges are building past the point of no return, Captain."

Damn, Kirk thought. He fought an urge to pound his fist on the armrest of his chair. "On-screen."

"Aye, sir," Ensign Jana Haines said from the science station, where she was filling in for Spock. The relief science officer usually worked the gamma shift, but these were special circumstances. She operated the sensor controls and Vok Populi appeared on the viewscreen. The shining metallic satellite looked deceptively in order, but Kirk knew that the photon charges embedded in its construction were only two minutes away from disintegrating Vok Populi. A digital display, superimposed on the image, let Kirk know exactly how much time they *didn't* have.

The turbolift door whooshed open behind Kirk. He turned to see Imogen Dare step onto the bridge, wearing a belted blue robe over her hospital gown. Her face was drawn and somewhat pale, although how much of that was from her injury and how much of that was from the imminent destruction of Vok's foolproof voting computer was anyone's guess. Her eyes were irresistibly drawn to the doomed satellite.

"Commissioner?" Kirk said. "Should you be up and about?"

She turned a grim face toward him. "Should I be anywhere else at this moment?"

Kirk understood. Her entire mission to Vok was in mortal jeopardy. He wouldn't be able to sit tight in sickbay either, not under these circumstances.

"I suppose not," he said. "Please take a seat."

She found an empty chair at the auxiliary environmental controls station, but not before making eye contact with her disgraced aide. A range of emotions, from disgust to pity, cascaded across her face. Clearly, word of Tanaka's sabotage had already reached her.

"How could you do it, Steve?" she asked. "You have no idea how disappointed I am."

He wilted before her gaze. "I'm sorry to let you down."

"We'll talk later," she said sternly. "Be sure of that."

In the meantime, Kirk turned to Uhura. "Can you hail the computer?"

"I'm trying, sir, but it's treating me as a potential infection, blocking me at every turn. I'm using all the right passwords and secure channels, but it's shutting down, cutting itself off from any attempt to countermand its programming." She threw up her hands in frustration. "I'm sorry, Captain. I don't know what else to do."

"No need to apologize, Lieutenant."

Kirk knew Uhura had given it her all. His heart sank as the countdown reached its inexorable conclusion with only seconds to go. He suddenly realized they weren't going to win this one.

Three, two, one . . .

On-screen, the photon charges ignited, flaring brightly at strategic placements deep within the satellite. The individual bursts swiftly merged into a single blinding fireball that tested the viewscreen's protective filters. Blinking, Kirk raised his arm to shield his eyes from the glare, which faded almost as fast as it appeared. Tiny blue dots danced in his vision as his watery eyes recovered from the flash. His gaze stayed fixed on the screen, where nothing remained of the satellite except a wisp of energized ions that was already dispersing across the vacuum of space. Kirk watched bleakly as even those final sparks dimmed and died.

He had failed.

Vok Populi was dead.

The taste of defeat was both bitter and unfamiliar. He shared a distraught look with Dare, who appeared equally stricken. There would be no fair election to observe now, with no supercomputer to tabulate the votes of an entire planet.

"Off-screen," he ordered, rather more sharply than he'd intended.

"Aye, sir."

Haines switched off the sensors formerly focused on VP-One. The empty space that appeared on the screen was not significantly different in appearance from the now-empty space it replaced and offered little solace to Kirk. He gazed furiously at Tanaka, who was being watched like a hawk by both Chekov and Bradley. Kirk was unable to resist lashing out at the compromised diplomat.

"I hope this was worth it, Mister Tanaka."

Tanaka averted his eyes from the screen. "They said they'd release Myp once the satellite was atoms. She should be safe now." He took a deep breath to steady himself. "You can throw the book at me if you want. I take full responsibility."

Kirk hoped he was right about Myp being safe. "What makes you think her captors can be trusted?"

"Because, ultimately, she's one of their own and they got what they wanted. They have no reason to harm her now." He sounded like a man desperate to convince himself. "And because, honestly, the alternative is . . . unthinkable."

Kirk didn't feel like challenging the man's hopes. At this point, there was nothing to be gained by adding to Tanaka's anxieties. Kirk wanted to think Myp would be okay as well, if only so some good came out of this debacle.

"Well, that's it," Dare said unhappily. She sounded more troubled by the loss of Vok Populi than by her own near brush with death. "The election has vanished along with VP-One. And you just know that Gogg and his followers are going to press to have him declared the winner since Ceff forfeited and they don't accept Prup as a legitimate candidate. That would have been a harder argument to make if Prup had racked up a majority of votes, but now?" She grimaced in anticipation of the strife to come. "Not that the executive committee is likely to cave to Gogg's demands without a fight. We could be talking an attempted coup or, worst-case scenario, a civil war, all because the election will need to be called off."

Kirk refused to accept that. "But surely there must be a backup system, some other way to tally the votes?"

"I wish!" Dare shook her head. "Less-sophisticated processes, such as those used in the past, have already been rejected as being too vulnerable to human tampering or error. You underestimate how unique VP-One was. There's no other computer on the planet that can match its capacities."

A thought struck Kirk. "On the planet, you say?"

"I know that look, Captain," Chekov said, grinning. "You have a plan, don't you?"

A hint of a smile lifted Kirk's lip.

"Possibly, but we're going to have to work fast."

Thirty-Nine

Ozalor

"Greetings, Doctor. I am pleased to find you well, if rather more hirsute than usual."

Spock reacted to McCoy's appearance with his customary equanimity, although he was gratified that their lengthy search for the missing physician had finally succeeded. McCoy stood in a doorway within Avomora's private chambers, his familiar face obscured by whiskers of dubious authenticity.

"Don't get me started." McCoy scratched irritably at his facial camouflage. "But it's good to see you, too, Spock, not to mention the rest of you."

"Doctor!" Chapel rushed forward, displaying rather more emotion than Spock. She beamed at the sight of her long-lost colleague. "You have no idea how glad I am to see you again. I've been worried sick about you!"

"Likewise," McCoy said. "They told me you and Levine had been left safely behind on Braco, and I had no real reason to doubt them, but seeing is believing." He nodded at Levine, who was hanging back with Godwin. "Nice to see you up and about as well, Lieutenant."

"We never stopped looking for you, Doctor," Levine replied.

"I would hope not," McCoy said dryly. "Still, imagine my surprise when Avo told me that a Starfleet shuttle had touched down on Ozalor . . . and that you were right here in the palace!"

"I could hardly do otherwise."

Avomora appeared in the doorway behind McCoy. Spock observed that she was standing on her own two legs, albeit a bit shakily. She leaned against one side of the archway as though in need of its support. Her face seemed paler and more strained than he recalled from their brief meeting in the gymnasium.

"Not with your life in jeopardy," she added.

"And what about your life?" Jemo hurried to the princess's side. "You need McCoy's help, now more than ever."

"My health is not worth another's life," Avomora insisted. "But, please, gentlemen, ladies, step inside my study and make yourselves comfortable."

Spock suspected that she needed to sit down as well. He turned to Godwin and Levine. "Watch the entrance to these chambers while we confer with the doctor and his allies. It is only a matter of time before our escape from the dungeons is detected."

"Aye, sir," Godwin said. "We're on it."

Confident that the security officers were on the alert, Spock followed the others into a somewhat cluttered study whose shelves indicated a wide and somewhat eclectic range of interests. Avomora sank with obvious relief into her mobile chair, eliciting a worried look from Jemo.

"Just how are you doing anyway?" she asked the crown princess. "I thought you were only faking another bad spell to give you an excuse to summon Doctor McCoy at this time of night?"

Spock understood that, as part of their plan, Avomora had arranged for McCoy to be waiting for them here after the landing party effected their escape from the dungeon. He considered extracting the miniature earpiece from his ear now that it was no longer necessary, but chose to retain it as a precaution, should events take an unwelcome turn and they found themselves in custody again.

"I was only kind of faking it," Avomora admitted. She gingerly massaged a watery eye as though it troubled her. She shivered beneath a replacement quilt. "Not feeling all that great, to be honest."

"Already?" Jemo asked. "Vumri healed you just a few days ago."

"Not sure 'healed' is the word for it," McCoy grumbled, "considering how frequently her treatments are needed."

The doctor's concern for his royal patient was obvious. Spock wondered if she had truly needed the chair when she visited the gymnasium or if that had just been a ruse to deliver the quilt holding the earpiece. Or perhaps she had merely exaggerated her actual symptoms on that occasion.

"I'll survive," she said curtly. "Now is no time to fret over my condition yet again." She looked at Spock. "Congratulations on escaping the dungeons on your own."

"We were not entirely without assistance," Spock replied. "Your associate proved an invaluable guide when it came to navigating the palace."

"You're welcome," Jemo said with a sarcastic edge to her voice. "Here's hoping I don't regret it."

McCoy ignored her remark. "I gather it's just the four of you come to liberate me? No reinforcements lurking in the wings?"

"Not at present," Spock said, "although the *Enterprise* should be aware of our location by now."

"Good to know," McCoy said. "And the ship's still at Vok, I assume."

"Affirmative," Spock said. "Captain Kirk remains committed to our original mission to observe the presidential election, which is underway as we speak."

"Right. The big election." McCoy shook his head. "I confess, I've been so caught up in affairs here on Ozalor that I've barely given any thought to Vok. That seems like a million miles away now."

"Thirty-four point eight light-years, to be exact," Spock clarified, "but further discussion of such matters can wait until we have expedited your removal from the palace."

Spock was already thinking ahead. Their next priority was to vacate the palace before they could be recaptured and then find a safe refuge outside the royal residence from which they could plan their escape from the planet. It was unlikely that they could return to *Copernicus*, which was presumably still under guard at a military base many kilometers away, so their best recourse was to devise a way to contact Captain Kirk and wait for *Galileo* or the *Enterprise* to come for them, as difficult as any such rescue operation was bound to be. Unless, perhaps, Avomora could contrive to smuggle them aboard a craft bound for Braco . . .

"Just one problem, Spock. I'm not ready to leave." McCoy nodded at Avomora. "I have a patient who needs me."

Spock was briefly confounded. He had not anticipated this complication, although, in retrospect, he probably should have.

"Doctor, with all due respect to your professional obligations, we have come a long way to recover you."

"And don't think I'm not grateful, Spock, but we have a situation here. I can't just turn my back on it, not at this point."

"But you have to leave," Avomora insisted. "Vumri and her pawns will never let you live if you stay." She leaned forward in her chair, although this clearly pained her. "I don't want you to leave either, but I can't have your death on my conscience."

"I'd just as soon avoid that too," McCoy said. "Funny thing about being a doctor, though. We're supposed to put our patients first."

"About time you figured that out," Jemo said, unhelpfully, as far as Spock was concerned. "Listen to him, Avo."

"But you tried to escape before," the princess pointed out, "and that was *before* Vumri tried to have you killed. Now's your chance to get away."

"At the time, I didn't know how to help you," McCoy said, "but now I have a new approach to try." He turned toward Spock. "One that involves you, Spock."

Spock contained his surprise. "How so?"

"Let me try to keep this brief," McCoy began as he proceeded to recount his failed attempt to cure Avomora by correcting an imbalance in her brain chemistry. He also spoke of *Lossu* Vumri's greater success at relieving the princess's symptoms, if only temporarily. "I've been observing Vumri's sessions with Avo. They do seem to help her in the short term, but the relapses are coming faster and stronger the more Vumri treats her."

"Could she be building up an immunity to the treatments?" Chapel asked. "So that she needs more frequent 'healings' just to get the same effect?"

"Possibly," McCoy said, "but I suspect it's more than that. I think that Avo—or to be more precise, her brain—has grown so dependent on Vumri's treatments that she's now suffering withdrawal symptoms if she goes too long without them, which would explain why she's getting worse, not better, despite my best efforts to treat the root cause of her condition."

"Wait a moment," Jemo said. "Are you saying that Vumri's so-called gifts are what's making Avo sick in the first place?"

McCoy shook his head. "No, not in the beginning. There was an imbalance in her brain, which my compound should have corrected, but the fact that her symptoms are worsening instead makes me think that maybe Vumri's 'cure' has become the disease." He looked at Spock, who found himself intrigued by McCoy's theory despite the precariousness of their situation. "Tell me, Spock. This is more your field of expertise than mine. Is there such a thing—could there be such a thing—as telepathic addiction? Telepathic withdrawal?"

"It is not inconceivable," Spock stated. "In the case of a Vulcan mind-meld, care is taken to fully disengage with the subject at the conclusion of the meld, to avoid any lingering connection that might compromise the individuals involved, but Vulcans are hardly the only species possessing telepathic gifts, nor our ways the only ways in which the powers of the mind can be exerted. It might be possible, in theory, for a telepathic contact to have lasting and pernicious effects such as you describe."

"Excuse me," Chapel interrupted. "I'm confused. Are Ozalorians telepaths? I wasn't aware of that."

"Not all of us," Avomora said, "nor even most. It's a special gift possessed only by a chosen few."

"Not unlike humans," Spock reminded Chapel. "Even your own species vary in terms of their esper ratings, with certain individuals capable of cultivating such gifts with the proper training, as in the case of Doctor Miranda Jones. Granted, the human propensity toward emotionality means that most humans lack the mental discipline to fully develop whatever innate abilities they may possess. No offense intended."

"None taken," McCoy said. "I'll take healthy human emotions over mind-reading tricks any day. But that's where you come in, Spock. As much as I hate to admit it, I can use a consult on this case . . . of a Vulcan variety."

Spock arched an eyebrow. "Indeed?"

"I've done thorough scans of Avo's brain and nervous system before and after Vumri treats her. Sure enough, the results show some unusual variations in her brain-wave activity, but when it comes to telepathy, I'm not too proud to admit that I'm out of my depth. This is your bailiwick, Spock. I was hoping you'd show up eventually, with or without the captain."

Spock was troubled by the direction of the conversation.

"Do I understand you correctly, Doctor? Are you suggesting that I join minds with Her Highness, for diagnostic purposes?"

McCoy nodded.

"It's asking a lot, I know," he said soberly. "I've experienced a mind-meld or two, so I understand that it's not something to be embarked on lightly. But I've gone as far as I can with my tricorder. I need you to tell me what exactly Vumri is doing to Avo . . . and how we can fix it."

Avomora leaned forward in her chair. "Please, Mister Spock, if there's anything you can do to free me from Vumri once and for all."

The heartfelt nature of her appeal stirred Spock's compassion, yet he questioned the advisability of McCoy's proposal, and not only because a mind-meld was always a daunting prospect in itself.

"I appreciate your distress," Spock said, "and do not wish to appear uncaring. I am concerned, however, about the larger implications. I do not claim to grasp the subtleties of Ozalorian politics as well as you must, but I gather that this is more than merely a medical matter, that there is a crucial power struggle involved as well. That being the case, I have profound reservations about meddling in the royal intrigues of an independent world."

"Forget about the politics, Spock!" McCoy said with characteristic emotion. "We're talking about a flesh-and-blood person in need. Look at her, Spock. Can't you see she's suffering and needs our help?"

"I am not blind to that fact, Doctor, but one cannot simply ignore the other factors involved. Even you must realize that there are larger issues to consider."

"What I realize and what I feel are not the same thing." McCoy spoke softly but with conviction. He looked Spock squarely in the eyes. "It's not about logic, Spock, or the big picture. It's about what I can live with."

"This young lady helped us find Doctor McCoy," Chapel said, weighing in. "We'd still be searching for him if not for her."

"If there's even a chance that you can break Vumri's hold on Avo, you have to try it," Jemo said forcefully. "Believe me, showing that witch the door is in everyone's best interest, including your Federation."

"Jemo's not wrong," McCoy said. "I don't know if you've had the dubious pleasure of meeting the esteemed *Lossu*, but she's not exactly a big fan of the Federation . . . or peace with Vok."

"We've met," Spock confirmed.

In truth, he was offended on principle by the possibility that someone might abuse telepathy to abuse and control another. That went against everything he believed—as a Starfleet officer *and* a Vulcan.

"I take it you will not come willingly, Doctor?"

"That's the long and short of it." McCoy crossed his arms atop his chest. "I'm sorry, Spock, but my oath as a doctor trumps your command status."

"Then it appears I have no choice," Spock concluded. "Logically, I cannot complete my mission and return you to the *Enterprise* without your cooperation, which dictates that we must first do our best by your patient." He approached Avomora. "Do you fully understand what is being proposed and all it entails?"

"I believe so," she said. "I've read about the Vulcan merging of minds and talked about it with Doctor Bones . . . I mean, McCoy. And it's not as though I haven't already had Vumri mucking about with my brain. Might be nice to have somebody else drop in for a change."

Spock heard the bitterness behind her humor. "Then I have your consent to proceed?"

"Whatever it takes, Mister Spock." She stiffened her shoulders. "And not just for my sake. Ozalor deserves an Heir who can reign without relying on a healer who cares only for her own ambitions."

"Very well, then." Spock surveyed the crowded study. "This setting will do, although a degree of privacy would be preferable."

"I'd like to stay and monitor her condition," McCoy said. "Given her ailment, we can't be sure how she'll cope with the meld."

"A reasonable precaution," Spock agreed.

Chapel lingered in the study. "Can you use my assistance, Doctor?"

"By all means," McCoy said. "Don't know how I've managed without you. It's felt like I've been missing my right hand all this time."

All eyes turned toward Jemo.

"Uh-uh," she said. "Don't even think I'm leaving her to face this alone."

"Doctor's orders," McCoy said. "The best thing you can do now is help make sure we're not disturbed."

"It's all right, Jemo," Avomora said. "I'll be fine."

"Easy for you to say. You're not the bodyguard."

"No," Avomora said. "Just the patient." She gestured weakly at the door, the effort obviously costing her. "Go. Let the doctor and his associates do their work. You can check on me afterward."

"You bet I will," Jemo said, giving in. "I'll be right outside if you need me."

She exited the study, drawing a curtain behind her.

Spock watched Jemo leave, then turned back toward the stricken princess. Acutely aware that imprisonment or worse awaited them should they be recaptured by the palace guards, he saw no reason to delay the meld.

"Shall we begin?"

Forty

Ozalor

"Are you ready?" Spock asked.

"I think so," Avomora said, putting on a brave face in anticipation of the mind-meld. "I mean, yes."

At her request, the lights in the study had been dimmed to ease her eyes. McCoy and Chapel stood by to monitor the procedure. Although the nurse's own medkit had been confiscated at the military base, McCoy was still in possession of his, so they were reasonably equipped to deal with any medical issues that might arise, despite the absence of a sickbay. Certainly, it was not the first time Spock had been required to perform a meld in less than ideal circumstances. He could only hope that there would be no unexpected complications, and that they would not be interrupted by palace guards in the process. The latter, unfortunately, was a distinct possibility.

"Let us proceed, then."

He circled around Avomora's chair until he was standing directly behind her. He took a deep breath to steady his thoughts even more than usual, then reached around to place his fingertips gently against her temples. She flinched at even the mild contact and a whimper of pain escaped her lips. That she was already in physical discomfort before the meld, due to her condition, concerned Spock, but as it was her recurring ailment that necessitated the procedure, they could hardly wait for her to recover before attempting it. The very goal of the meld was to discover what was preventing McCoy's cure from working.

"My mind to your mind," he intoned. "My thoughts to your thoughts."

The traditional mantra aided his concentration as his consciousness reached out to Avomora's. Making contact, he was immediately afflicted by a battery of torturous physical sensations that he now shared with the beset royal. Every sensory impression, from sight to sound to touch, became almost unbearably intense. Even the dimmest light stabbed his eyes, so that he squeezed them shut to keep out the piercing glare. The hum of McCoy's medical tricorder, along with the rustle of Chapel's uniform as she shifted her weight, grated on Spock's ears. Chills ran up and down his body, triggering a bumpy pilomotor reflex along his skin, while a throbbing pain radiated outward from his spine to his extremities, growing perceptibly sharper by the moment. His right eye twitched.

Was this what Avomora experienced on a regular basis? Spock's sympathy for the afflicted princess increased, as did his respect for her endurance.

She . . . I . . . we . . . hurt.

Rather than let the secondhand misery deter him, Spock probed deeper into Avomora's psyche. Gritting his teeth against the pain, as she was doing, he sensed also her nervousness over the meld, her resentment of her condition, and her determination not to let her medical issues define her.

The pain will not defeat us.

But he sensed something else as well, lurking deeper within her unconscious mind, entangled with her autonomic cerebral functions. There was another presence, another link to a separate mind, not Avomora, not Spock, but . . .

Vumri.

Through Avomora, Spock connected with the notably unpopular healer. He felt her presence in the palace, none too far away. He received a vague impression of her stirring restlessly from sleep, which only confirmed McCoy's suspicions: Vumri had indeed embedded a portion of her consciousness within Avomora's mind, creating a psychic link between them that, in time, had fostered a dependency on the part of Avomora, whose brain was no longer accustomed to functioning properly on its own, but required Vumri's telepathic assistance on a regular basis. Small wonder then that McCoy's compound had failed; even after the doctor corrected the princess's neurochemistry, her brain could not stabilize itself without Vumri's direct intervention. The crutch was now obstructing the cure.

You don't belong here, Vulcan.

Vumri's thoughts assailed Spock. She had clearly been alerted to the meld via her own connection to Avomora. Her anger and ambition crashed against him, muffled only slightly by the buffer zone formed by the princess's own consciousness. He sensed no genuine concern for Avomora's well-being, only fury from Vumri at her own power and position being challenged.

"Neither do you," he replied across their linked minds.

A cool anger, laced with Avomora's own animosity toward the alleged healer, suffused his thoughts. What Vumri was doing to Avomora was both insidious and obscene. He took strong objection to it.

"Release Avomora's mind. Sever your connection to her."

Never, Vumri declared. **The Heir is mine. Through her, I will shape the future of Ozalor.**

"That is unacceptable. If you will not sever the link, I will."

An empty threat, Vulcan. My hold on the Heir cannot be broken.

"We shall see."

Keeping his principled indignation under tight rein, he applied his Vulcan training to trace the pernicious link to its roots deep within Avomora's mind. Applied meditative techniques allowed him to visualize Vumri's presence as a knot of inky tendrils, similar to the tattoos adorning the healer's scalp, entangled with Avomora's unconscious mind, which he imagined as a band of polished agate. Focusing his own awareness on the knot, he attempted to unravel the strands binding the two women's minds to each other, as he might divorce his own mind from another's, but this was not easily accomplished. The strands were too tightly entwined with the bracelet, so that untangling them was akin to performing actual neurosurgery upon an exposed brain. He was reluctant to proceed too hastily or too forcefully for fear of harming Avomora.

Give up, Vulcan, Vumri taunted. **You cannot expel me from the Heir's mind. She cannot endure without me.**

Spock refused to believe that.

"What's happening, Doctor?" Chapel asked anxiously.

"I wish I knew," McCoy said. He'd witnessed mind-melds before, and always found them profoundly disturbing, but this one was obviously not going well.

Spock and Avomora were both shaking violently, so much so that McCoy marveled that Spock was still on his feet. Agony contorted their features, more or less in synch with each other. Avo's facial tics and twitches were echoed on Spock's usually stoic countenance. Veins and tendons bulged from the Vulcan's neck. Avo's trembling fingers dug into the armrests of her chair.

"His vitals are spiking!" Chapel monitored Spock with a whirring handheld scanner, calibrated to Vulcan physiology, while McCoy used his tricorder to track Avomora's responses. "Heart rate, respiration, cerebral activity . . . they're all going through the roof!"

"Same here." His tricorder hummed as he scanned Avo, the readouts on the visual display panel setting his own pulse racing as well. There was nothing normal about a mind-meld at the best of times, yet Avo and Spock were both being put through a wringer to an alarming degree. He wasn't sure how much longer their minds or bodies could endure the strain they were under.

"What should we do, Doctor?"

"Your guess is as good as mine." McCoy had a decent grasp of Ozalorian and Vulcan biology, but treating either species while they were telepathically linked to the other was not covered in medical school. He was just a simple country doctor at heart; he didn't know if he should even *try* breaking the meld—or would that do more harm than good?

"Aaagggh."

An anguished moan escaped Avomora as she went into full-scale convulsions, her arms and legs flailing wildly, her head snapping from side to side. Her eyes rolled back until only the whites could be seen. Froth bubbled from her lips.

"Damn it." McCoy held her down to keep her from injuring herself. He kicked himself for not restraining her earlier, although he'd had no reason to expect this kind of violent reaction to the meld. Straining to contain her thrashing limbs, he shouted urgently at Chapel. "Five cc's of dylamadon . . . stat!"

"On it, Doctor!"

She rushed to the medkit, which was laid out on a nearby shelf, and quickly prepared the injection. McCoy was reluctant to administer medication during the meld, but they would have to risk it. Hurrying back to the chair, Chapel applied the hypospray to the convulsing patient. It hissed as it delivered the sedative to Avo's bloodstream. McCoy hoped the dosage would be enough—but not too much.

"Come on, Avo," he urged her. "You've handled worse than this."

The drug quieted her convulsions, but only to a degree. She was still shaking and groaning and grimacing, just less frenetically than before. McCoy let go of her arms and stepped back from the chair, breathing hard from the effort needed to restrain Avomora. His shin felt bruised from where she'd kicked him during her seizure. Consulting his tricorder, he was unsurprised to find her vital signs still alarmingly askew. Her entire metabolism was running itself ragged. He was tempted to prescribe a larger dose of the sedative, but he had no idea how that would affect her meld with Spock.

"Thank you, Nurse. Let's hope that does the trick for now, or at least long enough for Spock to complete the meld."

"What about Mister Spock?" Chapel cast a worried look at the first officer, who was clearly going through hell as well. "Should I prepare another sedative?"

"Not yet," McCoy said. "From the looks of it, Spock needs all his faculties to cope with . . . whatever he's encountered in there. I'm counting on his sheer Vulcan cussedness to get him through this."

"Get him through what, Doctor?"

That was the question, wasn't it? In theory, Spock was just going to poke around in Avo's mind and determine what the problem was, but had he run into more than he could handle?

"Hell if I know." McCoy stared helplessly at Spock, who was all too clearly wrestling with unseen tortures. Guilt plagued McCoy as he watched his friend and colleague suffer for the young royal's sake. "I can't believe this was my own fool idea!"

———————

An alarm sounded, waking the palace.

"Uh-oh." Levine looked at Godwin, who winced at the shrieking siren echoing off the walls of the antechamber. "Sounds like they're onto us."

"Saw this coming," she replied. "I was hoping we could get clear of the palace before they let loose the hounds, but I guess that was just wishful thinking."

The pair kept watch over the mirrored entrance to Avomora's chambers. Their duty, as Levine understood it, was to allow Spock and McCoy to treat the sick princess without interruption. That assignment had just gotten a whole lot harder.

A stentorian voice, emanating from concealed speakers, replaced the siren:

"*Attention: All staff and residents. Four alien intruders have escaped custody and are believed to be at large in the palace. Non-security personnel are urged to remain in their quarters and report any suspicious individuals to the palace guard immediately. Repeat: Four alien intruders . . .*"

Godwin had her weapon ready. "How long before they sweep these chambers?"

"As soon as those guards we stunned don't check in," he guessed.

The guards, along with the governess, were locked inside a walk-in closet. In theory, they would be out for hours. Levine figured matters would be resolved, one way or another, before they woke up.

"Doesn't give us much time," Godwin said grimly.

Jemo sprinted into the antechamber from the hall outside the study. "We can't keep them out, but we can slow them down." She raised her voice while fixing her gaze on the mirror portal. "Initiate lockdown, priority level royal-slash-citrine. Authorization: YYVA-7191-Basalt."

A shimmering force field crackled to life on their side of the mirror. Levine heard doors slamming shut elsewhere in the princess's chambers. Closing off any back entrances, he assumed.

"There!" Jemo said. "We're sealed off from the rest of the palace . . . for the Heir's safety, of course. Couldn't do that before without triggering an alarm, but I guess that's academic now." She shrugged in resignation. "The good news is that these chambers were fitted to keep any threats to the *Yiyova* out, not to allow armed forces in. The bad news is they'll be banging on our door sooner rather than later."

Levine grasped the trade-off and couldn't argue with Jemo's reasoning; "later" was going to be all too soon anyway.

"So how is it you know that authorization code anyway?" he asked.

"I'm Avo's best friend. Who else is she going to trust with it?"

"And the king can't override the code?" Godwin asked.

"Not at this setting," Jemo said. "The idea is to protect the Heir even if the *Yovode* has been compromised."

"Works for me." Levine appreciated the irony of the palace's security systems working to their benefit. "Nothing like having some healthy paranoia on your side."

A gong sounded, as though someone was banging on the other side of the mirror. An amplified voice blared from the speakers:

"Open up . . . in the name of the Yovode!*"*

"Yeah, that's not happening," Jemo said.

Falling back on their training, Levine and Godwin took up defensive positions within two meters of the surrounding doorways, while Jemo headed back toward the study where the princess was being treated. Levine silently wished Spock and McCoy luck while wondering how exactly any of them were going to get out of this mess. At this point, he couldn't imagine that Avomora's father would be content to simply stick them back in the gym again. They were way beyond posing as the innocent victims of a forced landing. They were "alien intruders" and bound to be treated as such.

And to think that this all began with a bogus medical alert from Braco . . .

"Open up immediately. This is your last warning!"

"Not wasting any time, are they?" Godwin said.

"Would you?" he replied.

"Suit yourselves. We're coming in!"

Squealing disruptors targeted the other side of the portal, producing an ear-piercing ringing as the energy beams struck the mirror. Levine didn't need to see through the mirror to grasp that the guards were trying to blast their way past the chambers' defenses. He mentally counted down the layers between them and their opponents: the mirror and the force field.

Only two.

Not nearly enough, he thought. "Any idea how long we can hold them off?"

"Don't look at me," Jemo said. "I'm a bodyguard, not an engineer. They can't go all out without endangering the Heir, but—"

A harrowing cry came from the study. Jemo's cocky attitude gave way to a look of dismay.

"Avo!"

She bolted from the antechamber, abandoning the two security officers.

"What's wrong? What are you doing to her?"

Jemo charged into the study, drawn by Avomora's heartrending cries and moans, which the sedative had failed to entirely suppress. McCoy couldn't blame her for being alarmed, but he had enough on his plate without dealing with the agitated bodyguard too.

"Not now!" McCoy glanced back over his shoulder as he tended to his patients, despite the sirens and commotion coming from nearby. He barked brusquely at Jemo. "Let us handle this."

"Forget it!" Jemo stared aghast at Avomora. She drew her ionic blade and activated it, so that it glowed white hot in the murky study. "I'm shutting this down, right this minute!"

Chapel gasped at the sight of the charged knife.

"Blast it, Jemo!" McCoy kept one eye on his tricorder readings while standing ready to restrain Avomora if she started convulsing again. "You and Rayob brought me here to help Avo. Don't stop me now!"

Jemo faltered, her knife hand dipping. "But . . . she looks like she's being tortured. Do you even know what you're doing?"

I wish, McCoy thought. "No guarantees, but at this point all we can do is stay the course and hope for the best. We're on the same side, Jemo. You need to trust me to do everything I can for Avo . . . and keep out of my way."

Indecision showed on Jemo's face before she clicked off her knife. "This had better be worth it, Doctor."

From your lips to Spock's pointed ears, McCoy thought.

The meld was taking its toll on Spock.

His suffering and Avomora's were one and the same. Only his Vulcan stamina kept him standing despite the borrowed pain searing his nerve endings. Perspiration streamed from his pores as alternating fevers and chills lashed him. His fingers trembled as they remained pressed against Avomora's temples. Both of his eyes twitched spasmodically, tortured by the light striking the young woman's eyes, but he kept his inner vision focused on the task before him: dislodging Vumri's unwanted presence from the princess's mind. His extended consciousness, reaching deep into Avomora's psyche, poked and tugged at the invasive tendrils, which seemed to twist and tighten the more he fought to peel them away.

Leave us, Vulcan. Your mind is strong, but not strong enough. Let go.

"You are correct," Spock realized, "but mine is not the only mind opposing you." He reached out to Avomora's own consciousness, drawing her into the contest. His mind's eye visualized the earpiece that still resided in his physical body, evoking it in order to speak to her, mind to mind. "Can you read me, Your Highness?"

Yes, Spock! I can hear you!

Her voice was faint but clear.

"Listen to me, Your Highness. Doctor McCoy was correct. Vumri has indeed infected your mind telepathically, but I cannot expel her on my own. I require your assistance. We must drive her from your mind together, combining my skill with your spirit. Two minds against her one. Do you understand me?"

I think so, Mister Spock, but . . . I'm too sick. I feel like I'm dying.

Spock knew what she meant, literally.

"I share your distress, but we must push past the pain to focus on what must be done. We *can* do this, Avomora. We can set you free."

Don't listen to him, *Yiyova*! Let me take away the pain, as only I can.

Spock grasped how tempting the healer's offer had to be to Avomora. Their shared agonies cried out for relief. He was also all too aware that abruptly severing the link to Vumri was not without risks, considering how dependent Avomora's brain and body had become on the telepathic connection. In an ideal world, the princess would be carefully weaned from Vumri's influence under the supervision of skilled Vulcan adepts, but that option was not available under the circumstances. They could only uproot Vumri through sheer force of will—and trust in Doctor McCoy and Nurse Chapel to deal with the consequences.

"Hear me, Avomora. We must risk this . . . if you ever wish to be the ruler of your own fate. You, I, us . . . we can take back your life, together."

Empty promises! I alone can ease your torment. Do not heed the stranger's lies, child . . .

A sudden surge of fury amplified Avomora's resolve. Spock felt her willpower swell and he focused it like a phaser beam on the tendrils rooting Vumri's mind to Avomora's, which began to dissolve and melt away before the sheer force of his and the princess's combined thoughts.

"We are not a child! Our mind is our own!"

———————

"We are not a child! Our mind is our own!"

Spock and Avomora shouted in unison, startling McCoy. Spock fell away from the chair, collapsing onto the floor. Avo went limp in her chair, her spasms ceasing abruptly. Her heartbeat dropped dramatically. Her breaths grew shallow.

"Spock!" Chapel hurried to check on the fallen Vulcan. Her scanner whirred energetically as she shouted out its readings. "Major cardiac arrhythmia, sinking blood pressure, respiratory distress . . . he's crashing, Doctor!"

"What's wrong?" Jemo could not stay back any longer. She rushed to Avomora's side. "Is it over? Is she going to be all right?"

"Not if we don't move quickly," McCoy said. "For both of them."

He wasn't entirely sure what had just transpired inside Avomora's head, but both she and Spock were showing every sign of major, possibly life-threatening withdrawal symptoms. If McCoy had to make a guess, he'd venture that the mind-meld had "worked" to the extent of undoing whatever Vumri had done to Avo, but that the princess was now going through the telepathic equivalent of quitting "cold turkey"—with Spock along for the ride, thanks to the meld.

"Chapel, ten cc's of cordrazine for Spock, followed by a good slap, if necessary, to keep him from slipping into a coma." McCoy barked out orders, careful to keep his patients straight and tailor his emergency measures to their respective species. "Jemo, grab me a spare hypospray from that medkit over there!"

"On it!"

Jemo sprang across the study to fetch the device even as Chapel treated Spock. McCoy could have used a few extra arms, not to mention a fully staffed sickbay, but the private study was now an intensive-care unit. Returning in record time, Jemo slapped a hypospray into McCoy's waiting palm. With no time to load anything specific into the device, the doctor had to resort to one of the preloaded palliatives readily available to him. He quickly double-checked the dosage before administering the drug. Avo's skin felt cold and clammy to the touch as he propped her head up.

"Is that going to do it?" Jemo took Avo's limp hand in hers. "Tell me you can save her!"

Chapel slapped Spock across the face to rouse him, a drastic measure that was known to be effective with Vulcans sometimes. "Wake up, Spock!" she pleaded. "Come back to us!"

McCoy found himself torn between his patients, uncertain which was in the most danger. Standard triage criteria were of little use.

Please, he thought, *don't let me lose them both!*

"Does Ozalor have a death penalty?" Levine asked.

"Don't know," Godwin called back to him from an archway

at the other side of the antechamber. "Probably should've asked before."

"That's what I'm thinking," he said.

Their defenses were buckling. The reflective surface of the mirror portal glowed furiously red before evaporating into a silvery mist, revealing a mounted cannon on the other side of the archway, along with what looked like a small army of palace guards. Peering past the guards, through the crackling force field that remained, Levine glimpsed Salokonos, the *Yovode* himself, commanding the assault on his daughter's chambers.

"Surrender," he bellowed, "or no mercy will be shown you!"

Levine glanced over at the hall leading to the study. He wished he had some clue what was going on with Spock, McCoy, Chapel, and the princess, but in the meantime, he intended to hold his position for as long as possible, while counting on Godwin to do the same. That was the thing about working security; sometimes all you could do was follow orders and put yourself on the line, without knowing what command was up to.

Ours is but to do or die, he thought. *Preferably the former.*

The cannon battered the crumbling force field. Blinding flashes of bright blue Cherenkov radiation left fuzzy spots dancing in Levine's vision. The field gave every evidence of being a strong one, probably the best the royal treasury could afford, but he didn't need a tactical display to know that it couldn't stand up to such punishment much longer. Determined guards fired on the field with their rifles and disruptors as well, adding to the barrage. The force field flickered and sputtered, clearly on its last legs.

"Get ready!" Levine called to Godwin. "Here they come!"

"Hard to miss," she shot back. "Battle stations, it is."

With a flurry of sparks, the field gave up the ghost. A first wave of guards poured through the breach, roaring like blood-crazed Klingons, only to be stunned by the Starfleet officers' purloined disruptors. Using the archways as cover, Levine and Godwin set up a crossfire to slow the assault. The stunned guards dropped to the floor, but more guards stormed the antechamber, leaping over their fallen comrades. They fired back at the defenders. A crimson disruptor beam sizzled past Levine's head as he ducked back inside the doorway just in time. He wanted to think that the Ozalorians' disruptors were set on stun, but he wasn't about to bet his life on it. He'd seen what they had done to the force field.

"Keep going!" Salokonos urged his guards. "For my daughter's sake!"

Funny thing, Levine thought. *As I understand it, we're trying to save your daughter too.*

Not that he expected Salokonos to see it that way at the moment.

Firing with practiced accuracy, Levine thinned out another wave of guards, while Godwin stunned her fair share of invaders, too, but they were fighting a losing battle against a seemingly inexhaustible flood of opponents dead set on recapturing them—or worse. A red-hot disruptor beam melted away a strip of fiberoptic molding around the doorway, only a few centimeters away from his fragile flesh. He glanced over at Godwin and saw her similarly besieged.

Nice knowing you, he thought.

Gaining ground, the guards advanced like a category-ten ion storm. Levine saw the end of the battle coming in minutes, if not seconds, but kept on firing. He hoped Captain Kirk would someday get word of the rescue party's valiant last stand. It would be nice to be remembered at least.

"Halt, everyone!" a voice rang out. "Lay down your arms!"

Avomora emerged from the hall leading to the study. She looked a bit pale and shaky, but clearly up and about. She approached the guards, who immediately ceased fire lest they strike their crown princess by mistake. Levine and Godwin lowered their weapons as well, not wanting to catch her in the crossfire. Glancing toward the hall, Levine glimpsed Spock trailing after

Avomora, propped up by both McCoy and Chapel. Jemo had her glowing knife out, just in case.

"Avomora?" Her distraught father pushed through his guards to reach her. "Are you well?"

"More than you can imagine," she said, smiling. "More than I ever dreamed I could be."

Forty-One

"It's working, Captain," Uhura reported. "The votes are streaming in, billions of them."

The *Enterprise* had been drafted into service as Vok Populi's emergency replacement. The ship's computer was, by a considerable margin, the most sophisticated and powerful computer in the sector. It was generations beyond anything found on Vok, whose technology was more akin to that of twenty-second-century Earth. Uhura, Scotty, and his engineers had scrambled to adapt the *Enterprise*'s existing systems to the task of intercepting the votes that would have been transmitted to VP-One. The trick was harnessing all that processing power, as well as the ship's communications array, to receive and tabulate the votes of more than six billion Vokites spread out across the surface of the planet.

"Mister Scott?" Kirk asked from his chair on the bridge.

"So far, so good, sir." Scott manned the main engineering station. "But I can't promise we're out of the woods yet."

"Understood, Mister Scott."

Despite the *Enterprise*'s prodigious computer, the job was putting a strain on its systems, which were not designed for this. To compensate, all nonessential computer functions and communications had been suspended for the duration of the tabulations. Kirk wished that Spock was on hand to assist with the technical challenges, but the crew that remained was among the best in Starfleet.

"It's vital that this election take place today," Dare said, defying any suggestion that she return to sickbay.

The commissioner had used all her powers of persuasion to convince the planet's executive committee to accept the last-minute change in plans. She had *not* consulted with the candidates; she would have to get their approval after the fact. Kirk agreed with her; as he knew from experience, sometimes it was smarter to ask for forgiveness than for permission.

The curve of the planet could be glimpsed at the bottom of the viewscreen. "Status, Yeoman Zahra?"

"Steady on course, Captain," she replied from the helm. The *Enterprise* was slowly orbiting Vok, following the same path VP-One would have taken had it not self-destructed. "Feels like we're crawling, though."

"Take it slow, Yeoman," he said. "We have to give the entire world a chance to vote . . . in every time zone."

"Aye, sir."

It occurred to Kirk that he was going to have to relieve Zahra and the rest of the bridge crew eventually, given that the global election was going to take all day. Kirk found himself grateful that a Vokite day was only twenty-two hours long.

"Captain!" Scott said, frowning at his display screens. "We may have a wee problem."

Kirk pivoted toward him. "What is it?"

"The computer, sir, it's slowing down quickly, if you'll pardon the oxymoron. Too much data coming in too fast through too many channels; it's causing a logjam of sorts."

Kirk had been afraid of something like this. The *Enterprise* wasn't built to be a planetary voting tabulator and they'd barely had time to jury-rig it to that purpose, let alone run any trials or tests. Technical difficulties were to be expected but could not be allowed to undo the election. Too much was at stake.

"Uhura, any way you can regulate the transmissions?"

"I'm trying, Captain, but Mister Scott is right. We're not prepared to process so many signals at once. I'm trying to govern the flow by temporarily storing the excess data in buffers, but they're filling up faster than I can release them back into the pipeline."

Dare looked worried. "Just be certain no votes get erased or rejected. The integrity of the election depends on every vote being counted."

"We all appreciate your concerns, Commissioner," Kirk said, "and the importance of making sure every eligible voice is heard." He flicked a switch on his starboard armrest. "Computer, report status of vote tabulation."

"*Tabulation encountering difficulties,*" the ship's artificial voice replied. "*Efficiency impaired. Processing power insufficient. Tabulation procedure in jeopardy.*"

"Computer, access additional circuits as needed, excepting essential functions."

The overhead lights flickered briefly as the computer diverted more of its duotronic circuits to the task at hand. Kirk hoped that would be enough, but he was swiftly disappointed.

"*Nonessential circuits insufficient.*"

"Captain?" Tanaka said, speaking up. He remained under guard, his trip to the brig postponed on the chance that his singular understanding of VP-One could still prove necessary. "I may be able to help."

Kirk was in no position to reject Tanaka's input out of hand. "Talk to me."

"We anticipated a glitch like this, in the event there was a surge of voting at any particular moment. If you'll allow me access to a control panel, I can possibly fix this. I just need to tweak some crucial subroutines so that your computer can do a better job of breaking the flow of votes into smaller, more discrete packets, perhaps by region or district, tabulating each packet individually before adding each subtotal to the cumulative sum." He shrugged. "That's the simple version."

What he was saying made sense to Kirk. He often did the same thing when reviewing the ship's stores and consumption rates; it was easier and more efficient to add up several smaller totals instead of trying to calculate it all at once. But could he truly trust Tanaka after what he had done? Tanaka was the one who was responsible for destroying Vok Populi in the first place.

"Please, Captain," he said. "Let me try to make up for what I did, at least to some degree?"

Kirk attempted to gauge his sincerity. "How do I know I can trust you? What's to stop you from putting Myp's safety above our mission again?"

He doubted that Tanaka could trick the *Enterprise* into self-destructing—a *Constitution*-class starship was more secure than that—but it was possible he could deliberately make their current problem even worse by throwing more bugs into the computer's electoral programming.

"I've already done what I can to save Myp," Tanaka said. "I did what her captors asked. I destroyed Vok Populi, which they have surely confirmed by now. They have no way of knowing what's transpiring on the *Enterprise* or whether I'm cooperating with you or not." He smiled wanly. "If you pull this off, they'll blame your legendary ingenuity, not me."

Kirk was willing to take the blame. Sizing Tanaka up, he took the penitent diplomat at his word.

"Go for it."

He nodded at Chekov and Bradley, who stepped back and let Tanaka scurry over to Spock's science station, where Haines surrendered her seat to him. She watched warily over his shoulder as he accessed the main computer. Kirk observed him carefully as well.

Tense moments passed. Tanaka deftly worked the computer control panels while studying the various visual displays. He inserted a microtape into the reader, modified it via the manual input controls, then ejected it with a sigh of relief. He slumped back against his seat, breathing heavily as though he had just run a four-minute mile.

"There," he said. "That should do it."

Kirk couldn't—wouldn't—take his word for it. "Computer, report status of vote tabulation."

"*Tabulation proceeding,*" the computer reported calmly. "*Efficiency restored.*"

Kirk was glad to hear it. Was he just projecting, or did the computer's tone sound subtly more relaxed as well? In any event, it appeared the tabulation was back on track.

"Thank you, Mister Tanaka," he said stiffly, not quite ready to forgive the other man for his earlier betrayal.

"It was the least I could do, Captain." Tanaka returned the station to Haines. "And not nearly enough."

Kirk couldn't disagree. Tanaka's timely assistance didn't make up for putting them in this bind, but it was a start. Perhaps he had taken his first step on the road to redemption.

In the meantime, they still had a long day ahead. Even with Tanaka's fixes, would the *Enterprise*'s computer be able to keep up? Would General Gogg and his loyal supporters accept the result of the vote? Would Prup and her fellow reformers?

That probably depends, he thought, *on what those results are.*

———————

Twenty-plus hours later, Kirk was running on coffee and a short power nap he'd managed to squeeze in during a lull in the voting. The food slots had been shut down to free up processing power for the election, but he'd remembered Janice Rand's old trick of using a hand phaser to heat up a stale pot of coffee from the galley. In retrospect, she had deserved a commendation for that inspired bit of creativity.

"*Well, Kirk?*" General Gogg demanded from the bridge's main viewscreen. "*Let's have it. Who claims the victory in this contest?*"

Both candidates appeared on the screen, which was split between their transmissions from the planet. Kirk understood that both Gogg and Prup were holed up in their respective campaign headquarters, awaiting the election results. Vok's executive committee was listening in as well. Dare had chosen to notify all parties of the final tally before releasing it to the public, if only to stay out ahead of any possible challenges. She shared the command circle with Kirk, discreetly relying on a guard rail for support. Typically, Gogg had directed his query at Kirk, who refused to play along, letting Dare deliver the news regardless.

"The results are in," she said, "and the majority of the votes went to Prup."

"Holy jamborees!" The young activist clutched her chest as though to keep her heart from bursting through her ribs. She looked more stunned than elated. Jubilant aides rushed in from off-screen to hug and congratulate her. Prup shook her head, visibly struggling to process the news. She sounded as though she couldn't quite believe it. *"For real?"*

"The *Enterprise*'s computer has double-checked and triple-checked the figures," Dare stated. "In the end, you received sixty-two percent of the vote and General Gogg received the remaining thirty-eight percent. Voter turnout represented eighty-three percent, which is quite impressive. Your people can be justifiably proud of their determination to stand and be counted."

And that was despite the turmoil and intimidation, Kirk reflected. He had to wonder how high the turnout might have been had it not been for incidents like the one in the capital plaza frightening some voters away from the polls. Still, Dare was right; Vok was to be commended for that outstanding degree of civic participation.

"I see," Gogg said gravely. His stony visage hardened even more. If Prup appeared thunderstruck by the outcome of the election, Gogg was positively sphinxlike, making it impossible to anticipate how he would react to the news. Would he accept the results or not? The stability of the planet, and possibly the entire sector, hinged on whether the General chose to keep fighting this battle.

"*No!*" Sozz barged into view, proving himself much more predictable. He was red-faced and incredulous. "*This isn't possible! How could Vok choose this child—this puppet—over a true leader like the General?*"

Kirk had his own theories about that. His best guess was that the threats and violence from Gogg's outraged supporters, spurred on by the General's combative rhetoric, had produced a last-minute backlash against Gogg, causing Prup to come from behind to win the election. Whether Gogg had personally directed the violence was immaterial; by furiously inciting his followers to rise up against "the enemy," he had sabotaged his own campaign by reminding anxious Vokites too much of the draconian excesses of the old regime.

Or maybe the planet was simply ready for a change.

Kirk suspected that Prup had swept the younger generation's vote, while picking up enough older voters to put her over the top. She no doubt owed part of her victory to the likes of that elderly man in the plaza, Bloj, who was so committed to voting. Prup was the choice of those who wanted to put the old fears and wars behind them. Kirk had no doubt that, down on the planet, Bloj would be rejoicing soon—provided Gogg didn't throw a monkey wrench into the proceedings.

"The people have spoken," Dare stated. "Their reasons are their own."

"*Naturally you would say that,*" Sozz said, "*after your own computer usurped the election. How convenient that the* Enterprise *just happened to award the victory to the candidate the Federation wanted to win all along.*" His sarcastic tone came through the universal translator as clear as day. He turned away from the screen to address Gogg instead. "*Surely, General, we cannot let this transparent fraud go unchallenged. Are we to take Starfleet at their word? Let an offworld alliance determine our destiny?*"

Kirk felt obliged to defend the integrity of his mission.

"A comprehensive record of the voting results is being compiled and will be made available to your government and media promptly, but I can assure you that no bias toward either candidate factored into the computer's calculations. The Federation's preferences did not influence the tabulation. The numbers are the numbers."

"*Spoken like a loyal Starfleet captain,*" Sozz scoffed. "*How backward and gullible do you think we are?*" He shook his fist at the screen as he grew more agitated. Spittle flew from his lips in a way that made Kirk grateful that the other man was not actually on the bridge. "*You will not get away with this brazen hoax. The people, the patriots, will take arms to answer the General's call. They will—*"

"*Quiet.*" Gogg silenced his vituperative aide with a curt gesture. "*I can speak for myself, Adjutant.*"

"*Yes, General, of course.*" Sozz composed himself. "*I did not mean to speak out of turn.*"

"*See that you don't.*"

Looking distinctly abashed, Sozz retreated into the background as Gogg turned his attention back to the delegation on the bridge. Kirk held his breath as he tried and failed to read the General's granite countenance. Kirk hoped that Vok's first free election in living memory would not be disputed. The planet's nascent democracy depended on it.

"*Captain Kirk,*" the General addressed him. "*This is your ship and crew. Can you vouch for their trustworthiness?*"

"Absolutely," Kirk said. "Beyond a doubt."

"*And will you give me your word that you did not tilt the calculations toward my opponent?*"

"You have it."

Gogg nodded.

"*Very well,*" he declared. "*You proved your honor by clearing my name even when it was against the Federation's interests to do so. Therefore, I have no choice but to take you at your word. We will not contest the election.*"

Kirk felt as though they'd just dodged a photon torpedo. He tried not to let his relief show too obviously.

"But, General, you can't be serious!" Sozz couldn't contain himself. *"What about the cause, the security of our world?"*

"It's as the commissioner said," Gogg stated. *"The people have spoken, if unwisely."* A hint of bitterness inflected his voice. *"It may be that they will come to regret the folly of their choice, but so be it. I did my duty to the best of my abilities. To the victor go the spoils."*

"Thank you, General," Prup said. *"Vok will remember that you graciously chose to let the people choose when it mattered. Please know that my door will always be open to you as our divided people come together to forge our shared future, even if I don't always agree with your views."*

She spoke deliberately and without rancor. It seemed to Kirk that Prup's manner had already become more solemn now that the reality of her new responsibilities was sinking in. He could practically see the weight of leadership settling on her shoulders as she realized how many people depended on her now.

Kirk knew the feeling well.

"Madame President-Elect," Gogg acknowledged her. *"I will concede the election promptly if that is acceptable to all concerned. I would prefer my supporters learn of our defeat from my own lips."*

"That is more than acceptable," Dare said, "and probably judicious as well. We will release the official results immediately after your broadcast."

Kirk agreed. Better that Gogg's people get the bad news from their leader, and hear his concession speech, than from a third party such as the *Enterprise*.

"In the meantime," Prup said, *"I think I want to touch up my acceptance speech . . . now that I actually need to deliver it."*

"Congratulations," Dare said, "on behalf of both the United Federation of Planets and myself."

"And the crew of the *Enterprise*," Kirk added.

"Captain Kirk, Commissioner Dare," Prup said. *"Consider yourselves invited to front-row seats at my inauguration."* She smiled at Dare. *"I haven't forgotten that you took a spear for Vok."*

Kirk noticed that Doctor Ceff was not visible amidst Prup's ecstatic staffers. The former candidate had been keeping a low profile since the scandal involving her brother in order to let Prup's campaign move past that debacle. It was a shame Ceff couldn't take a greater part in the celebrations to come, but Kirk wanted to think that she would be pleased with how matters had turned out. Her risky decision to drop out of the race in favor of Prup had paid off.

"Just think twice about the entertainment at the inauguration," Dare said, wincing at the memory. "Please."

"*Duly noted,*" Prup said.

Only a few more pleasantries remained before both candidates signed off to deal with the daunting tasks before them. There was a victory to be declared, and a defeat to be weathered, so Prup and Gogg had much to do before the sun rose again in their respective corners of the world. For himself, Kirk savored the satisfaction of a mission successfully completed. The election was over and, in his estimation, the best candidate had won.

"Mission accomplished," he said. "And it seems that principles won out over strife in the end."

"I should say so," Dare agreed. Despite her injuries, she looked more pleased than she had since they had first arrived at Vok. "All's well that ends well, albeit not without some aches and pains along the way."

And we didn't compromise our principles, Kirk thought. Politics might be a dirty word to some, but this time at least it may have yielded an outcome they all could live with.

If only he could point that out to McCoy. Last he'd heard, Spock and *Copernicus* were heading to Ozalor, of all places, in search of their missing friend. No victory would truly be complete until he knew what had become of them.

The sooner the better.

Forty-Two

Ozalor

"But, Your Excellency, I was merely seeking to soothe the Heir to the best of my abilities!"

Vumri pled her case to Salokonos in the *Yovode*'s private sanctum, the matter of the crown princess's health still being deemed unsuitable for public airing. Vumri stood before the seated monarch, her arms outstretched before her, as McCoy and his would-be rescuers looked on. Jemo, standing off to the side, smirked at the healer's protests, clearly enjoying seeing Vumri in the hot seat. McCoy was not above taking a certain satisfaction in the same.

"Give me a break." He stepped forward to confront Vumri. "You kept your psychic hooks in Avomora to hold on to your power, obstructing me from helping her."

She glared at him. "How dare you impugn my motives, Earthman! My devotion to the throne is beyond dispute!"

"Hardly," Spock stated. Like McCoy and the others, he was still clad in Ozalorian garb. "You forget, *Lossu* Vumri, that I have experienced your private thoughts firsthand and can testify that there was nothing selfless about them."

"So you say, Vulcan." Vumri appealed to Salokonos, who listened in silence to the dueling voices before him. "This is utter hearsay, Your Excellency. Who will you believe, a Federation spy, who abused your gracious hospitality by assaulting your palace guards, or one who has always served you loyally?"

"It is not simply your word against Spock's." Avomora occupied a position of honor at her father's side, standing confidently on her own two feet. Her rosy complexion glowed with restored vigor and freedom from pain. "Thanks to Mister Spock, I shared your thoughts as well, Vumri. You are no friend of this court . . . and deserve no place in it."

Vumri clutched her chest as though mortally wounded.

"You don't mean that, Your Highness! These foreign devils have confused you, twisted your thoughts against me. Don't let them deceive you with their lies and trickery!"

"I trust them more than I ever trusted you," Avomora said, "and I feel more myself now than I have in far too long." She turned to Salokonos. "Please, Father, send her away, so I never have to look at her scheming face again."

The monarch nodded at his daughter. He fixed his steely gaze at the disgraced healer.

"It seems, *Lossu*, that your gifts are no longer required. The Throne thanks you for your service and bids you farewell."

Vumri's face fell. She dropped to her knees before the king.

"Your Excellency, please reconsider! You cannot just cast me aside, not after all I have done for your daughter!"

"Done for or done *to*?" McCoy said.

Salokonos appeared unmoved by Vumri's outburst. "Do not embarrass yourself, *Lossu*." He frowned at her display. "Guards, escort her from my sight."

A pair of guards came forward. They hauled Vumri to her feet and began to walk her toward the exit, despite her increasingly frantic efforts to break free from their grip. She shouted furiously at the royals.

"You weak-minded ingrates! The Federation is playing you for fools! You'll rue the day you chose them over me! You're a disgrace to your noble ancestors!"

A stream of vitriol erupted from her as the guards dragged her from the sanctum, the silver door solidifying behind them. Her voice faded away into the distance.

"Good riddance," McCoy said.

"You said it, Doctor." Chapel gazed at the door through which the unscrupulous healer had vanished. "She wasn't exactly helping her case there, was she?"

"Her case is concluded," Salokonos decreed. He swept his gaze over his visitors from the *Enterprise,* including the two security officers. "The question before us now, Nurse, is what's to be done with you and your compatriots." His forbidding expression did not seem to bode well for their prospects. "Despite your efforts on my daughter's behalf, I can't say I'm pleased about a Starfleet landing party trespassing on my world—and in my palace—under false pretenses."

McCoy didn't waste his breath denying it. There was little point in pretending that Spock and his team had not been intent on rescuing him all along. That would just insult the king's intelligence.

"With all due respect, Your Excellency," McCoy replied, "I wasn't exactly thrilled about being brought to your planet against my will, so maybe we just call it even and let bygones be bygones?"

That elicited a faint smile from Salokonos, as though amused by McCoy's audacity. "Never afraid to speak your mind, are you, Doctor?"

"You have no idea," Chapel murmured.

"We do not wish to pose a problem to you or your government," Spock said. "We seek only to return to our ship, preferably via the shuttlecraft we arrived in."

"Please, Father," Avomora entreated. "Let them go. They've done so much for us already. It's the least we can do."

Salokonos examined his daughter. Worry furrowed his brow.

"But what if you fall ill again? If Doctor McCoy has indeed helped you, as it appears, I'm reluctant to let him depart."

Should have seen that coming, McCoy thought, frowning. *Can't win for losing . . . unless I speak up fast.*

"That shouldn't be an issue, Your Excellency. In theory, my compound already corrected the chemical imbalance in your daughter's brain, meaning she should be fine from now on, but just in case there are complications, I'll be sure to leave all my data, including the particulars of the cure, with your own physicians." He looked at Avomora, gratified by how much better she looked than when they'd first met. "I also promise to check in with Her Highness periodically to make certain she's fully recovered . . . with your permission, of course."

Salokonos stroked his beard thoughtfully before rendering his decision.

"That is acceptable to the Throne. You will be allowed to depart our world, even if that means opening up a confidential line of communication with Starfleet."

McCoy relaxed. He hadn't been entirely sure that Avo's dad would assent to his proposal. For the first time in what felt like forever, it looked like he was really going home.

"A private channel between your court and Starfleet can certainly be arranged," Spock said, no doubt already figuring out the logistics of such a setup. "It may well be that this incident will lead to a new and more positive relationship between Ozalor and the Federation."

"Perhaps." Salokonos did not rule out the possibility, which struck McCoy as progress of a sort. "Recent events *have* inclined me to see your Federation in a somewhat more favorable light."

"Yep," Jemo agreed. "Turns out you Starfleet types aren't as annoying as you're cracked up to be." She winked at McCoy and lobbed a new carving over to the doctor. "Something to remember us by."

It was another quartz caricature of McCoy, this one boasting a very fake-looking beard—and *maybe* a slightly less ornery expression.

"Oh, trust me," McCoy said. "I'm not forgetting this house call anytime soon."

"Nor shall I," Avomora declared. "I'm in no hurry to assume the throne, but I would hope that by the time that day comes, your people and mine will have long overcome their differences."

"Absolutely," McCoy said, grinning. "What's a little kidnapping between friends?"

Forty-Three

"Spock to Colc. Can you read me?"

"Loud and clear, Mister Spock. What do you have for me?"

The reporter's voice issued from *Copernicus*'s dashboard comm unit. On course back to the *Enterprise*, the newly repaired and re-fueled shuttlecraft had detoured sufficiently to come within hailing range of Braco so Spock could fulfill his obligation to inform D'Ran Colc of what they had discovered on Ozalor—to an extent.

"Our time is short, and I have no desire to tempt fate—or Inspector Wibb—by returning to Braco, but let me convey the essential facts of the matter," Spock said, back in uniform once more. He selected said facts with precision. "A rogue element within the *Yovode*'s court *did* go to extreme lengths to surreptitiously obtain Doctor McCoy's professional services due to a serious medical issue affecting a highly placed member of the court. Salokonos and his daughter, the *Yiyova*, were not party to this unauthorized initiative and only became aware of it after the fact. As for Doctor McCoy . . . despite the questionable manner in which he was brought into the case, he did his duty as a physician, resulting in a positive outcome. Afterward, in appreciation of McCoy's humanitarian efforts, the *Yovode* graciously allowed us to retrieve the doctor."

"And?" Colc prompted.

"I believe that is an accurate summation of the incident."

"It's great stuff, but I want the whole story. Who was the mystery patient? Exactly what sort of medical issue are we talking about?"

"That, Mister Colc, is a matter of doctor-patient confidentiality, as you must surely appreciate."

"*I don't appreciate it one bit, Spock. What about our arrangement? You wouldn't have found McCoy without my help.*"

"That is incontrovertibly true, for which we are sincerely grateful, but our understanding does not supersede all other considerations. I have told you what is within my rights to tell you."

His statement involved a degree of verbal parsing. He had not revealed *all* he could tell, but only that which was prudent. In particular, he chose to omit the tumultuous details of their capture and escape and recapture since those would do nothing to promote more amicable relations between the Federation and Ozalor.

"*That's not good enough, Spock. You owe me all the dirt.*"

"I owe you the facts, Mister Colc, not irrelevant gossip. That being said, I can also pass along the news that Count Rayob has resigned from his position at the Ozalorian royal court."

"*Really?*" Colc's interest was audible even across subspace. "*Well, that's something at least. Am I correct in assuming that his departure might have something to do with a certain rogue operation?*"

"The only appropriate response to that query," Spock said, "is 'No comment.' That Rayob has retired is a matter of record. We can only speculate about the motive behind this decision."

A groan escaped the comm unit.

"*Anyone ever told you, Spock, that trying to pry secrets from you is like wringing blood from a Horta?*"

"Thank you, Mister Colc. I pride myself on my discretion."

"*It wasn't a compliment. I don't suppose I can interview the good doctor himself?*"

As it happened, McCoy was standing in the cockpit directly behind Spock, listening in on the conversation, while looking considerably more clean-shaven now that he had divested himself of his artificial whiskers. He shook his head at Spock.

"Perhaps another time," Spock said. "We are understandably eager to return to the *Enterprise* and will soon be out of range for secure communications of this nature."

"*Don't pull that on me, Spock! We had a deal!*"

"Speaking of which," Spock said in a deliberate attempt to change the subject, "may I ask if you have been in contact with Hynn V'sta?"

"And then some," the other man reported. *"I've got to admit, you came through for me there. She reached out to me not long after you took off for Ozalor, wanting to tell her side of the story. Our friends at the Tranquility Bureau aren't exactly pleased with me for airing that interview, but the public's interested in what she has to say, even if they don't all agree with her."*

Spock was pleased to hear this. "An open exchange of views is generally preferable to armed conflict."

"I'm not entirely sure Inspector Wibb would agree with you. I've offered him equal time, but so far he prefers to keep the free press at a distance. His loss, if you ask me." It was easy to visualize the reporter shrugging. *"Not that I go easy on V'sta, of course. I'm nobody's propaganda tool."*

"That much is evident, Mister Colc. I wish you the best of luck in your future endeavors."

"Hold on there, Spock! We're not done yet. I still have plenty of questions!"

Of that Spock had no doubt, but he judged that he had more than fulfilled the terms of their bargain, possibly to good effect where Braco was concerned. His fingers manipulated the comm controls to distort the frequency.

"You will have to forgive me, Mister Colc. The signal is breaking up. Spock out."

He switched off the transmission to forestall any further wrangling on the part of the reporter. McCoy chuckled at the ploy.

"Nicely played, Spock. The captain would be proud."

"My ego requires no boosting, Doctor, but I will accept your observation in the spirit in which it is intended."

"Well, isn't that big of you," McCoy said, indulging his customary irascibility. "That reminds me, Spock, you know what I missed about these little talks of ours?"

"I'm confident you are about to inform me."

"Nothing," McCoy drawled. "I didn't miss your smug Vulcan attitude one bit."

"Then I trust you enjoyed your vacation, Doctor."

"Vacation?" McCoy raised his voice. "You think what I just went through was a vacation? Why, you green-blooded, clueless excuse for a Good Samaritan . . ."

Spock's keen hearing picked up insufficiently suppressed laughter in the passenger compartment. He chose to take this as a reliable indicator of good morale aboard the shuttlecraft.

"Please take your seat, Doctor. We still have a long way to go before we reach the *Enterprise*." Spock pivoted toward Levine, who was at the helm. "Set course for Vok, Lieutenant. Maximum safe speed."

"Aye, aye, sir. You don't have to tell me twice."

"Naturally," Spock said, bemused by the expression. "That would be redundant."

Forty-Four

Captain's Log, Stardate 6787.2: *With my crew at last re-united, and the election on Vok concluded, we are making ready to depart the sector and return to Federation space, but first Mister Spock is briefing us on a scientific discovery of considerable significance.*

"The evidence suggests," Spock began, "that none of this sector's humanoids are actually native to the region. In my estimation, the Vokites, the Ozalorians, and even the Bracons are most likely the descendants of an interstellar civilization that colonized this sector long before the parent civilization collapsed or contracted eons ago. Indeed, there is reason to believe that the only actual natives of this sector are a species of primitive, cave-dwelling life-forms I encountered on Braco."

A peculiar three-legged creature occupied the triscreen in the *Enterprise*'s main conference room. Kirk contemplated the image with interest. Also present at the briefing were McCoy, a yeoman to take notes, and Commissioner Dare, who had been discharged from sickbay. Conspicuously missing was Steve Tanaka, who had chosen to remain on Vok to face charges for sabotaging VP-One. Kirk understood that the young man hoped to atone for his crime by devoting himself to the planet's welfare—and possibly Sergeant Myp as well. Thankfully, the policewoman had indeed been released by her captors following the destruction of the satellite. President-Elect Prup, as well as the planet's Civic Security agencies, were not taking her kidnapping lightly and had vowed to find and prosecute those responsible.

He's young, Kirk thought of Tanaka. *Plenty of time to make up for his mistake.*

"It is even possible," Spock continued, "that most of the other flora and fauna on Braco, and not just the humanoids, were transplanted to the planet eons ago."

Kirk pushed Tanaka out of his mind in order to fully concentrate on what Spock was saying.

"A provocative theory, Mister Spock. Please elaborate."

Spock gestured at the exotic life-form on the screen. "The possibility first occurred to me when I discovered that the trivets have copper-based blood, unlike any other known life-forms in this sector."

"A relative of yours?" Kirk quipped.

"Unlikely," Spock replied, "although one particular trivet seemed under that impression. It sensed the copper-based nature of my blood and was understandably intrigued."

McCoy nodded. "Chapel mentioned something about you picking up a three-legged shadow on Braco." He grinned at Spock. "Green blood is thicker than water, I guess."

"Its curiosity was quite understandable," Spock replied. "I was almost surely the only other copper-based life-form that this trivet had ever encountered. Its unique nature, compared to the other inhabitants of the sector, suggests that the trivets and the Bracons did *not* evolve from a common ancestor." He paused for emphasis before going on. "It is theoretically possible, of course, that two entirely different forms of life could evolve independently on a single world, but that is hardly probable. The simpler, and therefore more likely, explanation is that one strain of life-form originated elsewhere."

Dare nodded. "I grasp your reasoning, Mister Spock, but why assume that the humanoids aren't native to this sector? Perhaps these mysterious 'trivets' are the aliens?"

Spock called up another image, replacing the trivet with a picture of a tile mosaic depicting humanoid pioneers working their fields while curious trivets scurried about the borders of the artwork.

"This mosaic," Spock explained, "was found within a forgotten bunker on Braco. It dates back to before the apocalyptic conflict that leveled the planet's prior civilization. The image suggests that the trivets roamed the planet while it was being settled by early Bracons. I theorize, in fact, that the art depicts the original colonization of the planet by visitors from elsewhere."

He zeroed in on the upper left-hand corner of the mosaic, enlarging that section of the image, so that a trio of background figures could be better seen. Unlike the Bracon individuals in the foreground, these smaller figures were partially obscured by a shimmering purple glow, producing an artistic effect that rendered them much less distinct.

"I call your attention to the way these particular Bracons are depicted," Spock said, "as though they're beaming onto the scene from space by means of a Bracon transporter beam."

Kirk squinted at the image. "That's a bold speculation, Mister Spock."

"Quite," Spock agreed, "and in itself this mosaic hardly constitutes definitive evidence. It is merely one piece of the puzzle. Since we returned to the *Enterprise*, I have conducted an extensive search of the relevant databases and discovered that, in fact, there is no fossil record of humanoid life evolving on Braco or anywhere else in the sector."

"None?" Kirk asked in surprise.

"None whatsoever," Spock stated. "No evidence of early primates or hominids, nor any pre-apocalyptic cave paintings, stone-age tools, burial sites, or any other indicators of early protohumanoids once populating the planet."

McCoy poured himself a cup of water from a pitcher. "And nobody ever noticed this before?"

"The accepted explanation is that all such evidence was destroyed by the interstellar war millennia ago. With so much of their early history lost to the global devastation, it appears to have been all too easy for Bracon archaeologists to assume that any trace of their *pre*history had been swept away as well."

"What about the trivets?" Kirk asked.

Naturally, Spock was prepared for that query. "It required some digging, but, as it happens, there *are* stray reports of what might be fossilized trivet remains turning up over the years. Curiously, they have attracted little attention, and have even occasionally been dismissed as hoaxes, perhaps because they do not readily fit into the established narrative regarding the development of life on Braco."

"Not so curious to me, Mister Spock," Dare observed. "Speaking as a politician, not a scientist, institutions tend to resist data that runs counter to their agendas, especially if they're already heavily invested in another paradigm."

Spock nodded in understanding. "Such as the myth that Braco is the birthplace of their species, as opposed to merely an offshoot of some forgotten interstellar civilization."

"But who colonized Braco?" Kirk asked. "And what became of them?"

"An excellent question, Captain, deserving of further study." Spock switched off the triscreen. "As we are well aware, our galaxy is littered with the remnants of extinct races and civilizations, whose origins are lost in deep time: the Kalandans, the Zetarians, the long-dead inhabitants of Camus II, Sargon's people, and many others. Galactic history is vast enough for some ancient people to have planted their seed on Braco, only to fade from memory with the passing of eons."

"And a cataclysmic war or two," Kirk added.

"Sadly, yes," Spock agreed.

"Well, as for the who," McCoy chimed in, "I may be able to provide another piece of the puzzle."

"Really, Doctor?" Spock said. "How so?"

"I did a pretty comprehensive genetic profile of the Ozalorians while treating Avomora," McCoy said. "In the process, I discovered some markers similar to those found in the DNA of those humanoids we encountered on Gamma Triranguli VI a few years back. Maybe whatever ancient civilization set up that manufactured Eden also colonized Braco at some point, although apparently they refrained from installing any computerized serpent gods in these parts."

"Come again?" Dare asked, apparently unfamiliar with the Vaal incident.

"Doctor McCoy is referring to a world we visited some time ago," Kirk explained, "where a primitive humanoid species was being tended to by a computerized system that had obviously been put in place by a more technologically advanced civilization some ten thousand years earlier." He looked at McCoy. "So we're thinking that Gamma Trianguli VI and Braco were colonized by the same species?"

"Or that the Bracons and Vaal's creators shared a common ancestor, even further back in the depths of time," Spock said, intrigued. "I look forward to reviewing your genetic studies, Doctor."

"Happy to be of assistance," McCoy said dryly.

"In any event," Dare said, "I understand enough of what you're saying to see that the political implications are game changing. If it can be proven that Braco is *not* the sacred birthplace of this sector's feuding peoples, that makes it much less of a prize to be fought over . . . and therefore less of a bone of contention between Vok and Ozalor."

"That is only logical," Spock agreed.

McCoy snorted. "As if logic ever changed anyone's mind where politics and patriotism were concerned."

"Sadly, I'm afraid McCoy has a point," Kirk said. "Not everyone is going to accept, let alone welcome, Spock's theory at first. As noted, all three planets are deeply invested in a cause they've spent many generations fighting over. They're not going to abandon it overnight because of some admittedly intriguing science."

"Perhaps not, Captain," Spock said, "but they deserve the opportunity to better understand their own origins." He turned to address Dare. "I assume I have your permission, Commissioner, to share my findings with the relevant scientific communities in the sector?"

Dare only needed a moment or two to consider the issue.

"Far be it from the Federation to withhold the truth of their own past from this sector's inhabitants. Feel free to release your report, Mister Spock. I only ask that we share the data equally with all three worlds."

"I quite agree, Commissioner," Kirk said. "What they choose to do with the information is then up to them."

"Precisely," Spock said. "It occurs to me, however, that it might be best to make the data available to not just the scientific establishments but to the press as well."

"Oh," McCoy said, sounding amused. "You wouldn't happen to be thinking of any reporter in particular, would you?"

Kirk understood that an investigative journalist on Braco had been instrumental in assisting Spock in his search for McCoy.

"Most definitely, Doctor," Spock said. "I believe a valid alternative theory about the genesis of their people, of significant political relevance, would constitute . . . a scoop?"

"One would think," McCoy said. "But do we really believe the truth will make a difference when it comes to old hatreds and rivalries?"

"Hard to say," Kirk said. "Peace is a funny thing. Sometimes it takes forever to get going, then it comes on in a rush. In this case, at least the tide of history appears to be heading in the right direction, with the warmongers on the wane and the peacemakers gaining ground."

"Until the next election," McCoy said.

"No victory is final, Bones. It's up to every generation to keep up the good fight . . . and push the ball along just a little further."

McCoy sighed. "Sounds exhausting, if you ask me."

"Better than being complacent," Kirk said, "and taking our gains for granted."

"Amen, Captain," the commissioner said. "If you'll pardon the expression, politics is more than just a five-year mission. It's never-ending."

Kirk considered everything they'd gone through since the *Enterprise* first set course for Vok. It had been a bumpy ride, with plenty of unexpected swerves and detours, but he could live with where they'd ended up. "That being said, I'm inclined to pronounce this particular mission concluded."

McCoy raised his cup.

"I'll drink to that," he said. "And did I mention that I managed to come away with a few bottles of fine Ozalorian vintages, straight from the *Yovode*'s private cellars?"

Spock sighed. "You are incorrigible, Doctor."

McCoy smirked. "You just figured that out?"

EPILOGUE

San Francisco
Earth

The Golden Gate Bridge loomed majestically over the sunlit waters below. Imogen Dare took in the view as she sat on a park bench overlooking the bay. It was a crisp fall afternoon and she sipped on a hot latte, savoring the subtle flavoring. A man crossed the park and sat down beside her.

"Sorry to keep you waiting," Admiral James Komack said. Snowy-white hair, not a strand out of place, betrayed his years even as his trim, fit physique belied them. The insignia on his gold command tunic testified to his rank. "A strategic planning session, addressing the latest Romulan provocations, ran over."

"No worries," Dare said. "Gave me a chance to appreciate being back on Earth again."

"Welcome home," Komack said, "and congratulations on the success of your assignment, despite some truly formidable obstacles." A note of sympathy entered his voice. "I trust you're recovered from the injuries you sustained in the line of duty?"

"Very much so," she assured him, even as she cringed inwardly at the memory of the attack. She still had some bad moments remembering how close she'd come to being killed, but her Deltan counselor assured her that was to be expected and that she would eventually get past the trauma with time and therapy. "It's kind of you to ask."

"Least I could do," he said stiffly. "Now then, about that *other* matter I asked you to observe . . . what's your take on Jim Kirk and his crew?"

So much for small talk, Dare thought.

Months ago, before Dare had departed Earth to rendezvous with the *Enterprise*, the admiral had quietly approached her asking for a favor. With Kirk's five-year mission drawing to a close, Starfleet Command was weighing its options as to how best to deploy Kirk and his senior officers after the *Enterprise* completed its assigned journey of discovery. In that context, Komack had asked her to discreetly observe Kirk and company in action—with an eye to figuring out their next postings.

"Off the record," she reported, "the current crew of the *Enterprise* functions like an exceptionally well-tuned machine. At this point, they know each other's strengths and capabilities and rely on them without hesitation. Even after five years out on the frontier, none of the bridge crew or other senior officers struck me as bored or restless or ready to move on. I observed no festering personality conflicts nor slackening in discipline." She paused to finish off her latte as she collected her thoughts. "This particular assignment threw any number of unexpected curveballs at them, including ambushes and abductions, assassination attempts and conspiracies, but they did their duty, with Captain Kirk stepping up after I landed in sickbay."

A phantom pain stabbed her as she flashed back to the would-be assassin's spear piercing her body, but she didn't let it show. This "unofficial" meeting was not about her.

"Your glowing assessment does not surprise me," Komack said, "but the question remains: Given the caliber and experience of Kirk's crew, would we be better off spreading that talent around by breaking them up and reassigning them to assorted other posts throughout Starfleet?" He peered out across the bay as though looking beyond today into tomorrow. "Judging from the official logs chronicling this recent assignment, the individual officers certainly seem more than capable of succeeding on their own if they have to."

"True," she granted, "but what you lose by breaking up this crew is the superlative teamwork and camaraderie forged by five solid years of exploring the galaxy together, while facing pretty much every challenge imaginable. That's an asset that Starfleet should think twice about tossing away."

"Point taken." Komack's practiced poker face made it difficult to determine what he thought of her advice. "So your recommendation is that we should keep the *Enterprise*'s present crew together? Perhaps even consider sending them off on a *second* five-year mission."

Dare couldn't think of a better decision.

"Why mess with a good thing?"

Acknowledgments

This is the first book I wrote since my faithful old laptop bit the dust, so thanks to that venerable device for its years of service, as well as to everyone who helped me get my new computer set up since, unlike Mister Spock, such things are hardly my field of expertise. In particular, thanks to my friends Ken Meltsner and Janice Eisen for helping me install Word on the new device, so that I could once again sit down at the keyboard and reenter the twenty-third century. And to the local miracle workers at Chimera Computers in Lancaster, Pennsylvania, for successfully transferring all my old data to the new machine when others failed.

As always, thanks are also due to my editors, Margaret Clark and Ed Schlesinger, and my agent, Russ Galen.

And, of course, Karen and little Sophie, who are waiting patiently downstairs for me to finish this book so we can settle in and watch old monster movies for Halloween.

Finally, don't forget to vote on every Election Day, no matter what planet you live on.

About the Author

Greg Cox is the *New York Times* bestselling author of numerous *Star Trek* novels and stories, including *The Antares Maelstrom*; *Legacies, Book 1: Captain to Captain*; *Miasma*; *Child of Two Worlds*; *Foul Deeds Will Rise*; *No Time Like the Past*; *The Weight of Worlds*; *The Rings of Time*; *To Reign in Hell*; *The Eugenics Wars (Volumes One and Two)*; *The Q Continuum*; *Assignment: Eternity*; and *The Black Shore*. He has also written the official movie novelizations of *War for the Planet of the Apes*, *Godzilla*, *Man of Steel*, *The Dark Knight Rises*, *Ghost Rider*, *Daredevil*, *Death Defying Acts*, and the first three *Underworld* movies, as well as books and stories based on such popular series as *Alias*, *Buffy the Vampire Slayer*, *CSI: Crime Scene Investigation*, *Farscape*, *The 4400*, *Leverage*, *The Librarians*, *Riese: Kingdom Falling*, *Roswell*, *Terminator*, *Warehouse 13*, *The X-Files*, and *Xena: Warrior Princess*.

He has received three Scribe Awards, as well as the Faust Award for Life Achievement, from the International Association of Media Tie-In Writers. He lives in Lancaster, Pennsylvania.

Visit him at: **www.gregcox-author.com**